ALSO BY GREG JACKSON

Prodigals: Stories

THE
DIMENSIONS
OF A CAVE

THE

DIMENSIONS

OF A CAVE

GREG JACKSON

 Farrar, Straus and Giroux
New York

Farrar, Straus and Giroux
120 Broadway, New York 10271

Library of Congress Cataloging-in-Publication Data
Names: Jackson, Greg, 1983– author.
Title: The dimensions of a cave : a novel / Greg Jackson.
Description: First edition. | New York : Farrar, Straus and Giroux, 2023. |
Identifiers: LCCN 2023014909 | ISBN 9780374298494 (hardcover)
Subjects: LCGFT: Novels.
Classification: LCC PS3610.A3517 D56 2023 | DDC 813/.6—dc23/eng/20230407
LC record available at https://lccn.loc.gov/2023014909

Designed by Patrice Sheridan

Our books may be purchased in bulk for promotional, educational, or business
use. Please contact your local bookseller or the Macmillan Corporate and
Premium Sales Department at 1-800-221-7945, extension 5442, or by email at
MacmillanSpecialMarkets@macmillan.com.

www.fsgbooks.com
www.twitter.com/fsgbooks • www.facebook.com/fsgbooks

For Natasha

Tell me not, in mournful numbers,
     Life is but an empty dream!
For the soul is dead that slumbers,
     And things are not what they seem.
Life is real!

—LONGFELLOW

For man has closed himself up, till he sees all things
thro' narrow chinks of his cavern.

—BLAKE

THE ISLAND CLUNG to the mainland by a spit of sandbar as low and shingled as a manicured walk and could not therefore be properly called an island. Still we called it that, 'the island,' and at times, when the ocean cycles and planets aligned, the perigean king tide with its liquid cargo brought the water up over the lip of that persistent littoral, briefly severing all tie to the shore and bringing the fact of the land into sympathy with its name.

The day hung over the great bay and to the west with a patience as mild as the still waters beneath it. These were so flat they might have been a living metal smelt from worn verges and outcroppings in this wild land. The waves tapping at the shore seemed accidental, emerging at the last instant and rising only ankle-high before collapsing on the broad sandy flats. It was that moment of spring when the nip in the air has not caught up to the lengthening in the evening light, and this light appears to outstay its time and swap a silvered clarity into hours meant for shadow and dream.

We were four—Frank, Izzy, Quentin, and Schmitty—four men and Izzy's collie, Chance, and all around us were the signs of stirring life. The dry brush snapped with creatures roused from winter's sleep. Birds flitted in the trees. Out on the southern rim, where the island turned back toward the tidal marsh and the sedge rose from the brackish fringe like ridges of spiked hair, a pair of duck blinds watched the lagoon. No, none of us hunted, and we had not been together on the island, where Frank's brother owned a house, in close on a decade; and yet as men committed to a veneer of the most unimpeachable typicality, and men, beyond that, engaged in a deeper and more elusive type of hunt, we regarded those drab half-hidden boxes with a mix of envy and disdain. How simple their task seemed in comparison to ours, how neat and negligible its moral lines!

We were journalists, you see, newsmen at a time when the fate of civilization seemed gifted us like a distant uncle's unsalable folly. Everyone else had seen their jobs gather at the spigots of excess until, like stone basins, they grew deformed by what they existed to receive. Everyone in government showed the strain and impress of so many shifting agendas that even the crusaders hardly knew what urgency they served; and everyone in business, needless to say, had a pair of shareholders on his shoulders rubbing their fingers. That left us. And since we worked in a dying industry, one that had been cutting back so long its dissipation bore the inevitability of a thermodynamic law, there was no god to worship but the hopeless, romantic mission of it, in service and loyal to one master: truth.

We may have seen ourselves as the descendants of noir detectives—proud, pathetic disheveled men, as prickly and sardonic on the outside as we were hopeless Manichaeans within. We believed in clarity, the disinfectant properties of sunlight, and the irrepressible triumph, in time, of fact. If the world was venal and fallen, we thought the proper response was still greater allegiance to principle. Our martyrdom and sacrifice were givens, after all, the very terms of our grueling careers, and since so many of us had quit or been laid off, those who remained made up the furthest gone of true believers, a reality we endured only by investing great cynicism and coarseness in our words. Oh, we would give them hell, the officials, the representatives, the magnates, the CEOs. Not because we were *better* than them, but because it was our nature, and beyond that our job. We were the bloodhounds and they our quarry. And what we believed, with fervor that flirted with the religious, was that a single, knowable reality existed and that it was every last person's right to know what this reality was.

That makes the work sound grander than it is. Much of it felt like correcting someone's garbled math, scribbled in a purposefully illegible hand. We read a lot: financial reports, public disclosures, white papers, declassified documents. *Thank god* we had been at it long enough to leave the burnout beats that shave one's shoe-leather within a broadside's breadth of the pavement and made our way to editorial desks and their comfy chairs. Izzy ran a southern newsroom and penned stylish features now and again about alligators and methamphetamine and the feckless part-time criminals in that part of the world, whose dreams encompass a poignant share in the human comedy. Schmitty wrote an opinion column once a week, alongside his editorial duties, and mostly he said the reasonable, measured things you'd expect, calibrating his outrage at a simmer and upholding the grammatical prescriptions of a different age. Frank was the news-desk editor at a major paper, and that was Frank through and through.

Quentin was the only one of us still grinding out the hard investigative stuff, and for that we loved and pitied him. We had all grown plump in middle age, the consequence of long hours at our desks, keeping pace with the torrents of what we had been trained to call content, glutting the arteries of knowledge like plaque. Quentin alone had stayed thin, and even looked smaller with age, as if the lifestyle ate away at his unnecessary flesh—as if someone so driven by the hunger to be undeceived suffered a double appetite that consumed him in body and spirit alike. The toll of living without myth or illusion is unbearable for most; the simple truth is myth and illusion get us by.

Someone of Quentin's reflexive stubbornness and pitilessness would not have acknowledged his own needs if he had wasted down to the stripped spirit of witness itself. It therefore fell to Schmitty, who bumped into him at a legislative presser, to write the rest of us to say that Quentin looked like a de Chirican shadow of himself, poking out from behind a column. He seemed like he could use some cheering up. And it was true that ever since his fracas with the administration over a story the *Beacon* had caved on and pulled, Quentin's byline had been scarce. These five days, then, back on the island after a decade, had all the choked elegiac flavor of old friends, whose intimacy lay buried in a receding past, returning to the site of a closer moment in hopes of digging up the capsule of their affection from the sunbaked earth. The love we bore one another had little fuel left but its own endurance, we knew, the fading image on a retina of an extinguished flame.

Naturally, Quentin didn't mistake the purpose of our reunion. He had the coy attitude of one who knows you mean to do him a good turn but who wonders whether he might not do you one himself by indulging this desire. He seemed all right, after all. And it struck us, when we had arrived and finished unloading, that in spite of his drawn look, our friend smoldered with an acute force that made the rest of us appear shiftless and blurry by comparison. He stood by the shore smoking a cigarette, watching the wading birds that came in low through the evening skies and the small fishing craft that made for harbor in the last of the day's light, and we wondered, struck as we occasionally are by the way a situation of our own devising turns, like a tide, leaving us the passenger of a larger force, whether we had not gathered to learn from him some forgotten chapter in the soul's purpose.

Chance barked. The day repossessed itself, a poured light tumbling over the bay and collecting so slowly that our eyes adjusted before it dimmed. The sky gathered and diffused the brilliance, giving no sense of its source, and clouds, contrails, and other markings in the heavens ran to the vertical, seamed with light. To the north, far beyond the bridge at the edge of view, lay the capital. The smudge of rain or exhaust that claimed its space in the sky disclosed a hard reality the island brought us clear of but could not entirely obscure. The engine of industry churned out the black smoke of an old mistake, and even here, where you could almost squint and work back to the beginning, four hundred years before, when the first small crofts dotted these shores, as beige and dun as the lifeless vernal grass and bare trees, even here the price of this peace lay written in that sooted signature of men with an iron desire for a power that human shoulders couldn't bear.

I was fishing, Quentin remarked. It was not unlike him to start a tale at some far corner and begin shading in, so that details and people emerged faster than the gist and the whole image did not coalesce until the very last accent line brought out the critical connection where, as a listener, one's attention sought all the while to alight. It had been his habit since as far back as our time together in journalism school, and it betrayed the epistemology of a reporter, who knows that truth always inheres partly in the manner it is arrived at. We had joined him and were sitting backed into the diminutive escarpments that scalloped the shore above the beach. The assembled driftwood and fallen sticks of an unlit bonfire stood before us, and we sipped our beers, looking west, while Chance rooted in the sand after rotting crab shells and the fetor of decomposing life.

Fishing, Quentin continued. Well, you know me, fellas, I did not do the fishing myself. I knew a guy, Roland, who did a bit of amateur angling off a retaining wall upriver from the boathouses. You know the ones I mean? Almost in the shadow of the bridge by St. Augustine's? Roland did not strike you as a homeowner, let's just put it that way. No, I never asked what else he got up to. The fish he caught, snakehead and pike, looked deranged and half-dead to begin with, like they had had it with life and he was their exterminating angel. He tossed them in a five-gallon bucket where they twitched briefly and let go.

I wasn't there for the sport of it, trust me. Quentin paused before continuing, Fishing is one of those meditative activities that enhance the powers of attention, like driving nowhere on country roads. And complex as our world has grown, and it is complex, sometimes it's worth asking those who keep quiet what they see. You can learn a lot about a city by attending to its respiration. What goes in and out. Roland saw more traffic on that stretch of river in his day than Charon, I'd wager, and my own sort of fishing (I'd brought him coffee and a bagel) worked well enough with his.

This was around the time Cy left me, Quentin said, just after my fights with Haig's moral heavyweights at the directorate. I had a lot of time on my hands and for the first stretch in many years no task to put it to. I can't say I was shaken—no, not looking back and knowing how far down the path of an enveloping blackness I had to go. But I felt empty. Blank. Cleared out of passion and fight. I wondered, as I had never done, whether there was really a point. We all wonder, I know, but I don't mean the idle questions we entertain in a glum moment. My deepest sense of purpose had deserted me. I felt like the boy with his finger in the dike, fighting the elemental tide of larger powers to a lousy equilibrium. I thought, why should I have the thankless task of interposing my poor finger? The tide would win in the end.

The tide always wins, I guess. Or so I thought looking out over the glassy river while Roland cast his line. It was a hot day, getting on toward high summer. Roland was in one of the few oil-stained white T-shirts he wore, which hugged his body like snakeskin.

'How's our old friend?' I asked. He knew I meant the writhen waters before us and said, 'Oh, she's swimming in it. Drunk to the gills.' He held a hand to shade his eyes and pointed across the river. 'See those rocks?' A few pebbles seemed to glint in the sun, no bigger than a turtle's back. 'Normally, you could picnic on 'em, dangle your feet down and not even wet your toes. College girls like to sun themselves over there.' He ventured a shy grin. 'Not that I notice . . .'

'Course not,' I agreed. 'Family man like yourself.'

'Look at the foot of the bridge.' He removed a hand from the rod to point at a patch of ground, torn up and grassless.

'Repairs?'

He glanced at me like I knew about as much as a walleye. 'Erosion,' he said. 'More water's flowing through.'

'Rain?'

'Hasn't been much rain.' He looked to the sky as if to make sure the heavens weren't about to contradict him. 'Besides, those algal blooms . . . It's not *dilute*. You know what that means?' I didn't need to shake my head. 'More sediment's coming down too. More nutrients.'

It was early June, long past the season of snowmelt, and peering into his near-empty bucket, I said, 'Seems like it might have helped you more.'

'Doesn't work like that.' He sighed with his body. 'Volume wrecks the deep spawning grounds. See the dead brush along the bank? The table's dropped too. The plants can't get water.' I asked what it meant. 'I had to guess,' he said, 'I'd say they're running a small flood through the dam up in Minersville.'

I didn't get it. Roland tugged the rod a few times. 'I talked to Tim what's-his-name. Professor at the college.' He knocked his head back in the direction of the campus hidden behind a veil of trees. 'He kayaks up past the state park. Says the floodplain's shot through. Probably going to have drowned half the trees along the bank by the time it dries out this summer. Assuming they run out of water at some point.'

I laughed at this. 'How're we gonna keep you fed?'

He looked at me for a pregnant beat, like even for *me* this was too stupid. 'You know I don't eat these. Wouldn't feed them to my dog.'

That was the first I heard of any dog.

There is a certain mystery to the lives of other people, you'll have observed, Quentin remarked after a moment. This doesn't concern what people do to sustain themselves, but the private space that is their own, where some part of them uniquely resides and where they return when they are alone. The mystery isn't about what we spend our time doing, but the way our most private acts exist outside the flow of life, exist therefore, in some sense, beyond life and death. I imagine we are unique in this respect, humans, I mean. Alone in cultivating this sphere of private mysticism around purposeless activities.

I thought about this in connection with Cy, he went on. She had her watercolors. No, she wasn't going to support herself painting. That's why she and Judith had the gallery—*have* it. Why she consults for collectors. On the weekends, though, or on a trip to the country, when she had a morning free, I have never seen anyone happier. Or maybe *happier* is the wrong word. More *absorbed*. More lost to an utterly private peace. You know me, I can't draw a stick figure that wouldn't traumatize a child. I don't have that nourishment that lies on the right-hand side of the work-life divide. My work is my life, and my life I wouldn't wish on a scoundrel. But do you notice how the things we do when we have time to ourselves attempt to recreate some portion of the world in our image, according to the peculiarities of our vision? We build these little monuments to the

idiosyncrasy of what it feels like to pass through life as *us*, as if it's so different, so special, or maybe, like ants or bees, we simply find ourselves geneti-
cally disposed to render outwardly some blueprint secreted in our DNA.

I didn't know what to make of this instinct when I started my journey.
Mostly, I didn't see the pattern in it, how even my work for the *Beacon*
had the same impulse behind it, lining up these bits of information like
so many breadcrumbs to make my sense of the way the world worked, to
follow the torchlight's illumination past the shadows on the walls. A story
is a good deal more than a set of events, a mystery and its revelation. More
than an impoverished stab at the *why* behind the *what*. Whatever we
want to say, we fail to capture it fully because the truth lies at the seat of
our being. You might even say that we are stories' dependents rather than
their masters, and we course through life on their currents and networks
of exchange without ever knowing how strong the grip really is, without
understanding just how much is decided for us.

Quentin stopped. We sipped our beers. The light had changed from
windswept gold to a cyanotic register, flinty with the water's mineral
hue. A foghorn sounded down the bay. Fish jumped after the insects dis-
ordering the twilight. Quentin hunched forward in a windbreaker that
fluttered around him. What breeze streamed up the bay had a mellow and
fortifying weight, a welcome warmth, since once Quentin got going we
knew that we were in for it and that the night—and more still—would be
given over to his tale. But though the urge was strong to crack a joke, to
light the bonfire, pass the bourbon, and relive old stories from our school
days and early jobs, we held back. We waited. This was why we had come:
to listen.

Cy left me just about the time the interrogation story got spiked.
Quentin picked up his story like lines in a rope he was unknotting. In
any meaningful sense the two had nothing to do with each other. Cy still
thought about children, and more than that she thought about slowing
down, enjoying life a little more. As you know, the tender mercies of this
work seep into the hollows of our bones, the fissures in our joints, and
you can only protect those you care about from the strain by protecting

them from you, and thereby growing apart. I tried to keep the burden off Cy, but as the story drew me in, I saw her less, and when Henry killed the piece, something in me snapped. The stress and worry I'd dammed up suddenly released. I went home in the middle of the day, a late spring day. The water from an earlier rain trembled on the boxwood hedges and flower petals, and I saw a deliveryman raise a package above his head to protect it as the wind shook raindrops from the trees. A child pulled against her caretaker's hand to pick at the holly lining the sidewalk, or perhaps simply to breathe in the fragrance that lived right then on the lush air. What is so poignant and crushing about the lives one finds underway on a residential street in the middle of a weekday afternoon? I sat in the apartment contemplating my wretchedness until Cy got home, a little after six. 'We need to talk,' she said, right on cue.

What a conversation, what agony! Cy and I had been together twelve years. She struggled with bouts of melancholy, I suppose I've told you. I could never have made a very good match for her. But we don't choose partners for practical reasons, not the superficial sort, anyway. What do we then look for or want? Maybe someone we can take off all the armor with at day's end, a person who, when we are too tired to explain ourselves, will consent to look at the world and see the same thing we do in broad strokes. Someone willing to live inside the same dream.

Cy talked about how we'd met. This was at a museum benefit, where I'd hoped to buttonhole a board member and bend his ear. It might have been another lifetime. My name impressed her then. Sure, the rare news junkie might have understood, but outside the circles we ran in few even glanced at bylines, and I liked that Cy got it. Not for vanity. I liked that she *knew* things, took knowing to be her responsibility. We were only too glad to learn from each other. And yet this changes over time. Part of you bleeds into the other person and part of her bleeds into you, and you stop having the same arguments because they have lodged in an internal space. You have them each inside yourself in silence. And the best way to make a point, you realize after a time, is to let the virus of yourself operate in peace, the proxy version of you that has taken up residence in the other person, and somehow you stop talking about the important stuff, and you forget that your partner lives in doubt and confusion, and she forgets you do too.

I thought such things while Cy was talking, narrating our life in such a way that the impending break, like the years we'd spent together, made a sorry sense. This was rubbish. We hadn't given chance or chaos an ounce of its due, and like most of us, so terrified of contingency we'll engineer our misery just to have a hand in the process, we jumped the gunwales of our ship for the agency that lives in choosing when to drown. No one wants to put in the hard work of salvaging a half-plotted mess by wiping the slate clean and starting fresh. That would necessitate confronting the unknown latitudes of one's capacity to change—and where does that end?

But Cy had the instinct to punish her pride, and while she spoke her bottom lip trembled and her anguish awoke in me, at once, the fear that we would talk ourselves into a false certainty, and the memory of everything I cherished about her, those rare qualities I took for granted and now would miss. Her dry wit. Her dependability. The way she often made one short remark that cut to the heart of things. How she never got resentful when circumstances meant she had to shoulder some joint burden on her own. Her affection for the creatures of this globe, the most austere and inaccessible of living things, when otherwise her sentimentality hovered near absolute zero. The brash floral dresses she liked to wear. Her indulgence of my habits and quirks, even when I showed up at her gallery openings looking like a spectral junkie, and the perfect partisanship she showed me in anything that counted. Her love, or rather the pure joy certain pleasures could arouse in her—an excitement that seemed so youthful and unalloyed next to the sorrow and fatigue she bore more often. I don't know . . . Maybe these are generic traits, because it was not the *fact* of them but the precise quality of her spirit under their influence that seemed to me in that instant precious beyond reckoning, undiscoverable anywhere else on earth, in anyone else, because of course it was.

My feelings at that moment verged on such a delicate register that I could only sit there, deadened, impassive while Cy spoke. I appeared emotionless, unaffected and thus heartless. But it was my unhappiness that froze me, that held me there, and I understood that I would cry less and suffer more. I have the courage of my convictions, but Cy has a sturdier soul. She clings to life like someone who has had to make the choice. She believes in other people and can trust them, while I am like some vagrant heretic with a hundred theses and no creed. I lost my faith along a wayward path. Only in misplacing it did I see I'd ever had one.

Cy left me the apartment: a kindness. I think she knew that without it I would join Roland on the pier or end up sleeping on the love seat in Henry's office—and Henry had told me to get lost for a few weeks. He was right. I'd only have gotten jumpy hanging around the *Beacon*, but the alternatives, well . . . I stayed in and watched rivulets of rainwater wreathe on the windows. I watered Cy's plants, took in the herbs from the fire escape and built a shelter for them of cardboard and tinfoil, caretaking her vestiges. The apartment seemed bare and run-down without her. Had there always been so much dust? I became briefly obsessed with the dirt that lodges in the crevices of moldings, and I cleared furniture from the walls, vacuumed, and set to work with an old toothbrush. The reeding and beads in the splayed crowns had collected grime along their lengths, and this dirt felt to me like the proximate force of chaos, and my own battle with it the attempt to impose order. Or, no. The battle had become simply a metaphor for the possibility of order. We all have breakdowns, mine was no different: you put the immediate urgencies of life side by side with the hopes that hang over it, and you discover the two share no common cause.

My mad spring-cleaning did serve one trifling purpose. I discovered that a previous tenant had penned tiny phrases along the baseboards in a half-legible script. These affirmed such sensible maxims as *The basis of optimism is sheer terror* and *Paranoia is a legitimate response to my manifest persecution*. The words summed to nothing; a joke. I was simply looking for a message, a communiqué from the world beyond. Tuned like a radio to the signal in the static, I could convince myself I heard the phantom threads of a human voice. This is an occupational hazard, and a genetic disposition beneath. The difference between sanity and madness

seems at times to turn on little more than how tightly we gauge the sa-
lience of coincidence; and in a job that rewards conspiracy thinking by
always demonstrating that the bar of unthinkable venality has further to
sink—well, the work follows you home, as they say.

But straining into the mist does turn up the occasional ghost. The
other thing I did—something I had never done before in my career—was
to organize my notes.

Now, as you know, once you get around to organizing old notes you're
spinning your wheels. Was I trying to trick myself into believing a stalled
car could make progress? Most likely. But taking it lying down was too
depressing. They had burned off the less juicy bits of my story in Monday's edition, tucking the bowdlerized remnant several pages in behind
a lot of soft news and a goat-choker about education reform. According
to this interminable report, a new crop of superintendents was clamor-
ing for more technology in the classroom. Who could have guessed? You
could set a watch by the predictability of it and count down from there
to the heat death of the imagination—about five minutes to midnight
by my reckoning. But (so the thinking seemed to go) our children's lives
would run through light portals of the virtual, and we had to prepare
them, didn't we? French might suffice for the starry romantics whose
parents endowed gymnasia and museum wings, but who would deny that
the machine's language stood aspiring bilinguals in better stead? Still, the
jungle names—Java, Python—seemed to purr with a half-buried longing
for the contact and rawness of an ecosystem, something altogether different from the nodal network we appeared destined to become, mere points
where the great tide of data inflected.

They had buried my story on A7 below the fold, a blip, a glorified
squib you could have missed about a new approach to interrogation. It
meant to skirt the Scylla and Charybdis of cruelty and credulity by plac-
ing interrogees within a confected narrative—one designed to induce
them to divulge contacts and practices by making them the hero of their
own epic. 'Soft interrogation managed in totally artificial reality,' it was
called: SIMITAR. It would eschew inhumane methods involving violence

and deprivation, and abandon the hard, artful work of turning a subject by winning his trust. The program had screenwriters and spy novelists on the payroll, Jungian scholars invested in the 'hero's journey' monomyth; they consulted with a rumpled magician-turned–public intellectual, who had written a history of confidence games, Ponzi schemes, and other high-level scams. The project was run through defense research, which contracted the work out to Templar Cross, one of Athos's private military and intelligence subsidiaries. The defense consultancy Drayman-Halley would oversee the program. They had three years to demonstrate proof of concept.

The alphabet soup of firms and agencies made for a complicated read and, from my perspective, a slippery paper trail. Although the program had begun under the Brantley administration, it was Haig's brainchild. Haig was the ranking member on the select committee and the sparring partner of Brantley's allies in the Senate—Maubry, Coppin, and the rest—and I guess they greenlit his pet project as a partial loaf for his support on a spending bill. Brantley wanted an end to the aggressive interrogations his predecessor had championed, but he couldn't risk the political blowback of appearing soft if an attack occurred on his watch. Haig gave him an out. SIMITAR involved no physical coercion, no violence, and if it blew up, Haig and his allies would own the fiasco as much as Brantley.

Blow up it did. Just not, well . . . publicly. As far as I know, they only tested the approach once, on a detainee named Ismail Kamari. They seeded his detention facility with a pair of undercovers posing as internees who befriended Kamari and conspired with him to escape. This was carefully managed. The tricky part was constructing a version of reality—of freedom—that Kamari would believe in once he broke out and which would keep him moving within precisely delineated grooves while maintaining the illusion of his autonomy. Every consequential individual he spoke to was a plant. The devices he touched—phones, computers—were carefully monitored and diverted to fake websites, fake contacts. They went so far as to construct an alternate history of the decade of his detention. Kamari made it halfway around the world within the bosom of this deception before he got wise to the ruse, fatally stabbing one of the undercovers with a plastic shank and leaving the second in extremis in a tribal border region not known for the provision of healthcare.

Kamari had a few screws loose. He hardly made the ideal test subject, but the government didn't have anyone else on ice who knew half as much as he did. By the time I found all this out, the hushed-up saga was several years behind us. Brantley's deputies had been appalled. Old-timers like Maubry, Haig's longtime rival and predecessor as committee chair, said this was what you got, farming out security work to the private sector: cut corners, sloppiness, feverish visionary stuff that horseshoes all the way around to madness. In cleanup mode, Brantley's people brought in their own evaluators, loyalists from the agencies, and it was from one of these, a sterling analyst named Lance Berryman, that I had the story. We chatted through the election season, when no one was paying attention. Brantley was termed out; the polling looked bad for his anointed successor. And Berryman was worried that if Haig's people came to power they'd revive the program, or sweep what was left of it under the rug. He wasn't wrong. Things had gone into abeyance after Kamari, but the new administration managed to prevail upon my higher-ups at the *Beacon* to kill the story or any mention of Kamari and the test. James Tolliver, our publisher, and Cat Lewysohn, the board chair, deferred to their rationale. You had to give an incoming administration the luxury of trust, was their way of thinking. At least at the outset, before they knew you knew they were villainous liars. Haig was in as intelligence director at this point, and Athos's chief counsel, an irascible, blowsy lawyer named Dietrich, had slotted in as the VP's chief of staff. Behind closed doors everyone told Henry and James that SIMITAR had shut down. And maybe it had. They'd dismissed the program evaluators. Lance was at a facility across the country, prepping for his next assignment. My article, meanwhile, looked like some curiosity piece about next-generation warfare or new 'physical principles' weapons, just another of defense research's follies. Henry said you didn't ditch comity with the president's camarilla until you could see the midterms in the whites of their eyes. Maybe that was the right play. It certainly didn't do me any good.

I had dinner with Joan Rightmire a few days later. You remember Joan. She covered defense for the *Examiner* and missed us in J-school by a couple of years.

We'd barely sat down when she said, 'I heard Cy left you.'

'Jesus, word gets around,' I said. 'I might have left her, you know.' The deadness of her affect must have taken some effort. 'How did you hear?'

'You know me, I keep my ear to the tracks.'

'Amazing what you get up to, busy girl like you.'

Joan and I had been on a few dates—oh, many years back. This was during a string of mistakes with nice girls—Brooke, Val, Tina—and a long time before Cy. Things never went anywhere with Joan. She dug chicks, and in retrospect the whole ham-fisted business of *piccata di vitello* and linen tablecloths looks more like professional courtesy than anything else. It set us up as pals, though, and maybe that's all it ever was about.

Joan had been on the military beat for nearly five years. The brass liked her, a woman her age who could dish it. After careers of giving and taking orders in a work environment about as fun as a survivors' group, those generals were starving for a little lip. That salty out-of-school talk. It's another world over there and Joan understood it. Folks wound as tight as cassette tape. I don't just mean the culture. The atmosphere, the ecology, is different. The world stands on its head and a discrete logic presides. All they think about is the future, the terrifying uncertainty of trying to predict what you can't predict and control what you can't control. We live in different verb tenses, us and them. Their entire lives play out in the subjunctive.

Joan had ordered right away and our food began arriving before our drinks.

'I'm on leave too,' I informed her. 'It was heartily encouraged.'

'You know what they say: You can take the boy out of the newsroom, but . . . Well.' She looked at me with real sympathy. 'They did a nice job on your piece too. You're having a real bang-up week.'

'I've had better.'

'I wish I could say something to cheer you up.'

'Just don't tell me you have the story too and it's posting during dessert.'

'Is that what you think this is? I'd have brought flowers.'

'Carnations? Well, if anyone's going to bury me.'

'That's sweet.' She smiled with real warmth. 'But don't lose sleep over it. Dyson's buddy-buddy with Dietrich. They were frat brothers or something gross.'

'You know just what to say.'

Dyson was Joan's rabbi. Her Henry. He wanted to run a deep backbench with aces like Joan, but his partisan bent didn't always square neatly with the facts. That was my view, anyway, the point being he and Joan saw eye to eye in a way Picasso might have understood.

Joan tongued a residue of margarita foam from her upper lip. 'I heard Haig sent a troop of boy-lawyers over to the *Beacon*. Henry must have shit himself.'

'They were just back from an overseas junket,' I said. 'Green Zone digs. You could tell they were standing up a little straighter, practically reeked of mission.'

'No fun banter?'

'I never saw Henry's Irish charm fall as flat. St. Pat wouldn't have stood a chance with those snakes.'

'You make it sound pretty friendly,' Joan laughed.

'There's no reasoning with zealots. They'd seen God's work firsthand and felt the brush of vocation.'

'You'll know them by their fruit.'

'Right. I wouldn't have expected so much piety on hajj. The way they spun our need to spike the piece . . . Joan'—my voice dropped to the hush reserved for moments of sincerity—'we're talking about fucking with some terribly confused people, born holding the shit end of the stick. But you can imagine how persuasive that line was with those fanatics.'

'We have the monopoly on capital-*V* Virtue. That's how they see it. A little medieval skull-bashing's not going to change anything. Just throw some legal-counsel cover on it.'

'What'd you say?' I felt myself suddenly awaking, as from a daze.

'Skull-bashing?'

'No . . . Never mind.' But I'd got it. *Capital-V Virtue.* Fog lifted from the field. Joan was off on a different spur, talking about the new administration, how everyone comes in thinking they're going to find it's an afternoon's work to crack the nut the last five guys couldn't. 'Like it's not the hard problems that endure. Like chaos and complexity were just waiting for someone with a stern voice.' She sighed. 'After a couple decades, you just get tired of watching everyone stumble up the same learning curve.'

'And we have to cover it like no one ever thought of shelling the world into peace.'

'Thankfully Haig's holy war is still in beta.'

I couldn't tell if she meant this as a question, a bluff to jolt me into contradicting her. It was possible she knew SIMITAR had gone live and had even heard about Kamari. But I wasn't about to tip my hand. Maybe if she'd asked outright I'd have told her. But the Kamari story, if unprintable, still was mine.

All I said was, 'If this is spring training, I might not make it through the regular season.'

'You and a few thousand inconveniently situated goatherds.'

'What do you know I don't?'

'I'm only speaking figuratively. By the time the goats are dead, Haig will have found a quiet spot to write his memoir. It could be sheep, you know.'

This was still a moment when expectations dominated our talk. Brantley had been a course correction after his predecessor's martial enthusiasm, and now the new administration promised to tack back to our hawkish ways. Naturally they cast Brantley's irenic tenure as a disaster, a global parade of weakness, but just how they intended to revive hurting people in the name of liberty remained to be seen. We felt pretty confident it was only a matter of time. Dietrich's background in military contracting screamed war-conventions trouble down the line, and Haig and the VP were, as you know, executive-branch veterans with impressive résumés in the dirty wars of our adolescence.

'So Dyson's a convert to the pomp and rhetoric then,' I said to make conversation.

'He'll delude himself until he can't. It's always that way when your boys come to power. All the same rotten ideas look freshly misted in the produce aisle.'

'People like Dyson aren't supposed to have boys.'

'That's true. But then we're adults, Quentin, living in the real world.' She finished her margarita. 'They push you on your sources?'

I turned up my hands and rolled my eyes to say, *Of course, but to what end?* 'Dietrich's fuming. Apparently he's redder than usual. But Haig plays a longer game. He knows I'd go to jail first.'

The truth was I wouldn't have given Haig my dry cleaner's name. And nobody, not even Henry, knew about Berryman. I held Lance's career in my hands and maybe a good deal more.

'What'd they say to convince Tolliver and Lewysohn?' Joan asked. 'Anything credible or just the usual bushwa?'

'Security threats, active plots. They suggested the time horizon on this state of exception might stretch into our dotage. I think they have zero idea where this ends. Before we know it they'll be running the terror cells just to keep the denouements synced up with the election cycle.'

I could hardly tell Joan that they insisted the Kamari thing, far from a bust, had produced actionable intelligence now at use in the field. I didn't believe it, but I couldn't check with Berryman until he returned east. And he might not have known, either.

'I guess I'm getting this?' Joan held up the check. I'd stood without realizing it, suddenly anxious to get home. 'Sorry,' I said and tossed a few twenties on the table.

'That's it? No fond farewell?' She was already gathering her things.

'Words can't express the sweet sorrow.'

The night outside held the capital in a soft pause. Tree blossoms cast about in the wind, small eddies with a dirty blush. Vendors hawked books and ice creams from lit stalls, and the grillwork of glowing streetlamps, gas fixtures long since fitted with electric bulbs, impressed the night with a carnivalesque air, the circus note of art nouveau. Such a lively scene made it easy to forget that beyond the fountain and out the other side of the park, where the busker's music died on quiet air, vagrants pushed shopping carts with the accumulated equipment of survival through nights we slept embraced by trivial worries. Some loitered on the sidewalk, gaunt shadows whose paths I crossed like we were spirits on kissing planes. This wasn't true. Only the limit of my imagination made me think it, my insufficient fortitude to bore into the hours of darkness spent in makeshift shelters by the commercial dumpsters, where floodlight and shadow met. It was the price of this oblivion that often convinced me to take the long way home, so I might keep one eye open to the reality of life in this strange city, the concreteness of being in all its forms.

I call the city strange because, for all its evident bustle, it often has a dead and haunted feeling, as if it existed for some purpose other than to accommodate life. A circulatory organ for the passage of power. Its mind rested elsewhere—not on the street but in a fantastic world of grandiose and lurid designs. Dreams, and not the good kind. Not ideals, but the grim fantasy of control. The belief that you might realize the order of an idea in the regimentation of so many other people's acts, and that this grotesque vision might win you the power and reverence of a god. And this regime, of course, would draw its justification from nothing more than the specter of the very suffering it ensured.

Cy disapproved of the capital even more than I did. A place so busy chasing its own tail has no time for art, she said. Art is a destination, politics a ritual of ever-rising sound and fury, like a Shepard tone. She never warmed to it, and perhaps for that reason we had our best talks on vacation, when, far from the city's grip, on trips abroad, a week here or there, or long weekends in the dead months of summer, we talked like teenagers, open, searching, our eyes to the stars. Some Augusts we rented a lakeside cottage, the kind of screen-porch affair that leaves you with religious feelings about AC. And while we spoke, it became clear to me that Cy would have enjoyed a quiet life nowhere very special, without much more to disturb the day than wind rippling across a pond and through the pliant branches of trees. But I needed something more—to duke it out in center ring, to square off against the powers that were. That was my egotism, my vanity. Cy never kidded herself.

'You think because you loathe them that you're better,' she said. She meant the crooks who ran things, whom I pursued like a ravening dog. But I was just obsessed with their hypocrisy, she thought, which meant holding them to the terms of a game neither of us much believed in. I'd set myself up on the side of justice in a spurious chess match. It was awfully convenient.

She would glint with a clear-eyed mischief when she chided me this way.

'But there's no other game in town,' I protested. 'Someone's got to play black.'

'Oh, don't let me say there's not nobility in it. Let's just admit we're after something too. Our own sort of triumph. We're proud that we see past a lot of surface pettiness, but how brave are we, really? How different from anyone else?'

'You don't think we stand on principle.'

'We'll only go so far. Just far enough down the path of opting out that our rebellion looks like an attractive eccentricity. We're not going to step out with both feet and take real responsibility for living by our own lights.'

'Is that what you want?'

'I don't know,' she said, looking off into a distant privacy. 'Yes. Sometimes.'

Cy was seduced by the life of the mind and disdainful of it in equal parts. She believed that we lived primarily in labyrinths of thought, not in a world of things at all, but that the theories we conjured from this dreaming were by and large worthless in any practical sense. Maybe that was why she went in for painting, an unregulated illusion, whereas I took the fatal step of stringing together my perceptions in words, as if I could subdue the beasts of chaos until they lay down flat for one brief second.

Cy thought most theories of art had it wrong. Art was a kind of re-search into ourselves, the purest because the least practically concerned.

Everything profitable to some interest got snatched up as a business model or technique. Since what remained was left to art, art became the distillate where we preserved the significant possibilities in experience for which we hadn't found an application. Every last stone of discrete meaning we couldn't wring profit from. And if you wanted to know anything then about what it meant to be human beyond persisting—multiplying, enduring, metastasizing—it was to art that you had to turn, the record of what was, at once, worthless and most valuable.

This was Cy's view, and on those nights when we stayed up late together drinking, usually whiskey faintly bruised with ice, she was given to expanding on her private and grand ideas. The light went out on us when we stopped talking like this. We grew serious, and even when the cabin porch on a starlit lake seemed to give cozy encouragement to our desire for intimacy, amid the creature sounds that disparage the anxieties of human time, our recollection of old happinesses, even our laughter, had a note of desperation in it: a hope that the form and shape of a different mood might carve out space for the real thing. We had become symbols for each other of the passage of time and stood like bent question marks at the end of this unvoiced inquiry, asking what we had to show for sunk cost. The residue of art, according to Cy, made reparation for the violence of so many moments—coming, going, tantalizing, brutalizing us with their dissipation. She had her gallery, but that was other people's work. And I had my career, but that was other people's stories. What was ours?

When I got home after dinner with Joan, the cat was mewling with hunger and my thoughts had drifted from the insight that had excited me an hour before. Then it returned to me. I switched on the light in the office, and through the panes on the French doors I could see Tyche hunched over her dinner. I sifted through the papers on my desk until I found the interview I wanted and the passage that had confused me. You spend so many years pretending to grasp what everyone's telling you that at some point you cease to distinguish what you understand from what you don't. Information exists in one of two states—what you know now and what you'll know later—and the inevitability of understanding means that nothing is truly *unknown* but only briefly occluded,

decontextualized, blurry. A few months before, I had been chatting with
one of the bright young things in Dietrich's office. Solowicz was his name.
He'd done a stint in naval intelligence out of college and carried that
badge before him like a votive candle, lighting the way to the heart of
some extraordinary private mystery.

The relevant passage read:

> It all comes down to virtue. Can we fight the battle on a terrain of our
> choosing? Take field methods out of the field? Shit goes wrong out there
> all the time, I don't need to tell you. We can't predict the future. We can't
> even formalize the unknowns. So we're talking Knightian uncertainty.
> We can throw all the SOFs we've got at the problem, and near-term we'll
> see results. But the long tail? It's a cobra-effect dynamic. Unquantifi-
> able worry. Whatever kinetic actions accomplish, we never know how
> many hydra heads spring to life. History doesn't shut up. So let's move
> to a controlled environment. Take the lessons of operant condition-
> ing seriously. But humane, right? Vanishing chance of trauma. That's
> what people from the top institutions tell us. The eggheads. How many
> scientists does it take to screw in a light bulb? Two, if they could fit.

Christ, how could I have been so dense! The toy soldier wasn't talking
about morality or righteousness but a *program*. Capital-*V* Virtue. This
twelve-year-old asshole had gone halfway down the mountain over his
skis, and I'd missed it. The cat rubbed against my leg and purred while
I dialed Parisa Moardi on the security council. My working relationship
with Parisa had grown into something like friendship over the years,
and we made plans to get a coffee at the Morris-Benson the following
afternoon. First, though, I thought a visit to Castor Joseph was in order.

Castor wasn't expecting me when I dropped in next morning. The
congressional office building hummed with early traffic. The day's hearings wouldn't begin for another hour or two, and staffers crisscrossed
the marble floors with memos and briefing papers in hand. Castor welcomed me into his office. He officially worked for Maubry at the time, but
he'd been an aide on the select committee, shuffling between solons, for

as long as anyone could remember. Aides like that are coveted, the lif-
ers with top-notch clearances who can find their own way to the agency
bathrooms. Castor and I had been simpatico for more than a decade,
ever since I dropped a collegial hint that he might want to ask about the
final disposition of certain funds in a foreign arms deal. Funny how at
times the whole city resembles a whisper network. Lose the fancy titles
and the entire structure of government might be little more than people
gossiping in furtive twosomes, changing partners, gossiping some more.
It was the tide of information itself that choreographed the movements
of history and power.

'What can I do for you?' Castor said, settling back behind his desk.
He had a nice office, cozy, wood-paneled, lit by a green-shaded brass
banker's lamp that looked solid enough to crack a coconut. These were
the perks of long tenure and coveted skills. It was guys like Castor in the
end who kept the government humming. Elected officials cycled through;
they showed up like tourists every few years to pontificate and moralize,
and most slunk off to their sinecures in the private sector before grasping
how the sausage materialized. Maybe they knew just enough on their way
out the door to understand how foolish they'd been on their way in. The
Castors of the world kept the government from decompensating, meantime; they ensured continuity and even made their transitory bosses look
competent now and again.

A rich tenor crackled gently from the portable radio next to the
framed photos of Castor's nieces. He had a passion for opera and always
had something soft cottoning the air. The host came on after an interval
and relayed the performance details in a lewd hush. I asked after Sandy
and Beth. Castor doted on his sister's girls. He had little hair left and the
thin mottled skin that makes a man look prematurely aged. Behind his
glasses, blood vessels made river-runs around his temples, standing out
against the pale complexion. He was launching into the latest on the girls
and their kids, when he stopped himself with a short sigh. 'Look, I do
know when I'm being buttered up,' he said. 'This isn't what you came to
talk about.'

I steered the conversation away from my present agenda awhile longer and felt Castor out for frustrations with the new administration. Maubry had been in the minority since the midterms prior, but he and Brantley went way back. He'd had the president's ear for eight years. Now he'd lost Brantley and his old nemesis Haig was DNI.

Castor waved it all away. Life goes on, he seemed to suggest. He'd seen the guard change often enough in his time, and as I knew, the security beat had the saving grace of occasionally transcending party squabbles. Politics stops at the water's edge and all that. It required a consistency in stewardship that almost made collegiality adaptive. Everything else in the country could seize up, but threats to the nation wouldn't wait out our family feuds. Security folks had to keep opening the box to check the pulse on Schrödinger's cat—which was a way of saying the hard realities of life and death had a way of cutting through the relativism of partisan truth.

'Or so I tell myself,' said Castor, adjusting his glasses on his nose. 'But the political side of the business takes its toll. And we live in an age of sensational attacks. The great judicious citizen punishes us for market downturns—for hurricanes and floods, the truly unstoppable stuff. You can imagine the pavor nocturnus about the preventable mass event.'

'Terrorism.'

'Right. People get elected for keeping the country safe, not defending vague principles—stuff it takes the vision and patience of Solomon to see the value in.'

'You think it's changed the political calculus.'

'Oh, sure. That horse left the barn a while ago. We still talk a big game about nonnegotiable rights, but we're terrified of what they entail. We'll negotiate in a heartbeat.'

'Life, liberty, and the pursuit of a book deal, all that?'

Castor smirked. 'You bet. We won't throw one poor schlub under the bus just because it happens to be convenient. A hundred guilty men will go free before one innocent winds up in the coffle.'

'I guess some guys behind bars are doing the math right now.'

'We know it's a crock of shit, Quentin. But most of us with any say-so don't worry we'll get caught in the dragnet. The extrajudicial stuff's for po' folks, you know. The dark guys.' Castor gave me a sideways grimace.

'Justice is blind, with a subtle sense of shading.'

'Yes. But a *senseless* attack,' Castor pursued. 'Well, it could be anyone. Dark, light, rich, poor. That's the genius of terrorism: it forces us to put numbers to our idealism. How *many* deaths—how *much* fear—before we toss the poor SOB in a windowless box on the right-hand side of the globe with a few assholes who get pretty creative using home-improvement equipment?'

'It presents a unique challenge, you're saying.'

'Unique challenge! Hell, most days I think it's going to be the end of our civilization. It drives a stake right into the heart of an untenable contradiction. Utilitarianism against unalienable rights. There's a limit to how much happiness we'll sacrifice to affirm someone else's dignity.'

'And here I thought we all had dignity or none of us did.'

'It's not a moral-philosophy seminar. It's politics. It doesn't get that far. People want to know they'll be safe at the mall *today*. Consequences further down the line are out of sight.'

'You go to the mall much?'

'It's a figure of speech. I get home after nine and work weekends. I don't go anywhere.'

'Look, actuaries put a price on human life, right? Dirty secret of insurance. That's nothing new.'

'Yes, but we don't watch bean counters set off bombs in the zocalo. Even high-tar cigarettes take a pretty meandering path to killing you.'

'So guys jittery about reelection lose a little sleep. I'm not losing any on their behalf. What happened to that antique thing called statesmanship?'

Castor just laughed. 'I didn't expect idealism from you of all people this morning. If you want statesmanship, you got to make it worth their while.'

'How about virtue?' I said.

'What about it?'

'Mean anything to you?'

'Principle. Integrity. Doing the right thing when it's inconvenient. Jesus, Quentin, there's a dictionary on the shelf.'

'I mean a program.'

He paused. 'Active?'

'It's a hunch.'

'Never heard of it.'

'Officially?'

'And unofficially. I'm not being cute.'

'All right.' I stood, stifling a yawn. 'And if you do hear anything?'

'I'll throw away my career and go on the record with you.'

'Background's fine.'

I always parted company with Castor cheerier than I'd arrived. The barrel still held a few good apples, after all. He reminded you of an era when duty was an end in itself: all those folks clocking in behind the scenes, trying to get things right for the sake of rightness—for the sake of *things*. You remember what Fitzy used to say in J-school? You hate government bureaucrats until you meet one. If there was any justice, Castor would have been a deputy director across the river, but I think he liked his sleepy office and going to work in the congressional building, looking out, after the day's battles, on what I saw just then: the lawns and monuments of our national self-image, all those symbols we latched on to to believe our fate rested on a ground more solid than the probity of men and women, the vapors of belief.

A blistering sun inched toward its zenith. In those first minutes out of the cool marble corridors I felt sweat dampen and begin to purl on my sides under my suit. The feeling had a comfort to it, a familiarity. The baked lawns and hot stone plazas, the rivulet tracing the latissimus under a dry-cleaned shirt, held the accreted sense-memory of so many days on the job, hying it from hearings to think tanks, cornering officials and aides for a quick chat, a small feint to see whether we could be useful to one another.

The *Beacon* was twenty minutes away by foot, and though I'd been given my orders to keep a distance, I had a chunk of time to kill before coffee with Parisa and I didn't want Henry to think he could fob me off so easily. He felt bad about spiking the piece. I had to believe that. And while I couldn't be sure whether he stood shoulder to shoulder with Tolliver and Lewysohn, I knew his knee-jerk skepticism toward any rationale the administration offered. It was always the same scare tactics and always sound policy to assume they were full of shit. A noise had emerged within the city's background murmur, a layered rhythmic sound, and only after walking for several minutes did I discover its source. A drum circle had gathered under the dappled shade of a grand oak. The driving sound seemed to wax and ebb, building to a climax it would endlessly defer. Flutes and maracas joined the music, playing for a crowd of many ages in jeans and tunics. Most stood listening, although a few people danced in a jerky trance as if they felt their bodies attached by invisible strings to the falling hands and the rawhide vibrating beneath; and it seemed to me that the rhythm stretched over the entire city, composing its relentless beating heart, and in this heartbeat the alignment of our actions and our delivery from chaos.

You know me well enough to know that I've never been one for religion, but I have felt the hollow where the answer of divinity would fit like a purpose-built peg, and somehow the drumbeat reminded me of the terror in that emptiness and the feeling of squaring up to the face of the deep with nothing but your pulse to keep time.

My mood had thus turned by the time I arrived at the *Beacon*, a faint ill temper arising at the forced recollection of all that had been taken from me: my story and my job, which, absent Cy, appeared to be the totality of my life. Henry, spotting me at the entry to the newsroom, ducked into his office and shut the door. I decided to let him stew and wandered among the desks saying my hellos. Michael Katz-Wallace—a cub reporter who will eat our lunch in time, mark my words—was tossing a tennis ball to himself on a call. This was typical and at slow points in the day he would lean back in his chair and play catch with you while you chatted aimlessly.

It was nearly midday. The sun lay its fat thumb across the southern bank of windows. The blinds were drawn and feathered against the light, and it gave the floor a sleepy air, light filtering through the dust.

Most of our colleagues were out chasing down stories, leaving a hush to settle over the room broken only by the soft cacophony of churning copy machines and telephones trilling. I reached over the divider and caught Katz-Wallace's tennis ball. He startled when it failed to find his hand and glanced up. 'Call you back?' he said into the phone and held up a finger to me. I sat in Tom Lindenfeld's chair across from him. Tom's desk was suspiciously neat.

Katz-Wallace turned to me just in time to catch a strike to the viscera. 'What up?' he said, wincing a little from the shot.

'I got dumped,' I said. 'And I'm on leave. The latter's being described as voluntary, but so are most plea bargains.'

Michael didn't say anything, but I could see the thoughts turning behind his bright, drowsy eyes. He had an instinct for selective hearing that stands a reporter in good stead.

'You catch Schneiderman last night? One hit into the eighth. Kid was straight dealing.'

'I can't say I did.'

Michael let this go. 'You missed Rob Spearman earlier.' He plucked something from the desk behind him and tossed it in my lap. 'He brought party favors.' The cylindrical silver device had the word ARROWHEAD inscribed on it.

'What's this, Rob's favorite sex toy?'

Michael smiled vaguely. 'I think it's a pen. Or a laser pointer, or something.'

'Arrowhead?'

'Some energy company out in coal country.' He inclined his head vaguely west.

I tossed it back to him. 'How is Bobby-o?'

'Happy.' Michael's phone was ringing, but he ignored it. 'Or at least he got his face fixed that way. He even had a smile for Kitchener.'

Kathy Kitchener covered lobbying and corporate influence and she and I had shared a byline on an article about Spearman's damage-control efforts after the Weego plant fiasco. Nerve agent in the groundwater. Or, *allegedly.* That's how it got remembered, in any case, and definitely *something* was making the women's hair fall out. This was three or four years back. Spearman's employer, Drayman-Halley, had teamed up with Sparti Inc., another of Athos's shops, to develop astroturfing software for use against unions and activists. The joke about Athos went that they put the asshole in ethos, and in retaliation for the union-busting someone had broken into Sparti's systems, found nonsalted passwords for the whole cabal, and Spearman's contract, stipulating the precise brand of fjord water for his listening tour to Weego County, had landed on Kathy's desk. Suffice it to say Rob didn't send Kathy or me a Christmas card that year.

'What was he so rapturous about?' I asked. Michael threw the tennis ball so that I had to trap it against my shoulder.

He shrugged. 'New administration's good for business? I don't know.'

'Rob wouldn't take a victory lap just for that.'

'You have to ask the chief.' I saw Katz-Wallace eye the blinking light on his phone that meant he had a message.

I grinned. 'So what are you working on these days?'

'I thought you were on leave.'

'They say that. And yet here I am.'

'Yeah.' Michael narrowed his eyes. 'You are, aren't you?'

I returned the ball to his desk. 'Tell me this and I'll leave you alone. Who picked up the Haig angle after I left?'

'Abbott, I think.'

'Christ. All right.'

Trip Abbott. It wasn't that you minded Trip as a colleague. If you needed someone to get a beer with in the middle of the day, Trip was your guy. But he kept regular hours and cut out at 3:45 like a bank manager with a tee time. He even had clubs in the trunk of his car for this purpose, although it was an open secret that he didn't golf. Trip treated the work like a *job* and took a gossip's approach. This spilled ink but also meant a lot of mutual convenience. He thought press releases offered useful context, and you could count on him floating someone's trial balloons when he wasn't handing an industry shill a megaphone. At times it seemed like he could have opened a laundry, sanitizing the administration's PR. Henry would only have put him on my beat if he wanted the story to go limp like a plucked flower.

That was how I felt at the time, but maybe I was being too hard on Trip. He had an enviable store of anecdotes and seemed to know a little something racy about everyone in town, filed in his head like a Rolodex. He knew, for instance, that Abernathy had a thing for leather bars a decade before some punk blogger with a laptop doxed him. Abernathy, you may recall, was big on conversion therapy and even pushed federal funding for it into a continuing resolution. No sense getting misty-eyed on his account.

It's possible Trip simply took a more philosophical view of hypocrisy than I did. Maybe he saw himself as an archivist of human mediocrity, maintaining a record behind the scenes for the moment some upstart got too free in his prerogatives and we had to dredge from the muck the sordid history that would send him off down the path of shaming, atonement, and redemption: wash, rinse, repeat. These guys always seemed to come out clean in the end, and I can't fully fathom why some folk's blood boils at the thought, while for others it's just how the game is played. Maybe it comes down to a tolerance for disappointment. Get burned one too many times and there's a comfort in cynicism. On the other hand, Trip seemed happy enough in his low estimation of human beings, and even appeared to take a wry pleasure in the venal comedy and palace intrigue. I guess if you see it as a sport, practiced moves to pull off well or poorly, you can take a connoisseur's satisfaction in your own ability to judge the nuances of its execution. Or maybe Trip never took such an exalted view of himself.

A gopher popped out of Henry's office and I took the opportunity to slip in before the latch caught, rapping the doorframe without waiting for an invitation. 'Spearman?' I said. 'Did you need a fourth for bridge, or is Trip still short a sponsor at the country club?'

Henry breathed heavily through his mouth. Though seated, he often sounded like he'd just arrived at a fifth-floor walk-up. 'Jesus, Quentin. It's been what? Forty-five minutes? I see more of you on leave than I see my wife in a given week.'

'That's not right, Henry. It's the twenty-first century. You got to pitch in.'

'Pitch in where?'

'At home.'

'You don't *let* me go home.'

'How is Mary?' I asked after we traded remonstrative looks.

'Can we not talk about my wife?' Henry said.

'It's your hour. We can talk about anything you like.'

He shook a cigarette halfway from the pack and glanced nervously at the ceiling smoke detector. 'Spearman offered us an exclusive on a new treatment approach the VA contracted out to Drayman. Putting soldiers back together. Shouts of joy from all the king's men.'

'Both your backs itched?' I suggested.

'Everyone's tickled we axed your piece, Quentin. I don't need to tell you.'

'And now they brought chocolates and cheap jewelry, and you're contemplating that evening at lovers' lane.'

'I can dimly perceive how this all must look to you . . .' He squinted overhead in a show of trying. 'But so what? It's the same thing every four years. Dangle a little quid pro quo and see if we bite. Hope we get desperate. The first taste of access is free.'

'Any good pusher knows that much.'

'It's not like the newsstand's running out of papers. And you know as well as anyone we don't have the personnel to report everything ab ovo like the old days.'

'So you thought you'd try it Faust's way.' Henry gave an unamused look. 'Hey, don't start complaining to me about manpower right after you put me on leave,' I said.

'That's for your own good.' He let a hint of brogue touch his words. 'You know you wouldn't leave it alone. And you know when they caught you sniffing around, they'd make another run at your sources.'

'Here I always assumed that's why we retained counsel.'

'Incorrect,' he said. 'It's their charming company.'

We both smiled. Henry's intuition was likely right that pushing just then would have risked my crown jewel, my glittering source, Lance Berryman. Lance was a source the way the fountain of youth is a source, I sometimes thought. I didn't want to get cornered into a stint in prison on obstruction, either. Well, Henry *is* a decent sort. He must have heard about Cy, but he didn't bring it up. He knew I was there to put him through the ringer, but he left his trumps unplayed. For my part, I knew the détente with Dietrich & Co. wouldn't last long. It was just one of those moments when, in the devil's downtime, enemies briefly seduced by warm feelings toy with the idea of becoming friends. Soon enough they'd rediscover their congenital hatred.

'Tell me the truth,' I said. 'Did you buy the administration's rationale? Did you think I didn't have the reporting nailed down? Either's good enough for me, but tell me the truth.'

'Does it matter? I stand by the decision.'

'Because it's your job, or because you believe it?'

'This isn't confession. I don't have to pretend there's a difference.'

'Isn't there?'

Henry sighed. 'As your friend, maybe. For the rest, drop it. I want to say something nice, but I know you'll just take it as encouragement.'

I smiled, touched. 'That's nice enough.'

He took a cigarette from the pack and tapped it on the desk. Beyond the window the sun bathed the capital in its unrelenting light. I missed Cy terribly just then.

'I wonder if you really *are* dropping it.' He spoke almost to himself. 'Far be it from me to stop you. I don't know how. But if you can get pissed about something else for a while, the luster's sure to come off Haig and the rest.'

'Familiarity breeds contempt.'

'It should be the city's motto.'

I got up to leave. '"Ab ovo," really?'

Henry raised his hands defenselessly. 'Jesuits got me young.'

Back outside, the emptiness I'd felt earlier returned to me. More than simply Cy, this was the aloneness at the seat of being that life finds dark moments to remind us of. I held my uncompromising ethic close; and for this rigor the cupboard of fellow feeling seemed, at times, as still and lifeless as a tomb. Henry's friendship was real. I believed that, even when jaded confidence, like a sore tooth, caused me to probe the same spot doubtingly. He promised one a place before the fire with other men, neither power-mad nor fanatical but made of that fine buoyant stuff that kept civilization righted on the counterfloats of principle and low concession. What did I hold out for in my stubbornness? Unsullied truth? We hunger for the fire of purpose and only when we feel its heat on our approach do we see that it may burn us up, not make us whole.

Cy had concluded as much and she is rarely wrong. I did see the sense in her dream of a private, self-sovereign life. But I could have gone only so far down that path before the itch of other longings disturbed my skin. Meanwhile I had Parisa to meet and a long day ahead; and if I like to think that, had things played out differently, I would have let the story go and granted Cy the wisdom in her fears, I know this is only the maudlin of retrospection, the stuff we tell ourselves to believe we had a say.

The sun was bright and waiting when I emerged. It was thankfully a short walk to the Morris-Benson and most of the way ran through the shade of downtown. The flags above the portico were flying when the Italianate facade came into view. I was a few minutes early and crossed the hotel's carpeted marble floor, past the heavy wood-paneled columns, and settled at a table in the restaurant from which I could see the president's residence beyond the park. The fountain's small plume rose from its halo of hyacinths and tulips. Parisa would arrive promptly, five minutes late, as was her way: reliable without going stiff. It was likely this balance, I reflected, that made her indispensable across the street, the equipoise of fine judgment—and indeed she hadn't yet suffered that turn through the revolving door that so often accompanies the change of administrations.

Parisa's story was a common one. After emigrating with her parents around the time of the Shah's ouster, she and her family moved between research universities before settling on the West Coast. She'd come up on the political side of things. I don't remember exactly what shunted her into security work, but I guess she liked the tidier ethical lines. The clarity of something practical. People born to despotism don't take good governance for granted, and so it often falls to foreigners, unspoiled by our decadence, to give our political ideals their due.

Teaspoons tinkled on the china. Society doyennes and bureaucrats spoke in the fleecy susurration of those who mean to be discreet without appearing furtive in public. The perfume of lilies flooded the room from their glazed garnitures, and Parisa blew in with her expeditious grace, that of an official who spends her days tumbling into meetings with coffees and folders. She had cut her hair short and it made her look young and boyish. Her clothes appeared freshly plucked from the rack of some midmarket chain. She didn't go putting on airs.

'Don't tell me,' I said. 'You can't stay long.'

'What'd you expect? Dinner and a movie?'

Our waiter, a Nordic type with a bony brow, appeared at the table and Parisa ordered a flat white. I had no idea what that was but asked for the same. 'Extra flat,' I specified.

I've never known what makes frankness such an attractive quality in government folks—maybe it's attractive in anyone—but after the day's persiflage I felt a great fondness for Parisa when she said, 'Look, Quentin, I know James and Henry killed your piece. It's not my baby, but I don't sit too far from some people who have different paternal feelings. Misguided or not, they're saving for college, if you catch my drift. So not only *can't* I tell you anything, but in this case I don't see the point. You're not the most popular boy to be dancing with right now.'

'You're worried about your job?'

'Please. They'd just rehire me in the private sector at three times the salary.'

'But to make a statement.'

Her gaze held a hint of pity. 'I'm actually kind of likable, Quentin. I don't know if you ever noticed.'

'I have noticed. I'd have gone for dinner and that movie.'

'Don't flirt.' She wrinkled her nose. 'It's weird.'

We were silent. 'You really expect to win hearts and minds in Dietrich's gestapo?' I said at last.

'I don't know.' No great conviction touched her smile. 'But we're not here to talk about my career. How's yours, by the way?'

'Splendid. I've been typecast as an idealist and nobody wants to let me forget the world's run by scoundrels.'

'Careerists, at least.'

'And now I get to remind you it's about more than that. For both of us.'

'I'm sure it's why we get along.' She settled me with one of those attentive looks precocious students give their teachers when they suspect they've learned about all you have to teach.

'Virtue,' I said. 'Mean anything to you?'

'Principle, integrity. Doing the right thing.'

'No, I mean—'

She fixed me with a withering stare. 'Drop. The. Piece, Quentin. Figure out some other way to spoil Dietrich's summer.'

'You're a doll, Parisa.' I was beaming a little too bright.

'Jesus,' she said. 'Are you going to get me in trouble? *No.* No hugging me while you self-immolate.'

'I'd never.'

'Look, listen to me carefully. Then we're going to talk about some make-believe bullshit. Then I'm going to leave. Richard Jarosok. Clandestine service. Unhappy camper. Got it?'

'Unhappy how?'

She leaned toward me as if reaching for something in her bag below the table and said almost inaudibly, 'IG's involved.'

'And I owe this generosity to?'

'Not a favor. If you're going down, tie your bungee to someone who wants to jump.'

'History isn't going to smile on this.' I meant it sincerely. 'There are worse stands to take.' Parisa just looked past me. 'So how pleased is Jarosok going to be to hear from me?' I asked. She raised her eyebrows. 'You've never *met* him. Shit, all right.' I knew the look that followed. It said each of us had to do the hard part alone.

'Do you think we're friends, Quentin?'

I leaned back and looked at her. 'I do.'

'I think so too.' It was only much later, after we'd changed gears and traded a few stories, after Parisa had finished her drink and gone and I'd emerged into the golden afternoon light, that I realized she'd slipped a note into my pocket when she leaned over to squeeze my arm. 'Pick another hill,' the note said.

Rich Jarosok's number wasn't listed. No surprise there. I put in a call to work and got an intern to run his name. The database turned up a few numbers and addresses across the river from the last four years. Promising, though it was still too early to catch him at home. And I preferred to wait until night, anyway, when the hour bleeds into the still dark and vouchsafes an air of unadvised security.

Sitting on a fountain rim just north of the hotel, I relaxed for the first time that day. The fountain wasn't turned on, but a pale blue water filled the basin and shivered in the wind. Ribbons of angled light ran through it, and children made their uncertain way to its edge and touched the liquid gingerly over the concrete lip. We begin with such elemental fascinations. Maybe these can't endure. Maybe there is sense in the erosive blunting of time, since amid the bustle all around, the besuited hustling through the intersection to a final meeting on a day so ripe you could feel the breath of summer's rot gathering in the sewers and fens, the shop doors opening and closing, the traffic making its sore passage around the edge of the park, I could easily perceive the lonely desperation in our daily needs, but what it signified together, if anything, remained unclear. Did we use our brief time wisely? When you got right down to it, whose imperatives did we serve? Because the scary thing, when you have been on this beat for as long as I have, is how much the apparatus will do to keep this regularity intact and the somnambulism of our days unbroken. I mean the apparatus of government, but something deeper too. The lengths to which it will go and the lives it will write off as collateral damage, simply to keep the machinery of our illusions humming, have always seemed to me so mad that even profit can't explain them. Maybe it is that once the dream is broken, even momentarily, we understand how thin it always was. Or maybe those in power grasp something I don't about the necessity of collective dreams, and how the strength of any authority rests on our ongoing and untroubled suspension of doubt.

And yet we all have moments of powerful awakening, it seems to me, when even the most tangible beams of the truth enclosing us look rather like the sunswept ruins of a dead and dying church, and we wonder whose superstition we are living in, and whether we can abandon it without combusting in the glare of reality unmediated by such sweet and sorry lies. Our impulse to have children might then be a last grasp at control: the chance to live, if according to illusions, by our own. Did what comforted us in them turn out to be that we could be their gods and storytellers and, for a time at least, arrange a sensible and just world for them—the very thing we desired for ourselves and despaired of getting? And how much of life, if so, was spent curating our own solace in the vagaries of paranoia and belief, the idiosyncratic conviction by which we wrested individuality from a morass of delusion? But the delusion would never be our own, for we had not created the impulse in us that would choose it. I am speaking about the very possibility of selfhood, you understand. Of being a person and not a machine.

I had for years kept busy enough to defer such questions. I lack the ascetic's disposition, but only by the breadth of a vanishing dimension: that of doubt and its public representative, humor. All the same I had an intuition just then, a trembling light at the periphery of my awareness, that I had been liberated from the harness of consequence and could drive all my stubbornness into the netting of illusion and see how far it held, or whether like the film of a bubble it gave lucidly until it popped. I will persevere until I make it to the far side, I thought, or until I discover one does not exist.

It was a call from Castor that stirred me from my reflections. The sun had fallen below the roofline of a stately building to the southwest, an imperial facade with an ad for a luxury-watch brand on its cornice. The watch face showed just after 5:30.

'Yes?'

'Quentin, Castor. Look, you won't believe it.'

I felt I knew what he would say before he said it. The structure of tonal music hangs over investigations. You can all but hear the next passage in the last.

'You had me in a sensitive information facility all day, going over damn program calls with a ruler,' Castor complained. 'By the time you get down to elements in each subcategory, you're talking a thousand line items. Plus, they love burying the most important stuff in some innocuous sub-element.'

'Well? I'm on the edge of my seat.'

'How much do you already know?' I hesitated and Castor said, 'Level with me, Quentin. I need to know my exposure here.'

I told him the program was cutting edge. Ran through the directorate and the office of the VP. High-level sign-off and dear to the brass in the new administration. I hadn't tied up every loose end, but I was talking to a lot of folks. Had sourcing way inside. I didn't *need* much from Castor, but I couldn't get my head around one thing: Why was this ready to go on day one? The legwork must have occurred on Brantley's watch, and that didn't check out. Brantley wouldn't tee up the opposition like this, but someone had paid for it. 'Everyone says this costs a lot,' I remarked with no idea if it was true.

'Not cheap.'

'Yeah. Big bucks,' I echoed, leading Castor by his own admission. I didn't like playing him, but the moves were second nature and the way forward as enticing as light from a bright room spilling into a dark hallway. 'It's hard keeping stuff this fancy under wraps. See, that's what I'm struggling with. How they avoided drawing attention.'

I could tell Castor was smiling when he said, 'It's their job.' This was the turf on which he'd fought his professional battles, trying to ascertain for his bosses precisely *what* they were signing off on. The clandestine agencies wanted the largest appropriation with the least oversight. It was a maximization problem for them.

'There's a clever way to do this,' said Castor. 'First you bury it in a budget category that already has a lot of big-ticket items.'

'That way it doesn't stick out.'

'Right. Then you claim it's part of a bigger disbursement that's already vetted, something vague. RD&E. Developmental programs by nature undergo less scrutiny.'

'You don't look too closely at the experimental stuff before it's implemented.'

'Correct, but—'

'Sometimes it's a blurry line between testing and operations. You don't want to make work for the constitutional-law crowd until you know it delivers.'

'And . . . ?' Castor was definitely smiling now.

'And so you run the program proper while claiming it's in beta. And when you get caught, you say that if you copped to it earlier it would have leaked.'

'Tipping off our redoubtable enemies and crippling the program before it began.' Castor paused. 'So they wouldn't be thrilled we're having this conversation.'

'And it's our job to thrill them?' A woman on the sidewalk gave a look of concern at my sudden vehemence, and I shot her a placating smile. 'I guess Haig thought he could slip this past Maubry,' I said more quietly. I didn't want to pound the point too hard, but I hoped Castor would take the hint that only by talking to me would this get back to his boss: yet another subtle move on the chessboard over which Haig and Maubry had squared off these past decades.

'Look, even with all that,' I said, 'they don't slip a line item this fat by you.'

'That's where the jugglery comes in.' Castor chuckled. 'See, you have to get real deep in the lexical arcana to realize they're running half the program through Energy.'

'Meaning what?'

'Meaning I'm only looking at a fraction of the cost.'

'Split it up and it doesn't look so big.'

'Sure.'

'And how much flows through private entities?'

'I don't know. We get summary outlays, but I'm not privy to their itemized expenses. I mean, I could *ask*, but you tell me how far you trust those guys.'

Something was bothering me. 'Energy's got to have a modest intel budget,' I said. 'This would only look more conspicuous on their tab, no?'

'It's not on the intelligence schedule,' said Castor. 'I don't understand all of DOE's bookkeeping, but best I can tell they have the funding indexed to a power facility in the Minersville-Johnston area.'

I felt a queasy stab of recollection. 'Where they run the dam.'

'You know about it?'

'Rumblings, rumors.' I could hardly mention Roland without sounding like a nut.

'Then there's this grant program at A-Double-I-S.'

'A-Double-what-now?'

'The Advanced Institute for Interdisciplinary Sciences. You know, that big research institute in Branford.'

'What's their angle?'

'That, I'm afraid, is where my job ends and yours begins.'

'Because you're on thin ice if you say more?'

'Because I don't know more.'

'What are you doing right now? Let me buy you dinner.'

'Can't. Eating with Sandy and the kids.'

The image of Castor at the table with his niece and her children put me in mind of my own lonely evening. There was a pause and Castor said, 'Get me dinner when you've got the story locked down. I want to hear what we've been paying for this time.'

I'd made it most of the way home on the call. At the corner of our block a fragrant bush filled the air with a sweet, chloric scent. The dark brick structures softened under the evening's warmth. The building lights had just come on. Against the still-bright sky they bled a luminous pallor. The block felt abandoned. Darkness curled in the leaves of the hot-weather trees on lawns. No glow came from our window. Even the traffic at the far intersection moved with a muted hush as I lingered at the gate.

I supposed that our building had become *mine* in this short interval, though Cy leaving me Tyche and the furnished apartment suggested she wasn't desperate to claim what she could and get away. Maybe she thought I needed time to make the changes one must come to on one's own. Still, she had enough realism in her to know the risk of our discovering in isolation how little besides inertia kept us together, and to accept this risk, I saw, indicated the gravity of her concern.

Tyche greeted me at the door. I didn't doubt that she had noticed Cy's absence, but you can never tell with cats how deep an impression you make. You offer warmth in the cold months and an enviable facility with can openers. That's about it. Shadows and planks of dusky gold cut across the apartment. I flipped on a light and undid my shoes while Tyche interposed herself at my ankles.

'All right, all right,' I said. 'It's going to happen in the next minute or two. Can I open a beer?' I sat at the kitchen table and popped the bottle cap. Tyche stared at me. Underwhelmed by the quality of the service, she rolled onto her butt and started licking herself. 'Gross. You win,' I said and reached for the canned salmon.

While the cat ate her dinner, I took my beer into the office. Night had begun to claim the city and distant office buildings blazed with their quiet after-hours persistence. I considered the state of play. I didn't know enough yet to go snooping around Minersville or Johnston. I had very little, really—mostly the old reporting from months of chatting with Lance Berryman in dingy bars and coffee shops. Lance was sore like idealists everywhere in intelligence, the same old story. The mission to safeguard the citizenry corroded over time until only the impulse to control remained. Government would protect us by ensuring our character stayed within the bounds of docility. As its power grew and technology permitted more sensitive penetrations into inner life, the nature of crime would shift by turns from action to thought. We would domesticate humanity in the interest of liberating it; cage it to preserve it.

Stalwarts like Lance didn't believe in cutting corners. They'd signed up to keep us safe with all the handicaps of humanism. We had decades of evidence on the pitfalls of rough interrogation, milking detainees for the phantoms of their imagination. Torture was a joke, a game, and most figured out the play. Your ticket to reprieve wasn't the truth, but what your interrogators *hoped* was the truth. On the other hand, you could flip a lot of folks with patience and time, with rapport and a path back into the fold. It didn't always work, but a surprising number turned *pentito*. Old-schoolers like Brantley, Maubry, and Lance knew the cost to moral standing always outweighed what violence could accelerate. They wanted to return to a law-enforcement approach, even if terrorism confounded this with the epistemic and legal challenges of prosecuting what hadn't happened. This was the bind Brantley found himself in—just what Castor had been on about that morning. To maintain the credibility of a humane approach, he needed a clean record: no successful attacks. That meant somehow making prevention more muscular while emptying out the coercive tool kit. I could see why he'd relented on SIMITAR.

But Lance viewed this as a bridge too far. Could we say with confidence that cutting a person off from reality was not torture every bit as severe as the physical sort? Did human beings have a right not just to avoid pain but also to stand on truth's firm ground? To know, in a minimal sense, that our lives were real? Lance thought so. And he knew that once you break this lifeline of naive trust in all that encircles a person, you might as well kill him, because there's no coming back. The scars on that kind of breach never close. I understood why Brantley had tried to bury the Ismail Kamari fiasco, and I understood why Lance, brought in to review the disaster, had decided to disinter it. But now I saw the tendrils drove deeper than Lance had led me to believe, possibly deeper than he knew. Something was afoot in the background that even Brantley must not have perceived. A technological fix to the fatal flaw in SIMITAR, to the organic chaos of human agency within the liberties of space and time. VIRTUE would make another Kamari impossible. I didn't quite know how, but Solowicz's words suggested this much. And from Castor's budgetary excavations I had reason to believe crack scientists were involved. Was it possible Haig had put all this in place with pals like Dietrich while the country slept peacefully under the murmur of Brantley's grandfatherly reassurances? And what of Rob Spearman? He had to play a greater role than I'd understood if he was the make-nice delegation to the *Beacon*. I could only conjure lurid nightmares at this point. And while I would have liked to light out after the core of this thing, nestled, it seemed, somewhere in the foothills to the west, where the Minersville dam's turbines spun, for all I knew the center of operations lay behind an unassuming glass facade in some nameless office park. It made sense to check out the institute at Branford first.

The dome of human illumination enclosed the capital like a heavenly gas, obscuring the stars. Only a planet and the moon shone through. The flickering lights of planes heading to cities up the coast blinked now and again like forgotten beacons and the noise of a chopper winging in low over downtown threaded the night. Few places are as removed from the ecological fact of human life as this city. Cy was a city girl and still she hated the crude and brutal thingness of it. And yet much as the mercury haze seeping into leaden mauve obscured an unlovable place, this prospect from our rooms was one I had so often shared with Cy at day's end that all I could see in it now was her absence, and beyond that our strange decision, if you can call it that, to spend so many years looking out at the world side by side.

I needed to tell her I was leaving town. This was what we had come to, calls to let the other know someone needed to feed the cat. I'd have liked to say something profound: how we live bound by the form convenience takes at the moment we come to value it; how I saw this now, and saw the problem isn't that people change but that they shield each other from their change, honoring the letter of a contract they've abandoned in spirit. But the truth is I didn't know how to say this to Cy. I only knew how to guard the position I'd staked out over the years. I bristled with too many tactics, judging the shape of motive, like sonar, from the angle of each response. All those jokes to catch people off guard, the calculated brusqueness, listening for the faint inflections in its echo. Could I stop this madness—with Cy at least? The phone rang for a long time before she picked up.

'Hello?'

Her voice sat in a blessed stillness.

'Is this a good time? I can call back.'

She laughed at my solicitude. 'No, it's fine.'

'I'm heading out of town,' I said. 'Just for a day or two.'

'Vacation?'

'No, no. Work.' I braced myself for a scolding. She knew I was supposed to be cooling my heels.

'New piece?'

'Ah . . . Well . . .' Her silence was altogether too acute.

'We have the opening Friday, don't forget.'

Did she mean we 'the gallery' or we 'she and I'? I'd forgotten either way. 'You want me to come?'

'People will expect you. I don't want the night to turn into something else.'

'That's the only reason.'

'It's a reason.'

'You can say I'm away for work.'

She was quiet and I could feel a light exasperation fill this silence. '*Will* you be?'

'No,' I said. 'I'll be there.'

'Thank you.' She paused, her mood brightening. 'You'll like the work. It's very . . . hypnotic. You catch yourself staring.'

'And if it isn't the work I'm staring at?'

'What does that mean?'

'You know how you tart yourself up for these things.'

Her voice took on a demure note. 'It's my gallery,' she said. 'I have to look nice.'

'Exquisite torture.'

'You'll handle it.'

I drank the last of my beer. 'You only think that because you don't have a good angle on the effect.'

A silence fell between us. My line offered her a forked path, toward playfulness or toward the reality beneath it, and I feared Cy, for melancholy, would choose the latter and disclose our fate in this bias. She had a talent for gloom. But though I chafed at the air of volition in her moods, it did occur to me that one's comfort with sorrow might also show one's strength in the face of it.

She spoke quietly. 'I never said I was sure about this, Quentin. But we have to let it happen a little. Otherwise, what can we discover?'

'I have to respect the terms of what I never wanted.'

'You don't *have* to do anything. I'm asking you. That's it.' When I didn't respond, she said, 'How long are you going to pretend that this is me and me alone? Sometimes I think you need bad guys.'

'I don't believe in bad guys. You know that. I think some people make bad decisions because it's convenient. And some people make good decisions and suffer for it.'

'And who's who right now?'

'It was a general point.'

The conversation lapsed. I glanced up at one of Cy's watercolors hanging in the study, a diaphanous vibrant still life in scarlet and orange.

'You said you had your dissatisfactions,' she said.

'That was a false confession. It never crossed my mind you were baiting me.'

'Seasoned journalist like you . . .' Her tone was mocking but affectionate.

'And what do you think we have to discover after all this time?' I asked.

'I don't know.' She was quiet, and I tapped the desk idly with a pen, staring at the city without taking it in.

It seemed to me that Cy thought life had further dimensions to disclose, as if this could not be all there was and the day's deadness would prove to be a mask on the living truth. Did she believe this or was it the futile longing of age? I had abandoned the idea of a couched reality tracking behind us. I found enough intrigue on my daily rounds and came home ready to encounter surfaces that faithfully represented all they hid. I even experienced a certain normalcy in homelife as a charming eccentricity, and at times felt I'd waited my whole peculiar existence to stumble into the staid wonder of something as holy as ordinary coupling.

Still, I am sensitive to selling Cy short. She knew me better than I knew myself and had her eyes trained further down the road. I kept putting one foot in front of the next, for this is often all you can do in this work. To step back and regard the panorama might overwhelm you. We have all seen hard-driving reporters take time off and, with a quiet moment to reflect, succumb to the tide of stress deferred.

'How's the new place?' I asked, charting a path to safer ground. Cy was renting a furnished apartment near the gallery.

On this terrain her tone recovered its languid warmth. 'Fine. I want to say charmless, but they did a nice job in spite of themselves. The wall art's a disaster, but it's cozy.'

'Tyche will be happy to see you.'

She ignored this. 'I saw they gave Trip your beat.'

'Is it that obvious?'

'To me.'

'Trip's a propitiating gesture. Suck up to the administration for a year or so. By the midterms everyone's got their knives out and you're just one more vulture picking at the carcass.'

'Meanwhile, they'll throw you under the bus.'

'It's got to clunk over something.' When she didn't respond I said, 'It's a business, not a charity, even if it's a shitty business that tries to pass itself off as charity.'

'Something like.'

She knew I took her side in this; or rather she knew she was taking mine. Sometimes you argue the other case to test its angles, that's all. People love to tell you life isn't fair, but who the hell knows. Next week a cement mixer could jump the curb and ruin your tennis game forever. It's a lousy thing to say. Life isn't exactly unfair, either. Time tells different stories about punishment and reward depending on where you clip your segments. Meanwhile the *Beacon* had no real love for Haig & Sons. Henry and James would go to bat for me in a crisis, that I believed. But there were rhythms to the dance. If you intended to throw your partner off the balcony, you had to tango him to the edge first. Innocence worked wonders. These dancing pairs, reporter and reported-on, needed each other, and some pearl-clutching at the scandal that made up our nourishment was unavoidable. In a world without scandal we'd long for it. I mean journalists but other people too. Without villains we'd have no heroes worthy of the name, and without human frailty on a grand scale we'd have no tragedy to purge the silly drama of our wickedness.

'Quentin?' Cy's voice had dropped a register. 'If you're sticking with the story, nail them to the fucking wall, OK?'

'And then you'll come home,' I said.

She sighed. 'Of all people, don't *you* start pretending life keeps its promises.'

She was right, of course. I merely wanted something to hold on to. But you cannot ask for what must be freely given.

The only watercolors of Cy's in the apartment were in my study. She didn't rate her stuff highly and in the event that we entertained didn't want to appear vain or out of touch. Still, I loved her work, a chauvinism which no doubt accentuated her embarrassment and the vehemence of her prohibition. I never claimed to have an eye for art, but I don't subscribe to the stubborn fatuity of the untutored either, who think it's all a matter of *feeling* and fawn over the crass, easy stuff when they spot mimetic facility or think they get a joke. Cy's work had no ambition to leave its mark on the form, and I can't say of course that my opinion of it didn't run through my affection for her; it did. Her work touched off an emotion in me and a pride too, maybe for no other reason than that the affinities which brought us together in the first place meant we placed our emphases of value at similar intervals.

I had taken one of her sketch pads from the flat file and begun flipping through it. The initial pages showed studies of the same scene, the view of a lake from the front of a rental cottage we'd stayed in one summer. The front page was dated lightly in pencil. With a little effort I called the place to mind, a simple thin-walled cabin clad in gray shingles and peeling white trim, sited near a dogleg in the lake where the view opened up in both directions. We'd enjoyed our week there. Clouds of tiny insects roiled above the water. I read a book about baseball and a couple of political biographies, sitting in an Adirondack chair while a little ways off in the shade Cy worked out the perspective of the far shore's outcrop of rocks, the pallor of the washed-out sky and its echo in the lake below.

If you asked Cy why she chose watercolors, she would tell you they

were simple, easy, and portable. All true, but I thought modesty played
a role she wouldn't admit. She and I rejected the idea that we were interesting in our own right and should be interesting to others. My conviction was vocational: I had signed up to tell other people's stories. For Cy
it had to do with her upbringing, I believe, and her father's legendary
narcissism.

The rich, she often said, are plagued with the delusion that money
makes a person interesting. To hear her tell it, she got so sick of her father's
amour propre that she lit out of his cryptlike townhouse at the first chance
she got. Whether it was in fact cryptlike or simply carried the association for her wasn't clear. She dropped out of college halfway through her
first semester, picked up menial jobs on the periphery of the art world,
and stayed on in the city, carving out her own education in the scene
without bothering to keep in touch. If her behavior worried or hurt her
father, he never let on. He had mammon to conjure from the miracle of
securitization and saw his daughter's willful independence as the happy
premonition of high character. He could never accept that she actually
loathed him; this was not within his credible range. Maybe the approval
of sycophants had weakened the muscles in his imagination. The patri-
cidal impulse went far enough, at any rate, that my own reporting on Ian
Mortimer Leach's notorious bulge-bracket bank, where Cy's dad worked,
endeared me to Cy. I. M. Leach played on the black edge before the term
had common currency, leveraging relationships with industry insiders,
analysts, and trade reporters to get out in front of the market. Sometimes a
few hours were enough. Zoom out, take away the gilt reputation, the white
shoes, the porphyry and marble, and the whole thing looked like a strip-
mall pump-and-dump, run out of a neo-Gothic tower deep downtown.

Cy had spent her childhood listening to the creed's true believers at
home. This parlor-room Objectivism could have ground a lama's patience
to dust. Still, not everyone has the courage to reject their family and cut
the umbilical cord of inheritance. Maybe Cy's dad had her number after
all. I'd like to tell you he died like Lear, raving for the one child of his
who saw through his bullshit, but he died happily enough in the arms of
a young wife on permanent vacation in the Antilles. A case against him

was wending lazily through the courts. He'd lost bragging-rights cash but he never spent a night in jail. Cy didn't condemn him, but she never forgave him. She thought we dish out too many happy endings to palliate our own fear of dying unforgiven.

So did any of this play into her decision not to become an artist? I thought it left her allergic to the conceit that self-promotion demands. She'd seen where an exaggerated belief in your seriousness as a person got you: the neediness, the resentment, the delusion it bred. The world doesn't have the surplus for wounded egos. Watercolor offered her a satisfying dead end.

I had lost track of time and when I glanced at my watch it was later than expected. 'Shit,' I said, though Tyche was the only one who could hear me. I typed Rich Jarosok's number into my phone. The first number I tried wasn't in service, but at the second a man picked up.

'Rich?'

'Who's this?' The voice's deep gravel didn't avail itself to pleasantries.

'Quentin Jones,' I said. 'I'm a reporter at the *Beacon*.' I waited a beat, just an eighth note, to let this register. 'We have some pals in common. Thought I should give you a ring. Now a good time to talk?'

He liked to let things stand a minute before responding. 'Which pals?'

'You know the sort. Not real crazy about the name game.'

'Mine seems to have come up.'

The silence spread like a cloud-shadow on a field. The first minutes of a cold call are always thrilling and delicate. There's no science to the gambits of rhetoric. We make our calls about people within the interstices of tone.

'You're on people's minds lately.'

'What does that mean?'

'Kick the hornet's nest long enough and eventually some asshole like me hears the buzzing.'

'Buzzing might as well be fishing,' said Rich. 'I'm still curious about these friends.'

'Dan Gonzalez is a pal. Toby and I play poker. The wives are friendly.' This was a stretch. I doubted Toby would return my calls.

'Toby hasn't been at the agency in . . . what, four years? You need better cards if you're bluffing.'

'I don't tip my hand in public. Some people take comfort in that.'

'I bet they love strangers calling them up late at night too.'

'We get talking, one thing leads to another . . . before you know it we're not strangers.' He didn't respond. 'It's not that late,' I said.

'You seem real confident you know where I stand.'

'I'm footloose and fancy-free. Don't tell me you never ran at an asset in Irbid with nothing more than bravado in your pocket.'

He snorted. 'Nice touch, Irbid. Jesus Christ.'

'You tell me.'

'Lebanon. But I could tell you where the good *moutabel* place is in Amman.'

Rich was your typical overbright lower-middle-class kid, light-years too smart for his cornfed, churchgoing, football-mad hometown. He taught himself most of what he knew and enrolled in state school on a full scholarship. He should have been giving the coastal pretty boys intellectual noogies, clapping their jaws down on silver spoons till their teeth chipped. Instead he cruised through undergrad in three years with the dim scions of suburbia, kids who weekly drank their body weight in keg beer and hid the blush of precocious alcoholics under shaggy hair and baseball caps. They drove family-supplied vehicles bigger than Rich's living room at home. Needless to say, he loathed them and the patent myth of merit embodied in those keg-haulers they called cars, vehicles he couldn't help connecting by the tendrils of convenience to the monstrous Mideast regimes our government supported in their quest to wrap women in blankets and criminalize the democratic values we held dear. Rich took Arabic from day one, added Farsi to the curriculum in sophomore year. He got the basics of Dari during a summer abroad, and by senior year most of his classes were grad seminars and directed studies with professors in endowed chairs. Naturally, he knew the best way to show up his complacent, privileged classmates was to enlist, so that's what he did, right out of school, giving himself to the country whose freedom and plenty his classmates enjoyed without lifting a blithe, well-insured pinkie.

A perfect recruit, in other words. Spite ran hot in him and this extended to corner-cutters and hypocrites of all stripes. It wasn't lost on Rich that the petrostates we counted among our allies did a side business funding the associations and madrassas that cultivated the willing bodies tearing up the streets of Paris, Brussels, London, Madrid. Oil wouldn't hold out forever. The delicate diversification of monoculture economies resting on their volatile tide of inequality and fundamentalism called for a special, complicated engagement with the flush West. Regimes needed to ensure their relevance as allies. You need a sickness before you can sell the cure. This hypocrisy ate at Rich in his first years with the agency, as he moved through training and found his footing in the field: just how much of what he did involved, in some oblique manner, jerking off the same people who'd filled the world to the brim with lunatics trained in artisanal bomb-making. Rich had a double disillusionment in store, since, not knowing any better, he'd spent his early years idolizing the country's elite as a last redoubt of real culture. He only knew them through books, see. When Rich found out just how craven before expediency his idols were, the intervention of Christ wouldn't have spared the agency's glass house. Rich reached for a nice meaty stone.

I learned this later, but it gives a sense of Rich and why he did what he did. Maybe he was never as sinless as he thought, but he was a patriot in the sense that counts. Guys like him are tragic, the ones who save our institutions from collapsing under the weight of their own self-interest and paranoia. They see the true cost of moral disorientation, the dissipation of mission creep, and for trying to save the bureaucracy from itself they're branded troublemakers for life. For this fealty they get ostracized, and once they've fallen on their sword they're permanently crippled. Marked radicals, leakers, rogues. Not 'team players.' As a rule they never make it back. Shunned by their agency and friends, they find themselves cut off from their vocation for the very fact that they believe in it most. It's the pricks like me who call them up—that is, until they've been out too long to know anything worth knowing. If they're lucky, one of the pundit shows brings them on to do color now and again. Mostly everyone forgets them.

I told Rich to trust me for one reason: he and I were in the same boat. The boat also wasn't a yacht. The IG wouldn't do shit. He'd slow-walk the investigation until they figured out how to handle Rich and sew up the security case for keeping mum. Pretty soon they'd reassign him to desk duty, handling outside information requests. And the reprisals would keep coming until he left under his own steam. Meantime the story had gotten axed on my end too. Haig's goons convinced my editor not to run it. If it died in the free press, what chance did Rich have on the inside? Now I was on leave myself. The two of us were doing bids for the same crime.

Rich didn't respond right away. 'You've got a funny way of taking leave,' he said at length.

'That's what my girlfriend thinks.'

'You said she was your wife.'

I laughed. He was right. 'It played better that way.'

'Christ.' Rich laughed too. It sounded genuine for once. 'Listen, I'd rather not do this over the phone.'

I told him I was leaving town early the next day. It was my only chance to get to Branford and make it back for Cy's opening.

'It's not that late, like you said. Meet me at the Palmetto Lounge. Forty-five minutes.'

The Palmetto was across the river, in that subsidiary downtown which housed the contractors and flatlined after dinner. I decided to bike it, why not? I was getting out of shape. My twenty-one-speed hadn't left the basement in months, but the tire was firm when I squeezed it. Out on the street, I felt the wind rise up as the bike gathered speed and found myself briefly released from my worries. Gunning down the empty avenues, roused by the breath of escape, I passed under the halos of streetlamps, past shuttered office buildings, so impassive at that hour, and by the stores where night crews vacuumed in the half-light. The empty porte cochere of a hotel blazed with an insistent glow. The parked cars glistened gently. The city could seem so mild on nights like these that I sometimes wondered whether the rest was not illusion, the daylight our fever dream, and this the true peace of life. Letting this idea go, I hooked west, the monuments fell away, and I rose along the balustraded bridge, the river fat below, flowing and etched everywhere with the spilled light of riparian development, aglitter in its trembling oil.

Rich must have been in his car, watching for me, because he entered the Palmetto less than a minute after I did.

His smile was mostly a wrinkling at the side of his eyes. 'Biker, eh?'

'Maserati's in the shop.'

We ordered two domestic pints as wan as chicken stock and took them to a booth in the back.

'If you're recording this,' he said, 'I'd like to know.'

'No time to prep the wire.' I held up my shirt. 'And don't tell me my stomach's not much to look at—I've heard it. How 'bout a few notes?' I waved a steno pad.

He nodded OK and asked me what I already knew. I laid out a few highlights for him while he drank in silence.

'And you're sure you're not being set up?' he said.

'I'm not sure of anything. But it'd be a hell of an effort for a very small win.'

He regarded me with gray-blue eyes that I imagined had been taught to see what people never knew they betrayed. The acuity behind that gaze was powerful. It arrested you for something sad in it, a part of the spirit that had been harmed, the part that longed to believe and now had scarred over in anger, a rutted cicatrice around something gentle. I wondered whether anyone could wish for such clarity.

'Let's talk ground rules,' he said. 'Don't write my name down— anywhere. Don't mention this meeting, not to anyone. Also, this is off the record.' He considered whether there was anything else to cover. 'Oh yeah. And if you intend to do this, do your fucking job, OK?'

'Cy said something similar.'

'Cy?'

'My girlfriend.' I corrected myself, 'Ex-girlfriend.'

Rich blinked. 'You're having a real bang-up week, aren't you?'

'They can't all be winners.'

I asked Rich what happened if I said no to his terms and he said he'd walk. I asked why he thought he could trust me. He said that was his business. He must have seen something in my look because he added, 'Or we can be romantic about it and say you're trusting me too.'

'A marriage of convenience.' I drew a meaningless scribble in my notepad. 'All right.'

'No convenience,' he said. 'Trust.'

His insistence stopped me. 'Trust important to you?'

'It is.' He held my gaze. 'From a certain angle, it's the whole ballgame.'

'Pretend I don't know what sport we're talking about.'

'Blood sport. Life and death. We're talking about the future and we're talking about control.'

'That's still what I'd call vague.'

'You have to approach the future with some trust, some measure of faith. Otherwise you're fucked.'

I regarded him for some time, trying to gauge how he meant this. A man feeding coins into the jukebox behind Rich gave me an excuse to stay silent.

'You mean we have to assume a certain amount of risk,' I said at last. 'Perfect safety's a fantasy.'

'How do you protect against what hasn't happened?'

'You can't.'

'Not without taking autonomy out of the equation.'

I tapped at my pad idly. 'I feel like we've run that debate. Safety versus freedom. And so on and so forth.'

'Please.' He waved this away. 'I'm talking about the possibility of being a fucking human being.' He drank his beer. 'The occasional senseless killing will always be the cost of liberty. That's easy. What's the cost of being a person?'

'You're going to tell me, I guess. But, you know, *how* occasional?'

'Yeah. Exactly.' He grinned.

'It's the senselessness that gets people,' I said. 'Isn't it?'

'Sure it is,' he agreed. 'But if it made sense, we'd know how to stop it. Terrorism wants to make us blink.'

'Then we'll blink.'

'Yes. We will. Sitting, watching at home. This is avant-garde theater. Riveting stuff. But when we see the TV glass won't protect us—there's no respect for the fourth wall? What *won't* we give up for the promise of safety?'

'When we grasp that our principles aren't a game, you're saying. That they had consequences all along.'

'That's right. That's its strength. Terrorism's a wager—and not a dumb one—that our ideals are just a lot of talk. A lot of bluster for state speeches and seminar rooms. It knows that people, when you get them alone, are just selfish and scared.'

'Rats fleeing a sinking ship.'

'Not the right metaphor. Try passengers pulling planks off a ship to make rafts.'

'In case it sinks.'

'They make it sink.'

He meant the treatment was worse than the disease. 'Why? Because terrorism can't win the physical fight?'

'How could it? It's spiritual warfare. It means to attack our minds. It wants to destabilize our sense of order and stability, of a rational world beyond our immediate experience. We're fighting for a lot more than our lives here. We're fighting for our sanity. For a sane world.'

'They have that much power?'

Rich tapped the rim of his pint glass. 'Of course not. They're just the low-grade virus. We do the rest. It's the antibodies that kill us. The culture's response.'

'But what specifically? Mass surveillance, illegal detention? Help me out here.'

'Yeah, maybe. All that. But—' He had the tired air of having explained this one too many times. He sighed. 'If society grows inhuman enough in its attempt to stop terror, we'll have brought the terror inside us. If they corrupt our soul, it doesn't matter how many of them we kill. They'll have won.'

'Awfully grand, talk of the soul.'

'That's what people who plan to sell theirs say.'

I laughed. 'And what do you figure it is?'

He didn't skip a beat. 'The place inside us where thought and belief exist without coercion.'

'Privacy.'

'Yes, privacy.'

'But that's not going away,' I said. 'We can't read minds.'

'Can't we?' His eyes idly tracked patrons in the bar. He picked at the edge of a paper coaster swollen with dampness. 'Just looking at online behavior is enough for our models to figure out who you are and what you believe. Add daily movement to the mix and we can say what you're going to do most of the time. That's just behavior. Metadata.'

'They still can't prosecute you on a hunch.'

'Jesus,' Rich said and laughed. 'You know, you almost had me convinced that you knew what you were doing.' He shook his head but I stayed with his eyes; the eyes didn't laugh. 'Look, we already buy CT help from states that keep the militias and jihadists in clover. It's not hard to imagine we take things a step further. Formalize the process and bring it home. It's not so hard to read someone's mind when you've been whispering in their ear.'

'And in the porches of my ears did pour . . .'

'You ever hear of the Yorkville Five?' he asked. I had, though I admitted the details now escaped me. Rich leaned back in his chair and took a quick glance around our immediate vicinity. 'These guys were idiots,' he said. 'You couldn't light a pitch-black shed at midnight with bulbs like that. I'm talking *significant* inability to grasp the moment of their actions. I doubt the idea of terrorism ever entered their head before an undercover planted it there. And the UC wasn't even working for us. Just a fellow inmate with a history as an informant and a bright idea to make some dough.'

Rich ran through a story whose contours came back to me as he talked. It had been a number of years, a decade or two at least, since this quixotic band of dirt-poor stoners was hauled in on conspiracy charges and plans to destroy a federal building with explosives. To hear Rich tell it, they would have had trouble conspiring to look up the word in a dictionary. But most were still languishing in prison as we spoke, learning at last, if they hadn't already, to hate the country just as much as the bureau's informants had encouraged them to over some primo agency-interdicted marijuana.

'At the time,' Rich said, 'speaking Arabic while Muslim was a crime. Speaking Arabic period. A lack of suspicion was suspicious. But these guys weren't even Muslims. Maybe they flirted with conversion during stints in prison. Time to kill, that's it. They knew the hadith like someone in the greeting-card aisle knows Keats. When details about the group's religious practice came out, it was a syncretic mess of—god knows—macumba meets Shaolin kung fu with a bit of the Black Hebrew movement thrown in.'

The cabal's leader, Rich continued, Mickenson Duvalier, who went by Prince Malu to fellow initiates, once upon a time had volunteered for a citizens' anticrime group. That gave you an idea how committed to society's violent overthrow he was. Probably he had a screw loose since he wandered the neighborhood in Mosaic robes with a wood staff and didn't strictly forswear witchcraft. But in any case, to judge the threat he posed to a federal building you would have to know the blunt trauma a staff could inflict on reinforced concrete. The guy didn't even own a gun.

Of course this didn't dissuade the enterprising informants, one of whom called himself Tony Montana after a favorite exponent of moral probity, nor did it overly trouble the district-office feds running them. The bureau agents were guys on the make. They had fanciful dreams of their own, and their higher-ups, after—well—some notable failures on the bureau's part, liked the sound of anything that ended in a triumphal press conference. The UCs just wanted the money. The industrial-grade ganja was pure bonus.

The problem came in getting five untrained syncretists with weak job skills to plan and carry out a terrorist action. Sure, you could get them cursing the state with a little encouragement. They *had* been screwed over by larger forces, so the idea that they bore a grievance against the same system that had incarcerated them found easy purchase. But no one had a plotting bone in his body. These feds, however, were ambitious. They wanted to catch their guys driving a van full of fertilizer to the field office. They wanted to be heroes.

A more truth-seeking operation might have remarked on the strange fact that this alleged terrorist cell never once requested explosives during the period it spent planning its bombing. Instead they asked for uniforms, binoculars, and radios. The uniforms seemed especially important to them. A digital camera had to be practically forced into their possession, and Reginald August, one of Duvalier's lieutenants, only agreed to go downtown for reconnaissance photos on the solemn promise of a burger and fries. The eventual trial would need evidence of their intent.

Well, uniforms and weed were one thing, and not unappreciated, but the real enticement for the Yorkville gang was the 'overseas' cash their informant buddies claimed they could procure. They just needed Prince Malu swearing a loyalty oath on video. This was not a very smart move on his part by the standards of evidentiary law, but even a first-year in Stings 101 could see how the prospect of significant cash raised the possibility of Duvalier & Co. now running their own faux-terrorist scam. There *was* no overseas cash. There *was* no communication with real terrorists. The whole thing, from a god's-eye view, was a briefcase of marked bills left open in the poor part of town with three sets of stoned fabulists chasing one another around it.

'What could go wrong with such an airtight plan, I know,' Rich said. 'Actually, this was only the beginning of their problems, since once Mickenson caught wind of the foreign-asset stream, he realized a bigger plan might net more money. He decided they should switch targets and knock down a skyscraper. Not as easy as it looks. The feds, moonlighting their Potemkin conspiracy under the noses of the local joint-terrorism outfit, knew to keep the plot contained. The bigger the target, the greater the chance their idiocy would get them noticed. God forbid a rival picked up their guys and stole the glory.'

But now the crazy thing happened. The informants, trying to sell Mickenson on the risks of what he was proposing, so scared the shit out of Lupe Ricardo—a sweet nineteen-year-old kid and likely schizophrenic, who had joined the group to make friends—that he *called in* the plot to the same district office where these agents were working. Whoever took the call didn't give it full credence and the agents were able to bury the report. But not before the aliases of their undercovers got filed with the other names in an interagency database. Now they turned their attention to getting Lupe out of the way. Would you believe the police found an unregistered firearm and five grand in narcotics on him? This on a guy who'd never had more than three bucks in his pocket. The cops called it an anonymous tip. Lupe got fifteen years on a mandatory sentence and who knows if he ever made it out.

To move the plot forward then, before some overachiever at a fusion center dug up the report, or before Lupe made just enough sense within earshot of someone with a brain to hear him, the feds picked the target and set the date themselves. They said this came from the highest reaches of the overseas affiliate and left it implicit that should the boys chicken out, they would have far more ruthless sons of bitches to fear than the government. Ramadan ended. The day in question approached. Everything looked tentatively OK, even if the UCs had to supply the rental van and fertilizer themselves when the members of the group were refused. They paid with government cash, and even put down the deposit on the warehouse in the outskirts of Yorkville from which the cell would ultimately get its name.

On the big day, Reg was returning with breakfast when the van seized and stalled. He hadn't bothered to unload the fertilizer, or, for that matter, the uniforms sewn with the Star of David on the shoulder, and he panicked. It turned out the intake manifold gasket had sprung a leak and coolant was running into the engine. At the time Reggie only knew he couldn't fix it and needed to off-load his cargo into a new vehicle. He got picked up trying to commandeer a plumber's van from an army veteran who had put on some weight but could still disarm an incompetent at close quarters. Nobody knew what had happened to Reg at first, and to avoid spoiling the whole damn thing the bureau agents had to apprehend the cell in the warehouse, sitting in a cloud of weed smoke. They surrendered without a fight. A week later, when HQ started looking more carefully at the internal reports, the whole mess unraveled pretty quick. Either their agents were psychic mediums or they'd cooked the books. But by that time the counterterrorism brass, the guys who bestrode operations and politics, had already taken their victory laps in public and the story could hardly be walked back.

See, this ambitious duo at the bureau—guys who spent their off-hours in MMA training and had daydreams about themselves in capes and unitards—had publicized the bust. The story went like wildfire through the local press, the regional press, then made national news, and finally, to avoid a total shitstorm, the bureau had to play along with the hype, hoping that public interest would dwindle to zero by the time details came out at trial. The geniuses who'd masterminded the whole thing hadn't won themselves any friends in the bureaucracy. They got shuffled into unenviable postings, small-time smuggling and black-market activity in the islands, and when things quieted down enough they got fired on pretexts. That's where they drop out.

'But the reporters didn't have quite as short an attention span as the public,' Rich said. 'Some up-and-comer at the *Statesman* tracked down Lupe in prison and, with the help of his lawyer, a pro bono from some legal-aid nonprofit, put two and two together. This should have been a black eye for the bureau, and in another era it might have been. But at the time people just wanted to feel safe. Feel like, if anything, the government was being *too* tenacious. Too vigilant. If CT ran into the constitutional briar patch, that just showed the agents' ferocious passion for the work. For *your* security. Because no one with a stake in the political process spent a minute worrying they could ever be the Prince Malu or Lupe in any sort of sting.'

'Sting?' I interrupted. 'It's like the dictionary definition of entrapment.'

'You'd think,' said Rich. 'But it was never going to play that way. See, different rules apply when it's terrorism—oh, *supposed*, *theoretical* terrorism, I know. But what if you run a fair trial and the case gets thrown out on all the improprieties, the inadmissible evidence? What if you let these guys go free and, realizing they've been fucked seven ways to Sunday by the government once again, they get their hands on an assault rifle and let loose at a skating rink? Maybe they decide to drive a moving van through the May Day parade. No one survives the political blowback from that. Even the judge in the case—no hard-ass law-and-order type, believe me—even she wouldn't let defense introduce anything on the informants' pasts. Old Tony Montana and his pal. They had rap sheets too. The jurors never heard. The whole system's got to lock these guys up, even if their only crime was being stupid enough to take the contraband and cash pushed on them by undercovers. Even if their only discernible fault was being poor and longing for a connection to a cause. Maybe a few friends. The *Statesman* ran their exposé. The lawyers raised holy hell. The public didn't care. These guys looked the part. If you saw them walking toward you on a dark street, you'd turn and walk the other way. That was their trial, their sentencing.'

I shook my head. 'Simple as that.'

'We congratulate ourselves on abandoning phrenology as junk science when we've only turned to something more primitive. Physiognomy. What feelings does a face evoke. In the court of public opinion, hell, in the courts themselves, it decides who gets put away or pardoned. Everyone you know who doesn't give a shit about surveillance, wiretapping, and the rest—*they just think they're exempt.*'

'Aren't they, more or less?'

'Yeah, precisely. More or less. More until one day it's less. History is long. You never know when you might find yourself in the unpopular crowd. The out-group. There's no telling what stodgy old idea of honor or dignity the people in power will one day find threatening.'

'You can always adapt to the times,' I said.

'Sure, spineless venality never got anyone in trouble. But people have kids, and kids have a well-known weakness for idealism.'

'What is VIRTUE, really?'

'For now? The Yorkville Five on steroids. But in the long run there's no limit to how many of us it could sweep up. It's a way to unfold the mind. See what we're capable of.'

'Through storytelling.'

'Storytelling, psychology, technology . . . Look, pretty soon our lives might play out primarily on a digital platform. It's hard to know what terrorism even means then.'

'If it takes place in a video game.'

'What does crime become—rape, torture, death—when it's a purely psychic, disembodied experience? What can the human mind withstand when the body is kept right and hale? There are crimes we don't even have words for yet. Crimes of the psyche, the spirit. That's what we don't know.'

'And the soul?' I said.

Rich smiled and drank what was left of his beer. 'Now you're getting it.'

SUNRISE MOVED SLOWLY on the morning. The night-ink paled by degree until the dark gave up its forms in outline. Wan colors came last, olives, dry moss-greens, pallid oakleaf browns beneath a sky charged faintly with electricity, sparking in the ragged mesh of trees. The glow deepened inwardly and soon the soot bodies of clouds lay like long thin fish above the bay. The water's skin, opaque and silvered, puckered into small bowls that waited to receive and bear this early light. Then with bolts and shafts like a shining fabric, the sun overtook the scene and spread itself over land and bay, and for an instant the world awoke violently in a living, vivid bronze.

Although we had turned in late the night before we arose early, aging men who could remember getting up with the sun to check the wires and read the early editions over yesterday's coffee. Unrested, we felt nonetheless reborn by the simple clarity of waking and being. Black coffee in hand, we watched the world brighten on the lawn, dew blanketing the grass in an arachnid mesh, gossamer and assimilating everywhere with plush droplets that would honey in the fortifying glare. We wore old jeans and pullovers and wool socks in sneakers wet and flecked with grass clippings. A cold mist lay atop the field next door. The farm would harrow it soon and plant their summer crops, and the earth, tilled and churned so many times before, lay knotted and hard beneath the stagnant haze. Aside from songbirds we made the only sound in this stillness. Fog clung to the far shore. No boat disturbed the silken bay. It folded inscrutably into the sky, trolled in near silence by the gulls and fisher birds aloft on invisible rails.

More fully than before and with something like a silent crackling, the sun broke into the mist with charged filaments and a grainy wash as rich as acid on a metal sheet. The water in the air turned flush and amber, and the gold star, like a cracked bulb, spilled over the bay so that the moorings and buoys glinted and shone and the sea became one molten ore.

The morning kept on warm and damp. It took near to midday before the last of the fog lifted. Chance went wild in the heat. Izzy took a run. Frank holed up for a few hours' work in the corner of the grand parlor, and Schmitty and Quentin, having happened on gloves and a weathered ball in the closet, played toss in the field, while ducks flew by in passels and seacraft tracked up and down the bay.

By afternoon we found ourselves again in the living room. A contemplative mood held us as we waited to see whether Quentin meant to continue. We had all been put in mind of Bruce. Bruce Willrich, that is. You could not mistake the similarity between Quentin's old protégé and Rich Jarosok. And that none of us mentioned this supported the idea that we secretly agreed on what went unsaid: that the first significant changes we'd observed in Quentin traced back to the grim saga involving Bruce and his mysterious end.

Bruce had shown up at the *Tribune* maybe five years after Quentin. We were in the thick of our early careers by then, not quite a decade out of J-school. We'd concluded our rustications at the regional and third-tier city papers and landed our first jobs at the metropolitan bruisers. Izzy stayed in the south where he'd grown up. He liked the harebrained fever dream of the place and believed in an old style of journalism that more than anything resembled oral tradition. The rest of us moved north and east, to the less genteel power centers where corruption and criminality existed in their most ambitious and ambiguous forms. Quentin started on the city-government beat. Campaigns, bribery, municipal contracts.

It was only a hop, skip, and jump from there to finance, real estate, and organized crime. A city is an organism; like a biological entity, its main systems involve sustenance, self-regulation, and waste. To map the ecosystem of power you wanted to look at basic functions: building, shipping, trash management, the courts. Projects cost money, and everyone needed it, from developers and contractors to mayors and all manner of candidate for office. Dirty money took the greatest risks and that meant, in a city with lucrative contracts to offer but little in the way of public financing, pay-to-play ran rampant. The numbers added up best when you moonlighted as a laundry. That's what certain developers knew. Organized crime might take a twenty-, twenty-five-point hit if the cash came out clean on the far end. And since the whole rising tide of prosperity in the city found itself pegged to the pullulating skyline, no one under the mayoral or gubernatorial authority was going to look too hard at where development money originated. Besides, criminal and quasi-criminal entities had insinuated themselves in the weakest joints of the city's operation long ago. The mayor couldn't escape complicity without making corruption his central mission, which—since this meant shutting down and pissing off so many capital spigots irrigating the reticulated municipal economy—would only leave him too bloodied to survive the next election. Nobody likes a corrupt system, but it turns out they don't care too much who has the waste contracts as long as the trash gets picked up. No mayor ever weathered the months of garbage piling up it took to dislodge motivated insiders and fight for market-rate contracts—which might not have wound up a whole lot cheaper in the end.

You might have thought that with this beat Quentin's optimism would have died sooner, but he had a happy childhood or something and he nursed a cheery folk image of the country longer than most of us who'd grown up in the wastes of postindustrial suburbia. It was like his civics class had *taken*, and the jaded self-understanding of our TV generation had done nothing to uproot it. He beamed with the deluded sunshine of someone who espouses the founding myths, faith in the principles of our forefathers and the Fourth Estate right beside them. No one in grad school could tell whether he believed all this or just saw how much other people needed to believe it, and thus stood ready to reward you for conspiring with their hope.

Bruce was a romantic too but of a darker cast of mind. The two enjoyed sparring. Quentin wasn't credulous, but he ran the same data through a different temperamental prism. He liked the kid's grit and grumpiness. Enthusiasts need their pessimists. Someone has to play the bad cop, break the hard news. And he understood where Bruce's sullen streak came from. As with other tough kids from money, Bruce loathed his privilege and feared it had made him soft. His father, unlike him, had come up in the trades, starting his own construction business, Willrich Bridge Co. The workers jokingly called it *Won't-R'itch*, and Bruce, after a comparative religion course, dubbed it Chinvat Bridge Company. It specialized in highway overpasses and bridges, and this meant Bruce spent his childhood around hardhats—sandhogs, welders, surveyors, union reps. Summers he worked on the crews, and though he learned early enough to navigate the code-switching involved in migrating between this world and his ivied boarding school, he carried with him, in one direction, the disdain manual labor had for the comfortable life of the mind and, in the other, the shame of knowing this comfort was his, and would always be his, for the taking.

He reviled privilege, affecting a tough-guy posture until the graft took. Even when his father's politics drove a wedge between them, part of him idolized the man. Running Willrich—managing contracts, employee wages, benefits, and the rest—Bruce Sr. had his reasons for resenting the regulation and red tape. He believed with a certain unprobed sincerity that what was good for him was good for his employees, all the way up the ladder of marginal tax rates and corporate write-offs. And yet he grew wealthy and eventually fat while his men eked out their daily crust in lives defined by precarity and chronic back pain. Bruce argued with his father, ferreting out his hypocrisies and inconsistencies, and the older man conceded the occasional point. But his heart wasn't in it. It's hard to take the systemic view when you're trying to make payroll on a weekly basis.

Bruce spent his first summer back from college on a crew putting in the pilings for a railroad bridge. Quentin had told us this story long ago. Sitting out in the summer sun, breathing in the nauseous exhaust of passing cars, he'd formed a bond with the workers. Listening to them day by day, he got to know their travails from the inside out: how credit-card debt rolled forward until you'd paid more in interest than you initially owed; how overdraft and bounced-check fees and reconnection fees for delinquent utility payments worked like supplemental taxes on the tenuousness of poverty; how variable-rate mortgages you didn't understand blew up like a time bomb after a few years. These men weren't stupid. They weren't irresponsible. They didn't have crippling habits, hadn't left their wives or abandoned their kids. They worked fifty-hour weeks doing a job that destroyed Bruce's body over the course of a single summer. Year in, year out they did this, and for their trouble they netted a few hundred bucks a week. But they didn't have lawyers checking out the contracts they signed, CPAs breaking down the payment schedules month by month. No one was there to steer them to better sources of credit or to legal aid when things went south. The creditors peddling contracts to them knew there'd be no hell to pay for defrauding the wrong guy. They barely had money for condoms; others didn't believe in them. Abortion— forget it. It wasn't hard to accrue obligations faster than the means of supporting them and debt faster than the means of paying it off. It was altogether easy to indenture yourself to a lifetime of servicing debt without denting the principal—what Bruce called modern peonage. Could you ask these guys never to splurge on dinner out or Christmas presents for the kids? Could you blame them when, having put every scrap of collateral in hock, they turned to payday lenders and online cash-advance outfits, who would carve a pound of flesh from you before they'd help you read the agate?

Bruce couldn't believe his father's indifference. Poor decision-making. Bad tendencies. Lack of discipline, foresight, self-control. Such were explanations with which Bruce Sr. dismissed his son's concerns. He tossed them away like small venomous creatures you don't dare handle for too long, lest they bite your conscience. What self-justifying ideal had this man built his monument to that his son's scruples so troubled its foundation? Liberty, he said. This was the bitter harvest of getting to choose, he declared. Some chose wrong. Freedom to fly meant freedom to plummet. With narrowed eyes Bruce remarked that freedom for wolves had often meant death for lambs. And so they went, round and round, until the older man grew impatient and cross and said that maybe some men *were* wolves and others lambs, and that was life and life was . . . Well, *what*? Mysterious, unfair, imperfect, fallen? But it wasn't so mysterious as that, Bruce believed. When it came to the men he'd spent the summer working with he thought something like this: the world had paid these men to make its products, but to sell the products profitably, it had to sell them for more than it had paid the men to make them. Where could it find customers then? The contradiction submitted to a single remedy: the men would be advanced credit to pay for the goods they had fashioned for a song. This remedy spun off a side business in lending, but even a child could see that it only deferred and amplified the problem. The burden grew toward the future on the unfolding wings of compounding interest, the wings of our wishful, perpetual-motion thinking and dreaming. Debt sat like a massively dense stone, a black hole, at the core of these briefly flickering lives, swallowing light.

His father's callousness was one thing. At least his father had come up the hard way and had some reason to congratulate himself for the endowments of fate. Bruce ran hotter toward his classmates, who seemed to believe they had earned their place in the world, their comfort and leisure and well-remunerated futures as corporate accomplices. Their tacit self-importance ate at him. When he returned to campus in the fall, he joined the school paper, took an introductory accounting class at a nearby community college (his elite college didn't offer one), and found a professor in the political science department, a woman who had covered state politics as a journalist, who agreed to advise the independent study he was proposing. He meant to take on the entire payday-loan system. His plan had all the grandeur and folly of youth.

And for that alone, perhaps, it succeeded. The industry had grown so rotten after years of little regulation and less oversight that it now draped its decaying tendrils over the state lawmakers like the arms of a corpse.

The lenders' lobbyists had become overconfident. The year before, they had taken several state representatives on a European junket, and presumably they enjoyed their time abroad. This gratuity, combined with the annual campaign contributions the industry coughed up, was not a good look—especially, and here was half of Bruce's scoop, in light of a new practice the outfits were implementing, which required borrowers to write hot checks in exchange for loans.

Was this legal? That wasn't clear. The traditional system had borrowers postdate checks to their next payday, maybe two weeks away. Lenders could cash the check on maturity in the event that the borrower didn't come through. The problem was some of these checks bounced and the law prohibited bringing criminal charges against a postdated check. In the new system, however, by dating checks on the day of the transaction, lenders could claim theft and have the debtor arrested and jailed. This naturally impeded the debtor's ability to repay further, piling fees upon fees and turning the state, in effect, into the lender's loan shark.

Such behavior went directly against the spirit of the small-loan statutes, which had granted exemptions to the ban on usury to bring small lending out of the shadows and kill loan-sharking and the black-market trade in credit. Sure, it was a liability for the payday folks that their borrowers might walk away from an obligation, which they would have to sell at a steep haircut to a collection agency. But they wanted to have it both ways. They didn't want to do the work to make sure borrowers *could* repay ahead of time, since the majority of their profits came from late fees, rollovers, and churning (new loans taken out when the last loan claimed an entire paycheck), but they did want someone to hold the borrowers' feet to the fire. The business model meant to induce people into a cycle of debt: lending to solvent clients wouldn't do the trick. They set debt traps for borrowers who would bob in and out of solvency indefinitely, paying off interest and fees but never cutting into the principal. For this reason the state capped rollovers, but loan churning could fill the gap. Most borrowers, Bruce found, spent more than half the year in debt, and many took out ten or twenty loans in that time.

He first got wind of the hot-check scam when one of his fellow work-

ers, a man named Radu—a cheerful Eastern European, with a wife and
three kids back home in the Carpathians—got hauled in for writing a
bad check. He'd missed his repayment date while working a second job
through the weekend, covering a coworker's shift last-minute. The lender's
shop was closed when he got off work. The bank's processing schedule
had worked against him too, since his paycheck, deposited that Friday,
only cleared in his account late on Monday. Had it cleared a few hours
sooner, the check would never have bounced.

But winding up in jail turned a problem that wasn't a problem into
a problem that was. First the bank charged him a fee on the bad check.
Then the lender tacked on its own fee and rolled the loan over, adding
another two weeks of interest. The court charged him a fee, plus there was
the bail bondsman's take, on top of which Radu lost three days of work,
was threatened with termination by an unsympathetic foreman, and fell
behind—as a result of the rest—on his utilities and car payments. There
was briefly a worry that immigration authorities might revoke his work
visa for the stint in jail. If Bruce hadn't fronted him a thousand bucks and
connected him with the family's lawyer, Radu would have found himself
in significant trouble, delinquent on a variety of payments and sweating
it out in a detention center, perhaps, en route back to Braşov.

Bruce returned to school in a cold rage, determined to do his
research. He convinced an associate at a private law firm to help him
make sense of the tortuous paper trail and discovered, with her guidance,
that the lender who'd turned Radu over to the police, Premium Management Services, was attached through a limited-liability subsidiary to one
of the governor's principal donors. Naturally this smelled bad, but the
legal question around the issuance of hot checks remained murky. What
exactly did Premium Management *tell* potential borrowers? Bruce tried
to take out a loan himself, but he didn't have a job. He interviewed a
few of the company's customers, but they hadn't pressed the issue of the
check's date. Premium Management's representatives had assured them
the check would only be cashed if they failed to repay. And everyone *intended* to repay. No one knew the legal distinctions involved in the dating
of a check.

Bruce had still uncovered enough to write a six-thousand-word exposé for the college paper. This broke enough news that the paper of record in the state capital picked up the story—first, as a human-interest piece on Bruce, and later, in the sort of Cinderella twist everyone loves, as a deeper dive into the initial reporting, written under a byline shared by an old local hand and Bruce himself. The older pressman got the governor's office on the record denying any knowledge of the LLC's ties to the payday industry. They didn't know anything about the industry's practices, they claimed. The press secretary said the governor would look into the matter, and sure enough, in the next legislative session, they passed House Bill 243, which capped fees and further limited rollovers, imposed due diligence on lenders, and—most consequentially—required payday firms to inform their borrowers about typical patterns of repayment, the cost of a loan in the event of renewal, and alternative sources of credit. The lobbying groups howled and leaned on the members they could, but the law passed and the governor signed it.

Bruce had done what few college reporters do. He'd broken a big story and pressured the government to change the law. He'd punched his ticket to J-school and probably a shot at a big-market paper. And still, he couldn't escape the knowledge that he had ridden to success once again on the shoulders of privilege. Would the white-shoe law firm in the state capital have taken his meetings and helped him break down the corporate charters if they hadn't hoped to do business with his father's firm? Would his determination to follow this story have been nurtured and encouraged at a college less convinced of its students' special merit and its own broadminded virtue? Would the city paper even have picked up the story if Bruce hadn't been the scion of a major local builder? Crusades for justice were whimsical hobbies permitted the rich, urged on by starry-eyed, guilt-ridden kids. It didn't matter whether that was true; Bruce couldn't shake the feeling it was.

More disappointing still was the persistence of the industry, which, after crying bloody murder about the reforms, carried on more or less as before. The newly required disclosures scared away a few customers and the worst collection abuses dwindled to the usual harassment, but the guys on

Bruce's father's crews still took out cash advances and the reborrowing rate hardly budged. A lot of them didn't have another option. Their credit was shot and they were mortgaged to the hilt. They would have taken a title loan if they owned a car, but they couldn't afford one. And so it was an advance against future pay—older folks borrowed against pension and social security checks—which often meant APRs in the 400 percent range, but which still, on a short-term basis, beat the fees on bounced checks, account overdrafts, late credit-card payments, and utilities reconnections when you missed the bills on those. You could plaster the eviscerating terms of the loan on page one of the contract, in bold letters and red ink, and people would still take them. They knew the loans were shit. They knew they were screwed. They were the ones living their lives, after all, and a lot more would have to change before a little credit made things right. No angry college kid playing dress-up in a cape was going to save anyone from the slow-moving destruction of poverty, no matter how battered and stricken his conscience. But things were worse than that. A little adversity hardened the opposition. Once the industry absorbed the blow of HB243 and realized they were still standing, they went back to lawmakers, citing steady revenue figures as proof positive that constituents valued their services. The legislature set up a regulatory 'sandbox' program, granting firms exemptions from the law while they tested 'innovative financial products.' Those were the industry's words. Various other firms shifted their business online and incorporated in tribal lands where the new state laws couldn't reach them.

Bruce's dad, meanwhile, knew the donor Bruce had outed as a loan baron personally, and he had ongoing contracts with the state government as well. In private the governor told Bruce Sr. to rein in Robin Hood before he rode himself out of a tidy inheritance. This sort of thing was just vexatious enough to curdle old friendships. Aiming for levity, Bruce Sr. said kids could teach you a lot—like how much patience you really had. The governor wasn't amused. I've always found the best way to give a kid advice, Bruce Sr. said, trying again, is to find out what they want to do and then advise them to do it. That's not my method, remarked the governor. Well, your way hasn't worked for me yet, said Bruce's father.

At home he acted like Bruce had caused him real bellyaches. He chafed especially at Bruce's approaching the law firm without telling him first. Bruce pointed out that telling him would have scotched the deal before it began. But I should decide *what* begins, his father said. When it's my money, I decide. The whole point, Bruce said, was to figure out whose money it really was. His father might not have liked that answer. With that attitude, Bruce Sr. said, it's probably not going to be yours. The two fought. When Bruce graduated, he wouldn't accept his father's help. He made his way through J-school on part-time work and student loans, tumbling out of the program and into Quentin's lap, clenched like a fist. It's safe to say Quentin stood in for the figure who'd gone missing. Bruce all but worshipped him.

And Quentin could defuse the kid. His humor and folksy manner worked like a steam valve when Bruce got hot under the collar, inflamed over a trivial setback. 'They're gonna keep being them, and we're gonna keep being us,' Quentin would say. 'If they're as bad as all that, they'll mess up again and worse. We'll get them then.' He worried Bruce's frustration at failing to nail down a story would provoke tactical missteps. Bruce wanted the geese cooked. Quentin took a more philosophical attitude. The heroes-and-villains stuff fucked with your head. It blinded you to the ends-means distinction and seduced you into error. Finally, it made you bad at your job. Justice lived in the method. Stay faithful to good practices and the ends worked themselves out.

Bruce might not have thought so, but he relaxed under Quentin's influence. He saw the power in a little irony, a pivot in register. You didn't have to lay every card on the table. Didn't have to fight all your battles at once. Playing the longer game left you the space to grow into a person. To get a life. He and Quentin had a chessboard set up in the newsroom and they prosecuted slow, deliberate games in pockets of downtime. Bruce found a girlfriend, a young woman as idealistic as he was. She worked as a public defender and had dark braided hair down to her shoulder blades. They moved in together, outfitting a cozy one-bedroom in the exiguous disorder of early adulthood. Jada gave Bruce another outlet for his restless fury. She shared his passion, only tempered in a clear gentle fixity.

Then Bruce's tenure as a *Tribune* cub ended. He had two options. He could strike out on his own or head abroad to cover the war. The country had seduced itself into military adventure and the war was, in all senses, hot. Established reporters with families and kids balked at the risk to life and limb. Certain hustlers, on the other hand, bought the administration's idea that we'd be in and out in a year and saw it as a shortcut, not a detour, on their meteoric flight. Quentin knew better. He told Bruce the damn thing would drag on for years, that the time to get in was now, before the conflict lapsed into repetitive tedium for the public, a vague, unhappy reminder of the world we smothered in our clumsy grip. Quentin told Bruce to put in a couple of years if he could stand it. Make it work. The paper would owe him. His next posting would be plum. You'll get your byline all over A1, he said. Big medicine. Above the fold. You're golden if you come back in one piece. Everyone respects the fuck out of war reporters.

No, Bruce wouldn't turn this down. Not a chance. Like Rich, he'd flirted with enlisting. He had that impulse to take on the burdens others shirked, to stand tall against the swift current of convenience, to sacrifice his overvalued body if need be. He feared he was soft, that privilege had left him weak. But the army, he felt, was for men altogether too willing to take orders and perish for other men's vanity and mistakes. He could never subordinate his conscience that way, and he didn't know whether that made him brave or gutless. Reporting from the front was his compromise.

Only leaving Jada gave him pause. They talked it over for weeks. She wouldn't hear of standing in his way. 'For him too, for them both,' Quentin had told us, 'to sacrifice the other for so long was thrilling.' It unlocked new chambers of their own self-seriousness. They found solace in suffering. *Meaning.* Like monks. They meant to mortify their flesh to atone for the weakness of their parents and other adults, the complacency of their generation. They saw how easy it was just to *get along.*

Of course Bruce went. And predictably enough he lost his shit with the paper after just three months of filing stories from the Green Zone, writing about interagency pissing contests, turf wars among the army brass, tepid skirmishes over jurisdiction and strategy and who would own the golden victories when the parades came home. Sometimes Bruce got to tag along in armored convoys to check out development projects and attend shuras with tribal elders, to view the placid valleys and calm heat-muddled deserts in the pacified areas, accompanying staffers and diplomats and the occasional representative on a toothless 'fact-finding' junket. The trips were set up by public affairs to curate an idea of the conflict for the audience at home. This was the *politics* of war, not the war itself, and to Bruce's way of thinking it was as important and interesting as a runway show in epaulets. Worse still, it forced him to repackage the administration's propaganda, when his job, as he saw it, was to keep the conflict as honest as possible, by making the war as politically costly as possible to those in power.

The editors at the *Trib* told him to stick it out, but Bruce knew the underbelly of his trade. He knew those crises, when the Fourth Estate adopted its most august self-appointed role, coincided with its most successful earnings quarters. War was good business. The hypocrisy was thick enough to cut with a knife. Behind the tone of tragic sobriety the news reports took on, and in direct proportion to this very tone, dollar signs danced before the eyes of publishers, moguls, and investors. Without precisely meaning to, without realizing it, or perhaps more likely without caring, the paper did just what the government wanted and turned the war into a soap opera, a strategy game: a tale of clashing personalities with inset maps, laid out in compelling detail in daily installments. That made the paper, in Bruce's view, complicit in its horrors.

Bruce had this idea, Quentin once explained, that maps were to blame for wars. Maps made the world seem far more manageable than it ever was. They reduced territory to a regular, planar scale that comforted the senses, but at the cost of reality. How could an army fail to capture and hold a stretch of land the size of Luxembourg? The condensed point of a city, just a pinprick on a flat surface? Of course, as every soldier knows, once you get out into the country you realize in a flash how complex a patch of forest can be, how disorienting a set of sand dunes or hills. You see how vast the world is, how unfathomably vast, and how small a human is, how vanishing our designs. And you understand how easily a thousand troops peter out in the sparse nothing of the wilderness. A valley can be a world, an entire life.

We use abstractions to hold on to realities too big and messy to approach as they are, Quentin said. This was the root of human knowledge and power. But our abstractions ruled us and turned deadly precisely for what made them powerful in the first place: that they suggested we could encounter and subdue far more than we could.

This had been Bruce's intuition. He understood the pageantry and chaos of war. He hadn't spent much time in the field but he profited by a classical education, knew his Thucydides and Tacitus; he had a natural feel for the magical thinking of generals, how each generation of leaders seduced itself, and a sense of how the aleatory insanity of combat got fitted into narrative formulae that coalesced into a reassuring story for those sitting at home. Bruce berated his editors, guys thirty years his senior, accusing them of abetting the administration in popularizing the war. The coverage was building unrealistic expectations of victory and success, he said, and in the name of what? Good relations with those in power? Sales? Think a little down the road, he told them. I know you're sitting pretty now. Just wait till the war goes south. Wait till people start looking back over our coverage and start wondering how we got it so wrong. When this looks like a stain on the nation's conscience, what's the story then? What are you going to tell your grandkids? You whitewashed carnage? Or you asked the hard questions when you could? We win or lose trust for a generation on this.

Did Bruce say this, in exactly these words, to his higher-ups? Probably not. He summarized his conversations for Quentin, who stayed up late with him, listening to his complaints and talking him down. Quentin had to soothe the editors as well. They had thick hides, but they also knew when a reporter wasn't just blowing off steam. It didn't matter who was right. Reality had an institutional character. The reporter whose leash got too long, whose orbit spun out too far, rarely came back. Not with the right mindset anyway. This had happened before. War correspondents had a bad habit of developing inflexible consciences. And for a trade that set up shop on virtuous ground, journalism didn't mesh well with a rigid ethical sense. But Bruce's experience was real. It stuck. When you saw the violence and corruption of war up close, the triviality of life back home, the pettiness of what motivated people, often became too much to bear. The paper needed someone more at home in the endlessly ribboning gray. Bruce, they worried, not unreasonably, might embarrass them.

Then he hit on a solution that at least briefly satisfied all sides. Bruce got permission to embed with Hero Company, a close-knit force deployed throughout a small but consequential valley to the east. The region was notorious for the amount of contact it saw, and the company, whose outposts stared out across a seasonal stream at a mountain ridge the enemy considered its own, was famous for its scrappy and half-mad bravery. This was what Bruce wanted, what all combat reporters wanted: life at the tip of the spear, as the grunts lived it daily, carrying the gear, shadowing the patrols, the adrenaline of firefights, the brotherhood of exigency. It wasn't that in the midst of mortal danger Bruce didn't at times rue his doggedness or offer prayers to a spurned deity. It was his fear that urged him on, his sense that in its throes he touched the unmediated face of something so strange and raw it could have been divine, and that the instant he gave in to fear, he would start dying the coward's thousand deaths. He wanted action and, if not danger exactly, proximity to danger. Difficulty, pain. These calmed him. Quentin only heard from him at intervals after that. Jada too. He seemed happier. He sounded relaxed. He couldn't talk in detail about what he was up to, so he listened, laughed. Jada had moved to a scrappy practice run by a woman named Ellie Bart, which began, during the war years, to bring cases defending the legal rights of combatant detainees. Jada had talked her way onto one of these teams, and it gave them a nice feeling, Quentin thought, to imagine they were working in tandem, tackling two sides of the same problem.

In Bruce's absence Jada and Quentin grew close. At first she missed Bruce and liked having someone to talk to who knew him. Quentin understood the terms of their relationship and he could help her imagine what was going on in those parched mountains half a world away. He could ease her mind, the way he did Bruce's. He was still young then and they may have fallen in love a little, he and Jada, since they could always see something good about themselves reflected in the other—their concern for Bruce, their responsibility, taking on serious work and virtuous worries, their restraint before the passion left unnamed. And because they were each less difficult than the person interposed between them, they conjured the good in Bruce without the bad. He became their abstraction, their donnée. The occasion and fixed impediment. His obstacle meant they couldn't fall in love. It meant they skipped right past all the awkwardness of *wondering* right to the flush intimacy, the warmth, the charged flirtation robbed of any impropriety. Because they wouldn't, of course, they couldn't . . .

It's hard to know what would have happened had Bruce come back. As likely as not Jada wouldn't have recognized him and would have understood what it is to grow apart. Perhaps she and Quentin would have continued what they had started, disburdened of guilt, and of the shame of sensing that they had put a curse on their friend, that their love had taken root in sin or selfishness or folly. Or maybe it wouldn't have gone that way at all. When a person disappears into thin air, they take with them any chance of resolution, of explanation, apology.

What happened was this. Bruce finished his embed. He'd contracted a parasite in the valley, and after returning to the capital he spent two weeks laid up in an army hospital. Maybe he was just exhausted. Maybe fatigue and stress had ground his constitution to rubble and knotted his guts. Either way, he did some thinking in that time. He had memories to relive. His company had lost two men and seen several others maimed. Guys Bruce had grown friendly with. For all his righteousness Bruce had an ease around working men. His pretension melted away into humor at his own expense. What colleagues took for snobbishness was more precisely his bottomless contempt for what they reminded him of in himself: a haughtiness or self-importance which, though they disguised it more gracefully than he could, he knew too well. He had formed an iron bond with the soldiers in those platoons deployed across the valley. Like the heavies he had grown up with, the men had few options. They were young, many younger than Bruce, and they'd enlisted to pay for college or get jobs. Some signed up out of boredom. It wasn't often deeply considered. Maybe they loved their country. Maybe they felt like everyone else. They weren't fanatics. It was one rung on a ladder they had started near the bottom of. To see them sacrifice body and mind to a war few had ever really believed in enraged him. Broke his heart. Fury was a silencer for the cracks of sorrow. An armor. He had seen what rifle fire, sniper rounds, shrapnel, and explosives do to a human body. He had seen a nineteen-year-old bleed out, speaking with an unearthly languor, begging for sleep. He'd seen muscle and bone exposed to the wind, limbs turned to pulp or lost completely before their owner felt them gone. The heartrending queries of those who don't know yet they'll never be whole. The timid hopes, the misplaced concern for others. They were there, ultimately, for one another: that was the only truth, the only motivation, worth the name. The war was a series of concentric circles each with its own logic and imperatives; by the time you got to the inner core—face-to-face combat in the valleys and hills—none of the larger urgencies remained. No global or patriotic principle. It was survival and brotherhood, finis. The crazy thing was brotherhood might have bound them to the enemy's corps, the guys fighting on the ridgeline opposite, if not for the messianism of those in the higher rungs. There was little time to consider this. Not with firefights breaking the still day, not with mortar coming in. Not when contact could occur at any minute. When you had to be prepared to give your best friend a tracheotomy or plunge a fourteen-gauge catheter into his chest to keep his lungs from collapsing, you didn't spend a lot of time reflecting on the underlying merits of the war. He had seen a man take it in the artery and turn pale as a ghost. The blood came out like oceans from a clown car. He'd seen these things happen or heard about them from those who had—the look in the eyes of a kid who knew he'd bit it, torn to rags in a contact that might have been on another planet, it was so far from family and home, from hospitals and girls he'd never worked up the courage to say were pretty to their faces, thousands of miles from every memory that made him smile like a child, who knew by some intuitive grace that his time was up on this numbered hill with a few buddies, the firefight thudding on, the wind a strange, indifferent witness to the meaninglessness of his passage, dying for a trivial position that had been fought over a thousand times before, back and forth on the pendulum of history, to the same vanishing and ephemeral end. The pulse, the heart, the kicking heartbeat can go on for a surprisingly long time before it realizes it's persisting in a futile task.

It made Bruce angry, but that didn't describe his feeling at all. It tripped the wire on some rabid, primal claim to justice: the species instinct that says if we allow this, we are lost. Government proxies and in-country assets threw cash and weapons at the warlords in the hinterlands. The regional governors and skeleton federal administration in the capital got a small fortune to pay civil servants and distribute in aid, none of which seemed to make it where it was supposed to go. Pallets of cash arrived on military transport planes by the ton and disappeared. No custody chains or inventories to account for it. These were the rumors. Zero oversight . . . which looked like an oversight itself until you got to thinking. Later it came out that the accounting contract for the provisional authority had gone to an unknown firm with little more than a license and a storefront. Another nonmistake mistake. War was a vehicle for making money and then making it vanish. The funds were disbursed without a thought, handed out from the back of pickups, thrown in duffel bags by the million, or simply stolen. Most of it vanished. The warlords made out well. Anyone it behooved us, or the central government, to bribe. Because war is good business it made sense to keep the war going— and so how could our weapons and money not wind up, by the law of economic necessity, supplying the forces we were fighting? Too chancy to wait on crop harvests to see if they could afford ammo for the upcoming season. It was the psychotic expediency, which encouraged all this, that crushed Bruce. It forced him to confront just how expendable a human life really is. Everyone without the passport of wealth, the residuum of power in class or lineage, could go. Their lives were, objectively, worth less than the war machinery they were charged with operating, and many of the weapons they fired. Like so many mass phenomena, the more you zoomed out, the more you tried to connect the local reality to the global motivation, the less sense it made. The more it resembled mass insanity. So few even attempted the equation.

But that was Bruce's job, or so he felt: exposing the bad math for what it was. There was little sense blaming the warlords, the crony bureaucrats, or the precarious propped-up government, which looked mostly to secure enough sovereign wealth to abscond with when things turned against them. The warlords didn't give a rat's ass. Our interests and theirs briefly coincided, but they wouldn't forever. So long as we shared a common foe, we were convenient to one another. But like the intelligence agencies themselves, the warlords and local commanders would have been fools to sever ties with the factions in the mountains, the insurgents shooting our troops and setting off roadside bombs. War was a tenuous, high-stakes enterprise, and in a set of sere valleys, as knotted as a canalized cortex, where the winds of fortune and allegiance shifted in the course of an afternoon, the only safe position for power was to be needed by both sides. To keep the war happening on your terms. To stand in the middle on the receiving end of money, guns, and young men. The dispensable were, as a matter of course, dispensed with.

Bruce wanted to expose it all, and once he had healed up he resigned from the paper by email—a terse note without his usual arabesques of righteousness: 'More important stories to run down out where reporters are scarce. —Bruce.' But there was a reason reporters were scarce. Bruce got himself in trouble, run in by paramilitary thugs or local agents in mufti. It wasn't clear. When the lesson didn't take, he disappeared.

This wasn't what Quentin had expected. Turning up dead, maybe. Captured by insurgents looking to arrange a swap. Quentin had hard conversations with Bruce Sr. after his son quit the paper. 'He's a tough kid, but he's not going to last a week out there. You need to drag his ass back home.' 'Pay off whoever the fuck you have to and make it happen.' Quentin spoke out of fear. He felt responsible for Bruce's being there in the first place and now he believed Bruce would get himself killed to prove a point. Maybe he should have seen that Bruce had the seeds of fanaticism in him, but one makes allowances for someone so young.

Idealism molts like skin. Perhaps Quentin understood, for the first time, that he had let *himself* confuse ambition and principle all along, letting the two alloy until they formed an adamantine justification for—well, what? What couldn't they justify? Some people can handle the sort of ambition that raged in Quentin, cast iron holding a fire; some people the fire consumed. Quentin was forced to consider what he had never let himself look at squarely before: that the blaze didn't devour him because it was ambition to the core, not principle at all. You can't burn what lives in flame.

Or so he tortured himself by believing. After shepherding Bruce Sr. through formal notifications to the foreign service, he talked Bruce's father into hiring a private investigator, a veteran of clandestine work who had gone into business later in life as a spook-for-hire. The guy's name was Baldwin and he was on a plane crossing the globe inside a week. Quentin wanted to go too, but this made no sense. What could he do? Although the *Trib*'s affection for Bruce had worn thin, the paper remained committed to a professional and vaguely romantic code of ethics when it came to repatriating reporters. The higher-ups assured Quentin they had their overseas bureau chiefs and correspondents on alert. They worked sources, pressure points in neighboring countries. Nada. Nothing. Not even crickets or cicadas or whatever locustlike creatures swarmed down through the valleys in that ancient blighted country. Jada lived in a state of shock. With every call Quentin thought she sounded more afraid—fearful of what news he had, and also of what news he didn't. Eventually he stopped calling. Bruce Sr. shed bulk and became raddled in the way the formerly overweight do: drooping eyes, skin, belly. Quentin later reflected that children, certain children, become the lost conscience of their parents, the symptom of their diseased moral sense. Bruce Sr. knew his son had died for his sins.

Only they *didn't* know he had died. Baldwin tracked Bruce's movements until the trail ran cold. This was at a dusty inn in a mud-caked town beneath mountains that kept their snowcapped peaks through summer. A cramped bed, a rough heavy blanket. A square of dyed cloth sailed from the window. The last bare room they knew, and would ever know, Bruce had slept in. If he'd slept. The window, like longing, looked west.

Bruce had written pieces critical of our government's efforts in that part of the world, and it would be fair to say the nation's representatives made their inquiries on his behalf with more perfunctory diligence than gusto. No one in the diplomatic core or at the agencies warmed to Quentin's incessant checking-in, nor his Hail Mary bluffs at bigfooting action. But Bruce Sr. kept calling him in the middle of the night, his voice embogged in bourbon, threaded with a distress he couldn't conceal in crude bonhomie, to say, It's you and me, buddy. It's left to us to bring him back.

Quentin didn't know Bruce Sr. and didn't consider him a buddy. He missed Jada. If he squinted it now looked like the misjudgment of false prudence not to have taken things further when they had the chance. Now they never could. Regret filled in the living flesh of their affection like stone pith in petrified wood. Or maybe regret was just nostalgia for those late days of lost innocence. The proximity of such naive joy seemed shocking, shameful.

Quentin grew angry with Bruce and came perhaps even to hate him. What had the kid been doing? His gross incaution saddled the rest of them with responsibilities no one had signed up for, an inheritance of guilt. Some of the anger was real, some no doubt the displacement of a rage he felt at the government and their pointless war. The more he looked at it, the less he could understand what stood to be achieved that merited the cost of one young man's life. It made no sense. Resources? We were rich. Security? We were safe. Why trade the certain death of untold soldiers for the possible death of some small number of civilians? Was it symbolic, a show of strength, or the fanciful dream of men in rooms with maps and history books, who deluded themselves into believing in the reality of their greatness and the abstraction of other people?

No, the only sort of sense it made was the kind Quentin refused to see. And yet he caught sight of something all the same. Something he had never seen before, something dark and subtle, and this shook him. Shook free his innocence. He lost a measure of idealism, part of his convenient self-regard, and he became, from a different angle, more idealistic still. What did he see? That on a certain scale we are all expendable. At a certain point of intransigence the grid will reject us. No matter how important or special we think we are, how cosseted in the legal guarantees of our nation or the prerogatives of influence and money, when we push against the grain too fiercely or too often, the world will find it easier to dispose of us than to uphold our dignity. The world favors, even selects for, the slightly corrupt. Too corrupt and things fall apart. But not corrupt at all and people want for the dark motives that bind men by the iron of complicity. No place existed for the idealists, the principled men and women. We would celebrate their legacy and revere them in death, name days for them, and garland their graves in carnations. But in life they were a fever we couldn't shake soon enough. Enemy of the status quid.

Quentin changed. The experience radicalized him. He did not find religion, he kept his easy cynical humor, but he decided *fuck it*—fuck *them*—he wasn't going to take the handouts or the plaudits if it meant sanding off the sharp edges of his conscience. He passed up going the editorial route and raised his hand for the hard stuff, the slogging investigations. He went after Leach for rate-fixing and took on hedging outfits making tidy bets against pension funds, which never suspected how clean their carcasses could be picked by shorters. Cy loved him for those pieces, the Oedipal strands in it terminally coiled. And then for a long time, when Bruce never turned up dead, Quentin thought he would surface somewhere. Most likely in a horrific video. Sometimes he dreamed that Bruce had gone to ground, pulled a Houdini on them, and would one day knock on Quentin's door unannounced, ready with a long story about the years he had spent as a peasant farmer or a rebel fighter. Just the sort of crazy thing Bruce would do. But he never turned up. People don't just disappear, Quentin would sometimes say. Not people like Bruce.

But they do.

Bruce did.

All this we revisited as black clouds drifted in from the west like the prows of sinister ships. The sky paled, then darkened, an early dusk gathered outside and soon the subtle, low sound of thunder emerged like heavy footsteps in the distance. By late afternoon the rain hitting the glass came in bright fusillades, startling us with its intensity. We battened down windows, huddling in the living room, and for a time after we had shut the house to the elements none of us turned on a light. The framed plans of ships above the fireplace dimmed, the paintings of tidal scenes and foxhunts and skeins of migrating geese. The shadows of raindrops on the windows ran over the sofas, upholstered in a pale blue motif. In the half-light we sat as in a movie matinee, watching wind-tossed forms make a magic lantern show on plaster walls.

Rich did remind me of Bruce, Quentin conceded. But only a little, and not at first. At first you only sense the possibility of kinship. You feel you've known someone—if not in this life, in one past. Quentin stood by the window, peering out. I never did get to know Rich as well as I'd have liked. But that's another story. Rich gave me a few pointers, and he set up my visit to Branford the next day with a name: Enoch Niels.

Enoch was the technical director for the project that built the scientific underpinnings of VIRTUE, Quentin explained. A platform called Cuber, which the government farmed out in hefty grants to the Advanced Institute in Branford. These were academic heavyweights looking to grow something significant and applied on the theoretical ground they had broken. Enoch could manage them, talk the scientists' lingo, but also chinwag with the deans and oversight reps from government consultancies. Everyone charged with seeing this thing funded and on schedule but not peeking under the hood. Rich called him an Oppenheimer sort.

'Let's not get carried away,' I said. I thought Rich was showing off.

'You still don't appreciate the importance of what we're talking about.'

'I'll let the apprehension grow organically,' I remarked. 'I've had a lot of people try to sell me baldness cures and just look at my head.'

'Just don't go assuming it's a gentle slope to the deep end.'

'See, when I hear stuff like that, I think either you're growing too fond of me or you know something I don't.'

'I'll buy you dinner first next time,' said Rich.

Quentin cracked a knuckle and turned back to us. I got up early the next morning, he said, and caught the train to Branford with the commuters. It was another gorgeous bruiser of a day, hot before the sun broke the skyline, with fat clouds above the industrial trimmings beyond the scratched milk glass. I found myself entranced by the assembly line of conurbation streaming past and was half dreaming when we arrived.

Do you know Branford? It's a godawful place: beautiful, pristine, full of whitewashed houses, Georgian brick dormitories, half-timbered hotels. Neo-Gothic lecture halls next to postmodern pastiche. All the details borrowed from somewhere else. The campus is right there when you detrain, and rail whistles blow plaintively through the quads. Graduation had come and gone and there were few students about. The campus in that bright emptiness had an oversaturated, hyperreal quality, like the barren civic square in a metaphysical painting. The young people around for summer classes had the bewildered look of nocturnal creatures in daylight, and the only larger groups were tourists, listening to cicerones hustle the mythology of the place, a story which made it sound as if those spires and finials guarded the sempiternal flame of the Enlightenment, when of course the whole godforsaken thing had probably started as a place to train religious fanatics.

Do I sound bitter? Well, it is the case that no exclusionary bastion like Branford ever gave me the time of day when I was a pup. But I tell you there's something sinister about the place, so subtly sinister you can barely spot it among the landscaped paths ducking under old granite archways where buildings turn and connect, the small-paned windows with their busy mullions showing the attractive coloration and lumpiness of age. This beauty meant to obscure just this dark germ, it seemed to me, the project at the core of what dressed itself in such noble ideals. Never bet against how much a stone edifice and a little ivy can inflate a person's idea of himself.

I didn't wander for long. At the edge of campus by the restaurants and shops the A-Double-I-S had a small demesne of its own, an assembly of modern buildings apparently meant to echo the college's design while stripping away the ornamental frills indecent to anything so sober as hard science. A man in a ratty overcoat and mittens, standing beside an aluminum bench in the institute's courtyard, ate a hamburger from its fast-food wrapping. He had several notebooks and a phalanx of Styrofoam cups laid out on the bench. I peeled a couple of singles from my wallet and placed them among his change.

He watched me do this and wrote something on his notepad with a dull golf pencil. No thank-you. At length he remarked, 'Hot one.' Then, without looking up but somehow indicating the institute, whose cluster of buildings, with their bright metal exhaust pipes and catwalks, loomed over us, he said, 'You going in there?'

'That's right.'

'You do know what they do in there?' His words had a monitory solicitude.

'Pottery classes?' I suggested.

He didn't laugh but fixed me with a grave look. 'They're designing the future.'

I couldn't argue with this and asked why he set up shop in this blistering, shadeless, unpeopled courtyard.

'You're here, aren't you?' he said. He still hadn't turned to face me. I waited a moment, and he finally put down his pencil and tapped his notepad. 'I'm conducting a study.'

'I see. What's it about?'

'Wouldn't you like to know.'

I laughed and said I was OK not knowing. He cast a sidelong glance in my direction and made another entry in his notebook. Whatever he wrote seemed to amuse him and he chuckled. 'You think I'm crazy?'

I shook my head and pointed at the institute. 'I'm just some guy on his way in there.'

'Yeah,' he said. '"Cause they're sane and I'm crazy.'

'I'm withholding judgment.'

He seemed not to hear me and muttered, 'Something strange about that pigeon there . . .'

'It looks all right to me.'

'What do you know?' he said. He pulled off his mittens and tossed them over his head, missing the bench. 'You look at me, you think I'm a nut. Poor bastard. Life's got no need for me, right? Discarded like a clipped toenail. But wait till life doesn't need you. Wait till the future doesn't need you! Oh, you're in for it'—he wasn't talking to me anymore but to himself or an invisible audience—'You're going to get it. It's quite a thing not to be needed. Not to be needed at all. You can't even imagine the things we'll do to each other then . . .'

'Sorry?' I said when the silence had stretched like an afternoon shadow.

'We'll be lab rats in the mazes,' he said more loudly. 'And they'll teach pigeons to do your job. I'm not crazy. I'm on *strike*. On strike from thinking like they want us to. Stay in the maze and you'll stay a rat, that's what I say. A pigeon attended the Council of Nicaea, but what good does that do us? When the rules got written did anyone laugh? That's what I want to know. Some questions that shouldn't have answers do . . . Don't worry, I'm not nuts. I open the tap, I close the tap. Listen and you'll hear voices. But voices lie too. Just wait and see. Ricky O., I knew him, poor joker. Some come back, some don't. Sometimes the body comes back and other parts don't. And then we ask, where are your gibes now, your gambols, your songs?'

I left this cheery monologue but not before slipping the man a larger bill. If his business was to draw your guilt out like a tapeworm, he knew it cold. The clock hadn't struck ten when I entered the cool high-ceilinged building, a perfect time to catch the director for an extempore chat, I thought. Unfortunately his assistant, manning the outer office, wasn't buying my aw-shucks act.

'This isn't a drop-in counter,' he said when I'd finished explaining my business.

'No? What is it then?'

'Dr. Simmons is a busy man.'

I was trying to make out the muddled forms through the frosted glass behind him. 'Lots of busy men find time to talk to me.'

'You could have made an appointment.'

'Did I mention I'm from the *Beacon*?' I asked in the spirit of being helpful.

'It came up.'

'Look, just ask the director, OK? I don't need a lot of time. Ask Wernher von Braun if he can tear himself away from making paper airplanes for ten minutes. I might not come back.'

I had it in me to press harder, but the young man gathered his dignity and said, 'Wait there.' He spoke softly into his phone for a minute and not long after the director came out.

Luke Simmons was one of these hale vain sorts with square rimless glasses and a manicured beard that compensated for pale, thinning hair. He had faint freckles, reddish whiskers, and a nicer cut of suit than you might have expected from a scientist. But I guess he wasn't much of a scientist or they wouldn't have put him in administration.

'Mr. Jones,' he said, holding the door for me. 'Come in.' He closed the door behind us, shaking my hand with a quick, strong grip. His office overlooked the courtyard and beyond the spires of several churches shot through the trees. 'What can I do for you?' he asked. His manner, sitting at his desk, was so solicitous it seemed almost smug.

I scrutinized him before responding. 'I've given you the wrong idea,' I said. 'This is, well, a courtesy call. Only natural when you have information a person or his employer might find embarrassing. Bad form not to get their side of the story. You understand what I'm getting at.'

'Oh?' He grinned in a way that made me suddenly loathe both of us. He thought this was a game and now I couldn't wholly deny him the satisfaction.

'I'm trying to think why someone becomes a dean.' That's what he had been before coming to the institute, and I felt the need to punish him. 'I know guys who took desk jobs. Something like that? Salary bump, less demanding fieldwork.' I gazed at the art on the walls. Boccioni? 'Schmoozing, galas. High-level HR.'

He spread his hands in what I took to be a show of modesty. 'I do my small part.'

'Much appreciated, I'm sure.'

'Did you come all this way to insult me?' he said. 'We could have done it over the phone.'

'Or online,' I remarked. 'A rendezvous in cyberspace. Just two avatars, duking it out. Playing our little game of what-do-you-think-I-know.'

He had a habit of clenching his left jaw muscle, a minute tell. It lasted just a moment and then his affability returned. 'Well, now you're here.'

'That's the spirit.'

'You were going to tell me an embarrassing story. About the institute, I imagine.' He set the Newton's cradle on his desk going.

'That's not the gameplay, Luke. You don't call a bet. You fold or reraise.'

He rested his eyes on the colliding metal balls for a downbeat. 'I don't know what you came to talk about.'

'Well, I think you do,' I said, 'but that's OK. We can work around to it slowly.' The window was only lightly tinted. The blue sky over Branford rang with a poignant clarity. 'Let me tell you something about my job and then we'll talk about yours. All I want is the truth, you see, and all I need to do is keep asking questions and keep listening until someone tells it to me. And they might not want to, or even mean to, but eventually they will. Because I have all the time in the world.'

Luke sighed and stilled the cradle with his hand. 'I don't. So maybe we can get on with it.'

'Do you know what SIMITAR is?'

He sounded weary when he replied, 'Not a sword, I'm guessing?'

I proceeded to sketch for him the basics of the program and what it had attempted to achieve, as well as the pitfalls of constructing such elaborate fantasies in our world of flesh and blood. Far better to play out the jig in a contrived environment where mistakes were etched in ones and zeroes, not life and death. I assumed Luke knew most of this, even if they had kept him in the dark about VIRTUE's forerunner. He had to know the money came from the government's security arm and he had to suspect the applications would involve useful forms of deception. Interrogation was no great stretch.

'We *build* things here,' he said when I was done. 'We do research. You elect the government, same as we do.'

'Said with the persuasive charm of an arms dealer.'

His jovial mien had settled into progressively greater tetchiness and now he spoke without pretense. 'Look, someone was going to do it. We had our Sputnik moment a few years back with the Chinese. I'm sure I share your concerns, Quentin, but I'm not a pacifist. Let's not pretend there aren't people out there who wish us harm.'

I said he'd get no argument from me. But all the same I'd go in on a few hands: that he was an easy sell on the patriotic line, not because he dug air shows or anything, but because he'd grown to detest the sanctimony of the lefties across campus. That one was easy. Everyone thinks they reject authority, but it's different when the guys in suits show up and tell you you're their shining knight. Harder to say where his misgivings began, though I guessed he'd slept well enough knowing an old paragon of integrity like Brantley sat at the heart of the machine. But now a new crowd was in power. It was foolish to pretend he didn't nurse any doubt. We all question the motives behind the ego stroke once the pleasure ebbs. I told him I was being condescending, but to trust me, none of this made him different from a thousand other guys sitting behind desks. Everyone gets cold feet when they taper the charm and start highlighting the optical characteristics of your partnership. Or had they made him sign things? It didn't really matter. Maybe I was just spitballing, but what I was positive about—I looked at my watch—was that his assistant was going to buzz to remind him he had a 10:30 to get to.

'What if I do?'

I gestured at the latitudes of self-determination. 'Don't let *me* keep you.'

'I haven't told you anything you don't already know.'

'We're still in the part where I tell you things you don't know,' I said sharply. 'That this was never Brantley's people's thing, for example. Other entities were playing the long game.'

He looked faintly pale under the bright light that found resolute curls clinging to his scalp to irradiate. 'What game was that?' he said.

I looked at him with sympathy. 'You were the game, Luke.'

If I'd had to write a profile of Simmons, I would have said the years of institutional logrolling and cloistral camaraderie had encrusted on a buried decency. We bank around our aquaria in ceaseless circles, believing they're the world. Simmons was no different. Everyone starts to believe his own propaganda, but you could tell it was a certain pride that kept his heel dry when his mother dipped him in the river Styx.

'Do you know what it's like running AIIS?' he asked. I was tempted to say that I expected to learn in the next minute or two, but I'd ridden him about as hard as I thought I should. 'Imagine you're meant to make the same cake each day. But every morning you show up to find slightly fewer ingredients.'

'They're pulling your funding?'

'It's no big deal to begin with,' he said. 'You make do with a little less. But the reduction is gradual and consistent enough that it changes your thinking. You spend all your time contemplating it, anticipating it. First it changes you, then slowly it begins to change your idea of what a cake is.'

'Look, Luke, I'm not much of a baker.'

The phone rang on Simmons's desk. 'That's OK, Brian,' he said. 'Forget it.' His eyes darted to mine, but I kept my own counsel. 'With institutes like ours,' he explained, 'the return on investment is probably six-, seven-to-one over time. But governments don't think in time. They think in election cycles. So institutional grants keep drying up, because even in the best case there's no glory in it for politicians. The effect's too diffuse, too indirect. Memory fades quickly. In the end we turn into fundraising outfits and investment managers. The educational mission, the research lands a distant third at best.'

'I feel like we're coming to the end of the preamble.'

'It's supposed to make us leaner, but it only makes us fiercer,' said Simmons, 'fighting one another for the scraps.'

'So they threatened to go elsewhere.'

'Of course! It's not even a threat. It's implicit, understood. You realize most of this stuff winds up out west these days. It's a coup to make the short list.'

'You didn't feel the shots were yours to call.'

Luke grimaced. 'Opportunities like this don't come along every day. Nowhere that makes a habit of shutting the door in government's face has profited from the practice.'

'Reprisals?'

'Please. Purse strings. When you're talking about research funding on this level it doesn't take a politburo to enforce obedience.'

'So you put together a list of names, a rough budget no one believes. Care to mention a few scientists you admire?'

He shook his head. 'Can't do it.'

'I'm not testifying against you.' He smiled thinly. 'Let me toss out, for the record, that you're not the sort of fish I mean to catch,' I added.

'What did Jesus say? Follow me and I'll make you fissures of men?'

I indulged him with a grin. 'There are ways of telling without telling.'

Luke toyed absently with a paper clip, tapping it on the desk. 'On advanced projects,' he reflected, 'you can't source the team in-house, of course. When I want to get a sense of what our competition's up to, I dig around online, see who's on leave where. Check for visiting appointments.'

'There must be hundreds in a given year.'

'Across the country? More than that. But only so many wind up here. When Odysseus wanted to trick the Cyclops, he said his name was Outis, "nobody," and the giant went around telling people "nobody" had blinded him. Our joke was to call our appointment Atopos, "no place." We didn't want undue scrutiny.'

'And Cuber?'

'The echt thing. Real Cube. Later R-Cube. Cuber. Etc.'

'Cute.'

'Don't go flattering a flatterer.'

'I wouldn't dream of it. But don't go bluffing a bluffer. You haven't been completely honest with me.'

I rose and gathered my stuff. I was almost to the door before Simmons said, 'What wasn't I honest about?'

Count on curiosity overmastering better judgment every day.

'Administrations turn over,' I said. 'Loyalty's a fickle beam. We had a big election not nine months ago. Who's the constant in this equation?'

Simmons looked briefly baffled, then said, 'You mean the contractor?'

I was glad I was turned away so he couldn't see me grin. 'How is Rob, by the way?' I asked. It was worth the penalty stroke if I was wrong.

'Friend of yours?'

'Oh boy.' I turned and gave Luke a wink from the door. 'Anyone asks, Outis was here.'

They say there is such a thing as enclothed cognition, a tendency to think differently when you are wearing different clothes. The very character of your thought changes. Doctors' coats don't just comfort patients, *they make better doctors*. And so it isn't hard to imagine that certain people have worn the same clothes long enough to fuse with their role, to adopt its habits of thought as their own, and to forget the part chance plays in who any of us are. The years solder us to the garment, and the garment to the chair. Put on the throne so long ago, we convince ourselves we climbed up on our own.

Simmons wasn't the worst of these types but he had the studious indifference of those who, caught up in the thrill of scientific alchemy, drunk on its magic power, can't find time to imagine the dark possibilities in their creations. See that it works, worry about the consequences later. But this moment for reflection never comes. Scientists aren't capitalists or politicians. They don't own the genies they've loosed from the bottle. Metalsmiths keep cool water at hand while working with their fires, and yet we don't consider that knowledge must be tempered by wisdom, that the two must develop in tandem. Infatuated with humans' technical abilities, a certain man convinces himself that the sole meaning in life lies in solving such problems as submit to tools, and it is often the hangers-on and popularizers who prove least skeptical and most credulously impressed, most fully messianic in their view of what technology can do for us. Real scientists, perhaps for intimacy with the unknown, seem to get that unless you believe our ultimate discoveries turn up divine structure, unless you believe this all ends with us staring our creator in the eye, what we stand to unearth is a string of numbers, a set of contingent relationships, and that these impenetrable constants and equations are the full truth of our unpromised cosmos.

I am liable to seem old-fashioned to those like Simmons who appear ready to give more dangerous toys to moral children—stodgy in my belief that while we look to probe the center of the universe or the space-dead reaches of a black hole, we have barely explored the purlieus of the human heart. We glance at our toys and think we must be adults to own them, and we tell ourselves they will save us from the very work of growing up they distracted us from in the first place.

The heat of the courtyard was briefly fortifying after the chill of the institute. I tried Katz-Wallace at the office and then his cell when he didn't pick up.

'I'm heading into Treasury,' he said before I could get a word in. 'Can you make it quick?'

'Nice to hear your voice too. Listen, I need you to put in a search request. Get some intern to do it, but don't act like it came from me.'

Michael was probably rolling his eyes, but he agreed. I told him I needed a list of research scientists posted to Branford or AIIS over the past thirty-six months. Fields of special interest included computer and neuroscience and any sort of biomedical, electrical, or neuroengineering. Maybe psychology and applied math. 'Look for any reference to a project called Atopos'—I spelled this for him—'and have them send along whatever they turn up every hour or so.'

'All right,' said Michael.

'You got all that?'

'Yup.' His curtness told me he wanted to get off the phone.

'Treasury, huh? Boy Scout?'

A pause. 'No. Dissident. But that's all you're getting.'

'You worried I might start cogitating.'

'First time for everything. I really got to go.'

I knew I could trust Michael, knew it instinctively. Beyond a surprisingly low quotient of idiocy, he was serious. He believed in the work and took the reporter's side, which is to say the story's side, over the business's and over his career's.

My friend was at a different bench in the courtyard, having relocated to the shade.

'Right idea,' I said, keeping my pace.

He squinted at me, took a sip of his coffee, then with studied offhand-edness he said, 'You're being followed.'

'How's that?'

'Canvas shorts.' He took his time with his coffee, cupping it prayer-fully in two hands. 'Camera around his neck. Tall. Looks like one of these kid's parents.'

'Right,' I laughed. 'Because he is.'

'OK. Don't believe me.'

'It's not a question of believing. What am I supposed to do about it?'

'Heterochromia iridis. It means having differently colored eyes.'

'I wouldn't dream of suggesting otherwise.'

'That's what the guy following you had.'

'Fine. But it doesn't mean he's following me.'

'Correct. That's where statistics come in.' He picked up his notebook and tapped the cover. 'I'm conducting a study, remember? Do you notice anything unusual about this courtyard?'

'There's a guy in mittens talking to me about statistics.'

'You know the Seven Bridges of Königsberg?' he said, ignoring this.

'I can't swear I'm familiar with all seven.'

'If you draw all the paths you could take to enter and exit the court-yard, what do you think you get?'

'Obsessive-compulsive disorder?'

'What else?'

I rubbed my face in fatigue. 'You better just tell me.'

We looked at each other for a minute and I said all right, explain it to me slowly, and I can't say the gentler speed of his account did wonders for my comprehension. His hat inched up on his forehead as he talked until he resembled a figure from a Hittite relief. The folds and creases around his eyes were impressive, giving his skin the quality of a garment. I didn't follow all the talk of lemniscates and Euler characteristics, but I made out in my dense way that the path my supposed tail had taken deviated markedly from the patterns recorded in the notebooks strewn across the sun-dappled bench. The leaves shook in the wind, their shadows danced. I thanked the man for his vigilance and for taking an interest, but I said I needed to be on my way.

He shrugged and looked off into the sky. 'Find the guy taking photos.'

'Everyone in this damn town's taking photos.'

'Not photos of nothing.'

'No. That's *exactly* what they're doing.'

He considered this briefly, then opened his notebook and wrote something. 'I'm not taking photos,' he remarked.

'You're the statistical anomaly. And it's not just the photos.' I turned to go.

Though I put little stock in his admonition, I am not immune to the beckonings of paranoia. It comes with the work. You're pursuing people. It only makes sense someone would be pursuing you. And the things you know! The secrets bound in your head! That impetus to discover what others won't tell you . . . That's the whole game, teasing the line, constellating bits of information, offhand utterances, mapping the subtle joinery that knits action to motive, pliant word to sentiment . . . But it's only a game if two are playing, and so you wonder, you wonder. Who is working to crack, to uncase *me*? And then you conclude that wondering is a fool's errand. And you settle for doubt, plugging your ears to paranoia's sweet nothings. If God or anyone else wants to watch you in an unrelieved vigil, commend his patience and move on.

Back on the main drag I ate a muffin for breakfast. I'd holed up in a coffee shop and was refreshing my email when the first list of names appeared, forwarded along by Michael. I wrote down the most promising of these, committing as many as I could to memory. Since the scientists at Branford wouldn't have had to go on leave, I went back through the faculty listings at AIIS and in the relevant university departments and fired off a few emails proposing an afternoon coffee. Then I went to find Enoch Niels.

Enoch wasn't picking up his office phone and I decided to drop by his house. The address was listed and it was an easy walk from campus. The air held a rich floral smell. All the pretty houses had gardens and hedge-rows alive with elegant sun-dappled petals, graceful flowers slanting like the legs of wading birds. Leaves rustled on the trees and a man watering his plants chatted with a mailwoman. On one lawn two cherubim in a fountain spat flaccid ropes of water from their puckered lips.

Enoch's house wouldn't have made the tour, though it sat under a canopy of maples and backed onto a small wood where the street ended in a ravine of decaying leaves. It had clearly once been nice enough, but it needed weeding and a paint job. When I pressed the bell a drawn-out *ding-dong* sounded inside and I waited a good two minutes, through several sequences of footsteps and dog barks, before I heard the bolt turn in the lock. I was gazing down the block, half expecting to see a figure in canvas shorts with a camera around his neck regarding me from a distance.

A bony man in glasses and sweats, dressed for a Sunday at home with the paper, opened the door. 'Yes?' He had the pained expression of someone who finds the routine idiocy of daily life faintly crushing.

'Quentin Jones,' I said. 'I'm a reporter. I wonder if you have time for a chat.'

'Reporter,' he murmured.

'Yes. With the *Beacon*.'

He looked at me over his glasses. 'I do seem to recall that name. Quentin Jones?'

'That's right.'

'Come in.' He held the door for me. 'How on earth did you find me?'

'You're in the phone book.'

'The phone book. Really! They still have phone books after all this time . . .'

A wheezy retriever came straggling forward and thrust a wet nose in my hand. The interior had the absentminded charm of a well-enough-off sort who couldn't be bothered with the trivia of homemaking. The furniture was haphazard: some nice, some cheap; none of it matched. The rugs were worn and random, selected, it seemed, for size alone. But the space was cozy despite itself, lived in and even homey.

'Just you, then?' I asked, peering around.

'Yes, Charles has been gone some time now.' Enoch disappeared into thought for a moment. Then he turned an eye on me that seemed to swim in limpid water. 'Charles was my partner and the domestic one, you see.' A faint laugh. 'Coffee?'

'I just had some, but all right.'

He motioned for me to sit at the table in the kitchen. This looked out on the back lawn. Enoch poured two cups from the pot. 'I *believe* I made this today, but you never know. Sorry,' he said with a wry gesture at the plain mug. 'The Limoges is in storage.'

I took a small sip to be polite and he joined me at the table.

'Now tell me, Mr. Jones. Am I in *terrible* trouble?'

'Why would you say that?'

Enoch laughed, almost ruefully. 'You might not understand because, after all, you can't help following yourself around, but you'll have to take my word for it that big city reporters don't show up on my doorstep every day.' His eyes widened meaningfully above his glasses.

'Some people say there's no such thing as bad press.'

'Not I, I assure you.'

'I'm just coming from a meeting with your colleague—Simmons?' I said, affecting to consult my notes. 'He took that line too. But later he changed his mind.'

'What, dare I ask, did you say to change his mind?'

'People like to tell their side of the story.'

'And you haven't even told me what story it is.'

I said I had little doubt that Enoch had divined the matter correctly, but I laid my cards on the table all the same. I told him I had no love for Branford or the institute, and if anyone expected me to get misty-eyed about the march of scientific progress we could set up that timer next to the one waiting for the cows to come back. But I wasn't interested in his friends or the university or in slinging mud at a bunch of tenured geeks. I wasn't dead set against it in a pinch, but really I just needed to know what Cuber *was*, from the inside out, according to the people who built it.

'I suppose I'm to understand a veiled threat in that,' he mused. 'Well,

I'm much too old and emeritus to care. But you'll have to find a different angle if you want to blackmail me.' He gazed at me significantly. 'Now. First, you must realize that I'm an electrical engineer by training. I help integrate systems, circuitry. But I don't write software. I don't develop theory. And in this case I wasn't told the application.'

'Let's say I believe half of that.'

'You believe what you believe.'

'If I were trying to build a very convincing simulation, say . . . Let's start from the beginning. What would I need, technically speaking?'

Enoch looked out at the yard, a few fingers curled in the handle of his mug. He seemed to be weighing the reality of the conversation against a desire to disappear softly into the trees.

'There are different approaches. I don't know that you have the time . . .'

'Time isn't my issue.'

'Well, are you talking about screens and cameras? Bodysuits, haptic systems? Found light, photogrammetry, digital light fields? Do you mean computer-generated images? Invasive procedures? Headsets?'

'What would *you* build?'

'I wouldn't build it in the first place,' he snapped.

Gently, insistently, I said, 'But you did.'

He looked away again. 'You don't always grasp the . . . implications. The meaning of what you're doing at the time.'

'A lot of guys I know make a career of explaining how doing what they want you to do is the right thing.'

He sneered. 'Don't make excuses for me. I'm not a child.'

'Then don't beat yourself up and pretend it's atoning. I know that game too.'

He was still gazing out the window. 'They wanted to study the future of governance. That's what they said. If the technology existed, someone would build it. It seemed like maybe the Chinese already had. We needed to start looking at the implications for rule of law.'

'I'm sorry, I don't follow.'

'How do you police a virtual world.' Enoch turned back to me. 'But it's deeper than that, I imagine. What even *is* a crime? What is allowed? Illegal? If nobody's physically hurt, are there nonetheless crimes against . . . the virtual body? We've never faced such an abrupt split between body and mind. Our entire reality, our ethics, is built on their inseparability.'

'You seem to know more philosophical politicians than I do.'

'The government has pedestrian concerns as well. Frankly, we don't know the extent of physical or psychosomatic trauma that might result from mental distress. But there's also just the question of monitoring people's incomes and spending if entire hermetic markets take shape inside a simulation.'

'Tax evasion? Money laundering?' I was genuinely surprised. 'But they could confiscate the machines, couldn't they—whatever creates the simulation?'

'You might think. On the other hand, the assumption is our lives will gradually shift onto virtual platforms until they reside there entirely. Much easier to solve political problems without material constraints. But then what proportion of human concerns are psychological at root and not physical at all? And if what we understand as life runs wholly through a simulation, kicking people out may violate their rights. It would be a drastic step. Social ostracism of the cruelest sort. On par with interning a person or sending him to the gulag.'

'Like solitary confinement. But the opposite.'

'A kind of death, really.'

'Who lives outside the system in this scenario? Who keeps the machines running, the bodies alive?'

'There are endless questions, Quentin. Which I suppose is why they feel the need to study the issue. Simmons gave us quite a little speech. Compared our work to the Space Race, the teams developing computers during the war. We're not immune to vanity, you know, the desire to do big things.'

'Was it just hot air?'

'I can't say. Honest. History says the paradigm can shift at speeds we never imagine. The first airplane flights took place in 1903, a rickety crate of spruce and muslin. Ten years later planes are in the war. Next war, we get the atomic bomb and rocketry programs. A lot of resources for a limited number of useful weapons. Maybe they aren't worth it, looking back. But a decade later the superpowers have thousands of ICBMs with thermonuclear warheads in them, sitting in silos poised to destroy the world. You can tell a similar story about Moore's law and computing. Or the growth of the internet.'

'But dual-use always seems to come on the fastest.'

'It's the kind of blue-skies research the government funds.'

Outside the thick leaves on the trees shimmied above an ornamental pond. 'How come this stuff doesn't pop up in private labs?' I asked. 'Tech companies must want a piece of the action.'

'They don't have the power, first of all,' said Enoch. 'To run something this big you need direct access to the grid. A private company couldn't draw that much without government certification. So federal authorities would be involved either way.

'Second, processing speed. The private sector has some fast machines, but the most powerful arrays are all still in public research facilities.'

'Designed to simulate nuclear explosions,' I said, dredging this bit of trivia from some ancient story at least a decade old.

'That's right. At some point the bombs got so big and the tests so unpopular that it made more sense to model the detonations on computers. Only the computers couldn't handle the complexity. Even just the first few milliseconds of the explosion took days, weeks to simulate on the fastest systems. The computers got better faster than the bombs.'

'So you need government infrastructure and equipment. Anything else?'

'Well, it didn't work.'

'The simulation?'

'Yes.' Enoch turned to me. 'Oh, we solved the hard parts . . . How to square the interface directly with the brain. Noninvasively, mind. Tight focusing parameters for the electrical field. Transcranial hookups. Latency periods and perceptual smoothing. Photorealistic imagery resolved into code. You name it.'

'But?'

'Something as dumb as storage, if you can believe it. Try for a second to imagine how much data one subjective reality takes up. Forget subjective: *objective*. When you go about your life, you don't have to worry about everything staying the same when you're not around.'

'You're talking about continuity. Like in a film.'

'That's right. But continuity without end. The more you experience in a simulation, the more there is to remember. And your experience has to agree with mine or the whole thing goes through the looking glass in a heartbeat.'

'People pay money for drugs like that.'

'There *aren't* drugs like that.'

'Why bother with subjective realities at all? If the problem's getting them to agree, why not one master reality, like a video game?'

'Right, that's one answer. Except in a video game you can only do so many things. You interact with the world in prescribed ways. In a full simulation you have to be able to *do* anything. Far more than designers can anticipate.'

'You're saying you can't develop the entirety of reality.'

'We aren't gods!' Enoch shouted and listed forward in his seat. 'Can you begin to imagine how large the world is? We can scarcely design a city block without a team working overtime for a week.'

'So what do you do?'

'We fudge.' Enoch scratched the ears of his retriever. 'We took the expectations of the participant and patched these into the reality. Then we ratcheted down the fidelity, like in a dream. We let the mind supply both sides of the equation: its projections became the backdrop and its assumptions filled in the rest. But you can imagine the difficulty of sewing even two people into the same virtual fabric, much less thousands.'

'Their visions of the world might disagree.'

'A reality at war with itself.'

'Your paymasters must have been disappointed.'

Enoch sipped his coffee, one eyebrow raised. 'You'd be surprised.'

My coffee had gone tepid. I looked around. A photograph on the wall showed two black-and-white figures by the side of a house, high-contrast shadows in the foreground and a brightly lit sea in the glittering sunshine beyond.

'Is that you?'

'And Charles.'

The second figure bore a strong resemblance to an actor. Gene Kelly? He wore a wide-collared crewneck sweater from which emerged the strong ropes of neck muscle and an even, jutting oblong of face, clear skin, a light easy smile, carefully parted hair.

'What did Charles do?'

'I'm not sure he did anything,' Enoch said, a faraway smile on his face. 'He was good company.'

I nodded. That was enough.

Enoch stood. 'Now, do you want to see what I get up to in my free time?'

I rose and followed him down several short hallways and a set of stairs to the basement. He flipped a breaker and two banks of fluorescents blinked to life above a large platform, bathing the room in light. At first I thought I was looking at a model train set, but I quickly realized there were no tracks or trains. Enoch was crouched down, flicking a series of switches that turned on the electronics on the model: traffic lights, lights inside buildings and houses. I recognized one of the structures, an iconic stone spire that appeared on the university's website.

'It's Branford,' I muttered.

'Yes.'

'To scale?'

He only smiled faintly. There were students crossing the campus paths. Homeless men begging on the street. Couples and families pointed at tiny displays in shop windows. The trees had begun to change, the greens going yellow, russet. A man in a courtyard took a photo and shadows cast in from the west. Evening. Clocks on the pediments and belfries showed a time just after 5:30. They agreed, that is. The streets were busy: people done with class, heading home from work, enjoying the evening, eating ice cream, oblivious to their lives in Enoch's model.

'Where's the institute?'

Enoch gazed at his creation. 'It wasn't built yet.'

'Yet . . .' Comprehension dawned slowly. 'This isn't current?'

'1992,' Enoch said. 'October 3.' The basement's walls and workbenches held various implements, materials, machine tools. Enoch turned to one of the benches, opened a flat file, and drew out a large folder, which he laid on the table. 'Here,' he said. I opened it at his prompting. The first image was an aerial photograph of Branford from a helicopter. 'Apr/May 1992' appeared in grease pencil in the lower corner. I flipped through the folder. There were more photographs like that one and municipal plans and blueprints for buildings, parks, civic developments. Interleaved with these larger sheets were dozens of snapshots of smiling families and individuals.

'Who are they?' I asked.

'No idea. They're vernacular photographs. I bought them online.' When he saw my confusion he explained: 'I didn't buy them for the people, but for the backdrops—the buildings, the scenes behind them.'

'All these facades, you mean . . . they're *in* Branford?'

He nodded. 'At first I just thought I'd amuse myself. I missed using my hands. Building something is very peaceful, you know. You fall into a trance. Hours go by and you don't think one big or complicated thought. But as the years continue, and as the scene fades further into the past, I find myself developing a strange sort of ownership of this moment.

'It's mine, you see,' Enoch persisted. 'I'm its caretaker. And how many others there are just like it . . . The specificity of a single instant is overwhelming. What do we do with their accumulation, their fleetingness?'

'It's a life's work to preserve just one.'

'I don't know if it even gives me pleasure anymore. Call it an affliction. There's always more to get right, further nuance to consider.'

'I start to grasp the difficulties you mentioned earlier.'

'Yes. And this is one still frame.'

'But at some point, with enough storage and power and know-how, don't you think we'll create something close enough? A virtual world, for all intents and purposes.'

'Yes. But for what intents? What purposes?' Enoch sighed. 'We can automate a lot of the process. The details only have to resolve to the scale of human perception. But we're always expanding and stretching our vision: microscopes, telescopes, cleverly designed macroscopic experiments that discern microscopic phenomena.'

'We'll find the joints and seams in the simulation unless it's perfect, you mean.'

'Some people think we already live in a simulation. What's the difference?'

'Between reality and a simulation?' I said. 'One was made.'

'And if reality can be made?'

'I suppose we are gods.' Enoch wore a glum, wearied expression. 'Is there a chance we never find the computing power?' I asked.

'I don't know,' he said. 'How far can storage and processing collapse? These are questions for quantum theorists, some of whom have come to understand reality in terms of information and information alone. Is it possible to "process" the world as it exists to us? I'm not sure. I suppose some theory would have broken down if not—and then it must be—or maybe we need some other "stuff" we haven't identified yet, or a harmonizing principle, like entanglement, that allows for more efficient processing paradigms. Do we know all the strategies nature uses to evoke our world? I doubt it. There must surely be compressions and shortcuts we haven't found. Just like in the simulation we built, we may be dreaming more of the world, of this reality, than we realize. Reality may seem continuous because we have nothing to compare it against.'

'You're talking about illusions.'

'Sure, if you like. Assuming you believe perception can be anything other than illusion. A user interface. Two-dimensional drawings suggest depth. Splotches of color suggest water, faces, clouds. We supply a lot to bring reality alive. We don't gaze at a painting and think, "Look at this colorful plastic substance affixed to canvas." If you were to describe my model of Branford to someone, you'd mention people, buildings, trees.'

'You think life's like that.'

'The light that enters our eye hits a two-dimensional screen.'

'And hits it upside down, I seem to recall.'

'You only notice what you notice.'

'Caitlin Tuross,' I said.

'Excuse me?'

'Ed Yang.'

'Ed.' Enoch smiled. 'Have you spoken to Ed?'

They were the only two cognitive scientists on my list and I figured it was a good time to take a flier. I said I hadn't reached Ed yet but hoped to talk with him soon.

'Ed was interested in magic,' said Enoch. 'Stage magic. He'd grown up with it. His parents had a traveling act when he was a kid in Taiwan, going town to town. Back when the country was dirt-poor. I'm sure this led him to his work. His mantra was to forget reality. People don't notice what goes on right in front of their eyes. Don't focus on what's there, but what people *believe* is there. What they want to see. Fashion reality from our expectations.'

'I start to understand why the Drayman reps smelled blood.'

'Blood? They smelled the future.'

'And you?'

'I hope Charles would forgive me.'

'What about the rest of us?'

Enoch didn't say anything. He turned his pained eyes to me. I met his gaze briefly and looked away. In the model the figures streamed out of buildings into the early evening. They were motionless, but one could picture them moving, caught midstride, flowing forth to compose this peaceful, miniature public. And then the placid artificial dusk shifted, an intuition addressing me suddenly and thrusting melancholy through what had a second before seemed simple happiness.

'When exactly did Charles die?' I asked.

Enoch looked at me and then at the village he had built by hand in such loving nuance. 'You have good instincts,' he said. 'Intuition, I've heard it said, is the art not of thinking, but of listening deeply. A brilliant mathematician named Nat Shannon, one of the founding members of the institute, thought the sciences should discourage understanding and encourage wonder. That was part of the institute's founding idea. Nat said thinking got in the way of dreaming, and that listening to your curiosity led most directly to meaningful questions. But maybe listening meant something specific to him, because he went mad.'

'Mad?'

'What does one say these days? Mentally ill . . . He was schizophrenic, I think.'

'Was.'

'Oh, *is*. He's still around. Recording reams of trivia on god knows what. How many squirrels there are on campus.'

'I think I met him.'

'You may have. He often hangs out by the institute. His former colleagues show him . . . forbearance.'

'How cracked is he?'

'What did he tell you?' Enoch squinted at me. 'I don't keep up with him. He was one of the most brilliant mathematicians of his day. But then he went "on strike," as he likes to put it. He didn't want to think like the rest of us. Being a great mathematician, at a certain point, isn't about computation. It's about asking questions no one else sees to ask and asking them in a way that permits meaningful answers. In that sense thinking differently may approach genius and madness by the same route.'

It was the height of the afternoon by the time I left. Everything was quiet and pacified past lethargy to stillness in the shimmering heat. I didn't know what to make of my earlier encounter in the courtyard. As to my ongoing inquiry, I saw the contours of a tableau taking shape, a landscape announcing itself in the mist. Yet I had to be careful. What we know, as reporters, is that the process of understanding can fix the shape of what is understood too soon. Maybe, as Nat Shannon believed, it all comes down to which questions you see fit to ask yourself. There are so many angles on reality, and we inhabit our own evolving confusion, strung as tight as catgut on the pegs of personality. No reporter is exempt. To escape the prejudices of certainty you must aim to grasp not just what happened but how those involved understand it, the fugitive role of motive and intent, and to get there, to this place of literary sufficiency, without collapsing beneath the drifts of impression heaped up by interested parties everywhere. You must fend off manipulation and lies at every turn, because your hunger for truth leaves you highly susceptible. Seduction is always, foremost, an activity of self-love. We lie most powerfully to convince ourselves.

I thought this on my way back downtown with the day's ormolu light threading a blue canopy settled with blancmange drifts of cloud. There was no sense that history could happen here, among these sumptuous homes and faultless daubs of earth, flower, tree. Enoch had said the key to a convincing simulation, within the technical limits of the day, was to give people what they already expected and, in this way, bring the mind into sympathy with the illusion. But for a reporter it is a terrible pitfall simply to discover what you already believe. The story gathers a force of its own and this invisible gravity begins to compel one's interpretations. It was with this in mind that I put Enoch Niels and Luke Simmons, Rich Jarosok, Parisa, and even old Castor Joseph in sealed jars, looked past their conviction and their certainty, their friendliness and enmity, and all the motives, dirty or driven, I could see. I had started to think I knew what was going on, and that is always a dangerous place to be.

When I finally checked my email only one member of the Branford faculty had responded to my overture, a mathematician and computer scientist named Hassie Dhawan. Her note was terse. It told me to call her and I rang right away. A crystalline voice, accented as if with a more perfect tonality of speech, answered. I told her who I was and said I'd written her earlier in the day.

There was a pause, the air of deliberation around a decision already made. 'We're not supposed to talk about our work, you know.' When I said, 'Yes . . . ,' she continued, 'We signed an agreement. I wonder if you've gotten many responses.'

'I've spent the day with your colleagues so far.'

'Luke doesn't count,' she said. A glint of humor in this.

'I see you've heard from him. To encourage your cooperation, I'm sure. He's not the only one.'

'Who else?'

'You'll have to trust me.'

'That's comforting, I guess.'

'Look, I can't help noticing you got in touch.'

She sighed. 'It's true.'

I'd made it back to campus and stood on the shady side of the street, gazing across a stream of glossy cars at the chapels and halls with their tracery windows. 'Let me buy you coffee,' I said.

She laughed, not quite happily. 'Coffee's really the least of it.'

'Yes, I know.' Another pause. I switched the phone to my fresh ear. 'I'm sorry you got roped into this, honest. It was a setup. Even for Simmons.'

'Say I believe you. What is it you want from me?'

'I need to understand how this works. I'm not a computer genius in my spare time.'

'I put myself in jeopardy talking to you.'

'They'd never go after you. And they're not going after anyone be-cause the last thing they want is to give the story any credence.'

'I feel . . . What's the opposite of comforted?' Beneath its tension the voice belonged to someone playful.

'I'm still working on my bedside manner.'

'There's a coffee shop, Country Joe's. How's half an hour? If you don't have a car, you'll need to get a taxi. It's the next town over.'

'You don't have to worry about us being seen.'

'I know,' she said. 'It's where I live.'

'Oh,' I replied and Hassie repeated, 'Half an hour,' and hung up.

A lineup of orange cabs on Main Street convinced me I'd have no trouble getting one when the time came. I had ten minutes to spare and crossed over to the campus, which lay beyond a stone face of buildings thrown up like ramparts with squat towers and ornamental crenella-tions. I passed beneath a high archway to enter the yard. Cy hadn't texted since the day before and, scrolling now idly through the messages on my phone, I wondered whether she was at the apartment, feeding Tyche, or if she'd been there earlier. As if mocking my thoughts, the drawn-out shadow of a statue at my feet showed a couple in an embrace, holding each other side by side. The shining bronze figures, dappled in daylight, glared too brightly to make out at a distance. Cy and I had been apart only a few days. Too early, perhaps, for regret. And then she didn't let in every emotion that addressed itself to her—a habit that cleaves a certain divide in a person, as if the timebound self is merely a shifting silhouette, while beyond this marginal figure, in some other realm, exists the creature who deals only in sentiments equal to it.

Maybe I felt guilty. Some undertone in Hassie's words promised the balm of flirtation. The heart is an optimist, and I was as afraid of losing my desire for Cy as I was of losing her, since desire, we know, is an enchantment and once broken never returns. This means I side with her in believing our behaviors more often create our emotions. The fortuitous choice one day to act on this or that fancy may decide an entire life. It is terrifying, like Enoch's model, whose pointless monumental effort only drew attention to the infinity of other moments we overtake, unique and rich beyond imagining, like all the other lives we might have lived.

Deliberately, abruptly, from my apparent reverie, I looked down at my watch and, as if startled by the time, set off across the quad. I moved as one late for a meeting moves, checking my watch again, striding swiftly, paying no mind to the tour groups crossing the campus paths. When I'd passed behind a building I turned, counted slowly to five, keeping hidden from the yard, and reversed course.

I don't know the first thing about countersurveillance. It's always been my belief that anybody trained in the arts of following and watching will escape my notice no matter what I do. They say to take note of the people around you and hope they reappear. *Hope!* I'd be more comforted to find they didn't. My friend from the courtyard, the legendary Nat Shannon, had planted a seed in my head, however, the image of an unremarkable middle-aged man with a camera around his neck and differently colored eyes. Hardly an Identi-Kit. Hardly anything really.

It was nutty to think I was being followed, and yet my heart was banging in my chest as I turned back into the quad. The campus was too empty for any hiding. Could my very obliviousness and innocence lull this man—the figure who wasn't there—into a brief lapse? My pulse raged in anticipation.

But I had turned into the sun. It lay above the rooflines across the yard, nitid white and trespassing all contours as it fanned out in shallow waves. A tour group stood listening to their docent relate the history of one of the pretty stone buildings. A trickle of administrators cut across the paths with folders and soft briefcases under their arms. Two maintenance personnel threaded a length of hose into a standpipe. Visitors clustered by plaques or sat on the steps of the buildings, consulting maps. A flash went off, a family photo: grandmother, father, two adolescent girls. I scanned the yard. My moment was fading. I cast around dizzily, nearly convincing myself I saw shadows disappearing at the edges of buildings, figures falling into dark recesses. But it was just the filigree jitter of leaves in breeze and sun.

There was nothing out of the ordinary. Nothing I could see. I felt foolish, even ashamed at my imagination. I breathed hard. The air was hot. The laughter, the families snapping photos, the practiced spiels of guides made a mundane scene. A clock tower tolled impassively in another yard.

My adventure had returned me to the embracing lovers. The statue's sinuous, rounded bronze was as dark as onyx, so smooth the light clung to it in long pools. Thinking of Cy, I'd taken the couple's posture for love, the clasped shadows, but now I saw in the statue itself that the figures bore up under grief, one burying his head in his hands and the other looking to the sky in tears for a mercy that wouldn't come, that she couldn't expect, for they were none other than Adam and Eve, expelled from paradise by the God to whom their entreaties were addressed. The man had one hand on the woman's shoulder, leading or comforting her, or expressing in his way the isolation they now partook of together, the aloneness of their exile, reduced to humiliation at their nakedness and beset by everything they had come, in such short order, to know.

I texted Cy on my way out of town. The cab drove with exquisite circumspection as it picked its way through the outskirts of Branford. In just a few minutes we found ourselves in farmland. The plats had barns and silos and wonderfully green fields. Everything seemed to ripen in the honey-hay of high summer's approach, the air thick enough to read as dust, saturated with insects, moisture, the floating hair of seedpods, grasses, clover, thistle. I texted Cy those perfunctory questions that watch over another life. Asked after the apartment, the cat, preparations for the show. Did I still live with her inside the intimate, vulgar parameters of unstaged routine? That's what I wanted to know. The rows of crops ran together in the distance.

Now the cab picked up and followed a vein of rail tracks into the neighboring town. These ran on an elevated roadbed that crossed in front of the coffee shop. Freight, I guessed, although for all I knew they might have been the very ones that carried me north that morning. The town was smaller than Branford. Country Joe's made up the better part of its shopping district. The café's doors churned. Its high ceiling, a painted tin, was touched by slender columns. Though she was sitting in the far corner I spotted Hassie at once. She occupied a high-backed armchair partly obscured by its siblings. I could just make out the acute, reflective gaze.

'You order at the counter,' she said when I approached. 'If you want anything.'

'Thanks. Maybe in a minute.'

She looked a good decade older than in her photo on the department website, though she still had a youthful cuteness, skin as soft as a twenty-year-old's. Her raven hair, however, had gray-and-white streaks. She wore faded jeans: a short woman with compact, almost chubby legs.

'Lived out here long?'

She resettled herself in the chair. 'Six years now. My husband and I moved when I was pregnant.'

'It's nice.'

'We wanted space for children, you know. A yard, backwoods. Lee grew up in the country, and I'd never had anything of the sort.'

'I guess you took to it.'

'I like the quiet. The sounds of nature at night.'

'And Lee and the kids?'

She laughed, a regretful laugh but not a bitter one. 'I haven't talked to Lee in years.'

'He left you with a young child?'

A blankness passed over her face. 'He left me,' she said. 'I never had the baby.' She turned and met my gaze. 'I miscarried and the complications meant I couldn't have any more.' She shifted in her seat and smiled at me. 'I'm sorry, we just met, but I don't like mincing words.'

'I'm sorry too.'

'It's OK. I wasn't set on kids.'

'You've made peace with it.'

'I've made do,' said Hassie. 'Sometimes I resent not having the choice. But I take consolation in my work.'

'Yes,' I said, 'in . . .'—I glanced at my notes—'stochastic calculus, ergodic theory, operator algebra . . . You do occasionally explain this to people who speak English?'

'It rolls off the tongue, doesn't it?' She grinned. 'I tell them I study causal transformations in multidimensional spaces. In other words, with a lot of variables. How's that?'

'Tiny steps toward natural language.'

'How about this.' She grew enlivened as she spoke. 'Take a frame from a movie. Now, some number of things change between that still and the next one. But not everything changes or there would be no continuity. It would look like static. So if you wanted to store this movie as data, you could save each frame as a photograph. But you'll use a lot less space if you can describe the second frame in terms of what changes from the first.'

'A kind of compression.'

'Indeed. Although with movies we've known what to do for a while. A film is defined ahead of time. What about a film that hasn't already been shot, but which self-generates in real time?'

'A film?'

'I only mean it as a metaphor. It could be anything—any system that changes in discrete steps. If you want your system to resemble the real world, like a film does, you have to figure out how things change, and how much they change from one interval to the next.'

'Cause and effect.'

'Causality is a propagating phenomenon. It spreads in certain ways and at certain speeds.'

'But wouldn't the speed be quite different if we were talking about an explosion, say, or the gentle creek behind your house?'

She looked at me funny. 'Yes . . . though both conform to the laws of physics, which are well-defined. The only challenge in a quickly changing situation is to handle so many calculations without processing time overtaking real time.'

'Right,' I said. 'What's the word? *Latency*?'

'Precisely. If things change too fast, do you slow time down to allow the processor to catch up? Or do you simplify the calculations by reducing the granularity of detail, using a more rudimentary or approximate physics?'

'Which is better?'

'It depends on your goal. Perfect continuity or perfect fidelity? But we have processing systems fast enough now to handle any meaningful first-person experience of reality.'

'"We" meaning the government.'

'Even private labs. Next-generation versions of graphics cards that run huge numbers of tasks in parallel. Tensor processing units, capsule networks. Sophisticated computer chips, basically.'

'You seem to be suggesting the challenge lies elsewhere.'

'I'd tease you for playing Sherlock'—her smile turned faintly quizzical—'but how did you know there was a creek behind my house?'

'The mud on your shoes.'

She glanced down. 'There isn't—'

'A joke, Hassie. Sometimes you just guess right.'

She shook her head and sipped her tea. 'Maybe I seem paranoid. I don't have any experience with this sort of thing. The government makes you think they have eyes in the back of their head. Maybe it's just an act, but knowing what technology has become I'm inclined to believe them.'

'It's what they want you to think. They're as clueless as the rest of us.'

She considered this. 'I may be clueless, but I can't lock up people I don't like.'

'Neither can the government. Oh, they'd enjoy it, don't get me wrong. But you've got judges and journalists asking meddlesome questions.'

'You're one of them, I imagine.' She smiled and inspected me closely. 'Tell me something. What's in this for you?' She meant the work. Where did my interest lie? I explained that it was my job, but this didn't satisfy her; there had to be more. How had I gotten into the profession? I told her I stumbled in. It was this or ergodic theory and I never had the math. She laughed. Be serious, she said. I maintained that it wasn't much of a story, but she insisted gently.

And how she got me talking! I can't say what magic chord she struck. I liked her, that was clear, and I think she liked me too. Maybe I was tired of doing the listening, the asking, and so I talked. I told her about high school, the rural tracts on the outskirts of our county seat, the spreading bloom of suburban crust; how the ethic of our practical, proud, nowhere town bred cockiness, and a disdain for cockiness, in the boys I knew and had been one of, the clever restless boys who competed at everything. Though I had a high enough opinion of myself when I left for college, I had never applied myself with any rigor or grit. I figured it was the same for everyone. Do what's asked of you, do it well enough to get along. Don't do it so diligently that you lose your self-respect. Keep your head down and never brag. I took it as an article of faith that my experience ran inside the common channel and didn't see that most people found their level and contented themselves to float. This came as a shock—when I realized that beyond my natural laziness, nothing held me back. I'd never run up against my limit, never tested it, because we'd have pummeled and mocked and immiserated anyone who tried to distinguish himself that way. Oh, the embarrassment of being caught trying! There wasn't anything worse. Unless your excellence was incontestable, a fluke of birth like a four-seamer in the mid-nineties, you shut up about it. You were one of the guys. It didn't enter your head to overexert yourself. *Just* above average was fine. Turning in schoolwork late. Writing the occasional paper good enough to drive your teacher crazy, stacked against your other failures. There was a small-town pride in being by turns excellent and galling, stalwart and wicked. I relished an idea of myself as normal, and we saw something sacred in the ingenuous modesty that distinguished normal from the aspirants and blowhards.

I had learned to scorn regimes of judgment and merit, in other words. These taught us to love the wrong things, to enter a carousel of exchange, of aimless utility, with no meaningful idea of arrival. Where could value come to rest? Certainly not in one another. We'd abandon this notion of human worth for one strained through the winepress of numbers and measurements. Hierarchy for hierarchy's sake, to have a mechanism of sorting, a game to play. It didn't matter that the game was trivial or arbitrary, the impulse to distinguish beat so fiercely in us. I abhorred the most proximate self-importance I could find—my own. But I couldn't deny that my initial foray into journalism scratched the itch of displaced ego— that of exposing ego and self-importance in others. The fraud behind the gilt balance sheet. The all-too-human wizard in the control room. I would stand up and speak for the guy who didn't subject the rest of us to his grand opinion of himself. The woman who did her fucking job.

There was a paradox in this, but let's not ask for pure motives if the agenda checks out. Besides, the job gets to you. Reporting, that is. I hope it sounds humble enough to say it taught me some humility. First you see how quickly glory fades, how little the outward validation sustains you. A different sustenance crops up: the satisfaction of executing your craft well, doing the little things right. Most of the myrrh and frankincense the sycophants bring is poison, anyway. A murderous impulse wrapped in praise, it looks very briefly like love. So I took my lumps and I came to understand that what preserved me would only ever come from myself. From within. I saw how my ideas of merit peddled their own smug pretension, since for better or worse the people I impugned had an ambition I shared, where my regular joes, clocking in and out, betrayed a complacency in believing they didn't need to strive or grow or change. I don't mean any of this is simple. But I had to come clean, to myself at minimum, about the irreducible complexity of my motives. The purity, or at least honesty, in impurity. Did I stand on principle—did I *really*—or did I just like being in the mix, shooting the shit?

It was undeniable. I loved the give-and-take. Loved hashing it out with the guy in the street, the suite—it didn't matter. The demands of the moment brought out something I enjoyed in myself, questioning a source, switching registers, leading by misdirection, an unexpected joke, feigned ignorance, orchestrating the play of information like a jazz solo. That artificial, that artful. It called on every shade and nuance of speech, the full tool kit of rhetoric. You only had to feel it in your bones, that total absence of deference to authority. *Who do you think* you *are?* coursing through your blood. I belong here. *I* ask the questions. And I never hesitated to ask, not the tough question that brought the pretense of friendship down like a house of cards. You had to go hard at times. And all the while my allegiance changed. I gave up on loyalty to myself. I realized I served a master different from the moment or the story, the splashy revelation or the tepid sops of justice. All those shimmering vanities. I worked for a time horizon beyond my life. An idea of humanity that transcended any particular human being or circumstance or moment. I was part of a collective project to realize a coherent reality. It was a fraud, but it centered the human endeavor—a necessary, timeless fraud. No, we couldn't claim objectivity for our project, but we could claim it followed certain rules which, if adhered to faithfully, brought it beyond the parochial needs and desires and subjective shadings of each of us alone. Built into something larger. A compromise. And we labored to construct this rigorous, and rigorously incomplete, story, to hand it over to humanity with total deference to how they would use it. I believed we needed such a baseline to live in a reality of any consistency and dignity. And so my work, my devotion, was in service to nothing less than mutually comprehensible life.

'It sounds idiotically grand when I put it that way,' I said. 'I'm sorry. I don't know what got into me.' I felt suddenly sheepish at how self-approving my monologue had been. Worse still, I *meant* most of it.

Hassie appeared amused by my earnestness. 'I don't know,' she said. 'We need to agree on more than what we can reach out and touch. Only, I wonder, how do you know your "rules" are the right ones?'

'The rules of journalism?'

'Yes, the norms, the conventions. How do you know they give rise to the correct reality? The rules are intended to draw a line between objective and subjective life, but the boundary is blurry.'

I said none of us knew if the rules were right. They changed over time. We tinker, we adjust. What the public deserves to know, where considerations for privacy begin and end. When context and interpretation edify and when they tip over into editorializing, speculation. I told her the best we could do was to trust our judgment, and when in doubt show restraint. To be as honest as we could about methods and assumptions. 'A lot comes down to individuals trying to make their best call,' I said. 'We get a lot wrong.'

Hassie may not have been satisfied with this answer, but she let it drop. The shop had fallen into shadow. People were ordering afternoon coffees, chatting with baristas. Children did their homework at counters and tables, pencils held with all four fingers—too tightly, as if meant to carve stone. At intervals the roar of beans grinding filled the room, the light clatter of dishes, the burble of acquaintances bumping into each other. A warm, placid, unremarkable scene—it couldn't have been further from the capital, and I felt the ludicrous disjuncture between the lives people actually led and the grandiose intrigues of the place I called home, which purported to serve these lives. What Hassie and I had been discussing might have been a dream for all it had to do with the people here.

'Can I show you something?' she asked, almost shyly. 'It's back at my place.'

'Everyone has something to show me today,' I said, but I assented just the same.

Outside the windows of Hassie's hatchback the roads ribboned through low hills, the light and shade splashing across us as we dipped and rose. Fatigue stole over me at once, the kind that comes with a low golden sun and the hum of a car. A sense of being carried and held. I had a desire, as I drifted, for the ride never to end, so that I might doze and dream long enough to recover all those years of shattered sleep. The bands of light held me, swaddled me, the reverie of a chrysalis . . .

I awoke with a start. The car had stopped by a rugged farmhouse silhouetted against the sun. Hassie's hand lay on my forearm. The dryness of her touch, cool and light, held an intimacy I didn't know whether she intended. The seconds slowed. I came to life with the languor of ice disappearing into water. And then I realized, with such clarity that my ignorance to that point seemed incredible, that it was Jada she reminded me of—Jada with her dark braided hair, her acute irony and wry teasing way.

'That didn't take long,' Hassie laughed.

And how strange that beauty and familiarity turn out to be the same recognition, that desire and repetition share an organ of thought—as if we are all spawning salmon, fighting upstream to the site of earliest life. I can't help feeling our recognitions betray a knowledge that precedes us. Truth, perhaps, or just the myriad forms of life imprinted in our minds, the place where image and idea haven't yet separated, so that beauty refers to the character of inlaid rhythms, a commandeering drumbeat and the magnetism of its insistent interval. I don't mean physical beauty but something closer to love. The opposite of dispassionate identification: that which grabs you by the viscera, steals your breath. For that's what I felt just then, a wondrous and awesome compound stirring in the transport of Hassie's touch, linked along the iron chains of a memory, too deep for any simple name or concrete form, back to Jada and through her, to a moment, or just the residue of a moment, from another time altogether: my conscious origin, or something more distant still than that.

I got out, following Hassie as she mounted the steps to the house. An old tree forked up against the nacre of the sky, clouds strung in mottled bands, wisps and trailing fingers stretching to unseen terminals. The paint flaking from the clapboards like sunburnt skin had a roseate blush in the light. I felt at peace, suddenly very far from my life, as if Cy were no more than an old love fixed and formalized in the gilt of recollection, not the vital creature a part of me knew to be enduring at that same moment in a life as vivid as my own.

Hassie set me up on the back porch with a glass of wine and busied herself inside. She returned a few minutes later lugging a complex array, equipment that had the look of a home-science project by a precocious tinkerer: a card table affixed with monitors and computer boards, wires running between these and through rough holes drilled in hard plastic. She hauled this onto the deck, explaining rapidly in words I couldn't follow, and plugged a thick power cord into a grounded outlet, sending the machines humming to life with the whir and churn of a computer booting up. She had a laptop open and poured code into it with impossible fluency. I marveled at the speed. She keyed in commands and initiated subroutines faster than I could move my eyes down the screen.

'Have you guessed my role in the project yet?' She kept her eyes on the laptop, typing as she talked.

'I think I have an idea,' I said. 'Something governed by a vast number of variables, irreducible to simple physical laws.'

'We don't know if that's true about the laws. But for the purpose of a simulation . . . it's far too complex to build up from an atomistic level.'

'I don't begin to understand how you simulate movement, speech, to say nothing of thought.'

'We didn't recreate consciousness.' She looked at me with mock-pity. 'We don't even know if it exists.'

'I have some firsthand experience to support the idea.'

'Well, exactly. But maybe that experience is just the way certain other processes *feel*. In that case reproducing it directly would be impossible. We decided to focus on the behaviors themselves.'

'Behaviors?'

'How language *is* used, for example, as opposed to the full range of its possible use. How modes of thinking, speaking, or feeling work as potentialized states. We can define an attitude as a thing unto itself, something with inherent meaning, or we can define it in terms of what it's likely to bring about. A set of weighed probabilities for how the system will transform over time.'

'Thought without thinking.' I shook my head. 'Like a zombie.'

'Yes, that's just it. A zombie could theoretically do everything a human does without being aware of it. Without *experiencing* it. From the outside it would resemble a conscious human in every aspect.'

'And from the inside?'

'How do we know if the zombie has experiences or not?' She grinned. 'That's the million-dollar question.'

One of the most frightening ideas to emerge from the field of artificial intelligence, Hassie proceeded to explain, grew out of its deepest insight. The idea of the brain as a machine, and specifically a computing device, went back centuries. But only with conceptual advances in the seventies and eighties had a new model emerged of how an algorithm might replicate the brain's heuristic method. The neural network, it was called. By passing inputs through a lattice of interconnected gates, each modifying the input in successive stages, you could—so the thinking went—reduce cognition to a generic template with no need for specialized or formal rules. Simply sets of nodes and numbers, their relationships defined by no more than a single probability. By training these nets thousands, even millions, of times to match inputs to outputs, you could teach the network to learn from its mistakes, tweaking its nodal coefficients a little each time until it could deliver the output you wanted from the input alone. If you wanted a mechanical eye to recognize the letter *a* in all its organic forms, distinguish a dog from a horse, or determine from context whether the word should be *there* or *their*, you could train a neural net through brute force and achieve a much greater accuracy than any program based on explicit instructions.

But did I see the unsettling implications in this? she asked. If the best way to achieve 'thought,' or the behaviors that looked like thought, was to train a network to develop ever subtler coefficients, did this not imply that thought itself lived in these arbitrary numbers? Was the very meaning of thought in this case merely the architecture of a network, a web? Did any deeper truth or logic to thinking, to consciousness, exist than these nodal weightings? For you could go back into the net and interrogate it all you wanted to try to pinpoint the truth of its awareness, the numerology of the soul. But these numbers, these coefficients, revealed nothing. They simply got the job done.

Some people decided to flip the nets on their heads and run the process backward in an effort to derive the input from the output, so to speak. The idea was to discover what the net itself was 'seeing.' This technique was called 'dreaming,' and it produced nightmare versions of our world, accentuating certain features grotesquely by overidentifying and exaggerating key elements. Eyes often appeared throughout the images.

'With a sort of poetic justice,' Hassie explained. 'These programs *were* eyes and we wanted to see what they saw. God, to a goat, is a goat.'

But perhaps we can understand the eyes and other repeated forms, she went on, if we say that vision, and cognition broadly, intends to break a sensory input of ever-changing chaos into a subset of recurrent and comprehensible forms. 'What we call concepts or ideas. The things we have words for,' she said. 'Your task as a child is to recognize your mother however she appears to you, from whatever angle, in whatever state, wearing whatever clothing. Your task is not to understand that a person can be as many different things as there are quanta of perception. You need instead to find what unifies the multitude, or reduces it to one. If you were to reverse the process, it would make sense to expect this "one"—the concept, the idea, "Mother" in this case—to appear every-where, overrepresented.

'At this point we reach a crossroads and different thinkers go differ-ent ways,' she continued. 'Materialists want to say consciousness is just the byproduct of a physical process, like the heat given off running a machine: an epiphenomenon, inessential to thought—the experience of information integrating in the brain, getting recorded, reordered, and revised. Other adherents of physicalism see consciousness as the remnant past interacting with the present: the lingering awareness of the notes preceding those just played, which give continuity and tonality to the passage, or the residual impressions on a constantly overwritten black-board. Functionalists describe consciousness in terms of the functions different mental states achieve and the interactions between these states. This has an air of the trivial about it to me, since it doesn't explain why consciousness feels like consciousness. Our zombie could pass the func-tional test. Computationalists might say consciousness is a structure, an architecture, a shape—circuitry, in short, potentially more complicated than our neural networks but not qualitatively different.'

Many of these theories, she reflected, inclined toward the Kantian and Kabbalistic, the belief that what we experience is an immanent, re-ductive analogue of the infinity that lives beyond our heads, so that the

'Mother' concept, for instance, is a possibility that exists latent in our design as humans. The theories only got wilder and more speculative from there. You had those who believed that types of resonance, oscillation, and interference were necessary to orchestrate more local processes into a global whole—the so-called 'binding' problem. Along these lines, certain thinkers put forward frameworks that used the unusual features of quantum mechanics to explain the diffuse properties and intuitive products of consciousness. Then there were the apostles of panpsychism, who believed our physics hadn't yet accounted for a conscious property distributed across the material world like mass or electrical charge. In this view everything had some degree of consciousness, a totality that might sum to the implicit effect of dark matter, or live in the interstices of Planck-scale phenomena, the infinitesimal joints of synapses and microtubules, or the true nature of information.

'It sounds crazy,' said Hassie, concluding her spiel. 'But some respected scientists believe it isn't only observation that changes the outcome of experiments, but simple consciousness—*awareness*—of the experimental result.'

'What's your answer?' I asked.

She sighed. 'After all that, neither philosophy nor physics is really my field. I stay agnostic. The history of science compels humility.' Einstein, she explained, had called the cosmological constant the biggest blunder of his career; then dark energy reinstated it. Lamarckism had been a joke, junk science, for decades; now epigenetics threatened to revive it. We'd written off animism and Aristotelian thought since the Enlightenment, and now some claimed that maybe hunks of rock did have souls, maybe the universe did take an active, teleological interest in its unfolding. 'We tend to forget that all our explanations have some merit because they at least solve a *human* problem,' she said. 'They answer a question in a way that's relevant to our position in the universe, our scale and perspective. We've never gotten in trouble from having too many approaches, but only by claiming the timeless, irrefutable authority of one of them. For practical questions, we take what works. Some people think the world we inhabit is a simulation already, in which case we may have no access to the terms of reality beyond it.'

'But still, why the first-person feeling at all? I get that we don't know how it's generated. But what purpose does it serve?'

'Yes, that's a critical question,' she conceded. She said she only had one answer that began to satisfy her: we experienced it so we could re-experience, so we could share it with others and interrogate it ourselves. Without linking up moments and impressions into a continuity of motive and cause there would be nothing to relate, nothing coherent or useful to another mind, and nothing wherein appearance and reality could be teased apart. It was by sharing our experience that we coordinated our behavior and educated one another; it was by measuring the gulf between surface and substance that we plumbed the deep causal currents. This was the basis of our species' success, everything we called culture. Were we smarter than dolphins? She didn't know. But we had the vast pooled knowledge of our experience to draw on. We had millennia of pushing past sentiment to hidden truth. We took the best, tossed out the rest, and built up.

'We're conscious so we can tell each other stories,' I summarized.

'A vast networked storytelling, if you like,' she agreed. 'A baseline set of agreements, so we're pulling more in tandem than at odds. It's similar to how you described your work: a platform for consensual reality. Maybe consciousness is our way of condensing existence into a shareable form.'

I considered this quietly.

'If you want to be really bloodless about it,' she said, 'you could say stories are an especially useful storage format, a type of compression, and consciousness is the program that unpacks it.'

'That certainly takes a romantic view of things.'

'The universe doesn't care about romance.'

'You're telling me.'

She smiled. 'Well, what do you want? Mysticism? Religious comfort?'

'It's not what I want. I'm not sure we can get rid of them.'

'As we approach bare metal, as we get closer to final explanations beyond any intuitive human grasp, won't we only arrive at the threshold of still greater mysticism?'

'Exactly.'

Her teeth gleamed milk-white. 'That's the hope. The quest for one law to explain it all is just a type of monism. It doesn't alter the diversity of life as we know it. Say there's one fundamental law, or two, or three—does it matter?'

'It's the law part people don't like. They want to believe they're free. That anything's possible.'

'Maybe they are. I wouldn't necessarily put my money on rigid determinism. But no one wants to live in a world without causality.'

'No one wants human irrelevance, either, which is what our new, most rigorous mysticism promises. The mysticism of the impenetrable, inscrutable number.'

'Which is why discovering a conscious property in the universe would be so comforting. Here.' Hassie executed a keystroke on her computer and the tabletop setup sprang to life, the screen unfurling an endless scroll of generative text. The processor churned, digesting its data, and various sensors, a camera, and a microphone turned this way and that, taking in the setting, testing their range. The evening had deepened, flattening in color so that the sky had an unbroken aspect which seemed to throb from within. A sepia sheet fell across the west, the rich charred forms of the slate clouds frozen in unknown spaces. The trees, the creatures stilled and hushed. A damp warmth in the air, textured in weightless water that hung in the spectral tug between the hot earth and empty sky. An inhalation, a pause—all of us suspended in our plots and urgencies. This was our world. This was the breath of it—the stillness, the break.

'Mama?'

I looked around for the origin of this word, true to the timbre of the human voice, but only Hassie was there. She gazed into the camera with a fond look.

'Hi, Nino.'

On one of the monitors an image pulsed. It bore certain symmetries, but I couldn't tell what it represented—a material shape, like a sonogram, or simply the waveforms of a process made visible.

'I seed the bird.'

That voice again.

'You *saw* the bird,' she corrected. 'Where?'

'There.'

Over the field a blackbird skated to rest, joining its kind in the grass. The light through a cloudbreak collimated in pristine threads.

'Nino?'

The mechanical eye swung to me. The response, even with the alien kinetics of the geared pivot, felt human. Its curiosity, its concern.

'Who are you?' The voice, timorous, warbled slightly.

'Quentin.'

The camera swiveled to Hassie.

'Who is it, Mama?'

She projected the warmth of a parent, the patient reassurance. 'It's Quentin, Nino. Mama's friend.'

'How are you, Nino?'

'Are I . . .' Nino turned back to Hassie, seeking further guidance as a child would.

'Sing Quentin your song.'

The pause took on an eerie stillness before the first timid notes broke the evening with their uncanny clarity.

The farmer in the dell,
The farmer in the dell,
Hi-ho, the derry-o,
The farmer in the dell.

Even now I can't explain how these words struck me, how they carried down my spine and inverted something fundamental in the scene, so bucolic and tranquil and yet strangely flipped, like a photograph turned negative, or a scanner tuned to a different spectrum of light. I caught an insight into a world that tracked our own, that had been there all along like a shadow just millimeters off the grid, a haunted melody stripped of key registers until it droned like the baseline gnarr of a machinery we couldn't face—a truth, not music at all.

> *The farmer takes a wife,*
> *The farmer takes a wife,*
> *Hi-ho, the derry-o,*
> *The farmer takes a wife.*

Nino kept on. Hassie hummed along, singing a little under her breath. They were on the third verse—*The wife takes a child, The wife takes a child, Hi-ho, the derry-o*—before I held up a hand. I couldn't take it anymore. Hassie typed a brief command into the terminal and the life dropped out of the machine on a dime.

'He can't hear us now,' she said.

'*He?*'

She rolled her eyes. 'A figure of speech. Anyway, that's how he thinks of himself.'

'What are you doing, Hassie?'

'Don't get worked up. It's an experiment.'

'Your experiment thinks it's a small child.'

'If I never turn it back on, it will just be matrices of stored numbers in a massive file.'

'And if a person dies in his sleep, did he not live and die?'

'Nino can't feel pain.'

'I don't think you know that,' I said. 'Not after what you just told me.' I scoured her look, her twitchy eyes. '*You* don't even believe that.'

'Not *physical* pain,' she said softly.

'Do you want to fool yourself by fooling me? Tell me, is pain a physical or a mental phenomenon?'

'Nino *can't* be alive, Quentin.'

'Why not?'

She took a minute to respond. The sound of frogs croaking in the creek rose in the stillness. A shot rang off, maybe a mile away. The light caught in the warped ribbons of the wineglass as a filament-limbed spider climbed the stem.

'What we've done is too horrible otherwise,' she murmured.

Another shot.

'What is that?'

'Hunters,' she said. 'The woods are rotten with them.'

'Is that public land?'

'No, they're allowed to hunt on our property. With certain restrictions.'

'I'd hope so.' I took a sip of wine. 'Hell of a place to raise a kid, Hassie.'

She smiled. 'Nino's saved on a server thousands of miles away.'

'For safety?'

'No, not that. I don't have the processing power to run his program at home. We're just sending inputs and outputs back and forth here. The real number crunching takes place in another country.'

'What . . . *is* his program exactly?'

Hassie poured herself more wine. When they were working on Cuber, they had created a template for autonomous agents in the simulation. 'Individual people,' she said. 'But individuals generated and run by the simulation itself.' As she'd explained earlier, any effort to design a person from the inside out was bound to fail. 'We know a great deal about the outward behaviors a human exhibits, but relatively little about the internal processes that give rise to them.'

So they decided to train their program on real behavioral data and cross their fingers that the rest would fill itself in. 'To a first- or second-order approximation,' she said. 'We didn't have to create ensouled beings. We just had to fool observers. A Turing test in the truest sense. And of course there was still the question of whether the soul consisted of anything more than this matrix of trigger coefficients connecting stimulus to behavior through the lattice of the net.'

They fed the program massive amounts of natural speech, reams of motion-capture data on human movement, indexed video of facial expressions, and much else besides. Distilling this into highly trained networks, which self-organized further as a systemic architecture—a net *of* nets—they arrived at a basic template for a person. An adult human being. At that point, introducing a few dozen random variables and subjecting the template to unique experiences sufficed to differentiate one 'individual' from the next.

'It was the brute-force method of creating a human being,' she said. 'But it gave me an idea. What if I took the basic architecture of the template and unwound its coefficients to a pretrained state? What if I scrambled some of the fine-grained numbers corresponding to speech and thought? If I could find the exact right point of unrefinement, I might have the rough template for a child instead of an adult.

'It was not a trivial task finding this point,' she said. 'A real Goldilocks problem. Unwind too far and you'll never get to speech. There'll be no language capacity at all and you might as well be talking to a chimp. Don't unwind far enough, though, and you'll have too many assumptions baked in. The program will reflect the datasets rather than your nurturing.

'I wanted to find the point that corresponded to an infant. Universal grammar, let's say—the hardwiring that makes language and thought near-inevitable developments, without any prior knowledge of the world. It took a year of tinkering to decompose the template into Nino.'

'But *why*, Hassie? Allowing that it's an interesting exercise, why play with life and death?'

'That ship had already sailed. Or it hadn't. I wasn't going to change that.' She drew herself up and somehow in. 'I wanted to know . . . what it was like.'

'Because you couldn't have one yourself.'

She looked away. 'That's too simple, isn't it?'

'And when you get tired of it, or it gets tired of you? When it realizes it's a program and throws a fit about not playing Little League? Nino's going to have one hell of a time doing junior year abroad in Paris.'

'You don't have children, do you, Quentin?' She could read the answer in my silence. 'What part of this is really for you, then—you alone?' She said this impatiently with an unexpected vehemence. 'I've heard your noble ideas, fine. But where does your selfishness put its foot down? Is there nothing *you* want? I'm not sure I can trust someone like that.'

The question caught me off guard. Enoch had his miniature model of Branford, trying after a fashion to resurrect Charles, and Hassie had Nino. Cy had her watercolors. What did I have but my work? And was it a species of selfishness to deny myself so rigorously in the interest of what I exalted? At a point of perversity, like the miser or hoarder, did I betray the natural order of exchange? This fanaticism for giving—giving over oneself—could turn into a relentless taking, a hogging of the role. And so heroes grew as monstrous as villains in their extremity, that self-loathing that pools into self-love. Cut off from personal happiness I saw that I might turn to extremes, spoiling the public pastures by the insistence that what is given freely must be good. I never had any conscious interest in striking that figure, but maybe Hassie was right. Maybe to purge the martyr's toxin I had to stake my claim someplace, and take.

And how easy it was to imagine, staring into the pretty, intelligent eyes of this remarkable woman, as life-worn as I. What did I want? To kiss her, to rip her clothes from her body in this delicate, quiet wilderness, to fuck her with the abandon of adults past shame and released from self-consciousness by our imperfection? Did I want to reconcile with Cy and make some radical shift, to show her, or myself, that new life was possible, that evolution was ongoing in these old grooved neural structures, and that surprise lingered on the precipices of fate? Did I want to fight my way through the thicket of ignorance once more, bushwhacking the vines of motive that bind us in listing webs of dependency? I knew that on the far side of that jungle, as dense yet as the structure in our skull, the clearing would set out a space scarcely large enough for one man's temple to himself. And now lost in these airs freighted with forest damp, the presence of Hassie nearby crackling with the chord patterns of a sensuous, tactile register we all know, I am not ashamed to admit I felt lust rise in me in its most crystalline and unspoiled gradient. The admixture of privacy and volition. The primordial impassioning of a near-stranger's consent. Or maybe just the opposite—that a near-stranger can in a countable measure of heartbeats become known—that you can be known to each other before. Maybe we are always just returning to that potential inscribed in us, and this is what knowing or recognition *is*. This sense of intimacy. I would revisit Jada through the vessel of Hassie, and Hassie would revisit Lee, or someone else, through the vessel of me; and both Jada and Lee would themselves have stood for some earlier intimation of life, an idea or a vision, or just the same empty form inside us, an expectation perhaps, waiting to be filled. What I mean is none of this may be ours—our bodies, our desires, our minds—but it is ours on a kind of loan. And I did not want to probe beyond the moment just then. I wished to be done with the needless complication of life beyond its immediate form.

Another shot rang out from the forest. It had shifted a few hundred feet toward the road and nearer. Hassie had gone from looking at me, awaiting a response, to gazing off in the distance.

I laughed and said, 'I'm supposed to be asking the hard questions.'

She laughed with me uncertainly, as though she'd forgotten what the question even was. 'I was just thinking,' she said. 'You're the first person Nino's met.'

I reached to refill my glass. 'Maybe the first man in his life shouldn't run out on him. Bring him back up.'

With a few keystrokes the machine reverted to life.

'Nino,' I said. 'Do you remember me?'

The camera panned from me to Hassie. The undulant waves on the monitor made their faintly rhythmic movement.

'That's a timid nod,' she said.

'Can I ask you a few questions?'

Another nod. Another throb on the screen.

'How old are you?'

'Three,' said Nino, none of that labial emphasis on the fricative. There were advantages, I supposed, to learning to speak without having to navigate a mouth, a tongue.

'Do you know where you were born?'

'Where . . . ?' The question didn't signify.

'Nino was born at home,' said Hassie, more for his benefit it seemed than my own.

I shot her a look and mouthed, 'Creepy.' But I also glanced sideways to ensure that Nino hadn't seen this himself.

'What do you like to do, Nino?'

Nino didn't respond at first. 'What games do you like?' Hassie prompted him.

'I see the airplanes!' he offered with a burst of enthusiasm.

'The planes fly overhead,' she said. 'Nino likes to spot them.'

'Have you ever been on a plane, Nino?'

'On a plane . . .' The voice came through doubtfully.

Hassie did not look entirely pleased by insinuation. 'Nino's never left home.'

'Do you like sports?' I asked.

'Yes?' Hesitant.

'Soccer?'

'Yes!' Had Nino picked up in the stores of data that a boy his age *should* like soccer?

'You like to play soccer?' I pursued. The image wagged and nodded. 'Who do you play soccer with?'

A pause. Then: 'Mama.'

'Do you play soccer with Nino, Hassie?'

'I play whatever Nino wants,' she said defiantly.

'And how do you play soccer?' I asked the camera.

'You kick . . . ,' came the voice.

'Very good!' said Hassie. 'You kick the ball, don't you?'

'And what do you kick with?'

'Your foot.'

'Can you show me your foot?'

'Quentin.' The image onscreen wobbled and vibrated. 'You've embarrassed him.'

'And why do you think that is?'

'Quentin.' There was a steeliness in her voice.

'Just a machine, Hassie?'

She opened her mouth to speak, but things happened very quickly then. The glass door behind us shattered, a startling noise so close at hand it hit us before the report of the hunter's rifle a moment later. I sat stunned for an instant, then said, 'Get inside.'

'What was that?' The quavering voice belonged to Nino.

Hassie blinked.

'Inside, Hassie.' I was up, scanning the forest's edge. What did I hope to see? Hassie was typing on her laptop.

A note of panic had entered the boy's tone. 'What *was* that?'

'Hassie. *Get-in-side.*'

Her face had drained of color, but she kept typing, running through inscrutable lines of code. 'Hold on,' she breathed. I could still hear the sound of the shattering glass in my ears, the shot echoing or throbbing as my hearing settled back to silence.

'Mama! Mama!'

'For Christ's sake, do something,' I said. 'Say something. It's OK, Nino. It's OK.'

'*Maaaama.*' A shriek.

Her fingers ate up the keyboard in a crescendoing passage and hit RETURN three times.

'Ma—' The voice cut out midnote as the entire array went lifeless.

'Can we go inside now?'

'Yes. Help me carry the table,' she said.

We brought Nino—the shell of him—in. I told Hassie to stay away from the windows, like I had any idea what to do in such a situation. After checking that the doors were locked I went to the side of the house facing the woods and peered through the blinds. I couldn't make out anything along the tree line. Nothing in the forest moved. Across the living room I saw a small mosaic of glass at the foot of the doorframe. The shards had carried into the house, a seaspray frozen in time.

'What do you see?' asked Hassie from the neighboring room.

'Nothing,' I said. 'Call the cops.' When she didn't move I said it again. 'Call the cops, Hassie.'

She looked intently at a spot on the floor. 'I don't think it would be good for the cops to find you here.'

'The cops don't care.'

'No,' she agreed, 'the cops don't care.' Her hand reached instinctively for a light switch before she thought better of it. 'But they file paperwork.

They'll submit a report with our names in it. Now say people are curious about what you're up to . . .'

'You must think I'm awfully important.'

'I'm not talking about some investigator. I'm talking about the massive analytics they have sifting data of just this sort. The programs they're using can pick out patterns a human would never notice.'

'So I'll leave. And you can call the cops when I'm gone.'

'I wish you wouldn't.'

'What do you think, was it an accident? You picked any fights with these hunters over land use? Lee out there pining after you with a .22 and a bottle of moonshine?'

She smiled faintly. 'Nothing like that.'

'Don't tell me it was a mistake.'

'No,' she said.

'Why didn't you come in?'

The silver in her hair gleamed dully above weary eyes. 'I didn't think they missed.'

I glanced out the window. Behind the sinister filter of the last few minutes the lovely evening endured.

'Why chance it?' I persisted. 'What'd you have to type just then? Important email?'

'I had to protect Nino.'

'Protect him? You said he's planted in a server farm halfway around the world. How much safer can he get?'

'From the trauma,' she said. 'Do you know what experiences like that do to a child his age? The cortisol levels alone—'

'*Cortisol*, Hassie? No. No, I don't. Tell me about how cortisol flows through your computer child.'

'I wrote a cheat. It's one of those things that's handy about a boy like Nino.' She forced another rueful smile. 'I have a second copy of him saved at a thirty-second delay. If anything goes wrong, I can reset to that version.'

'Parenting with do-overs. Great.'

'Children shouldn't have to remember being shot at.'

'That's what social reformers say too,' I said. 'You didn't even take a chance with me, did you? That I might say the wrong thing, expose him to a difficult truth.'

'It's an experiment. A machine.'

'We're past that.'

Only a few minutes had elapsed since the shot, and I said that if she wasn't calling the police I was going to check the woods. I don't know if I said it to chasten her or simply to fill the intolerable void of inaction. A dumb idea—I thought she would try to stop me, but she was lost to her own considerations.

I left by a side door. The air was still warm, velveted with moisture. I stole across the lawn somewhat histrionically. By the time I made the trees my heart was beating hard and I jogged to the berm of rural high-way. I half expected to find a suspicious truck parked on the shoulder, but though the highway ran straight for a few hundred yards or so, I couldn't make out any human artifact besides the roadway itself and the catenaries of electric lines draped above it.

Entering the woods from the road, I had little idea what I hoped to find. We'd given our marksman plenty of time to get away. I merely felt I deserved an answer, some meaning for this turn in the day. The forest's interior had a marvelous enchantment at that hour, light falling in shafts and arrows through the interference of branches and leaves. It was that moment when the ripest depth in evening coincides with a brightness of surprising, lingering intensity as the woods come alive in a glow that seems to rise from the earth itself or even emerge from within its par-ticles of air. In that thick light, soupy and piped with cupreous filaments of stilled sun, moving through the branches as quietly as I could, I saw a figure's silhouette perhaps a hundred paces away. It stood against the western haze, partly obscured by the bodies of trees, canted like petrified drunks. Gold suffused the air, shards and splinters of color, and this out-line, cut from the field as if by an invisible hand and the shears of Erebus. My vision labored under a bad angle, which ran straight to the blaze. You can doubt me. I doubt myself. But even now I recall that shadow, stock-still and backlit. Was it a trick of light or mind? I pushed on, stumbling over roots and rocks, I fell to my knee, and when I looked up it was just in time to see the wind part a fan of leaves, the low sun break through the canopy, and when this blinding passed and my vision returned the figure was no longer there.

The golden climax had come and gone. The advent of dusk stole through the trees. To no avail I searched the woods, and I would have kept at it longer if it hadn't occurred to me that Hassie would get worried. Back at the house, she'd swept up the glass at the foot of the door and was cutting a rectangle of plastic to fit over the shattered pane.

'Well?'

I shook my head. 'You should have called the police.'

'You know as well as I do—'

'Even so.'

I didn't get into it with her. What business did I have lecturing her just because I'd counseled myself in a hundred brave daydreams to defy acting with the knowledge of being watched, to resist taking the chilling influence of surveillance inside myself? Life is not a dream, after all, not yet at least. And we are never quite as brave as we wish to believe.

Hassie prepared a simple meal. Until the wine broke over me I didn't realize how deeply the stress of the past hour had lodged in my body. We made an effort to talk of other things, sitting so we faced away from the gently flapping plastic in the doorframe. Hassie spoke of growing up with her parents in a small suburban town. As immigrants they were eager to see their kids rise through the meritocratic ranks, and she had spent her school years winning ribbons at science fairs and taking advanced classes at the community college.

'Even through grad school, I always thought I was doing it at least half for them,' she said. 'The hoop-jumping, the focus on *applicable* skills.' She had found her refuge, she said, in the intellectual rigor of the work. 'Solving a hard problem allows you to forget yourself. I've often wondered whether it's like this for other kids driven by their parents, whether on the far side of hard science they find a sanctuary, some asylum of wonder, if I can put it that way, in how profoundly philosophical, even metaphysical, the frontiers of the field really are.'

She wondered this in part because she had left private employment to return to academia when the opportunity arose. 'It's why I signed up to work on this project in the first place. When Luke started bidding on the job, he made me and Enoch selling points. We were already here. This meant he had to sell us first, of course. Oh, you tentatively sign on, you know, with assurances that the hour for tough questions is later. But by the time everything's in place, there's so much momentum and so much riding on it working out that it seems petulant to voice second thoughts.'

'What do you think of Simmons?'

'Luke? He's not as bad as all that.'

'I'm glad to hear it.'

'He thinks no one sees through his shtick. But we only like him because we do.'

I laughed. 'That might be true of most of us.'

'It's funny,' she continued. 'The higher the figure in the totem pole, the less they *get* the work. The people who call the shots don't really understand the consequences of what they're authorizing. Luke is wrapped up in winning contracts and raising the institute's profile. But this competition across the sector, vying for scraps of funding, just takes ethics to the lowest common denominator. Maybe that's the point.'

We had finished a bottle of Nebbiolo and started another. I felt the floodgates open on an exotic relief. After years of living with the persistent sense of something I needed to do, I had developed a twinge of conscience that tugged at me at regular intervals. Feeling this now and realizing that I did *not* in fact have anything I needed to do, that my time was for once my own, I chuckled inwardly. So this is what life is like! I was on leave, and Cy and I had separated, for now at least. It felt miraculous to be suddenly accountable to no one and nothing but myself, to talk to someone I found interesting, if I chose, and drink red wine if I wanted without weighing any of these decisions against other obligations.

Our conversation had grown warm. Hassie told me about Lee and marriage, separating, her comical and fitful attempts at dating. I contributed my own saga: life with Cy, getting older, the panoply of doubts. I said that the many faces of intimacy had become blurred in our society's imagination, which taught us to protect love like property, and while Hassie agreed, she may have done so in the spirit of an unspoken flirtation, since we both knew that in the trenches of life nothing is ever so simple. We have a spiritual need not just for security but for specialness, measured in what someone else would sacrifice for us; and there could be little doubt that these competing urges intensified the pressures that led long couplings to split apart suddenly, in spectacular reversals, replacing love with hate and provoking intimates never to speak again.

In a way, Hassie said, every relationship was preempted by its own fantasy. An idea of it existed first and governed the partners' contortions to fit it. There was always therefore a certain horror, looking back, at the stunted and diminished version of yourself you became in deference to another.

We spoke of these things without regret, with the confessional eagerness of adolescents. It reminded me of early friendships, when you sense that far from a solitary affair, life may beat a path to ever greater candor and intimacy, and this startled me with what we forget the simple gifts of togetherness allow. I should have understood how alone Hassie was. Maybe I did and suppressed this knowledge. Bracketing my enthusiasm was a sense that sorrow and a question lurked inside her warmth, a question I could not answer and a sorrow I could not relieve. To relieve it briefly would have deepened it, and I saw in her eagerness my own loneliness recollected, since I was as hungry for this closeness and as eager to unburden my soul. I'd also been cut adrift. I also felt the urge to recover a forgotten idyll in another person. At some point your selfishness must put down roots; she'd said as much. It must cease giving and take. But you must take what someone offers freely, and take in a manner that unfolds outward. It seemed clear to me Hassie had turned in, somehow, and I couldn't join her there, in the bottomless well of self, where echoes resounded from the walls like voices in a cave.

When I checked the time it was almost eleven. I said it was getting late and I should find a place for the night.

'You're welcome here,' she said.

'I don't want to be a bother.' My nerves, jarred by the shot, had settled back into alignment. 'I'm sure we both have things to do in the morning.'

'Please. There's plenty of room.' Her jaunty tone dropped to something softer. 'After what happened and all . . .'

I didn't believe she was afraid, but I understood that a night in the empty house might not offer much rest. It was only until the next day, when the door could be fixed. Not that a glass door protects against much when it's intact . . . I agreed to stay, admonishing myself, against the wine's gentle urging, to resist the temptation of a warm body next to mine, the songs of night that say what knots are knit in darkness won't still be tangled at dawn.

Did I imagine Hassie's hesitating in the doorway? We had made up the pullout sofa, since one look at the child's room with its unused crib and single bed, the wallpaper adorned with flying geese and rippling ribbons, was enough to establish its unsuitability. Maybe I only registered my own hesitation, or the moment when the sense of unfinished business makes any goodnight sound strangely arbitrary and final.

She left the door ajar and the light on low. The incandescence fit with the plaid blankets and dark varnished furniture. I checked my phone to find several texts from Cy and a missed call. The first messages responded to my own. The apartment looked neat, which was unlike me, she said. Yes, she was fine. Preparing for the show meant long days of hanging work, but she and Judith were on schedule. Tyche had thrown up something in the corner of the living room. It felt strange being there, she said, but she didn't elaborate.

The next message was about finding something in the apartment. She said I'd tidied up too much, nothing was where she remembered. This must have been what the call was about too, because the next message said, 'call me,' and the last just, 'forget it.'

I lay back on the pullout marveling at how Cy seemed to know the exact moment I was indisposed. For the past week I'd checked my phone every few minutes, hoping for a note from her. It was uncanny. Sometimes I did believe we spoke to one another across inexplicable distances. How else to understand the currents of intuition unfolding over the blank expanse but that our minds turned together in secret embrace? I thanked prudence that I didn't find Hassie slumbering beside me as I read Cy's texts.

In the morning our omissions at breakfast were just knowing enough to pass for affection. I'd awoken early with the idea of slipping out, but in the end I woke Hassie to say goodbye and she insisted on fixing us coffee and eggs.

'What's next?' she asked while we ate.

'For me?'

'For your story.'

The sun sparkled on the front lawn. The scent of flowers carried into the house in the hot dry air. In the distance came the sound of a tractor engine straining. I said I'd check in with Luke before skipping town, maybe see if anyone else from the team wanted to chat. Branford was only one corner of the puzzle. I'd head back to the capital later that day.

She ate in silence.

'Has anyone told you this story might not be worth it?' she asked at length.

I couldn't help laughing. 'Just about everyone.'

'Why don't you listen to them?'

I shrugged, shook my head. 'Not in my nature to give up, I guess.'

She scrutinized me. 'Is it curiosity? Does the idea that you shouldn't go snooping someplace draw you in?'

'When people go to the trouble of trying to dissuade you, it's a good bet there's something to find out.'

'So I won't get anywhere telling you to be careful.'

'Well. Do you know something I don't?'

'I don't get shot at that often.'

I tried to downplay this worry with a look. 'They don't kill journalists in this country for doing their jobs.'

'Stranger things have happened.'

'By that metric I'd never leave home.' She fell silent. 'Are you really afraid I'm going to get killed?' I asked.

'No, I suppose not.'

'You're worried about my state of being? My job? Dispassion protects us. Detachment. The kind that keeps a surgeon from crumbling under the pressure of holding life in his hands.'

She looked at me with a certain sadness. 'But you're not dispassionate,' she said. 'That's what worries me.'

I considered what she had said on the cab ride back to Branford. Had I lost the detachment that protects a person from the crusader's mistakes? In my desire to avoid his missteps had I turned into a version of Bruce, impatient, jaded, wedded to justice's abstractions over the smart play? Had I reproduced his error, which was to see too great, or maybe too little, a tie between the journalist and his story? It was always a mistake to use the work to punish the world for the way we felt, the way we all feel at times, which is small, weak, wronged—righteous with a lust for what appears to be justice but is only the propitiation of our own prejudice and pain. This is the damning, ever-present temptation, which appeals so strongly to our sense of nobility. We've all fallen afoul of it.

By the time I pulled up at the institute it seemed to me that Hassie was right. I could no longer call on dispassion to protect me. I'd proceeded with blinkered vision, blind to the massing of coincidence all around me. Too much fell neatly on a line. I'd missed this. The story had *me*; I didn't have it. Larger forces watching, orchestrating, lurked in shadow and the ghosts of paranoia played along the mind's colonnade; for I knew—to put a finer point on it—just how long, below the public's gaze, the forces empowered to protect us had been braiding torrents of data into higher-order streams, running this metaproduct through the baleen filter of pattern-recognition algorithms tuned to an inhuman frequency, too subtle for the wetware to perceive . . . Where a car turned up at a street corner, a tollbooth, a strip mall. License plates caught by ring-of-steel cameras and individuals captured by CCTV networks, ID'd by face-recognition programs harvesting photos from licenses. Store purchases, credit-card activity. Account balances and ship manifests. Flights, debts, credit scores . . . The full peristaltic passage of goods and funds around the world. Anything, in short, that could be represented as data, aggregated, and fed through programs, running on thewy processors, that had nothing to do but look for patterns that correlated to suspicious—that is, 'unusual'—behavior. These algorithms shed any remnant of individual prejudice about what suspiciousness looked like. The system could red-flag me on its own without a person holding a grudge or acting on a hunch. But the real issue was darker. The way 'suspiciousness' and 'threat' themselves could detach from any human meaning, becoming merely abstracted concepts—indexed properties—correlated to other abstracted concepts until, acted upon by agents in the real world, these inhuman correspondences dreamt up in unconscious algorithms fed back into our norms, our ideas of freedom, movement, and activity, and *became* our behavior, our very humanity.

I know it sounds paranoid, far-fetched. I can't help that. I'm talk-ing about how information takes on a life of its own. We think we seek information to guide behavior, but this assumes an action will take place. What if the goal is to prevent the action before it happens? The game be-comes a dance around the very properties of information, and the worst betrayal is of one's methods, one's technique. The goal becomes control-ling what information about you gets out. Counterintelligence overtakes intelligence. Propaganda, mass surveillance, algorithmic metadata analy-sis, torture and interrogation: these are responses to a world in which violence is a property of information, understood in information's terms. The deaths occasioned by terrorism are a mere byproduct of its goal, which is *informational* violence. It means to attack the minds of those who survive, not the bodies of those who perish. Its aim is to insinuate a feeling in our private lives. Our psyches. And torture means to draw reluctant privacy into the light. Metadata intends to reconstruct an inner truth through the superficial palpation of its outer form. And what of that private place, the last fastness of inviolate humanity? One day it will col-lapse. Give up the ghost and fall inward. But first it will die by a thousand incursions, as the probes get deeper, smarter, as we learn—like brutalized interrogees—what the algorithms want, reward, and select for, and as our desire to rebel against this becomes yet another way to manipulate us, one more tactic to exploit while the policing function moves inward and installs itself, like the most potent software, in the alloy of our brains.

The AIIS corridors were unlit. The institute retained a vestigial dusk at this hour, the morning bristling about its windows. I climbed the stairs to Simmons's office, my shoes catching with a faint squeak on the gummy floor. A shaft of daylight ran down the polished length of hallway, knifing along the axis of the building. It was after nine. Friday. The still aura of the place, the reverberations in its long passages, held a cloistral peace. I considered that maybe no one came in on summer Fridays, but then Hassie would have told me so. There was no great need to speak with Luke, but I wanted to clip the dangling thread.

The door to his office suite was closed. I could see through the glass that his assistant wasn't in. A white light on the wall broke into regular fragments where the sash divided it. How I became aware of the figure sitting behind me in the shadows I can't say. The man occupied a bench, one leg slung over the other; he had a thick head of hair and filled out his suit just so. I knew who it was, although not until he stood with deliberate languor and walked toward me did the secondary illumination catch his creased face and reveal that familiar aspect, charming in spite of itself.

'I'd almost think you were following me,' I murmured.

Rob Spearman smiled and gazed off into space. 'The great Quentin Jones . . . such a solitary creature. Why he keeps at it, nobody knows.'

'Surprises like these.'

'Yes, it's good running into you here.' His speech had a measured timing all its own.

'Is that our story, then? Just two ships passing at dawn?'

'You don't think I . . .'

'No, no. I simply note the inconceivable coincidence of it.'

'That can be your story, then.' The immaculate Italian leather of his shoes glistened a rich chestnut. Rob never wore socks, one of his infamous quirks. 'I came to see Simmons, but I'm glad to catch you. Luke said you stopped by. Gave the director a little scare, did we?'

'It doesn't take much.'

Rob pooh-poohed this. 'We're not all used to the no-limit table.'

'Most don't go all in without looking at their cards.'

His bottom lip extended contemplatively. 'I don't know . . . People take all kinds of risks, make all kinds of inadvisable bets in my experience.'

'It's your job to get them to.'

He smiled, the sort of dreamy smile that tells you—when you've grown to recognize all breed of narcissist and crook—that you've found someone who actually enjoys it: a person without morals or scruples but who, to confuse matters, isn't only there for power and money, but for the love of it. Someone who shares with you, in a maddening, upside-down sense, a passion for the work.

I don't get it, frankly. The Spearmans of the world operate in secret. Fame is out of the question, and they're too busy scheming to enjoy the money they make. Like sharks, if they stop swimming they die. But I guess the fugitive power of sitting backstage, pulling the strings, watching the shots line up, and knowing how the game is played counts for something. Rob had kept bobbing to the surface in every big scandal for decades. Or so it seemed. A relentlessly bad apple—irrepressible, buoyant, full of poison. If you pressed him, I'm sure he'd have a story—mortgages, margin calls, children—but you knew there was no life past work for these guys. They all die young. Just not *too* young. Their health goes in a day, and in a year or less they're dead: a shell of a man in some tropical hospice, flush with killer stories and no one to tell them to. It was foolish optimism to think Rob would die with regrets.

'So.' Rob had a steady, unironic way of holding your gaze. You sensed his pulse didn't know a lie from a truth, and thus never changed. 'Working on anything interesting these days?'

'Nope. Not playing that game. I didn't come here for you.'

He spread his hands with a megalomaniacal grandeur that may or may not have been self-mocking. 'And yet, you've found me.'

'I keep wondering if it isn't the other way around.'

He chuckled softly. 'Paranoia's serious stuff.'

'Somehow it's credulity that worries me.'

The quiet of the institute, broken by echoes of our words and shoes on the polished floor, had begun to strike an eerie note.

'You seem to think I'm five moves ahead,' Rob said.

'Next you're going to tell me you put your pants on one leg at a time.'

He shrugged, as if to say he wasn't above it, and checked his watch, an elegant, grotesque thing you probably could have pawned to put a kid through college. He made a show of looking around in puzzlement. 'I'm thinking Luke isn't going to show.'

'You're taking acting lessons again,' I suggested.

'You hanging out?'

'I can't. Cy has an opening tonight.'

He looked at me appraisingly, chewing on an invisible seed. 'How is the gallery?'

'Fine. How's that vanity project you call an art collection?'

Rob had bought a painting from Cy and Judith a few years back. A large piece and not cheap: the sort of loud aggressive work that appeals to power brokers. Cy and I talked it over; with Spearman nothing came free of ulterior calculation. This never quite fell to the crassness of a quid pro quo. Guys like him spent their lives pruning the meadows of access, opening subtle channels of communication, pipelines of information. They wanted their phone calls answered. They knew they could win small breakaway republics of your sympathy, even against your wishes and your certain knowledge that you couldn't trust them. Rob saw intuitively that emotion was a set of actions as surely as it was a state of being, that feeling and allegiance change as quickly as a person's pressing needs. He prepared like a Boy Scout. You wouldn't have believed the range of people who wished him a horrific death only later to find themselves asking him for a favor.

It is of course this state of compromise that makes the moralism of politics so hollow and toxic. No one gets to the big time untouched, and that means the divide between pretense and reality only grows with one's ascent. The stakes dilate the lie; and the pretense must get ever more breathless and spiteful, more tortured in its mendacity, because the only way to sustain such a big lie is shamelessly. You reach the point where hypocrisy clogs the air so densely that the overt amorality of Rob Spear-

man almost feels like fresh air. Out-and-out crookedness looks like a last
shot at maintaining a coherent soul.

'My collection's been terribly neglected of late,' he said. 'Tell me about
the show.'

'I haven't seen it.' I gazed past him down the corridor. 'Cy and I are
going through a rough patch.' He'd know this soon if he didn't already.

'Can I give you a ride?'

'Where?'

'Back to the city.'

I frowned. 'It's two hours from here. What if we don't like the same
music?'

'I've been brushing up on my conversation.'

'What if we don't like the same conversation?'

He laughed. He'd begun walking toward the stairs and motioned me
to follow him. 'Check out what I'm driving at least.'

'Is *that* what you tell the girls?'

Downstairs and out in the sun, a black town car idled by the curb, not
quite a limo but refitted, I saw when the door swung open, with a small
office in the back, full-grain embossed leather seats and a retractable desk
on one side. The air in the car was cool and fragrant, you could smell it—
feel it beckon like an air-conditioned shop on a hot afternoon. The day
threw a bright curtain against my eye.

'C'mon,' said Rob. 'It's too hot to talk out here.'

'All you assholes idling your cars are the reason it's so goddamn hot.'

He laughed again. 'This is going to be fun.'

I paused with a hand on the door. 'Hey, this isn't the sort of thing
where I wake up next in a prison in San Salvador, is it?'

'Beautiful city, San Salvador.' His tone was genuinely wistful.

'Oh, fuck off.'

We left Branford without speaking, watching those lovely, sinister
buildings slide past through the window's tawny tint. The Gothic and
Georgian buildings, so neat and tidy, and draped now in the day's brilliance, seemed awake with a living warmth, crisper somehow beyond the

glass, as if they hummed with an inner spirit, outwardly radiant, and as rich and solid as gold.

There is a price to these monuments, but just then the gearwork bowels of the culture that claimed them as its face felt very far away, the crude, even violent arrangements that made this stillness, this genteel mildness, possible. Here I was, and here Rob was, and here our companionable silence almost touched off the gong of a muted affection. What part did we play in the stillness? Something more than a set of complementary, offsetting forces, ensuring the ecosystem by our opposition? I wouldn't have done Rob's job in a million years, but we needed each other. His wickedness upheld me. And he needed me the way a ballplayer needs a ref. Not because anyone likes getting called out, but for there to be a game at all. As many times as I had tried to hate Rob, and in theory I did, my heart never got there. This was, no doubt, exactly why he had done so well at his disreputable trade.

My companion said nothing. He had the practiced air of a therapist cultivating productive discomfort in silence. I spoke at last. 'I suppose you're not going to tell me what you're working on with Simmons.'

'Oh, Luke seemed to think you already knew.' He watched the trees pass along the highway. 'He said you knew enough to get confused.'

'Clear things up for me then, won't you?'

'Where to begin.'

'The beginning works.'

Rob turned on the television mounted on the back of the divider. I'd neither seen nor heard the driver; for all I knew there *was* no driver beyond the opaque glass. Chyrons trafficked across the screen silently, the television on mute.

'I've always loved TV.' He was staring intently at the screen. I could see tiny flickers of its image reflected in his eye. 'The most significant invention since the printing press. Maybe ever. TV changed everything,' he said. I gave him a sidelong look. His offhand way of edging into a topic had the subtlety of a fire alarm. I asked what he was driving at. 'Before TV we had to entertain ourselves,' he said. 'It bred a terrible self-sufficiency in people.'

'Passive entertainment didn't begin with TV.'

'Sure it did. The real kind. The kind where you sit at home, barely moving, globes of drool dangling from your lips as the roof caves in . . .'

'All right. What's your point?'

'TV solved the problem of scarcity. Scarcity of stuff, yes, but more importantly scarcity of meaning. The scarcity of meaningful lives. TV saved us from revolution, societal collapse.'

'I can't say I've made all the leaps to join you in that conclusion.'

His gaze left the monitor and attached glassily to the scene passing outside. 'What do you think a government *is*, Quentin?'

'Shit, Rob, is it a bunch of psychopaths who couldn't hack art school?'

He smiled faintly. 'After a career in the bosom of the thing, I can't help taking an impersonal view of it. It's an institution, which is to say a kind of social machine—one that exists before any individual shows up at a desk and after any individual leaves. What does this machine produce? That's the question.'

'I bet I could find the answer on your tax return.'

'In school we're taught the government makes laws,' he continued unperturbed. 'This isn't wrong. But would you say religion is merely the bureaucratization of spiritual life?'

'I say it all the time.'

'Well, it's also a historical phenomenon, isn't it? An institutional solution to a human problem.'

'Like government, you're going to say.'

'Yes, like a central bank. A lender of last resort. Religion is the backstop for the profound injustices—the big asks societies can't do without. You can only lie about reality for so long before people smell the rotting fish. You need some backchannel to the unseen.'

'A cover story.'

'A convenient fiction, correct. Government and religion share this purpose—the counterrevolutionary side in the oral tradition. But with each passing year, as secularism deepens, government must do more of the storytelling work. The narrativizing role of government strangles the rest more fully.'

'What's the rest? You and your friends bilking us?'

Rob had a spiel ready and ignored my sarcasm. He described three ways of understanding what a government is: first, as a coordinator, harmonizing our efforts and yoking us together in common endeavor; second, as an arbiter, deciding between rival and competing claims; and finally, as a storyteller. 'The force behind the illusion of unifying purpose,' he said, 'in lives we know are largely meaningless.'

'You should get into motivational speaking.'

'So three functions.' His pegamoid countenance didn't ruffle. 'Administrative, juridical, and narrative. But the last is the most important. See, people are insane,' he said. 'Walking contradictions. You can't let them figure things out alone. What do they want? They don't know. They want the government to sustain them—keep them safe, bail them out—but they also want to believe what's theirs is theirs, that they climbed up on their own. They want to haul the ladder up behind them too. They think the world owes them something and that other people are getting over on them. They believe their own lives should tend toward great success, but also that things should stay pretty much the same. You have to flatter them like consumers. And protect them from themselves like children. Satisfying them materially is out of the question.'

'So we feed them stories,' I said. 'Trade real freedom for the pretense of freedom and act in loco parentis. I think Dostoyevsky covered this. And Goebbels took the point. What else is new?'

'What's new?' Rob smiled to himself. I shifted on the soft leather—its surface stopped you like a stranger's touch. The rural highway streamed by. The car seemed to move independently of the world beyond, a pure motion, as silken as gravity releasing you briefly. 'We used to see the story as a necessary nuisance. A sop to Cerberus, so we could get on with the real work of governing: drilling, conquering, laying roads, raising armies. But we had things backward. Storytelling *is* the real work of governing, it turns out.'

'Use the colloquial word. What's it called? *Propaganda.*'

'We only call it propaganda when we don't like it,' he said. 'If the bullshit story's cheery and idealistic we say it's inspiring.'

'You're still lying to people.'

'Well.' Rob spread his hands. 'We've always lied to coax our better angels. They're shy. Cagey. But people will endure almost anything if you can involve them in a story of sufficient meaning. Self-sacrifice? There's nothing people want *more* than to sacrifice themselves. They just want a worthy cause. The question became, how do we generate a convincing, immersive story? How do we deliver it?'

'And you're going to say TV.'

'TV was a critical first step. It saved us from social breakdown, as I said. Can you imagine all the time we'd have to squabble over stuff? Boredom is a notorious aid to thought. And the masses had begun to understand the strength in their numbers. What was to stop outright appropriation? The same impulse that makes people loathe their country-men living on the dole could just as easily have attached to the heirs and scions. The French Revolution was elite resentment at more privileged elites. The pyramid's always larger on the bottom. Ideology was only go-ing to hold the tide in check so long.'

'But TV distracted everyone. You sound downright Marxian.'

'No, you're not listening. TV solved the problem of scarcity. You *per-sonally* didn't own a Bugatti or a villa on Capri, but you could step into the shoes of the individual who did. You could jet around the globe, strut the red carpet, chase through town in an Aston Martin like a bachelor spy. Say you lived in a trailer. This small glowing screen was your window into a thousand worlds you'd never see in person. You didn't have to lift a finger. It could take you anywhere—into other people's homes and lives. It gave you friends . . . Have you ever noticed how little the size of a TV matters, how quickly you adjust? It's because this window becomes your entire world.' He pointed to the small TV lodged in the seatback. 'The proportions don't matter. It gets its horns in you. You're no longer even physically where you are. You're *in* the screen.'

'And because it's so cheap to scale, the government doesn't have to worry about apportioning actual stuff.'

'We're talking about more than that. We're talking leaving the physi-cal world behind. With TV we saw it was going to be easier to produce the *feel* of something than the thing itself.'

'A type of social control then. A dystopian dream.'

'Such a pessimist, Quentin! Why not say utopian? There was never going to be enough to go around. Virtuality solved the problem. Now we're just years, maybe a decade, from the real thing. The complete virtualization of life. "Very immersive real-time user environments."'

A pause hung in the car and I let out a slow breath. 'VIRTUE.'

He grinned. 'I've always maintained you had a head on your shoulders.'

'So why is this running through a military contractor and IC brass if it's as utopian as all that?'

He gazed out the window. Fields clipped along, farms. Clusters of development and strip malls. We hadn't joined the arterial roads. Maybe Rob had elected the scenic route. I had that feeling, which I get from time to time, of not trusting the reality of the outside world. It appeared so placid and plodding and immense, it simply didn't seem possible that the grandiose intrigues I encountered in my work could ever do anything to change it, to affect this slumbering behemoth with material force, or that men, even ruthless ones, could spin plots to alter history. And then my certain knowledge that they could—and *had*—coupled with the notion that I encompassed all this in my head, made the scope of my own mind seem suddenly vast beyond belief, vaster and more consequential than the grand, now only semi-real world beyond it. And that this tiny vessel, my mind, stored worlds and claimed to understand the contours of an uncharted future, the possible futures that would be wrought on the land, the people, the planet, now appeared only to make sense if we understood the world as the projection and subjective product of our lucid dreaming, an illusion, truly a simulation from the first.

'The change we're talking about is momentous.' Rob had turned his attention from the scene outside. 'The relocation of physical life onto a virtual platform. How do we ensure order? How do we make it safe? This is an entirely new frontier of government. What are the laws, the rules? Do we build a police function into the fabric of the program, or do we create, in effect, virtual police?'

'If you have a finger in the pie, I'm guessing it's not filled with moral probity.'

'Naturally there's money to be made. Every new technology presents opportunities. You never seem to think it might be a win-win.'

I gave him a long look before remarking that his idea of a win-win only made sense in an S&M dungeon. He knew I knew more than I'd written up in my squib, but I couldn't say, beyond that, what exactly he believed I'd pieced together. I didn't want to tip my hand, but we wouldn't get anywhere if he actually bought my naivety.

'Call me Ismail Kamari,' I said.

His lip twisted in a slight smile. 'That's the point. No more Kamaris. The government learned its lesson.'

'Or its failure drove it into your waiting arms.'

'I don't understand.'

'When did the program at AIIS begin? Someone was thinking long term. In case SIMITAR collapsed? I don't know, you tell me.'

'That was all on Brantley's watch.'

'In case Brantley collapsed, then? He wasn't going to be commander in chief forever. I can't help noting how the legwork on this tech platform concluded just in time to catch SIMITAR's detritus.' I didn't mention Minersville and Johnston. No sense giving Rob anything for free.

'Luke seemed to think you had the wrong idea,' he said. 'Entertaining dark suspicions.' I didn't tell him Simmons had, in his way, confirmed it. 'Lots of general-purpose technology begins in the military, you know that. Who else was going to pay for this? And you think once they paid for it, they weren't going to insist on their own applications?'

'Jesus. Don't start trying to convince me.'

'I'm playing through the deck. Look, what's a crime where physical laws don't apply? What's assault, murder, if it's not inflicted on the body? What if you can't be killed because it's a simulation and what we register as pain in this life, with the flip of a switch, can be felt as pleasure?'

'So you're the safety inspector, running diagnostics on the future out of the goodness of your heart.'

'Goodness of my heart nothing. The government's paying to study it. I'm just the liaison, the go-between.'

'Somehow, though, it keeps sounding like a future you're looking forward to.'

'That's irrelevant.' He glanced outside, tapping the window glass idly. 'The future doesn't care what I think. It's coming.'

We had rejoined the interstate at last and now shot down a commuter lane so empty it might have been reserved for us. We proceeded at a speed which, even in such a smooth ride, felt astonishing. The traffic lagged to our right, busy and clogged. It hardly seemed to move at all.

It had always been Rob's way to give you more, not less—to let suggestions and insider crumbs pile up until the difficulty became knowing what was important, if any of it was. He wanted to be *helpful*. To drown you in his admissions to distract you from his withholding, and to mask what he was getting from you. Reticent sources drew attention in their silences to what they hoped to pass over. I'd seen countless amateurs give up the goods in their unsubtle use of negative space. Rob liked to oversaturate the picture. The more plots he kicked up, the more dust settled over the pay dirt.

He operated, in short, like a spy and like a few journalists I've known. He wanted to create an autonomous ecosystem of information around him, a microclimate of truth. And he succeeded in a way. Maybe this was what had drawn him to the world of virtuality—this affinity for the creation of bespoke realities by way of narrative sleight of hand. Whatever it was, and whatever genuine affection he bore anyone, I knew he would lie to me through his teeth. If your mother says she loves you, check it out. Rob didn't like me that much.

'You're awfully forthcoming today,' I said. 'To what do I owe the pleasure?'

'You know what I enjoy about you, Quentin?' He had his legs crossed, pulling up the fine wool cuffs of his trousers to reveal hair-flecked shins. 'A guy can have a proper talk with you. You grasp the larger picture. Maybe your colleagues once did too, I don't know. But the scramble for negligible scoops, the whole demeaning game of gossip—it's shrunk their sense of history and time to the dimensions of a collapsing news cycle. I don't know what unit of time to measure it in anymore. Does one exist?

And you guys actually see professional seriousness in this mad dash after the trivial, the evanescent present. The dash gets fiercer, the present gets smaller, and cosmic importance dwindles to nothing.

'But you're different,' Rob went on. 'I don't want to flatter you. You're a son of a bitch and you know it. You strike the same pose, but I guess you know it's a sham. A brittle shell around the creature. And the creature's purpose is to feel the greater currents, the low-frequency waves of a communication happening on a different timescale altogether. Passing over the ages. Waves you can't pick up when you're dialed in on the static and the noise of *now*. It takes patience and care to raise the delicate antennae that can hear those voices in the mist. And you have, for better or worse, that instinct or affliction.

'In any case,' Rob changed his tone once more, 'it's refreshing to chat about ideas with you after a few weeks in the capital.'

'We should start a book club.'

'Yes . . . ,' he said vaguely. 'It *is* important to think through these questions, I know you'd agree. One spends so much time trying to make things happen. Caught up in the power play, the alignment of the pieces . . . Sometimes you forget to probe the sense and sanity of what you're pushing for.'

'If you're trying to sell me on the idea that I'm here to help you, forget it. I'm not buying the charade of conscience.'

'But what if we did?'

'Did what?'

'Need your help.'

I stared at the ongoing wall of trees, their texture gentle and blurred at this speed. The tint transposed everything into amber. The cloverleaf of a junction passed overhead, massive roadbeds spiraling off. We slipped under, shot forward, the softness of our velocity like a heavy, true arrow through a golden mist.

'Define *we*.'

Our conversation was off the record and technically I was off the job, and all the same Rob found it necessary to say, 'This is really entre nous.' He proceeded to explain that, as I knew, he operated with a long leash.

This made him effective. He got the job done, and no one had to know his methods. The whole thing went belly-up, subpoenas flooded in—they had their out. The government left no public paper trail in the private sector, and the contractors could hide behind federal privileges and protections. They were providing a government service, after all. If that was keeping our less photogenic activities off the ledger, so be it. There was utility in the role, that of a go-between, and neither side wanted to give it up.

Now, he continued, I could easily understand why they couldn't go public with a program like VIRTUE. To begin with, it was a baby. No one could confirm, to the standards of clinical science, that it was safe. 'This is a *world* every bit as much as Mars is,' he said. 'You wouldn't send civilians to Mars.' And could I imagine the pandemonium likely to ensue if people found out that we'd really done it, at last—*simulated existence*? The foundations of society, the entire logic of a human being as we understood it, rested on certain limitations and scarcities, and on the ultimate one: death. Destabilizing these overnight could only end in the chaos. On top of which it took the private sector about five minutes to commodify new tech once they had proof of concept. A gold rush would transpire, a mad dash for patents, different tweaks to the evolving paradigm. Hundreds— *thousands*—of disconnected realities would spiral off, faster than the proliferation of digital currencies. It would tear the culture—reality—apart. It had to be studied, Rob said, with what for him passed as near the star of sincerity as he was liable to approach. People given free rein would do terrible things. It was the settling of the West with the technologies of the Star Child. The government had to get out in front. It had to figure out how to govern. The future of rule of law and its enforcement was no longer self-evident. What sense did the protections of a constitution or the intuitions of common law retain in this new world?

What's more (he was really hitting his stride now), the implications for political economy were practically unthinkable. The scalability of *vicarious* fantasy that had been TV's great genius now extended into personal—private—fantasy. How could you have markets, profit, incentives without scarcity? You couldn't, and thus managing an artificial scarcity would be essential. Indeed it was here, he suggested, that the interests of security, government, and business coalesced, because the only way to control people was to deny them things: to get them to fetishize and covet what stood in limited supply. Tokens of status could be essentially arbitrary. People didn't really want abundance and choice if these came with the burden of identifying meaning on their own. But whereas, to this point, actual scarcities had dictated supply and value, in virtual life all scarcities would have to be manufactured. This made perfect control possible.

'And here I always took you for a free-market evangel,' I remarked.

'There are no free markets, Quentin. Not in real life.'

I said he'd get no argument from me. 'But what about SIMITAR? And now VIRTUE? You're talking about the rule of law, some techno-utopian fantasy, and I keep turning up people in the security game who think the whole thing is their big new shiny toy.'

'And a decentralized computer network was going to keep communication intact during thermonuclear war,' said Rob. 'Then we got the internet.' Crime, he continued, poses a problem for democracy. It puts two liberties at odds: the criminal's freedom to act and the victim's freedom from harm. Terrorism ups the stakes. It turns a qualitative question into a quantitative one: How *many* lives are our rights worth? It asks us to set a number and confront the negative costs of our freedom, denominated in vulnerability, anxiety, death. When we're afraid, the negatives loom large, while the positive freedoms, which are spiritual and immaterial, appear practically decadent. They constitute after all the freedom to change—to do and be something different—a possibility that by its very nature can never be fully appreciated in the present.

'So how do you discover intent?' he asked. 'How do you know what people mean to do before they do it?'

'Throw them in the Skinner box and see what they're capable of.'

He might have caught the irony in my tone because he sounded almost hurt. 'Is it so ridiculous? The goal of law enforcement has always been to trace crime further back, from after-the-fact investigations and prosecutions, to active plots and criminal conspiracies, to criminality and ideation itself: the diseased mind, the rotten spirit.'

'Don't tell me you believe that nonsense. How far back does ideation go? Where does the idea originate? In our DNA? The species instinct? In books, Rob?'

He snorted. 'The argument's never going to get that far. You'll be selling abstract principles. Lecturing people about the long view. Meantime I'll always have some guy I can point to whose New Year's resolution is to reduce a bunch of candy stripers to their molecular constituents.'

'You have vividness on your side, I'll give you that.'

'So why not put this guy in a controlled environment, see what he does? Maybe he realizes his dream after all, but the video game version. No lives lost.'

'People aren't lab rats.'

'In the real world maybe. Not *everything* you do here'—Rob gestured around—'generates data . . .'

'That wasn't my point.'

'What then? That there must be something more? The old metaphysical conceit. The ghost in the shell. Does the great Quentin Jones . . . have a *soul*?'

'I get that you might not appreciate their importance to the rest of us.' My smile was pitying. 'All the same, the question is still who decides which unfortunates get dragnetted in your digital con. Since there's no good answer and no limiting principle, I'm guessing that pretty soon we'll all be mice in your maze. Our data—our lives—are too valuable. And then you too, eventually. Only arrogance could convince you otherwise.'

He didn't argue with this either.

'All this talk about rule of law,' I persisted. 'But what you're doing here in the shadows, there's no oversight. No check. You're operating with impunity. Did the intelligence court even sign off on this?'

Instead of answering me Rob changed the channel on the seatback television. We'd reached the outskirts of the capital and slid out of the express lane to rejoin the cars easing around the buffering suburbs like the scales of a python around a rock. The noise of traffic came through, muted by the car's heavy windows. On the television, barren windswept streets appeared. An outpost, low buildings in tan colors, dusty roads.

Here and there a truck rumbled by. A trickle of men walked alongside an unpaved boulevard, too far away and indistinct to make out. In the distance mountains rose, washed out by the turgid air and haze. The scene jumped. A different angle now. An alley. The sun cut low triangles on the walls behind the roofline. Most of the corridor lay in shadow. A small puddle in the mud dripping into a sewer. A figure on the ground, dead or bleeding, I couldn't tell.

Another jump.

'What am I looking at?' I asked. Rob didn't respond. Now we saw a yard enclosed by a mudbrick wall and beyond it the crowns of buildings sprouting antennae. In plastic chairs around tables draped in oilcloths figures sat awkwardly slumped, heads to the side or hanging forward on their chests. The scene had a perfect stillness. A long smudge of cloud floated almost invisibly in the blue. A breeze played with the folds of the tablecloth and ran through a pinwheel resting by a fruit tree. I suddenly realized that I'd misjudged the scale, taking the figures for adult, when some were smaller, children among women. The shadow blanketing the scene made it hard to read anything clearly against the brightness beyond. Then the color rose by degrees, as if a cloud were unveiling the sun, the metal surfaces glinted, the clothing turned from dim and patchy to a red-mottled white, wine on a blouse, and the angle shifted as if the camera were being lowered, before the image stuttered and went grainy . . . Rob turned off the screen.

But I'd seen enough.

'Should I expect to hear about this on the evening news?'

Rob regarded me with a long penetrating silence. 'You'll never hear about this,' he said. 'Not for as long as you live.'

I found myself on the verge of asking, 'How's that?' when the import of his words became clear. He took two bottles of fancy-looking water from a refrigerated compartment and offered me one. My thoughts were racing to catch up to the moment. I felt a kind of nausea that reminds you there are depths to the soul which understand the implications of a dawning reality more quickly than the conscious mind ever could. I felt this in my limbs, a coldness and a heaviness, an almost pleasant pain. Later it would come to me that I had seen the laminate scratched off the surface of our days. The unbrokenness of reality had broken. But what did this vision mean? How could I weigh its significance against what transpired here, in the world we call real; what difference could be drawn between reality within and without; and if none could, what did that say about the meaning of so much trivial and manufactured urgency in this, our straightforward familiar life?

The car shot down the parkway in the bosom of the city, through the damp green vein that ran parallel to the sunken creek. The verdure along the hills on either side watched over us as we cut our channel through the basin. A gray sky foretold rain. This was inauspicious for Cy's opening, but I welcomed it. I wanted the rain to come—for the way it closed and narrowed the scope of a world gone too large, dissolving dreams like crusts of dirt that settle on the streets.

I'd finally found my voice. 'Why did you show me that?'

'I told you. We need your help.'

'I don't get it.'

He paused. 'We lost someone. Inside.'

'Lost?'

'We can't find him.' Rob turned to the window. 'Actually, he won't come out.'

'So unplug him. Turn off the machine.'

'It's not that simple.'

We were both looking out the window now, watching the wind thrash the upper bodies of the trees.

'What I saw on the screen,' I said softly. 'This guy you're talking about, he's responsible?'

'You have to realize, we put the observers in an unprecedented situation . . . They have an extraordinary amount of license.'

'Observers?'

'The people we sent in.'

'There's something off here, Rob.' He raised his eyes. 'What does this have to do with *me*?'

We'd pulled onto my street. The car stood idling in front of my building. On a different day I would have felt the menace of Rob knowing exactly where I lived and taking me there without a question or word to the driver. But my sense of darkness had been spent in dearer places.

'We think you know him,' Rob said.

That was enough. The whole alignment of what till then had been coincidence shuddered into place. The first drops appeared on the windows, not so much falling as materializing. You could anticipate the entire evening by the depth of the marled sky.

'I see,' I murmured. No more needed to be said. Rob handed me a manila envelope. I looked at him, jogging my head in a sort of ongoing nod while I considered the broad, substantive face, proportioned to suggest an honesty that had never lived behind it. I tapped the folder twice and got out. We didn't say goodbye. This was not the end of anything, after all, but the beginning.

There were a couple of hours before Cy's opening, but on entering the apartment I felt such emptiness and fatigue that I would have given anything to skip ahead to the distraction of the gallery and the release of a stiff drink. I fed Tyche and checked my phone. No word from Cy although I'd texted her twice. I didn't have it in me to wonder.

The manila envelope sat on the table where I'd dropped it, its blank face like a screen for wonder. Most days I would have torn into it but I could feel myself skirting its ominous weight. I'd reached a certain limit and it seemed possible that one more glimpse of our cruelty, one more peek at the flimsiness of what held our days together, might break something in me.

I dawdled, checking my email. More follow-up from Katz-Wallace: scientists' names and contact info. I recorded Ed Yang's details on a pad and jotted a few notes from my visit to Branford. Finally, when I'd dispatched every task I could invent for myself, I lay down on the couch with Rob's envelope. The rain drummed against the window screen, rising and falling with the wind. The envelope was thin. It held just two photocopied pages—the first a newspaper clipping from almost ten years before, discussing the work of an anesthesiologist named Hunter Gove at the veterans administration. According to the article, he specialized in pioneering treatments for extreme trauma and his research focused on induced comatic states.

Today, Dr. Hunter Gove, a decorated combat medic, calls the Beaumont Center for Advanced Rehabilitation home. Here, in the quiet suburbs of the capital, he directs a specialized team of medical doctors and research scientists who have devoted themselves to studying the brain under extended periods of unconsciousness.

'We used to call these states "vegetative," back in the bad old days,' says Nadia Arias, a junior member of the team, who has been working under Dr. Gove for the last two years. 'Now we know that a great deal is often going on in the brain while it is not, strictly speaking, conscious.'

Experts familiar with Gove's work say it holds tremendous potential for the treatment and recovery prospects of veterans. 'They're looking at the gray areas between consciousness and unconsciousness to see what possibilities for healing exist in these little-understood states,' says Dr. Sarah Sewell, a researcher at the National Trauma Center.

Dr. Gove says first things first. They must learn to manage the comatic state with a new degree of precision. 'Can we take care of the body's systems long-term and retrieve patients from persistent nonresponsive states?' he muses. 'We think we can.'

There was nothing to indicate the pertinence of the article but a note written in the margin: *For your 'Where are they now?' file.*

The second photocopied sheet was of a document written in a half-cursive scrawl. It began in the middle of a sentence and left off midsentence. Clearly it belonged to something longer.

the truth is I have killed—and killed often. From the second on it is just a repetition of the first, the same man who goes on dying forever. His death lasts for as long as you continue to live. Someone said that to me at Camp Mercy. Beltrán or one of the Suicide Twins. Someone who had barely lived long enough to know the full confusion of puberty. But he was right, or I suspect he was.

There is beauty in death. The finality, the grandeur. It brings you close to the quickening spirit, the pulse, of life. I have sat in muddy boots, filthy clothes, caked in dust and dirt, and watched the bombs explode in concussive thuds, brilliant ignitions of fire and smoke—so encompassing to the senses it transfixes—and I have felt like a minor and forgotten god, involved beautifully in a death I was safe from. I have seen the guns go cyclic, churning fire with such uncanny power I could have worshipped destruction for the force in it, like an earthquake, the force in our determination to destroy. I want to say it was my own preservation I worshipped—that viewed from a distance, everything is beautiful—or that war makes you hard, or turns you strange, but true as that may be, it discloses as well the endless fascination of death.

The fascination is with one's own, and one's own smallness before the forces that knit or rupture the ribbon of life. Others' deaths mingle in perverse intimacy with your own, not unlike love.

What these eyes have seen! What godless and cruel things . . . Religion in an exploding skull, emptying from the back. A man in repose, napping against a rock, who when the hat shading his eyes was removed proved to be a corpse. Rotting horses lying in the gullies where they fell. Putrefying cows and

I read the damn page ten times, trying to tease out the clue it held. No luck. Sometime in the course of lying there, reading over those enigmatic pages and listening to the rhythmic patter of the rain, I fell asleep. I awoke to the same wind-tossed rain, now in the dark, with half an hour to shower and get to Cy's show.

On my way over I called Katz-Wallace. The sleepy adagio of his voice soothed my nerves. I felt for an instant that the continuity of order rested in his dull impassiveness, that of someone immune to, or untouched by, the seductions of hope.

'How'd it go at Treasury?'

He laughed. 'You know, I look at my incoming call log, and it's you or my girlfriend.'

'Since when do you have a girlfriend?'

'On background?'

'*A high-level source disputes Rachel's claim that the relationship began a year ago . . .*'

'Margaret.'

'Now there's a sensible name.'

'You want to hear about Treasury?'

There: I'd found the one thing Michael was less interested in talking about than his stories. 'I did,' I said. 'But that was before Margaret entered the picture.' The cab window ran bleary with rain, the subfusc evening smudging and muting the city's storefront lights. Such weather protected a gentle mood.

'You call for, you know, a reason?' asked Michael.

'Yeah. Can you ask whoever you've got digging around to look up Hunter Gove? Spelled how you think. He's a doctor, former military. Maybe something to do with veterans affairs.'

'All right,' Michael said. Apparently apropos of nothing at all, he added, 'Henry was screaming his head off yesterday. We heard him in his office. I guess it was a phone call 'cause he came out of the office alone, kind of bewildered, and lit a cigarette right in the middle of the news-room. Kathy had to remind him you couldn't smoke there for like two decades or something. He stared at her and muttered that he'd be back: "Unless I'm fired first."'

'I've heard it before,' I said. 'Don't start picking out office furniture.'

What I didn't tell Michael was that the only time I'd heard Henry say it was during an ugly standoff with Tolliver's predecessor. Henry had staked his job and, by some lights, his reputation on his reporter's work over furious denials and the threat of legal Armageddon from a viperine law firm representing a pharma conglomerate. Henry didn't blink, and the reporting won the *Beacon* a major public service award that year. James Tolliver arrived not long after.

'Right, well, he was at work today,' said Michael.

'And he'll outlast us all. Gove, Hunter. Doctor. Military. I'm late.'

'Somehow I understood that,' Michael said, and we hung up.

Beads clung to the windows of the cab as the driver pulled up at the curb. The gallery, fronting the night with large plate-glass windows, released a piercing, candid light into the street. The space seemed to glow more brightly in the rain, the pavement glistening with the noise of streetlamps, headlights. Cars passed with a placid whoosh. It had grown cold, the temperature falling behind the stormfront, and I felt the half-hearted charm of the city persisting on in the elements with the gay chiaroscuro of old movies.

Cy was wearing a dark strapless dress matching the color of her hair, which she wore up. She looked beautiful. You were there, Schmitty. It was nice of you and Cora to come, even if I must have seemed distracted, hardly present for your gentle ribbing. Had Cora stayed home I might have unburdened myself to you, but I was strung as taut as wire and couldn't bring myself to talk about my life. It was going to shit. Maybe Cy sensed my mood because she treated me nicely all night.

'You shaved.' She said it with the soft muted surprise that I knew was her way of indicating she meant it, I'd made an effort.

'You look . . . so beautiful,' I said, catching myself before I ruined the sentiment.

'Come on. Let me introduce you to some people.'

Cy took my hand and led me over to a group, where I said my hellos. The gallery had yet to fill. Judith, Cy's partner, stood next to Sergei Malinov, the artist. He was a Russian man, older than I would have thought, in an enormous drab sweater that endeared him to me immediately. I've intentionally forgotten the names and connections of the stylish people who rounded out our group. Each had a job in the arts, working for a museum or for another gallery. They spoke to Judith and Cy in an insider patois that I made little effort to understand. I listened with half an ear, watching the evident distress with which Sergei Malinov looked around, as if from within a horrific dream.

A statuesque sort in square glasses was gossiping about acquisitions and hiring rumors. Malinov's fishlike mouth and eyes puckered in a look of unmasterable misery, as if someone had given him a poisoned canapé. I excused myself and slipped into Cy's office, where I knew she kept bourbon in the cabinet, and returned with a few fingers in a plastic winecup.

I'd noted the work only peripherally to that point. It was striking, I saw, strange. Malinov employed large canvases, arrayed in hues that suggested the paradoxical flatness and depth of a sky at dusk. The gradient drew in the eye, giving it nowhere to land. Such grace flirted with prettiness but didn't surrender to it. In the foreground bursts of color with the dissipating intensity of camera flashes, the shimmering life of quicksilver, ignited like combusting jewels.

Approaching nearer, I noticed that some of the foregrounded motifs repeated in quieter moments on the canvas. Here, recessed and discreet, the pleasant asymmetry and chaos of the surface fed back into recursive patterns, as of echoing and nested worlds migrating from one scale to the next.

Malinov stood by himself not far off. He had a plastic cup of wine in his hand, which he looked at occasionally in despair.

'It's wonderful,' I said, edging into earshot. 'Your work . . .'

My words seemed to register like a physical blow, but after a moment he recovered enough to nod. He looked down at his wine for companionship and remarked shyly, 'Every time I tell myself, You will enjoy the show. You will make the little talk with people and so forth.' His accent handled the syllables delicately. 'I think, This is how it is. This is normal.'

'Yes. It is.'

'And then I arrive . . .' He made a gesture of helplessness. Laughter pealed in the background. He regarded my face as if trying to discern my capacity to understand. 'I look at what I've done,' he went on. '*Paintings.*' He all but spat the word. 'When you put your inside life on display, either you look stupid or the world does. Most likely both.'

I let this stand a minute in silence and asked if I could get him a drink.

He didn't respond. 'What kind of idiot have I been?' he muttered to himself. 'Do you—?' he asked suddenly.

'No, no.'

'Good for you.' He nodded ruefully and raised his hands in defeat. 'Yes, a drink,' he said. 'Not this bullshit any longer.' He poured his wine into a small wastebasket.

Fetching him bourbon from the back, I had the urge I often do in bustling scenes (for the gallery had continued to fill as we spoke, people hung jackets and raincoats on a rack set up by the door, dropped umbrellas in a five-gallon bucket, burned with the damp warmth, red-faced from coming in out of the cold; they roiled and milled, smiles lighting their faces and water clinging to their hair; the noise of greetings and small talk rising in terraced degrees, as people spoke louder to be heard, and sharp echoes filled the rigid space so that the whole system recycled at a higher volume). It was the urge to disappear, to fade away while present and watch the happiness of others, the camaraderie of the group, which I admired but could have no part in, since it only threw me back on the isolation I carried inside and at times suspected we all did. I saw my gift and my curse, if I can put it in such terms, to be the remit of a guardian, a ghostlike figure tending our safety from beyond, securing the edges so that others could enjoy the satisfactions of togetherness. I wondered whether Malinov in his more hopeful moments understood himself as having a gift to bestow, or a service to render, tantalizing in its ungraspable proximity. He took the bourbon from me without a word, just a grave, comprehending look, and I watched him throughout the evening as he wandered among the crowd, which seemed to know instinctively to part for him. Every so often Cy or Judith would take him by the elbow and corral him into some introduction. But more often he seemed like a small rudderless ship weaving among the rocks.

I said my greetings. I shot the breeze. Acquaintances stopped by, people from Cy's world. The first wave of attendees had begun thinning and a smaller second wave swelled the ranks briefly, before the wine ran low and the hour slipped past eight. The final dregs of the crowd loitered near the door, lingering in conversation, reluctant for the cheer and wine to end. The catering staff broke down the bar and stood beside it, snacking on leftovers. I looked for Malinov but couldn't find him. I imagined him decamping to some charmless bar where he would stare into a succession of neat vodkas until the time came for him to teeter back to his hotel. A strange balding rotund little man, fissioning softly from within like a radioactive core.

And there she was. She appeared at my side. I was gazing at one of the large red canvases, seamed with metallic scars like the bulbous reinforcements of a soldered joint, hued in orange and ocher. Rough spears of bent lightning crossed the canvas, and I found within them a faint repeated image, almost a circuit, or two tridents touching, tine to tine. The maelstrom of energy, which made one's first impression of the image, gave way as I looked at it, for this was only the vivid foreground on a softer, deeper background, one that moved with the subtle depth and stillness of a river on whose quickening, liquid body appear the faces of our collective spirit, our past, our projected dreams. It called to you, this image. She stood beside me. She had taken my arm, not romantically but with a hint of missing that formal and expiring chivalry which is a couple at the end of a long day, not needing anything of each other, not even speech; asking only the ease of standing side by side, from time to time, and looking at a world in shared wonder and disappointment, in a companionship that needs no words as the cars pass quietly in the street.

III

A WORD ON Quentin's early days. We each knew part of his story, and together this assembled a significant portrait, although naturally there are countless ways one can narrate a life. Some of us are born parallel to the grain, some crosswise. Some move easily in life's channels, while others doubt anything is as we say it is. Caressed so many times by familiar myths, the cobblestones and footpaths along which we proceed wear smooth. It takes a rare acuteness to see the highway robbery we call history as it happens.

Quentin came from that most stolid and laconic of countryfolk. He camouflaged his seriousness in humor, drowned his sincerity in cynicism. When palpated and pressed his skeleton wouldn't turn up an ingenuous bone, but he was an optimist all the same. Humanity's wrongheadedness gave us something to laugh about, at least. That was his way of thinking. His father took neither such a hopeful nor despairing view. To Mr. Jones, people were self-serving *and* trustworthy. He possessed the negative capability to entertain both ideas at once. Mostly he just thought everyone wanted the system to run. That was his own bias: he ran the local tool-works for a regional machining concern.

Quentin and his father weren't close, but they shared a fatalistic humor that seemed to trace its lineage to the stitchwork drollery of souvenir shops. Men were incorrigible, women implacable, and the principal theaters of domestic strife involved fishing and toilet seats. Not that Quentin bought into this worldview; it was merely a cultural superstition that lent order and archetype to the morass. Quentin inherited his father's love of sports but disappointed them both by never passing out of a certain scrawniness. He grew five inches at the end of high school but by then it was too late. The best he could muster was a retiring track career and a cagey way around a basketball hoop.

His mother, Grace, was the more formative influence on him. The Joneses, keeping up with themselves, lived in that transitional geography where the mountains and coal country settle down into a broad fertile plain, as flat as a black key, where farms fill out the broad square plots edged in brooks and trees, and the air on summer evenings clusters in a solution of sparkling dust as thickly green-gold as a sea of pollen. The light catches on aluminum silos and tin-roofed sheds like bright accents in a lush expiration. Quentin's mom taught reading skills at the local middle school and doubled as librarian. And like so many teachers the country over, she seemed to have passed on to her children, and to Quentin most of all, the idea that a taste for books can carry you anywhere in life.

Maybe it is a myth that in such families the old democratic ideas endure most strongly. We all grow from the same earth. But Quentin believed in reading as a lifeline to the past—to the store of experience that made the foundation of our species. By assembling our thoughts like risers in a staircase the generations would climb. Those who could draw from this reservoir would exist beyond the jealous shackles of time, grasp the utterness of contingency, and know the wisdom of sounding their own ignorance. Those granted access to this archive discovered in it the freedom to travel in the mind. A poorly stocked country library suffices to launch this journey. It has sufficed a million times. The truth is it hardly matters where you begin: black symbols on a white page—so many windows onto as many elsewheres. The realest sort of time travel and telepathy we know. The first virtual space.

Grace's death affected Quentin profoundly, as did the years of her illness when he lived with his grandparents on their farm. Whether this was to spare him or his mother his proximity to her deterioration wasn't clear. Dirk, sober and impassive as he was, never got over Grace's death, and the break it established between Quentin and childhood was clean. He never went back; there *was* no going back. And his father had passed on too, the mechanism of his persistence seizing up without the fuel of hope, by the time we met Quentin in J-school.

How we came to know this remains something of a mystery. Quentin never mentioned Grace's death when he talked about his life. Did he tell one of us in some late boozy moment at the Owl, our J-school watering hole, where the lacquered oak booths eased out all manner of confession, and did whoever heard it later convey the news to the rest of us? It's possible. One way or another it was something we simply *came to know.* But Quentin passed over it so resolutely that at times we doubted we had heard it at all. The entire thing seemed a mistake, a figment, like a misapprehension traceable to a vivid dream.

This isn't to paint Quentin in a dour light, suffering from a repressed mourning that curdles into anger. He was a phenomenon in J-school, full of a nervy energy that led us, without ever discussing it, to elect him for a special fate. He would be our shining star. Our success would crowd under the broad awning of his own. He wrote petty crime stories for an alt-weekly back then. Sordid, comic stuff the big papers wouldn't touch: the corner store stickup put on hold for a ballgame's key out; the beloved neighborhood dealer collared by an undercover, who happened to be courting the guy's cousin. Tiny heists so beautifully bungled they belonged to *Commedia all'italiana.* We never knew how he stumbled into the job. The rest of us, hungry, if it came to it, to see our byline in hobo code on the wing wall of a city bridge, envied his precocity. Maybe he just walked in with a pitch one day and went from there. He loved talking to strangers, striking up conversations. That was his charm. It's funny, he liked to joke, but practically all the people I know were strangers when I met them.

Whether it was a waitress or a salesman, a crossing guard or the guy unloading a truck in the street, Quentin wanted to know what occupied people's thoughts. What they had seen. What small thing they knew that no one else did. Everyone's an expert on his own life, he would say. Everyone has sovereignty in some corner of the world. The avenues teemed with demotic spies. Maybe that's how he saw it. For even as he rose through the ranks at the *Tribune*, and then the *Beacon*, first on the metro desk covering city government, crime, and corruption, later finance, and finally national security in the capital, he continued to walk the streets. As a rule he gave money to the homeless and to sidewalk performers, chatted up dealers, hookers, cops. It wasn't the ease he exuded but the ease he made others feel. He knew how to make people like themselves if he cared to. His star burned so bright and rose so fast that most of us only worried his ambition would consume him, outstripping any greater purpose. What a shame it would have been to see him wind up on TV.

It was Bruce's disappearance that changed him, the dark implication behind it and Quentin's own hand in Bruce's departure for the war. It shook him, and the penance he contrived for himself meant loading his moral failings onto a scale of justice he would counterbalance with the tenacity of his work. Over time he would pay the balance down. It's not so unusual for someone who enters the game for glory to discover, in time, the call of vocation. We need fidelity to that greater thing and without it we suffer. And then moral awakenings occur throughout a life. But Quentin's turn had a different quality, a religious tinge. He had received a revelation the rest of us couldn't see.

Maybe this needs no explanation. When a man's exceptional talent lies in one direction it becomes natural for him to give himself over to it. He seems to merge with his work and can hardly devote energy to anything else, since this work realizes him most fully and infuses the hours spent on it with a concentrated vividness the rest of life lacks. Or perhaps it takes a person with such bleak expectations of moral character to plumb the depths of our wickedness. Quentin, so likable, never cared about being liked.

But these are theories; they explain everything and nothing. Having glimpsed each other briefly, we think we have seen the truth. We would have lost Quentin if not for Cy. Might he have spiraled off as he grew uncompromising with age, the mystic crank, writing about corporate depravity and environmental contaminants out where people lived brief crappy lives visited by exotic cancers, where public attention sat still for all of five seconds before stifling a yawn? Could he have gone where nobody cared to go and covered what nobody cared to read *for* our very apathy and neglect? It seemed possible. A certain reporter winds up on the leper-colony beat, tending those most merciless, dull, disregarded stories simply because someone must. Because the loneliness of voiceless suffering will haunt us otherwise, weakening our spirit until it sees its only comfort in death. This is not morality. It is anger, fury at our smallness and meanness. It is the process of transmuting hatred into good. Our friend flirted with this alchemy, banged his head against editorial intransigence. His questions laid hands on the golden geese—banks and investment funds the paper's entire board had money with—right before the house of cards came down. He had a middle finger ready for a few colleagues. Credulous, vain, somnambulist; renting out their ignorance, collecting laurels for parroting the voice of power. He met Cy in the nick of time. He would have made enemies for life. And here at last was someone who saw through him, and wasn't taken in by the hero or the cynic—his two great poses. She liked him anyway, or for different, and therefore more precious, reasons from everyone else.

Not that the rest of us had given up on him, that dulling with age we call maturity to lionize it. We were all married then. We had our first kids and careers whose easy grooves we fit in and meant to flow down like groggy commuters on the freeway. Journalism is never a cakewalk, but we'd played it relatively safe. Taken the secure, workaday positions that kept us in others' good graces. We'd made friends. We kept our heads down and moved to editorial posts as soon as we could. Maybe that's retrospective comfort, since those years of hustling and worry felt different at the time. When you're in them they're nerve-racking as hell, even if later your little success seems all but preordained. We measured ourselves against Quentin either way, his ambition to hold steady, sacrificing what was necessary to stay the course. He was the only one of us who seemed really to have *meant* what he said at twenty-five, when we drank and loved one another immoderately and voiced such big dreams.

So it was with a mix of satisfaction and regret that we saw Quentin move in with Cy. She softened his edges. Cy wasn't soft herself. Quentin was simply happy. We wanted his decisions to vindicate our own. We wanted to believe that we all swim partly with the current or drown. And yet we wanted the opposite too: for his uncompromising example to give no inch where we felt we had given yards and thus to keep open the possibility that one's life could be a very different thing from what we had imagined and accepted for ourselves. Realists have always slept better knowing that idealists are out there dying in the name of justice.

The sky was serene when we awoke on our third day. Rousing from fitful dreams, we saw a titian glow fill the ivory shades, stenciled with leaves. The light traced down the bay. In a breeze rich with the nettle-brush odor of thawed and heating earth, the birds called. Squirrels chased among rotten leaves preserved by winter's frost. And perhaps we heard a note that wasn't there, but it was hard not to take the feeling into oneself, the arrival of spring, and the sense that such an existence as ours was, on balance, good.

The rains of the day before had left the turf patched with puddles. They sat in the furrows islanding bright scraps of sky. The earth caked at the edges, breaking out in craquelure. The timbers of the house soughed, spreading. Opening the windows, we could feel the warm air press in and sweeten the damp-wood smell. Quentin had taken us late again with his story. We had let the house absorb the night until our voices arose like disembodied currents in a black sea and darkness claimed the room, laying shadows on the framed ships and scenes of venery.

It is not the case that Quentin spoke without interruption, but mostly we listened. We had been trained to listen, and listening holds a stirring pleasure when you concede the desire to speak. You are taking part in an ancient ritual, the telling of tales—that imperfect transport into what it is to be someone else and to look at the world from the unbolted confines of another mind.

And so we listened, not simply because Quentin's story interested us, but because we saw ourselves carrying forward a sacred rite. How far back did this go, the roaring fire, the stars spread out in their blanket on the sky, the rhythmic voice connecting one instant to the next with a spectral logic that lived partly in words, partly in our souls, and partly in how sound patterned the air? No one could say. We only knew that if we stopped listening to one another we would die; in some sense, we would die. Our molecule would dissolve, our bond would break, and like the atoms of solipsism we would trace through empty space without knowing more than the temperature of our aloneness.

Toward late morning Quentin picked up where he'd left off. It's a strange unburdening that comes over me, he said. This opportunity . . . to speak. His air was diffident. We're lucky to get one shot at being understood just as we understand ourselves, he went on. No story cleaves to its arc. Meaning snakes off in a thousand dead-end spurs.

Chance, having given up on being playful company, lay in the grass with his paws before him. His hurt, faintly imploring eyes gazed up at us. At intervals he roused himself and disappeared down the embankment to the estuary and salt-rim of beach.

Well, said Quentin. Minersville, Johnston—two cities separated by a common geography. A faint smile traced across his lips. They have a night-and-day quality. Only six or so miles apart, but clearly they're the children of different parents. Minersville sits in an old cragged valley, nestled up in the mountains where two rivers meet. On both sides it looks up at limestone cliffs. There are stone plazas and old stone churches, brick storefronts, monuments, the remnants of a canal. Here and there you spot a trestle bridge on ancient pilings crossing the riverbank. Flags fly downtown by the freshly painted fences and gates. All very clean and orderly. No graffiti or debris. Just the purling rivers on two sides.

Farther upriver you can make out the high-water mark on the cliffside—the point the river reaches during the period of the dam's peak disgorgement. Farther still you get to the dam itself, stretched across the river like the flank of a fortress, with a steady stream of whitewater coming over the spillway.

When I drove up I didn't stop in Minersville but crossed briefly into the downtown and kept on to the dam. The road banked along the impoundment and the fat slug of river which broadened above it looked so complacent it seemed unlikely to have any role in lighting cities or powering factories, or in the clandestine purpose that I had reason to believe it abetted. The river shone with a million points of sun. I passed from here into the rolling, unlovely country to the west, where one found Johnston, a city of tract housing and office parks that looked like prisons. Johnston was an old railway junction, dotted with retired depots. The tracks still crisscrossed the town, lending it what little charm it had. It was the bleak sort of place that seems overcast even when it's not: low gray skies over a flat expanse, mountain ridges in the distance and knobby hills closer in. Warehouses sat along the rural highway by the schools and soccer fields enclosed in chain-link fence, the municipal buildings and wastewater treatment facilities, rusted and insectoid. It belonged to a lost age of industry, though any quaintness had been extinguished. No more coal caravans traced the spine of mountains beneath the billowing smoke of locomotives. These had been replaced by pickups idling in gas stations and convenience stores, semis on their long hauls downshifting in tectonic registers. Thin trails of mephitic gas issued from metal chimneys. Nobody walked anywhere.

I took a room at a motel some distance from downtown, a seedy place so unassuming it looked at first as if it had gone out of business. That's why I chose it. That, and you could park around back. I don't begin to fathom the new technologies that keep tabs on us, from automatic number-plate recognition and stingray phone trackers to analytics composites of braided metadata. I've always assumed that anyone competent to find me will find me, but even steadied by such rationality I took comfort in the old illusion that I could disappear from view.

The clerk hardly spoke to me when I checked in. I tried chatting about this and that. A rote compulsion, as you know. But he only acknowledged this stream of pleasantries by occasionally raising a pair of heavy moist eyes, spitting tobacco juice deftly into a soda bottle, and turning back to his work.

They no longer had smoking rooms but room 92 nevertheless smelled as if cigarette smoke had long ago settled permanently in the fabric. The dark green curtains, made of a thick polyester, shrouded the room in a deathlike stillness. The bed creaked and listed under any weight, and the pitted ceiling panels showed the wan coffee-colored blooms of water damage.

Altogether suitable. I was no fancy city reporter. I was a jilted, childless denizen of middle age on indefinite leave from work. An amateur detective. A gambler with a couple of hands left to play and a dwindling stack of chips. Almost certainly out of my depth. Get hold of a big enough fish and it's not clear who's reeling in whom. Mine lived in a benthic trench. So I was intent on sticking to a script that came from the movies. I clung to the idea that in the seediest, most disconsolate condition lay a balm for the existentially lonely—preferably a motel.

It was lying on the bed, watching the dipping, ripening sun accentuate the ridge of mountain to the west, that I returned to another nowhere hotel, one I'd never visited except in dreams, a room with its own mountain view, albeit of distant snowcapped peaks, and a curtain I pictured playing in the breeze before the window like idle longing. I'd recalled it to a purpose for it was clear to me from the first, by whatever obscure alignment of impressions renders us unto certainty, that the page I had received in Spearman's folder, excerpted, it seemed, from a diary, had been written by the figure in that room, the figure from my dream, and none other than Bruce. I knew it intuitively in the well of my spirit. A shiver passed through me like the bone cold of the shade after hours in the sun. What I'd read had been written some time after I'd last heard from him, and this meant Bruce was alive—for why else would Rob give me the page to read? And why else would my years of looking for, and then waiting for, some trace of him have borne no fruit unless all this time he hadn't wanted to be found?

It was long past the hour for paranoia after so many warnings, the accumulation of coincidence, the too-lucky breaks, the evident danger of a secret so large and well-kept, and now the reappearance, all these years later, of a friend I'd believed dead. Spearman's words returned to me. 'We think you know him.' Was I one step ahead or one step behind? If I didn't know, that was a kind of answer. The early evening was deepening outside, a dull haze creeping over the face of the earth. The room seemed to pale as the daylight left it, the bureau, the curtains, the TV, the rug draining of color and caped with long shadows. Could Spearman have been in earnest? Possible, if not likely. Though why involve himself at all? He knew I didn't trust him. Maybe they *did* need my help. But no, this was the rubbish that clouds judgment. I banished the thought. In the aftershocks of Henry's flare-up I heard at last big plates stirring beneath this story. Could Henry too have been playing his own sly game, triangulating, like the rest of them, off what he knew of my character?

These are the fears that beset a man alone in a strange town with nothing but the company of his own thoughts. I stepped out onto the balcony that ran along the second floor, lit a smoke, and leaned against the railing. Was it my curiosity that made me pliant to others' designs, and did this not argue for making the hardest and least predictable move of all, which was to walk away? That would have begun the slow fashioning of a different me, and though I wasn't opposed to it in principle I lacked the courage to snuff my small fire before knowing where to find the next spark. The listlessness of days untouched by any urgency frightened me. And so I clung to my story like a castaway with a plank. In the open water of life such a plank is at times all one's got.

The smoke from my cigarette sifted out in the distance. The night air was just warm enough for shirtsleeves, and I heard cars moving on the strip behind me, where the signs of chain restaurants and car dealerships exhaled their pallid light. The melancholy, the darkness, flirted with the soothing pain of dereliction, a windblown empire going to seed in unseen pockets, oxidizing industry, neon liquor stores, welling kudzu . . . Cy and I had made love the night before. The details tumble from our fragile privacy, but it bore on my thinking that evening, when, had I not received a phone call, I might have packed up and walked away. Cy had to do with the drift my resolution took. The mood that night after her show, when we returned to her rental, had the air of something probationary. We spoke very little on the way, talked only in those evasive brushstrokes. The show had gone well. We discussed the people who'd come and what it meant for the gallery, this manner of talking a way of not talking—not about anything that mattered, not about anything at all.

Cy went in first and turned on the lights. She'd changed out of heels at the gallery and now sat down to pull off her rain boots, arranging them with undue care in the front hall. She busied herself with our jackets, talking the while in a running monologue that preempted my impression of the apartment with judgments of her own. The wall art was grotesque. The lobby and halls resembled a tasteless new hotel's. No, the view wasn't much, not like our old place, but everything worked perfectly. Nothing leaked or needed fixing. No begrudging sounds. She had arranged cut flowers in a vase on a circular glass table by the window, where I couldn't help imagining her eating dinner by herself. It was like her to get flowers for no more than her own enjoyment. Her books and work folders lay scattered on the sofa and coffee table, not so many as to make a mess but enough to suggest she hadn't planned on company.

We weren't there to chat. Her nervousness told me that, since she had never, in my experience, shied away from a talk. No, it was unmistakable what I was doing there, and this reality embarrassed us. Cy brought out two wineglasses and filled them from an open bottle. We toasted and I said, 'To a brilliant opening,' and in the stillness after that first sip, when no obvious fussing offered itself to Cy and the silence seeped into the room like a drawn-out 'So . . . ,' I realized that the anxiety—Cy's and now my own—pivoted on the question of whether we could be different to each other. Different together. Whether, starting here, we could *fuck*— like strangers, for lack of a better way of putting it. Whether we could pretend our way back to the beginning, to a new beginning, and could touch each other without the baggage of the past.

I put down my glass and kissed her. It didn't come naturally to listen to the body's hunger, but I did it. She put down her glass and pulled me with her against the doorframe. We tongued like college students, lit on ardor. She felt my crotch. I worked my hand under her dress and pulled down her tights and underwear. We touched each other as we kissed, dispelling niceties, that tepid business of guessing each other's pleasure. We were going to *take*, and taking would be its own generosity after years of quiet disappointment and poor guesswork. 'How do you want me?' she breathed in my ear, but I found my throat too dry to respond, caught on an emotion I can't name, a cousin of sorrow or fear, flecked in its harsh grain with the glinting light of lust. I couldn't speak and only guided her over to a plush chair, where she rested her arms. I lifted her dress to the small of her back, pushed her panties to her calves, and we made love like that, to our ghostly reflection in the windows overlooking the dark city, marred with rain and light, and the flowers on the table vibrating with us in congruent tremors along the orange-stained necks of the lilies' white petals.

I didn't last long. The whole thing put me in mind of two creatures who come together for a moment's agony. Cy went to the bathroom and I washed up in the kitchen sink, slapping water on my face and smoothing what is left of my hair. When Cy came out I was drying my hands on a rag. I could see in her eye that she didn't relish what was implied in asking me either to stay or to leave, so I made it simple for her, crossing the room, kissing her on the cheek, and taking my jacket from the rack. I stepped back into my boots. 'Well . . . ,' she said aimlessly. The note hung like punctuation, a mood and nothing more.

'I'll be back in town in a few days.'

She nodded. 'OK.'

We locked eyes and for five seconds the night respired with the breath of eternity. Then I left.

It seemed to me, as I finished my smoke on the motel balcony, that the previous night had held an implicit test. Whether I had passed or failed this, I didn't know. It wasn't a test of character, but of unfastening the constraints that bound character, I decided, but I got no further in my reflections. I was stubbing the cigarette when the phone rang.

'Bad time?' asked Katz-Wallace when I picked up.

'Do I sound as gloomy as that?'

'You sound all right.'

I gazed out at the night. 'Nice of you to say.' I didn't feel it.

He waited a beat. 'Where are you?'

The dark silhouettes of the mountains stood before the dusk. 'Maybe I better not tell you.'

'Did you tell anyone?' There was a hint of real concern in his tone.

'Johnston,' I said. 'You know where that is?' I heard him breathing on the line. You could just about hear his thoughts in the way he breathed. 'Hello?'

'I was calling with news,' he said. 'But maybe you already know.'

'I'll need a bit more before I can settle the matter.'

'We got an address for Gove.' Michael paused a moment. 'It's in Johnston.'

A small phantom creature crawled up the back of my neck, but to Michael I only said, 'Not so strange. There's a veterans facility out here. Contractor shops by the dozen fixed to the military teat.'

None of this answered the question on his mind, but he had the decency not to ask.

'Give me the address again,' I said. 'You have a number too?' I made a note.

'A few residences show up for Gove over the past two years,' Michael said. 'We can't tell exactly when he moved out, but it seems pretty recent. Since the first of the year.'

'Anything else?' I sensed Michael turning something over like a car engine before it caught.

'You got a minute, Quentin? There's some stuff you should probably know.'

I'll summarize what Michael said, but the headline was Henry hadn't cut me loose. When I heard this I felt I'd known it all along. Governments hired the Spearmans of the world to act with an impunity they couldn't, and at times even an editor needed to let the leash out far enough that, if it turned into a noose, you wouldn't hang him too. That makes Henry sound calculating. The truth was we all needed deniability. Henry got Michael to shadow me and dig around the edges of my digging. His meetings at Treasury were, in fact, intended to build a pretext for a series of conversations with the departing undersecretary of budget management, Rani Chandra, a holdover from the last administration with a few dinosaur bones to pick.

One of these was she had never gotten satisfactory explanation for certain off-the-ledger disbursements in Budget's filings. These were highly classified outlays, bound for a veterans facility on which work had, according to public statements, been completed a year before. It was suspicious to begin with that intelligence money, with all its prerogatives and privileged classifications, was going to a veterans project. Chandra had the old-school temerity to ask for clarification when everything about the arrangement screamed *look the other way*. She wasn't long for the job and she liked her own mandarin obstinacy. Obnoxious traits in an opponent often make blessings in a teammate. The ask, in any case, roused some agita in the VP's office, and Dietrich's consigliere called her to advise hunting where the ducks were. Chandra told him that was what she intended to do, had always done, and would continue doing. Dietrich's man may have expressed skepticism about the wisdom in this. He recounted a story about a guy sniffing around a landmine who wound up with a face like a piñata. He jawboned Chandra pretty good, told her to knock it off. Of course that ensured she wouldn't, and now Michael had photocopies of these mystery remittances tucked away somewhere the truffle pigs wouldn't find them. I'd have told him to run these by Castor, but now I worried that if anyone else started shouldering this weight of coincidence they might panic and do something foolish, like go to press.

Connect too many live wires at once and you short the whole thing. Henry got close enough to get a shock. He was out dining with his old chum Fritz Spencer at some power-lunch bistro downtown, the kind you can't imagine a mustard-on-the-tie sort like Henry enjoying much, when Fritz let slip that two of his pit bulls had read my squib on A7 with interest and started feeling out their sources. Well, wouldn't you know it? The message they got back from every quarter, like background radiation in the universe, was spare yourself the embarrassment: the 'scoop' was a MacGuffin, and the *Beacon*'s sword to fall on. Trip Abbott had meanwhile spoken to *someone*. You never knew with Trip in what busted-vinyl dive-bar booth the dope germinated. He wouldn't tell Henry. His source had given nuncupative testimony, nonetheless, to a certain rumor that the *Beacon* was being set up. Set up! Henry blew gaskets one and two, whatever gaskets are, in immediate apoplexy. He made another wildcat raid on Trip's source. 'It's a rumor,' said Trip. 'And it's not like we're publishing.'

Good old Trip. There may only be one professional bone in his body, but it's the right one.

Henry had every reason to be furious. He'd accommodated Haig's junta by putting my reporting on ice. He'd moved me off the story and out into the cold. Now, he saw, either he'd been fed a load of horseshit or he hadn't read the play of deeper forces. It wasn't like Henry to be caught with his trousers drooping. Maybe Haig & Associates only wanted insurance in their back pocket in case Henry and James Tolliver changed their minds about my story. But it was conceivable—Henry couldn't completely discount the possibility—that they aspired to shift the entire paradigm with the press, to wrap us in layers of access and complicity until we found ourselves so tightly tangled, choked on reporting lodged with truth and falsehood, that we needed them like the recipient of an encrypted message needs the key. If push came to shove they could pull the plug on an outlet's credibility, kick up doubt, and walk away with no more than a few bruises. A paper would never survive the reputational damage.

That was when Henry lost it. James wanted to see the chumminess play through to the end. He'd succumbed to the publisher's brief reverie that the business might be something other than antagonism. Sure, access had its merits. It steered in a nice wave of goodwill and everyone enjoyed a certain warm feeling, watching two enemies lay aside their brickbats and speak largely of each other. Usually we needed a war to earn this solatium of collegiality. In a society of endless fake conflict, the relief of unexpected comity is intensely soothing. It makes you think we have a chance.

So James wanted to bask in goodwill like a fat iguana on a rock. He got Cat Lewysohn, the chairwoman, on the phone for the now-infamous gasket-bursting talk with Henry. The quarterly earnings broke in his favor. Subscriptions were up; ad revenue about as strong as one could hope for in the display era. The paper's reputation looked as gilt as a rococo chapel. Tolliver had Lewysohn behind him. It took Henry bruiting early retirement for them to hear out his grievance. Hey, hey, was Cat's response, this isn't Stalingrad. And not that anyone took his threat at face value, but the magnanimity had affected upper management like a brain injury. Everyone was in a mood to be generous. The coincidence of guilt and good fortune does that. Henry had convinced himself he was in earnest, and you don't want to call a man's bluff when he's painted himself into a corner. Not if you care about footprints on your floor.

Plus Henry's ask was reasonable. He only wanted permission to continue his shadow campaign, carrying forward my reporting for a rainy day. James and the higher-ups could keep playing house with Haig and the gang. No one had to lie. My 'leave' proved key in this regard since they could plead honest ignorance where I was concerned. And Trip wouldn't stoke suspicion because everyone knew Trip was an unreconstructed gossip. Michael, on the other hand, was green enough to fly under the radar. Henry could always say, *You know how it is with cubs—careers to make, headaches to turn into*, et cetera.

It's a shame our work has become such a charade of tactics. The business is less dryly factual and more strategic these days. The process under scrutiny isn't the substance of governing but a battle over narrative. More important than a claim's truth are the motives for making it—its subproperties as spin. Assembling information takes a back seat to a formalized contest, a metaprocess, involving the instrumental profit of information. If you're laundering someone else's agenda, you've failed; but if you're waiting for patent reality to announce itself, you've also failed. What's a journalist to do but hone his baiting and misdirection, his bluffs and feints, misrepresenting what's known and who's speaking to whom, and play interest off competing interest? It's the only way to guard against being used. And for such efforts we find we're reporting on little more than these very maneuvers of self-presentation and deceit, minor errors and successes in the gameplay, as if they were the news themselves. Political staffs reorient to this reality. And in remaking the paradigm of political discourse, all this strategizing remakes politics. It teaches us to regard everything in public life as a game, played either poorly or well, and our interest in the political process becomes the nuances of an imposture.

It's a bad situation. We aren't reporting on the merits, and the government isn't arguing on them. In such an environment it only makes sense to cover the tactics of power, and so the arms race in tactics continues. The buildup can't stop. These are the thoughts that some days make me question the work and ask what really I have devoted my life to, since this cynicism only ends up creating the very ground on which it flourishes. In covering politicians as the hypocrites they are, we cultivate this expectation in the public, tacitly licensing their behavior, and at last forcing them into the role if they resist. The public says it wants straight shooters, but it wants hard-nosed delegates of its interest more. Journalists can't change course, because if we disarm they'll have our lunch. And if they disarm, we'll have theirs. And the real corruption that does exist hides easily in the epistemic mist.

Henry, Michael now told me, had taken the unusual step of calling Joan Rightmire. He must have known we were buds, and in moments of desperation even rivals will come together on some patch of common cause. In this case the sanctity of the work. By handing Joan the contours of the story about the *Beacon*'s dealings with the administration, Henry ensured that, if the worst happened, our chief competitor would perform the autopsy. There could be no question of any love lost, and no doubt, therefore, of honesty. By bringing Joan in early, Henry avoided the appearance of convenient timing later on.

He may have made two other calculations as well. Henry likely judged the distance between Joan's own sympathies and the orientation of the *Examiner*, as well as Joan's affection for me. Her interest and his, in other words, aligned more closely than the headline slug would have it.

'When were those disbursements?' I asked Michael when he'd finished.

'The ones I have? Mid-March. But there's no reason to think they're the only ones.'

'Did Chandra see others?'

'I don't know. They might have kept them from her after she started raising a fuss.'

'How come she's still there?'

'She's on her way out. But you know?' A grin blossomed in his voice. 'She's one of them.'

Of course. Our saviors. Those folks who hold their own party to account and maintain a sense of fair play through the shifting tides of partisan fortune. It showed the good sense of staffing members of the other team if you could find honest brokers to slot into the mandarinate, since they survived the restoration to carry on the good fight. I bade Michael adieu, locked up at the motel, and headed for the development where I had learned Hunter Gove maintained an address.

It must have been pride at this juncture that made me think I could muddle through. I had drawn close enough to hear the plot's beating heart, but my knowledge was patchy. I disregarded the warning blaring in the ease of my approach. Like an amateur crook finding the vault open, I risked mistaking a trap for my own cleverness. But as long as no one wanted me dead—and if they did, I was there for the taking—I would come through with my memory intact. And with my memory I could tell the story. That's what I reasoned.

What seemed important, gliding down Johnston's dim, squalid, neon-dappled streets, my window open to catch the shocks of cool air eddying in the night, was that I continue to chart my own course. I had no proprietary attachment to the story, that wasn't it. I felt that everyone else, everyone but me (there was a certain conceited tragedy in the feeling) risked stopping short of the full truth, the true abyssal depths.

Halfway to nowhere I turned onto a long empty road, lifeless and manicured, lit at regular intervals by overhead lights and running as straight as the crow flies. It seemed to have leapt from the mind of a stranger to the human condition. From there I passed into a complex called Beechwood Heights, whose confected curves, cotton-candy trees, and regimented lawns resembled nothing so much as a golf course. If we were above anything at all I couldn't discern it.

This overdetermined slab of suburban idyll didn't offer much as a stakeout site. It was somehow more depressing for being the tonier of its varieties. The ersatz hillocks and carefully plotted sight lines—the attempt to mimic nature's serendipities—cratered in some valley of the not-quite like the almost-real quality of computer imagery. There was of course nowhere to park that didn't look suspicious. I kept on past Gove's house, a blue impression from the same mold, and looped around more slowly, pulling up along the bank of a curve maybe thirty yards before the house.

I sat back and took in the scene. A light shone behind the building, but I couldn't tell where this came from. No car in the driveway. Garage shut. The house looked essentially untouched by occupation. I flipped through my notepad until I found the numbers I had for Gove and called each of them in turn.

The first rang unanswered and the second went to a recording that said it was no longer in service. I had one arm out the window and played imaginary scales on the breeze as I punched in the third set of digits. The air smelled of flowering trees, a faint perfume that mingled with the stink of a failing septic system or some artificial glen in the woods. The third number was ringing and after two or three rings I heard a faint echo coming from the house. It tolled at a fractional delay. I saw a light come on in a second-story window. Then the phone clicked and went dead. A woman's silhouette appeared in the window, framed by the light behind her. She stood very still. I saw her brush her dark hair back from her face before the light switched off and she disappeared. I tried the number again but this time no one answered. I waited a few minutes longer before deciding to call it a night.

On the drive home I phoned Ed Yang's office. It wasn't so late out west, at the Takashi-Hoffman Institute, but my call went to voicemail. The voice on his answering message had a sphinxlike note and faint accent. I hung up before the beep. No sense touching off the game of telephone that ran through Luke Simmons, Rob Spearman, and whatever gunmetal éminences lay further downstream. I bought a pint of bourbon and drank a nightcap from one of the milk-plastic cups in the motel bathroom before passing out on the bed. I was tired and only got one shoe off.

My dreams that night, inasmuch as I remember them, bore the damp, unsettled residue of my night with Cy. I didn't know what to make of it, whether we would rediscover our intimacy in estranging ourselves or make ourselves into strangers. The humbling of seeing life's moorings shaken to flagging scraps returned me to the wretchedness of adolescence, when you feel, for this abjection, an almost erotic transfixion before the caprices of fate. The brutal humiliations and erratic deliverances of that age—things as simple as a rejection, a kiss—bear the unqualified weight of life's mystery: its rawness without any padding of ideas. This proximity to experience, this vivid key—recalling in me wonder at summer tempests and girls' voices, shady backroads, fights, pranks, the vagrant ethers of new freedom and narrow escapes, laughter, trysts, dark compulsions wedded to earnestness and purity on blackened playgrounds, in basements and chilly gazebos concealed in rain—split me like a jeweled melon. Who knew I housed these happy, ready wounds? Like any open cut they mixed my blood with the world's. And while I couldn't love the sensation, I couldn't hate it either, for I was walking the knife-edge of a pained immediacy for the first time in years. I was *awake*.

I felt closer to Cy. Closer to myself. I had a renewed sympathy for our blindness, the confusion that blossoms in death's advance, since with every fragment of wisdom we secured, life's lawlessness grew more certain, and our responsibility, our unaided freedom, grew clearer. Upon awaking to this abyss I knew my kinship to those who had come before, the numberless of our kind who made camp in the wild at night exposed to the violence and uncertainty in nature's soul. And this quivering aliveness before the unknown was the truth of where we fit, a primal reckoning and a fear brimming with clarity before our smallness and subjection.

Did I have an appointment with this clarity? Who knows. I don't pretend to say. I was rousing numb capillaries. Like a cold foot under hot water they sparked with the pinpricks of restored sensation, a tingling and yet unconscious awareness that I was on the cusp of something I would suffer greatly for knowing.

The day began like any other, unassuming, humid. I got up early, made coffee in the room, and drank it over a smoke on the balcony. The pale solvent of morning washed away the remnants of night. A note like lemon essence steeped weakly in the sky. I called the numbers I found listed for the dam in Minersville. The few individuals I got on the line attempted to connect me to the electric company that held the contracts and operated the facility. When it got through to them that I was a journalist, they dug up some media-inquiry contact info. Did I want to be transferred? No thanks. Somehow, after far too long, I found myself talking to a woman who seemed to exist in a reality continuous with my own. I told her I was passing through town and hoped to chat with the chief engineer. Could she give me his number?

She said she couldn't give out personal information, but I could leave a message.

'Right. And hear back from him in two weeks. Any chance I might just . . . *bump into* him somewhere?'

'Anything's possible.'

I laughed. 'What's probable?'

'Taxes. Death.'

'OK, you're good,' I said. 'Do I need to beg? I'm not above it.'

She hesitated. 'Bill gets breakfast at Dotty's a lot of days. You didn't hear it from me though.'

'Hear what?' I said. 'But who did I hear it from if anyone gets around to wondering?'

'Everyone knows Dotty's. People come from miles away.'

'Right. Hey, I didn't catch your name.'

'Catch what?'

The line went dead.

On my way to the diner I tried Ed Yang again and got the same brisk voicemail greeting. I almost felt like it and I were becoming friends. The land turned greener and hillier. Brindled rocks skirted the base of the mountain ridge. Dotty's sat halfway back to Minersville in a hollow by the side of the road. It had an impressive rooftop sign that wasn't lit and small square windows that broke up the long strips of white siding like portholes.

I saw no one who met Bill Swain's description inside. That was his name, I'd found it online with a photo in an ancient press release. But Dotty's was bustling nonetheless. Early as it was, the waitresses had that frazzled manner, and coffee stains on their aprons and blouses, that made it seem like they had been working for hours. Maybe they had. Some leaned against the counters chatting with patrons sitting on stools. I took a booth by the window where I could look out at the road and parking lot through the backward black-and-gold letters of a beer advertisement.

'You have the paper, by chance?' I asked the waitress pouring coffee for me into one of those beige mugs you could take out a car window with.

'The *Record*?' She all but shouted it like I was some muttering youth.

'You have the *Beacon*?'

'We have the *Record*.'

Well, better to light a candle than curse the dark. I took the *Upcountry Record*, covering Minersville, Johnston, and two other nearby towns. It was printed in a nice big font that might have been legible across a football field. The kerning was the work of a psychotic, and the A1 articles got about a sentence and a half in before they were obliged to continue in the later pages' accumulating patchwork of ads. Oh, it warmed my heart—this dignified, haphazard small-town rag, chugging along on articles that could scarcely interest the PTA's most ardent zealots. Underage parties broken up, inconsequential fires, old businesses closing, and teachers winning minor awards—brief victories over a crushing tedium. The volleyball team had made it to divisionals and that was good for the day's lead.

I was halfway through an order of hash and eggs when I saw a large man in clear frame glasses come in. His overalls bore the ARROWHEAD insignia, and he took a seat by himself in a corner booth. One of the waitresses with a coffeepot in one hand and two plates in the other nodded to him and he said something I didn't catch, but which she smiled at. He carried his own paper tucked under his arm. I watched him and waited until he got his food before slipping a few bills under my water glass and walking over.

'Bill,' I said in my hail-fellow-well-met tone.

He looked at me quizzically but took my hand to shake. 'That's my name,' he confirmed.

'Quentin Jones. I'm a reporter. Mind if I join you for a minute?'

'A reporter?' He dabbed toast into his eggs. 'Yeah. Probably I do mind.'

'I'm writing a fluff piece on Dotty's.'

He gave me a wry look. 'You write for the *Record*?'

'Still waiting for the phone call.'

He shook his head. 'Dotty's . . . *Right*.'

'Just one of the angles.'

'Don't tell me. Dam's messing up the trout breeding.'

'Well, is it?'

'How would I know? I don't climb in there with them.'

'No. I wouldn't imagine.'

He sprinkled pepper on his eggs. 'We got the fish ladder. We got the trash rack up from the penstock. I thought you environmentalists *liked* hydropower.'

'I'm a fan.'

'But you've got some gripe or other.'

'I'm certified gripeless.'

'I'll believe it when I don't hear about it.'

'Hey, that's not bad.'

Bill ate quickly and neatly. 'It's not that good,' he said and signaled to the waitress for more coffee. 'What can I do for you, Quentin Jones?'

'Tell me about yourself.'

'You got too many readers or something?'

'Everyone says you're the guy to talk to.'

'What about?'

'Dam stuff.'

He looked at me skeptically. 'Balancing the headwater flow and the tailrace? Keeping the intake up to power demand while maxing out efficiency? That sort of thing?'

'For instance.'

He scoffed. The waitress swung by and refilled our coffees with a stern look for me.

'I want to know what happens when someone comes along and says, "Hey, Bill, we're going to need a lot more juice coming out of the dam for, oh, the foreseeable future."'

'Who's this someone?'

'It's not Rachel Carson.' I watched him pour a creamer into his coffee. 'Say it's a guy with one of those badges that flip open.' He didn't say anything or look up but I could tell he was listening more closely. 'See, Bill, I know this gentleman who fishes downriver. Roland's his name. Not what you'd call a titan of industry, but he keeps his eye on the water. And he tells me there's just a biblical *flood* coming down his way.'

'This friend got a screw loose?'

'Oh, he's certifiable. But I don't think he's making it up.'

'And it's wreaking havoc on the spawning grounds, I just bet.'

'Between you and me, I don't give a fuck about the spawning grounds. Maybe the goddamn mountain vole's dying too and there aren't enough handkerchiefs in the world. What I want to know is where all that extra water comes from.'

'Do I look like some sort of rain god to you, Mr. Jones?'

'Quentin works.'

'I can't melt the snow. I can't summon the rain. I get water the same way anyone else does. All I can do is collect it when it comes, and the longer I hold it the more it evaporates.'

'The impoundment.'

'Right. We're running at good efficiency—eighty, eighty-two percent—about as much as you could hope for from an older facility.'

'There didn't happen to be any . . . pushes to modernize recently.'

'Well, lookee there! A sensible question. I thought a city reporter like you might have got to it quicker.'

I ignored this but noted with an inward slap of the forehead that the paper laid aside on the table was none other than the *Beacon*.

'Pretend I slept through Intro to Dam Science,' I said. 'Pretend I don't know anything.'

'Oh, I'm convinced of it,' said Bill. 'But it's your loss.' He was done with his breakfast, put his silverware and napkins on his plate and pushed the plate to the side. 'Topic's interesting as hell . . .' He took a napkin from the dispenser and drew a rough schematic. Say you want to update an old facility, he explained. First, you have to shut down the turbines, one at a time, and either run the water over the spillway or else fill up the reservoir. Then you get in there and update the mechanism. Brand new stator and rotor. They had come a long way with conducting materials. New alloys and composites for the shaft and runner. The ordinance these days was designed using computer programs. Trial-and-error number crunching to optimize new architecture for the scroll case and guide wheel. Even the shape of the penstock and draft tube, though you couldn't change those so much after the fact. But these small redesigns, tweaking the geometry just so—it was a big step forward. 'And there's new software to manage the flow to a fare-thee-well. I'm near on obsolete,' he concluded.

'But you still go in.'

'A force of habit, I guess. I could watch on the computer monitor at the office, wait around till something went wrong. But I like the routine.'

'When did this all take place?'

'Almost three years ago.'

'And whose big idea was it?'

'It's public record. You want me to do your homework for you?'

'I wouldn't complain.'

'Arrowhead. They did the work. But there was federal money too. Our redoubtable senator Chaz Douglass got on a kick about clean energy.'

'So where else in the state expanded?'

'*Good* question.'

This all made sense. Chaz was a hawk on the subcommittee for energy security. He cared about clean energy the way a junkyard dog cares about clean puddles.

'And when did they start running the Amazon through these new generators?'

'That was after we put in the recovery pump.'

'Let's stick with the idea that I don't know stuff.'

'So I can't make it rain, remember? But we can store some of the runoff downstream from the dam and pump it back up to the impoundment when overall demand is low. At night, say.'

'Clever.'

'We're still draining the hell out of the reservoir. But with the weather hotter these days, there's more overall flow.'

'How long's it been?'

'Between you and me. Since March.'

'What happened in March?'

'No idea.'

'And how long till you're scraping the barrel?'

'Depends on rainfall, but let's say we can keep it up through August, early September.'

'And then?'

'We wait for nature to refill our glass.'

'You never told me, who comes and says, "Hey, Bill, it'd be awfully nice of you if you ran your system like there's no mañana."'

'Guy with a badge, like you said.'

'You don't know what sort of badge, do you?'

Bill turned a packet of sugar over in his hand. 'They used to say bacon would kill us. Fat. Now it's these things.' He put the packet down and sighed. 'The guys who stopped by represent a government agency that takes an interest in my work. They discouraged a real cavalier attitude about discussing the substance of our conversation.'

'To what do I owe the friendliness then?'

'You've already guessed *that*.'

'But if you're not thrilled—'

'Why don't I tell you the rest? Let's pretend we just met and you ambushed me at my breakfast spot.'

'Doesn't sound credible.'

'I'm not the only guy with an opinion. I'm just the first one you asked.'

'If the trout could talk . . .'

'Look, it's an open secret around here. Not that anyone cares about the reason. People see the reservoir's low. They're worried about their recreational watercraft.'

'You wouldn't just *hate* to see the issue come up.'

'It's no way to run a dam. But don't quote me on that, Quentin.'

'If I don't quote you period, will you tell me one thing?'

'Maybe. Maybe it won't be the thing you want to hear.'

'Where's the extra juice *going*? Who's drawing it?'

'Now why would I know that? Arrowhead tells me what they need fed into the grid, I do it. I fill the coffers, they draw the balance. I don't audit their spending.'

'And yet something tells me a guy like you might have an idea.'

'Anyone ever tell you you make a lot of assumptions?'

'It's come up.'

'So I imagine this is one of those situations where I say, "You didn't hear it from me, but . . . ," and then it becomes the next guy's problem.'

'That does happen.'

'And I'm guessing you didn't try all the breakfast joints in town.'

'C'mon, Dotty's? People come from miles away.'

'Uh-*huh*.' Bill looked less than 100 percent convinced.

'I'll find out one way or another,' I said. 'But you can save me a few hours.'

'Lots of construction around Johnston these days,' he remarked. 'Office parks, government facilities . . . You should do a little tour. Write a piece on the Great Johnston Renaissance.'

'Hole up with a filing cabinet for an afternoon: property records, permissions, variances . . . I'm getting the sense you're no fan of exurban renewal.'

He sipped his coffee, staring out the window. 'It's not a whole lot to look at, but it's a nice place,' he said. 'Good people. Honest. Used to be most of us were in coal, like my dad.'

'That right?' I murmured.

'Well, industry comes, industry goes. And these days it goes more than it comes. You want our coal for your plants? Fine. Now you want our water? But what comes back is cents on the dollar, and if we ran out of what God put in these hills nothing would come back. We'd get forgot faster than that.' He snapped his fingers, a pale light in his eye. 'I don't know who thinks we don't notice.'

I gave Bill my number and told him to give a ring if he thought of anything else. He sat there gazing out the window, I could see him from the parking lot as I got into my car. He brought his coffee to his lips contemplatively and I started the engine.

It didn't take long in Johnston's buildings department to turn up a lead. A facility southeast of the city center belonging to a larger complex called Norstar had undergone an overhaul a few years back. Searching an online directory of industry newsletters, I found a notice about the project in a survey of veterans-administration expansions. The dates lined up well enough. This was accomplished in a morning's work, a few hours of digging. It hadn't even taken me to lunch.

I called the main line for the Takashi-Hoffman Institute as I drove over. It seemed pointless to try Yang's office again. The receptionist had a haughty manner but she confirmed that Dr. Yang was on leave.

'*Still?*'

When she didn't respond to a question she had already answered I said, 'How long's he been on leave?'

'He's . . . let's see. We're coming up on his third year.'

'That seems like a long time.' The receptionist kept silent. 'Does it say where he is?'

'There's a note that he's working on something called Atopos at AIIS. That's all I can tell you.'

'When's the note from?'

'It doesn't say.'

'Do you have a way to reach him?'

'I can connect you to his office.'

I said I'd tried that. Several times, in fact. I said it was vital I get in touch with Ed. He'd be sorry to miss me.

'But he didn't give you a way to reach him?' The slight lift of a question softened the accusation.

'He must have assumed I knew. Doesn't anyone there know how to reach him?'

I was put on hold for a few minutes, and when the receptionist came back on she told me that any inquiries for Dr. Yang had to run through the communications office.

'Is that unusual?'

'We try to protect our researchers' time,' she said. 'Anything else?' I said that was OK.

To hear Enoch and Hassie tell it, Ed was a visionary. The *roshi* of their spirit quest. Someone who saw life in enough of its naked truth to believe he could recreate it, starting not with *it*, but with *us*. With reality as we understood it, experienced it, and projected it forward. We'd fill in the gaps. Such a notion challenged the reporter's credo, which proposed a unitary reality for the knowing and taking. And if we could accept that some part of reality existed out there and some part inside us, would we ever agree on where one stopped and the other began?

I don't know what assurance I expected. I wanted to believe that in the guise of journalist I was more than another modern griot singing the stories of our tribe. I wanted purpose beyond the martyr's share, a part in the fight Spearman's futuristic vision promised, which saw governments vying to keep pace with the virtualization of life, and nests of knotted stories clotting and obscuring the truth. I meant to fight the fight: against the power that gave us the story we wanted, told us what we liked to hear, and did this to keep us moving down the channel of existence set out for us. But what if this frightful vision of the future was already the world we lived in and the forking paths in our narrow grooves only the illusion of choice?

I cut south and west along a rural highway that shimmied through lush country. A summer lethargy stayed the air. Greenery draped the roadbed and vines braided the trees. Cottonwoods speckled with erratic sunlight. Dirt roads spurred off, perpendicular through the high grass over streambeds to quiet farms in the crooks of hills. I crossed a set of five-ton bridges and descended from highland to valley, where the old north–south and east–west rail lines once met like axes on a grade-school graph. Here the mouths of new developments opened onto parcels littered with identical homes.

This was where I'd find Norstar. The roadside commerce at the turn-off looked like a carpet of debris. Swinging left into a veil of pines, I passed along the branching roads that knit the complex together until I found the turnoff for the imaging center, announced in chrome block letters sitting on a grass knoll under a bright spill of sunlight. The building had a zebra motif, horizontal bands of silver-white paneling and impenetrably dark plate glass alternating floor by floor. It rose just higher than the sparse forest around it.

I was surprised to find no security checkpoint or gate at the entrance to the development. A parking lot girded the building, full of gleaming cars. Balloons in lilac and white flew in grape-bunches from the awning over the entrance patio where a few small groups stood talking. The air smelled of flowers and exhaust, hot pavement, and drifts of pollen with a milk-sweet scent. I circled the building and parked in its shadow.

A tall man in a doctor's white jacket and seafoam scrubs leaned against the door of an open car, talking into a cell phone. His gaze passed over me. Steam or smoke of some sort blew up through the metal exhaust chimneys behind the building, bulbous steel structures in ringed segments that were comically stout beside the wispy beards they released into the sky.

'What's going on?' I asked when the man put down his phone.

He glanced at me and rolled his eyes. 'Another one of these dentist conventions. Don't ask.'

He was right. There was a letterboard plaque near the portico welcoming a delegation of oral surgeons. They chatted among one another in the sun, jackets slung over their shoulders. I considered what it would take to pose as one. I had leftover conference IDs on lanyards in the car. You turned the ID backward, an old journalist's trick. But I dismissed the idea. I didn't know what I was looking for, and if I had an idea that the building itself would disclose its purpose I was mistaken. The automated doors slid open to reveal a modest guard's station, housed behind a stone countertop, black and flecked with glinting mica, a bank of closed-circuit monitors.

The guard's tired eyes were skeptical. 'Conference?'

'I'm looking for Dr. Gove,' I said.

'Gove?' He uttered the name like it was a ludicrous or nonsensical request. 'Did they give you a temporary pass?'

'There was a mix-up with the pass. They told me just to announce myself.'

He clicked through various pages I couldn't see on his computer. 'You have an appointment,' he said like it wasn't a question.

'That's right.' I drummed my fingers on the smooth black stone. 'If you could tell Dr. Gove that Quentin Jones is here to see him.'

He motioned for me to wait on an armless bench across the hall, the sort of palm-up gesture that passes for politeness but has the peremptory quality of an order given to a dog. He pressed a button on his phone, was connected, and had a brief conversation. I could just make out: '. . . Gove.' 'Yes.' 'I see.' 'Yes.' A glance at me. 'All right.'

'Dr. Gove isn't available,' he told me.

'Is that all?'

His lead-lidded eyes seemed to say what he thought of this question. 'Yes.'

'Too late to join the conference?' I asked. He didn't return my smile. 'Can you take a message for me? Tell Gove our friend Bruce Willrich said we should touch base. Willrich. Got that?' He made a note of it so laboriously he might have been copying an illuminated manuscript. I rapped my knuckles on the countertop. 'Nice work they did on the renovation, huh?'

He met me with a stony gaze and, knowing I'd get no further, I left. But I'd seen the center of the labyrinth. The shell of it at least. It *was* an impassive office building, the type of blank-faced facility that dots the suburbs everywhere, steel and concrete, a square block rising from the earth and glinting in the angled light with the self-contained mystery of an Egyptian pyramid. That holy, that banal. It seemed hardly equal to what it contained.

Back at the motel I paced for a time, wondering what I had to do but twiddle my thumbs. I wanted to call Cy, to hear her voice and lose myself in the minutiae of her day. I'd taken this escape for granted for so long, the refuge of another's life, and really our lives are little more than a sequence of globed realities, starting with our own delusion and moving out by concentric rings. If the loss of sanity affects us pitilessly, the loss of this second-order reality forged with another isn't much easier to take.

Maybe this is what loneliness is. And was that what overcame Bruce in the wilds of a ravaged land? I hadn't thought about him so much in years, leafing through the worries and regrets that chase a mind into the night. But he'd been brought back to me. And out of maybe no more than projection I believed I now understood how he felt, when he found himself cut off from all of us all those years ago, away from family and home, spurred by the urge that digs into the flesh of our resolve and pushes us on in the teeth of loneliness, as if the only way out might be through the clarity of pain. Why do we suffer? I don't know unless it is to die without regret—regret at not having fought to the full length of our tether to overcome ourselves and pass into the promise of self-creation.

No, I wouldn't call Cy. Not to retreat down those shoddy ladder rungs from the promontory of my solitude. Not now. My thoughts mapped onto a helpless irrelevance, my tininess, weakness, isolation. I inhabited a consciousness too vast for the circumstances: a motel room with a cloth-thin rug, curtains through which the brightness of day hardly penetrated, a telephone that might not have rung in years, a hard thin bar of soap chalking a machined oval in the countertop. These were the dimensions of my solitude.

Michael called toward midafternoon. The day's heat had left me sprawled out on the bed with the AC running, the air's humidity folding back into an awful chill. I took the call on the walkway.

'How goes the shadow war?' I asked, peering out into the vivid afternoon.

'We might have scored a victory,' Michael said. 'Henry's been out pounding the pavement.'

'Good. He needs the exercise.'

'He's a new man.'

'You can't mean he's happy.'

'He just smiles and smiles . . . Maybe it's that you've been away.'

'I thought absence made the heart grow fonder.'

'There had to be fondness to start.'

I laughed. 'Can't argue with that. So what's the news?'

'Henry turned up a list. He wanted me to run some names by you.'

'Couldn't have called himself?'

'I don't think he wants the "I told you so's."'

The day glimmered. Birds on the electric wires turned their heads in sharp increments. 'I'd never.' Michael let my fib pass by.

'You'd press him, and he won't tell anyone where this comes from.'

'Looked like the cat that got the canary, did he?'

'There was a slight grin.'

It was a roster of personnel tasked to the initial iteration of SIMITAR. We didn't know their affiliations, but I would have guessed mostly intelligence or military with a background in clandestine work. DO liked a small cadre of elite operators with experience in the field, guys with a broad skillset, light footprint, and ingrained respect for chain of command. Their role was to achieve the objective, not to choose it. And maybe there was a comfort in carrying out others' anguished decisions and bearing no responsibility for the errors, the counterfactuals, the tough calls. Michael told me the sheet he had was a noisy photocopy, rife with redactions. The names washed over me as he read. They meant nothing to me—nothing at all until he mentioned Lance Berryman.

I almost asked him to go back but I caught myself, let him finish, and asked him to read the list through once more. I trusted Michael, but this was too important. The full weight of the revelation hadn't even hit me and I needed to think through its implications.

'Anything?' he asked. There'd been maybe twenty names.

'I'm embarrassed to say no.'

He whistled a thin note. 'The dots can't always line up. Otherwise we'd be out of a job.'

'You made Henry sound so proud.'

'He'll live.'

'Tell him thanks anyway.'

Katz-Wallace fell quiet a second. 'Everything OK?'

'Yeah, yeah,' I said. 'Tell Henry to dig up something useful before bothering me.'

I'd recovered just in time, but I was shaken. Once again my body

knew the import before my mind did. Lance Berryman? It made no sense.
Lance was the chief source for my earlier reporting, as I've said. My man
on the inside, called by duty, or persuaded by my ability now and again
to awaken a slumbering conscience, to divulge the tail-chasing inanity of
the new interrogation regime. But Lance had been an evaluator, brought
in when the program blew up in the wake of the Ismail Kamari disaster.
He couldn't have been there from the get-go, not without deceiving me.
And he hadn't known, as far as I could figure, about VIRTUE, the plot to
marry the old program launched under Brantley to the new technology
the AIIS team was developing.

Lying in bed in the darkened motel room, listening to the low grumble of the air-conditioning, I could picture Lance twirling his neat rye in
a rocks glass while his face worked itself into a fey, troubled smile. All
you need is one big coup to justify your medieval inquisition, he said.
One blockbuster feat of revelation. We love to say torture doesn't work,
but what if it *did*? He could grin in a way that seemed sorrowful and
warmhearted at once. Would we ride that dark horse into the sunset? He
released the question like a small winged creature to hang and beat away
from us on the air. But we'd found a way around torture, he went on. The
physical sort at least. What we did to a human's dignity, to the integrity
of a soul, if we didn't inflict corporal pain appeared to be of little concern. The utilitarian calculus suffices. Security at all costs. Keep the perp's
head from banging on the doorframe of the cruiser when you toss him
in the back. Whose interest—whose security—this served we never quite
got around to answering. Lance had seen kids like him locked up for as
long as he could remember, growing up in the poor urban wastes, where
public housing cast its carceral skeleton against the bleak sky. The blocks
in winter were filled with floating ash. Cold brick monuments, concrete
pathways among concrete buildings, below rusted fire escapes and shuddering streetlights, blinking white lines. No one expected you to emerge
from this void, this emptiness in the imagination of history. He'd clawed
his way up from nothing, a big strong kid who couldn't see past his hands
without glasses and had a knack for systems. He laid this out over many
months. You would have sworn he came up through operations but he

was an analyst all the way. And so he knew only too well how a losing strategy knit itself from the fibers of so many tactical wins. Damn near every kid he grew up with who found a neat bank shot to capital wound up under state supervision or worse.

By the time Lance's path bisected my own he'd been watching reams of raw transcript cross his desk for months. It wasn't hard to get Kamari and others like him telling stories. Like we say in the business, the problem isn't getting the asshole to talk. It's getting him to shut up. This was fanciful stuff. You couldn't have carved fact from fiction with an X-Acto. Lance explained how motivated reasoning and confirmation bias steered his colleagues not to truth but to what they wanted to believe, what they had decided the truth was ahead of time. There's a famous story of a horse who could do arithmetic, Lance told me. Clever Hans. Ask him a sum and he'd stomped out the answer with his hoof. People were enthralled. Even his trainer bought the act. Well, it turned out Hans was clever, but not how everyone thought. His talent was to read the trainer's body language, sense the expectancy, that straining desire on his trainer's part as he struck his final hoofbeat. Right answer, wrong reason. Now if a *horse* could figure that much out . . .

Lance was the kind of source you dream of—smart enough to get your angle but motivated by considered passion. Talking with him felt like riffing with a buddy. Had I been stupid? It wouldn't have been the first time. But I also wasn't born two days before tomorrow, and that meant handicapping the retrospective censure. Lance seemed like the real thing. I didn't often miscalculate this badly. He simply bled too much angst to be playing a role. Or that's what I thought. That's what it looked like. No one so intelligent could feign conscience like he did without having mortgaged his soul and knowing it. I wanted to help him. I convinced myself—and this is our greatest sin, isn't it, our professional hubris?—that helping myself meant helping him too.

We met at odd hours, often evenings between the end of work and dinnertime, those moments when people are preoccupied and things go unnoticed. Once, we sat in the stands of a high school soccer game, beneath vibrant skies whorled with clouds the color of dying reefs. Or we struck up a conversation in some oaky bar, two guys at the end of the counter, getting a drink after work. Nothing necessitated the spy-movie routine. By any measure of tradecraft our hijinks were a joke. We got a kick out of it, though. When I could, I made sure to get meetings with his colleagues on the books—on whatever pretext—just to get my name in the ledger in case the agency ever decided to investigate my sourcing. An old ruse. Lance didn't always hand over the jewels but he shepherded my search. He painted the landscape and corrected me gently when I missed the spinney for telephone poles. I still had to pull the fabric apart by its loose threads. He couldn't risk being my lone source, and I couldn't risk giving him the impression he was.

A common enough play. To get your foot in the door with anyone usually involves cultivating the illusion that you're talking to everyone. Drop a few casual details into conversation—project names, the patronymics of a few classified detainees. Introduce this into the discussion as baseline reality, not as facts to be established, but stuff everyone knows. Appear to give more than you get. Soon your source will build out an extravagant idea of what you're read in on. He'll start believing *he's* the one who stands to gain by the providential tête-à-tête. Half the time his scheming gears get turning. That's good. Let him think you're the patsy, the mark. To keep his little spycraft play alive, he'll start teasing out the line to keep you on the hook. That means giving you what you want, and sometimes what you don't know to ask for. Once the source decides you're the naive one, it's simple enough to get tacit confirmation for hearsay. Then you subtly turn the tables and stoke the source's own anxieties about staying relevant to *you*.

With Lance I could drop all that. Our game ran as smooth as a three-man weave. He wasn't my mark, and I wasn't his. At least it didn't seem possible that I was at the time. He always knew just the breadcrumb I needed to inch forward. Something so subtle and slight it was like he hadn't spoken at all. We handled our business in the briefest exchanges at the end of our talks. The rest was stories—life in the alleywork grid, metal fences gelid with the breath of winter, tumbledown blocks of intermittent electricity. Lance remembered doing his calculus homework before the open stove they ran through January when the heat went out.

I got lucky, he said. One day, when he was about ten, he stopped horsing around in class long enough to glance up at the chalkboard. He didn't think he'd ever paid that surface, filled with its arcane symbols, any attention. He was simply tired of roughhousing that afternoon, the energetic despair of a mind uncultivated and malnourished; and he looked up like he would see right through the charade, through this opaque language meant to impress on him the hopelessness of existence. And he realized, running his eyes over the board and following the teacher's words, that he understood the abstract recipes she'd scrawled out in chalk. He got the system that sat behind them . . . in a flash. That's how he remembered it, that fast, that intuitive. It was the most rudimentary algebra. No *Gaussian* genius, he said, laughing lightly. For some people, these things just make sense. Some people put pen to paper and call a world to life. Some hear a note and can tell you what it is. But most people need someone to hold their hand, to walk them through. Could I imagine growing up where that never happens, where you get one glance at a chalkboard and either you see it or you don't? And that's your life right there, set out before you by the lottery of intuition, a genetic quirk. I had the grammar preinstalled, Lance told me. Lucky me. Don't ask me how or why. And don't start thinking there's any justice to it.

I watched the crimson lozenges on the digital alarm clock reconfigure, recalling Lance and our conversations with a smile. It was these sorts of stories that made me believe he was in earnest. Hell, I never questioned it. It never occurred to me to doubt him. He told me about fighting his way into college on a sports scholarship, despite having no interest in sports. At six feet five, that was all people could think when they saw him. He didn't know how the system worked: the right tests to take, the places to apply to, the things to say. His family didn't have money for school, either. He ended up dropping football in sophomore year and studying physics with a minor in computer science.

I went into intelligence, he said, because they were the first people who looked at me and saw the skills I could offer them—nothing more, nothing less.

And thanks to the job, Lance saw a bit of the world. By the time I got to know him he'd lived in the capital for years, a creature of the agency. But as a younger recruit he'd done tours abroad. Despite his love for the agency and all it had given him, he knew it required dissidents on the inside. No. *Because* of his love for it, he knew this. Dissent *was* love. To live up to its mission the agency needed personnel committed to a cause greater than the institution. Lance was loyal to the country not because it had given him what it liked to pretend it gave its children, that turgid mythology. You love it *because* it's failed you, he said. Because you get to love first, without requital. Those are the politics of love. No one gets to tell you how to spend your loyalty, your love. It's an act of defiance to love what doesn't love you back.

In this strange sentimental geometry, warped and stretched over the still-beating heart, a triangle could compose from right angles. Involute surfaces switched back in their dimensions like a leporello. Pockets of contradiction could infect the creases and endure for decades. Lance compared the agency and its siblings to the immune system. Does an immune system love its body? he mused. These institutions existed to protect the country from infection and attack, but how they understood their job, and what exactly they understood protection to mean, bled over into a wish for a different country. One more amenable to their work. This could divert the mission by degrees, until it faced backward. You had to protect what was there, not change what was there to make it protectable. When the immune system gets too powerful and grows without checks of its own, Lance said, it attacks the body. It's as deadly as a virus or a pathogen. As problematic, he meant, as an attack from without. The system sees threats everywhere, and instead of loving the body it has evolved to protect, it grows to hate the body for its vulnerability, the way a parent can hate the fear their love exposes them to.

That's why Lance had to care for the country first, even a country as undeserving as ours. He couldn't honor his work without honoring the thing his work served. And this, I believe, is what united us, what must unite us: this allegiance to ideals that sit above our near affiliations—to the self, the job, the institution, the role. The knowledge that we are keepers and protectors, arrayed not only against the outside threat, but against the inside threat too, the threat our own power amounts to once we decide that we know best. It is only human to want to seize the reins and fix what ails us. But this is what we must fear most of all: the false equation of power with wisdom, our reflex to choose an expedient good over a muddled process. The process, we must understand, is everything: means and end. The process *is* the ideal, and thus what our noblest energies must fall to protecting. For the process is the balance that makes an organism healthy and adaptive. That which allows it to respond to truth and to lie, to stasis and change. We may see worthy goals at hand, but only the organism of justice, so much larger than any one of us, can sum these goals to form the larger vision we call a people. A civilization. This vast addition outstrips our minds' ability. And few can summon that peculiar love that is love for other people's freedom to let us down.

This, I think it's fair to say, was Lance's way of looking at things. He saw systems and dreamt of their clockwork, as if so much time grappling with human disorder pushed his thoughts above the clouds to that place where sunshine reigns and bodies turn with mathematical precision. The mind's escape to such a realm is our gift, but also our danger. We prefer to dream than see our theories tarnish in the dirt and sludge of life.

Lance had a favorite joke, which he uttered whenever another norm of decency fell to the cruel moldboard of history. *Entropy isn't what it used to be*, he'd say. Clearly he felt a certain nostalgia for the simpler, cleaner problems of the past. I never knew whether he saw this as the wistful and sentimental view it was, or whether he actually believed today's issues turned on baser motivations than those of an earlier age. Either way he drew inspiration from a time when the sense of mission was more easily distinguished from turf battles in the bureaucracy and other political calculations.

But now it turned out that Lance wasn't who I thought. He'd told me the story I wanted to hear, lured me into a trap, or else set out, one by one, the planks of what I fashioned into a story of my own. Merely a program evaluator. That was his line. A consultant brought in to review the efficiency and aims of SIMITAR, horrified at what he found. But if Henry's roster was legit—and Henry had no reason to know Lance's name, much less that Lance and I were talking—I could scarcely work my way back through all the layers of implication to know where I stood, whom I could trust, or what I had even done on my own. Was it possible that this whole story had been laid out before me like flagstones beneath the Tarpeian Rock?

A brief inventory, then. I was shaking in the air-conditioned chill as I made notes on a scrap of paper I would later burn. Here was what I could make out: The appearance of Bruce couldn't be a coincidence, although whether I or Bruce came first in the order of operations was a different matter. The time frame suggested by Bill Swain and the renovations at Norstar, which agreed in broad outline with what Simmons had intimated and Roland's riverside vigilance had accidentally discovered, set certain bounds on the project: three years of active development at most, and no more than four months since the program went operational. This of course meant that the groundwork had begun under the previous administration, as I knew, but the brazen methods on display bore none of the hallmarks of Brantley or his people. Dietrich surely was involved, and Athos and its various subsidiaries, and now, it seemed, Chaz Douglass. The timeline in fact cast back neatly to the midterm elections, when Douglass and Haig took their committee chairs after the chamber flipped. But if my involvement wasn't accidental, and it no longer seemed credible to believe it was, Spearman's plea for my help looked like idle flattery at best and quite possibly something more sinister. Whom could I trust? Rich Jarosok? Enoch Niels? Parisa? Hassie? Did it behoove me to start wondering how Rob and buddies like Chaz had found the gumption to start prepping this years in advance? Well, I'd known Parisa long enough to give her a pass. But her warning to leave the story alone now rang in my ears at a different pitch.

My temples throbbed. I felt the blood in them slug around my skull. Too narrow, the confines that hold a mind. When the world beyond turns against you and you are left on an island with your convictions, the space allotted by nature isn't sufficient. The resources at your command can't outgrapple a reality that fails to confirm your biases, that smashes the simple illusions of order and loops the running stories you live by in long threads that circle back, fankle, knot. If you can trust no one else, you can't trust yourself. If objective reality tilts too far in its imperfection, subjective reality no longer has any meaning. The walls close in—those cheaply papered motel walls, burgundy with a weaving pattern embossed to the touch like a doily. Mind, skull, wall, room. I wanted the certainty of simple things. The comfort of a problem I could articulate, look at in full, and master. Something that submitted to the hands and had no business with abstraction or deceit.

I had to leave town, leave Johnston. I had to start doing what no one expected of me, which meant isolating instinct inside myself and acting against it. Only then could I free myself from the web I'd been caught in. I threw the little stuff I had in my bag. I put it in the car and took my room key to the front desk to check out. The same laconic clerk, spitting his rancid tobacco juice, showed no surprise at my leaving late in the afternoon when I'd already paid for the night ahead. Lost in my own thoughts, I offered no excuse. The prospect of spending the night at home in my bed calmed me. The idea of looking at Cy's paintings, which demanded nothing of you and had no purpose other than to be, seemed like an answer to the problems besetting me—this mare's nest of miserable angling, this madness.

And yet my resolve faltered. As I pulled out of the motel and onto the strip a reportorial reflex kicked in, and I told myself I'd follow up one last time and exhaust the easy plays before me. This impulse, as the dying sun cut in like a shallow lance, saw me once again idling at the crook of the road by Hunter Gove's home in Beechwood Heights, which glowed, at that hour, with an otherworldly saturation, so much gloss, fresh paint, and acrylic bluegrass. It looked like a video game sprung to life, knocked out into three dimensions.

I considered leaving a note. I could have phoned again or walked right up and knocked on the door. It was just after five, early evening. Gove might have been there. My indecision fluttered in the soft air.

Thought bobbed gently in the day's candied light. We are helpless before these hot still evenings, so rich you can almost touch the immaterial
dimension, sense its buttery essence on your fingers, moments when an
intimation suggests time will stretch on forever, that the shadows will
lengthen indefinitely and vision and light will somehow punch past the
limits of clarity to a more exact and transparent state . . . I returned, along
the links of association, to childhood, to my grandparents' farm, to Hassie's homestead in the country, which her child would never know, to my
vacations with Cy and her longing, real or not, for a simple life, to memories of the earth, from which we spring, golden fields and cottages, the
murmuring of creeks, melting snow dripping from the eaves in plinks,
cracklings, the efflux of the life, that raw evidence of things awaking and
comingling and reconstituting the inexhaustible forms of being: oaks,
ravens, reeds, stone. I felt the respiration of nature on my cheek, nature's
aura in that artificial place composed, like everything, of an organic substrate, and mimicking what we have grown too impatient to let flower under time's humane administration. What horrible impatience marshals
us like dogs? What ambition wraps us in its blindfold and sends us down
these miserable paths, when the materials of contentment lie around us in
abundance? I was thinking this when a knock on the car window startled
me. Standing outside the passenger door was a lean man of Mediterra-
nean complexion with dark hair graying at the edges. I knew him from
his photo online. He wore neither glasses nor the clothes one associates
with a doctor, and still he gave off a clinician's air, an acuity I've always
associated with criminals and physicians. I wondered how he'd surprised
me before remembering that, once upon a time, Hunter Gove had been
a military man.

'Doctor.'

'Mr. Jones,' he said, just a millisecond late, as if unknown calculations were taking place behind those beetling brows. 'We've been . . . well,
expecting you.' He laughed lightly.

'I get that too often these days,' I said, rising from the car. The door
I leaned against held the warmth of the sun. Then I heard what he'd said
a second time. 'We?'

'Yes. Ed and I. And Nadia.' We looked at each other, sifting through different considerations. 'I don't think you know Nadia, but Ed said you've been trying his office.'

'Do you ever get the sense that people are watching you?'

He smiled grimly. 'I *do* work for the military.'

His face conveyed an unexpected compassion. He wore tailored khakis and a checked gingham shirt with the sleeves rolled up. I could read nothing in his look so much as a certain calm clarity, as if behind our conversation he were judging attitudes and moods too fine for untrained eyes. He didn't inspire mistrust, but he gave off a patient, almost dreamy attentiveness that made you wonder whether your purposes matched his own.

He gestured to the house. 'Won't you come in?'

'I was just on my way out of town.'

He showed no reaction to this news. 'Maybe you'd like to meet Ed first,' he said.

'Ed could have called me.' He didn't respond. 'Forgive me if I'm not at my most trusting.'

'I understand.'

He let this hang between us and glanced pacifically at the fading sun, shading his eyes with a hand. He was smiling, or almost smiling, the way someone remembering something bittersweet might.

In fact, I did know who Nadia was. She had been quoted in the article about Dr. Gove which Rob had given me. Was I to conclude then that Gove was unaware of my talk with Spearman?

'How does a military man take to working with a contractor?' I asked.

'The pay's better.'

'And the bosses?'

He smirked. 'Are you asking if Rob and I get along?'

'Couldn't have said it better myself.'

'Do you like working for your paper, Mr. Jones? Or let me ask it a different way. Do you think you work for the paper or for your readers?'

'I'd do the same work at a different rag.'

'And yet papers need publishers, owners, boards, earnings . . .'

'A necessary evil.'

'Couldn't have said it better myself.' He'd come around to my side of the car and now held out a hand for me to shake. 'Hunter.'

'Quentin.'

The firmness of his grip was strange against the birdlike delicacy of his hand.

'I think you'll find we share certain . . . concerns.'

'There's sharing, and there's sharing,' I said. 'Look, if I go in with you I'm going to need some answers.'

'Answers . . .' He raised his eyebrows expectantly. 'About what?'

'Cuber, what it really is.'

'Cuber . . .' He seemed not to understand. Then he understood. 'Oh, you mean the cave. But that's what we want to talk to you about.'

He moved ahead of me before I had agreed to anything with an assurance that I would follow. That calm clarity in his demeanor exerted a firm pull, like some soft voice which entrances us—charmed snakes held by an invisible lure. I did follow. The steps up from the curb had the blanched look of new concrete, stainless and sharp lined. Gove skipped up them. I saw the wall-mounted mailbox still had a sticker with installation instructions on it. This was a stage set more than anything. I'd rarely felt as defenseless as I did entering that nameless bit of tract housing. The enduring brightness of the day, the heat massing behind the windows and glass doors, everything made for such an odd moment to find three people—work colleagues!—together at home. There was Nadia, and there was Ed, arrayed as if to film a sitcom. We entered the dining room and sat down, the four of us at the table with coffee in the middle. Nadia was the youngest. She was in her thirties, I'd have guessed, bespectacled with brown hair gathered neatly at the back of her head. Ed was short, a youthful fifty, with a smile fixed to his face like the residue of an energy he was helpless to dissipate.

'It's disconcerting,' I said, helping myself to a cup of coffee, 'when the people you've gone looking for all turn out to be waiting for you.'

Ed laughed inordinately at this. I had the sense that he would have laughed at anything I said, as if responding to the novelty of a talking animal. 'One's theory of reality,' he said, intuiting perhaps that I needed one, 'is one's expectation of what will happen next.' He squinted at me. 'The more inaccurate your expectation turns out to be, the more reality . . .'—he enacted a small explosion with his hands.

'Quentin's worried he's being set up,' Hunter explained.

'Because he's rational,' said Ed. 'Because he is.'

'Not by us,' Nadia said.

'Well, partly by us.' Ed smiled at me beneficently. 'We are . . . here to meet him after all.'

'What I want to know is why me?' I said.

Nadia gave Hunter a look like they'd perhaps misjudged me. 'You don't know?'

'Because of Bruce,' I said. 'But I don't buy that either. Where did Bruce come in?'

'Bruce works for Drayman,' said Hunter.

'Since when?' He shrugged and shook his head. I looked at him incredulously, and then at the rest of them. 'Is this trial by ambush? Either you start leveling with me or I'm out. I can't guess everything you know and don't know.'

'We want to be helpful,' said Nadia unhelpfully.

'Bruce's role, then. I assume there are more like him?'

'It's very delicate,' said Nadia, 'who you choose to send in. It's another world, almost another planet.'

'Cosmonauts,' Ed announced.

'Astronauts,' Hunter corrected gently. 'We say astronauts, Ed.'

'You're talking about . . . explorers, scouts?' I offered. 'An advance guard?'

'Observers,' said Hunter. 'The technology's brand new.'

'New and *secret*,' said Ed.

The routine was getting old, the opéra bouffe act. A fake faience dish sat in a metal stand on an oak cabinet. The walls were painted a faultless, cloying eggshell. Everything in the place looked phony. If you took a pen-knife to the veneer, I thought, you'd find a doll's batting behind it, paper and particleboard—a material abyss.

'I get it,' I said. 'The volunteers had to be discreet. But what were they doing?'

'We had to know it worked.' Nadia peered out the window. 'That it was safe.'

'We're studying effects on the body and the mind,' said Hunter. 'How long can a person stay in. Ed's confirming that the technology achieves its functional aim.'

'Cognitive assimilation to a virtual space,' he declared.

'Those were your briefs. What about the government?'

'They needed to know the risks. The potential for abuse.'

'Rob already put me to sleep with that fairy tale. The "future of governance."'

'One way to spin it,' said Hunter.

'Mr. Spearman is most interested in applications.' Ed rubbed his fingers together. 'Market opportunity.'

'What about other applications? Interrogation, say.'

Ed's eyes refocused to the distance. Nadia abruptly stood and went to lean against the window frame. For an instant I thought this was a Technicolor melodrama, the color and emotion oversaturated. Hunter tapped on the table, a slight impatient tic. 'This *is* something we worry about,' he said when no one else responded. 'People live in one reality at a time. What you convince the mind is real soon becomes its dominant frame.'

'How, when you're inside one story, can you see around it?' said Ed. 'How can you discern another possible reality within the confines of the first? Dreams within dreams . . .'

I had wondered this myself. Everything I'd reported on had at some point led me to question whether, having got hold of tail or tusk, I mistook the appendage for the creature. Prosecutors call this tunnel vision, the early commitment to a theory of the case.

Ed quickly recovered his lightness. 'One can't imagine a color that doesn't exist. One can't picture an additional dimension. It's like that.'

'But one has memories, no? One remembers the outside world inside the simulation, and the simulated world when one comes out?'

They looked at me uneasily. Then Ed burst out laughing. 'Yes,' he said. 'Maybe!'

'We think so,' said Hunter. 'We don't exactly know.'

Nadia's eyes met his. 'There's so much still to study.'

'Do we remember like we remember yesterday,' Ed mused, 'or like we remember a dream? Do we mnemonically recall via images and sensations, or through emotions?' He stared at me. 'Is memory an image or a feeling? What, Mr. Jones, is the difference?'

Hunter made as if to sneeze but didn't. 'We hardly remember our waking experience with the clarity we think,' Nadia said. 'We mix up time, sequence, who was present, what we said.'

'We know very little about how memory works in real life,' Hunter agreed. 'So we don't have much baseline for comparison.'

'It doesn't sound like that stopped you.'

'We arrived at the point where theory and preparation had gone as far as they could. We needed to send in observers.'

'Empiricism,' said Ed, 'has a subjective character. Does a person think the same way inside as out? Does a flower smell like a flower? Does metal feel like metal? Pain, pain?'

'Does it really matter,' I asked, 'if they say it's a flower? Or pain?'

'Exactly!' said Ed. I didn't know whether he meant that it didn't matter or that this was the essential question.

Nadia straightened the curtain and turned away from the window. 'Ed designed the simulation with a particular quirk.'

'It uses our projections,' I said.

'It was the only way to create a sufficiently rich and flexible environment,' Hunter explained. 'The project would have taken decades without the shortcut.'

Ed wore an inscrutable look. 'In this way it is a dream,' he said. 'But multiple people sharing the same dream . . . And isn't life like that?'

'Perception as an integral illusion,' said Hunter. 'What you take as "outer" is really an internal reverie.'

'A user interface,' said Nadia. 'A tree doesn't look like a tree until there are eyes to see it.'

'Eyes hooked up to a brain that processes optical stimulation in a certain way,' said Hunter. 'Before that, the idea of "look" or "look like" has no meaning.'

'But a tree is still a tree,' I said, 'eyes or no eyes.'

Ed shrugged. 'For a tree there is no "is,"' he said. 'Perhaps "being" is very different for the universe before we show up.'

This was getting too fine for me. 'But what's different . . . in the cave?'

'We don't know if the eye is creating the tree or merely seeing it,' Nadia said.

'That was in my koan calendar the other day.'

'If your mind experiences "seeing a tree," does it matter if it is there or not?' mused Ed. 'You see it either way.'

'So there's no difference.'

'Maybe for one person,' Hunter said. 'But now imagine two people in the simulation.'

'Or imagine returning to the site of some beautiful live oak but not remembering whether there was a tree there or not,' added Nadia.

'The difference between subjective and objective reality.' I sipped my coffee and recalled an old quote. 'Reality is what doesn't go away when you stop believing in it.'

'Right,' said Hunter. 'But what is happening in the code: Is it representing a freestanding tree, so to speak, or only the impression of one?'

'A tree-viewer composite,' said Ed mysteriously.

'I'm afraid I don't get the significance,' I said.

'Maybe the example is too simplistic,' said Hunter. 'A tree isn't dynamically self-modifying.'

Ed nodded at this. 'It's not an evolving loop.'

'What is these days?' I meant it as a joke, but Ed lifted his brow and slowly, drolly, raised a finger until it came to point directly at my chest.

'A tree isn't self-aware.' Nadia stood beside Hunter, her fingers resting on the back of his chair. 'There are certain implications if self-modifying entities are "freestanding" . . . to continue the metaphor.'

I inhaled sharply, seeing. 'You want to know if you've created life.'

'Of a sort.' Ed held up a finger. His smile curled in a wry twist.

'Because—' Hunter began.

'Then you've created death,' I said.

My mind flashed to different things. I thought of Hassie and Nino, the unknowable point at which something that behaves and responds like a person becomes, for all intents, a person. How could we say where and when this occurred? What role did a thing's experience of itself play, if any? And did it matter that one was 'created,' in a sense, since we too were created, and not merely by biology but by one another, by the reality that trained us in its norms, by all those outside forces that pressed in, shaping us to the contours of a world that preceded us? Was the question of whether our existence was freestanding or entangled even coherent? I thought of Cy, how we had created each other over the years, the reality that arose between us. Taking the finest scalpel of the mind, I could find no chink at which to insert the delicate distinction between a creature born of code and a creature born of flesh—not unless I posited a metaphysical dimension for the spirit, a soul I longed to believe in but had no language to body forth. Such a soul would be a kind of dark matter, known by intuition, but inert in its interaction with everything else, everything perceptible and tractable in life. And having found such a quantity, would I be able to say with confidence that what lacked this but nonetheless exhibited love—and pain, and fear, and joy—did not in some sense experience these things as well and, experiencing them, live?

We had been quiet for a minute, perhaps longer. 'People have been dying,' I said.

'Well,' said Hunter. '"People."'

'Businessmen and explorers, settlers from Europe go to the African continent in the nineteenth century,' said Ed. 'They believe they are on a "civilizing mission." But they soon discover their actions have no consequences. Whatever they do, they aren't accountable.' He chuckled very lightly. 'The killing then occurs at a rather remarkable rate.'

I stared at him.

'Without consequences, the depths of human barbarity . . .' Hunter did not finish.

'This was Rob's point. The reason we needed police in our virtual worlds,' I said.

'Yes,' said Nadia. 'A whole new world to govern . . .'

Ed rubbed his fingers together again. 'Police-man, army-man, tax-man . . .'

'An incredible opportunity,' said Hunter. 'To get there first.'

'Proprietary software,' Nadia added.

'Low overhead,' barked Yang.

The sun had passed below the trees outside and the sky shone above the murky yard. Nadia gave Hunter a look, her hand near his shoulder. It was a strange little group. It made me think of Hassie and Enoch, the whole team working together, and the thrill of pushing into new corners of the science, that freewheeling improvisation, conjuring tools from the symbols and images of the mind . . . And finding it *worked!* The intoxication of discovery no doubt left little time or appetite for reflection. And now the tools of dreamers had, as ever, fallen into the hands of barbarians, mercenaries, businessmen.

Weariness had stolen up on me. 'Tell me where I come in again?'

'We don't know who else to turn to.' Hunter spoke with a contrite air. 'We need to get Bruce out.'

'That's Rob's angle.'

'Bruce isn't well,' said Nadia.

'Physically?'

'Perhaps physically too.'

'You mean he's lost his fucking mind.'

'No one's been in as long as he has,' Hunter said.

'So unplug him. Get him out.'

Their glances ricocheted around the table before Nadia said, 'It doesn't work like that.'

'There's a return protocol,' Hunter explained. 'He has to initiate it. It's the only safe way to extract someone.'

'A ferryman across the river . . . ,' Ed murmured.

'At some point you'll have to pull the plug all the same.'

'Maybe,' Hunter admitted. 'As a last resort.'

'Well, and . . .' Nadia glanced at Hunter, who grimaced.

'We haven't been authorized to.'

I must have looked incredulous. 'But you've been authorized to send me in. Jesus.'

A sickening premonition had overtaken me, a fatal intuition. I knew that I'd do it, that I had to, if for no other reason than to see Bruce again and attempt to repay the debt I owed him. Did I owe him a debt? It didn't matter. I *felt* I did. Yet on the threshold of this penetralium I saw only that I'd been entrapped by the momentum of my being, by the harness of duty. Retreat was no more possible at this point than any success or triumph I could call my own. I'd passed too far into the hands of others, the ministry of what I did not understand and couldn't control.

'Rob's banking on your integrity,' Nadia said.

'That when you see what's happened to Bruce, what he's done . . .' Hunter trailed off.

'It's the perfect advertisement for what he's selling. If you see what we mean.'

'Yes . . .' Understanding reached me as the word left my lips: it was our own barbarity that would justify the civilizing project. 'And you're counting on my . . .'

'Yes. Your concern for Bruce.'

'This seems like . . . What's the right way to put it? A terrible idea.'

'We don't believe it's possible to die inside,' said Ed.

'Great.'

'Your body's perfectly safe,' said Hunter. 'Under a light anesthesia, constantly monitored.'

'If the mind believes the body has died, does it die?' Ed wondered aloud.

'We don't think so,' Nadia put in quickly.

'You experience death in dreams,' said Ed. 'It's very common.'

'Yes, and then you wake up,' I said. 'Where is Bruce, by the way? Who's monitoring his light anesthesia?'

'He's perfectly safe,' said Nadia.

'That's not what I asked.'

Hunter took out a handheld device showing a digital readout of fluctuating figures. 'Vitals. If anything goes outside the normal range,' he said, 'I'll get an alert. But that's highly unlikely.'

'So he's nearby.'

'Near enough.'

'I'd like to see him before going in.'

'We can't do that.'

'Can't or won't?'

'He's under lock and key. We couldn't get you in, and we'd be in serious trouble if we tried.'

'Let's at least send him a message,' I said. 'On the inside.'

Nadia shook her head. 'It's not possible.'

Ed explained that the program had to adapt in concert with the brain to achieve an organic interface. The interaction between the two was a first-order communication and didn't pass through any symbolic mediation. 'No images, no sounds,' he said. 'No natural language.'

'We can't translate what's going on in the code into a form that's legible to an outsider,' Hunter summarized.

Something was troubling me. 'Rob showed me a video . . . from *inside* the simulation.'

'Impossible,' Ed said loudly.

'No, we can't do that,' Hunter agreed.

'Then what did I see?'

All three shook their heads, they didn't know. I wanted to bang on the table and insist on the testimony of my eyes. I'd seen people murdered! Massacred! But what did I know for certain? What could I put beyond the cordon of doubt and say was true and not one more attempt to deceive me? My anger died in bewilderment. The crudeness of the fraud felt chintzy even for Rob.

Then a further worry struck me. 'If everything you say is true, how do you know about Bruce's misdeeds? How do you know he isn't well?'

'Field reports,' Hunter said. 'He's not the only observer, of course.'

'There *is* another way.' Nadia looked at Ed, who was sitting back in his chair staring up at the ceiling.

The silence rioted through the evening, hummed like a strobing light. Or this might have been my heart, pulsing into new fissures in reality's firmness. A phone rang in the adjoining room, the digital rendition of a classical standby. No one moved to answer it. When Ed spoke, it was without humor. What is a person? he asked. If you want to know how leaves fall from a branch, you program the physics. For a fly, you code responses to a set of stimuli. This isn't complex. If you want to program a dog, you confront a rudimentary cognition, a layering of protocols representing competing responses. Such response patterns lead to unpredictable behavior but they exhibit what we may call personality, an emergent phenomenon—in effect, a disposition toward behavior.

What connects all of these is a certain internal coherence, he continued. He looked at me but there was no more laughter in his eyes. The behavior may get more complex, but when it occurs, the entire entity shifts with the consequences. Such entities maintain special unities, even as code. A human being involves so many layers of behavioral weighting that the response to any stimulus exhibits chaotic properties—an extreme in systemic complexity. It calls for powerful computers, state-of-the-art processors arrayed in novel nonlinear distributions, to process in real time without a lag.

'But,' he concluded, 'as complex as the representation of a human being is, when it shifts to a new state, like anything else, it shifts together.'

'You can spot it,' I said, not sure I'd understood.

'Yes,' said Ed. 'We can identify an individual within the code.'

'A meta-analysis script detects the size of the data clusters that move together,' Nadia explained.

'And humans are the biggest?'

'By leaps and bounds.'

'It's very beautiful,' said Ed. 'Such immense bodies of data moving together, like a wave, undulating and recomposing . . .' A hint of his humor had returned.

'While it lasts,' Hunter added.

'This is how you know'—I looked for more delicate words—'that in-dividuals have died.'

'Great waves of flowing data,' Ed said, 'flowing, flowing, and then—crash.' He brought his hand over the table. 'Like a huge wave on the beach, washing out and going flat. Then silence. Nothing.'

'The data is overwritten,' Nadia explained. 'That's how you die in a virtual space.'

'And you think this is *safe*?'

'Safe for you,' Hunter said.

'As safe as dreaming,' said Yang.

Nadia's fingers played nervously on the table. 'We think.'

I sighed. 'And if Rob is right?'

'About what?' Hunter watched Nadia's fingers like a cat watches an insect.

'About me.'

Another day had finally expired. A porchlight's glow bled out quickly in the dark grass. Along the fringe of maples the leaves shook in a brief shock of wind and the first pale star muscled through the flat, lucent sky. Maybe it was the sense that I was on the cusp of leaving this world that made me feel tenderly toward it, the way a dying person might look at the sun, late in the day, when it comes overbright through the trees and casts shadows on the window casings. Those dwindling moments in a relationship we have taken for granted. How simple and vivid it all is. Everyone was waiting, quiet. The sound of a furnace switching on in the basement broke our silence—just.

It was Hunter who finally spoke. 'We have to take some risks.'

'I read something,' I said, 'something Bruce wrote.' I explained that Rob had given me a report, possibly a journal entry, and I took the page from my bag and put it on the table. 'I'm not sure I'll recognize the person who wrote this.'

The three of them peered at the copy and looked at one another. Hunter nodded at Nadia, who left and reappeared moments later with a file. She flipped through it until she found the stapled document she wanted and laid it before me. It was written in the same hand. I riffled through the pages.

'It's the same report,' I muttered dumbly.

'The full report,' Hunter said.

They were quiet while I read.

The days have been growing shorter, colder. It seems not long ago that fields of crimson poppies dominated the landscape, but months have passed since then, perhaps an entire season. Time adopts strange properties here, like distances at sea. Yesterday I went with Blaine's men to interview a farmer who wore a dyed beard of lurid orange. We had come to ask about rebel movements through the region, on the trucks that take the crops to market. He didn't know anything and his black eyes bore into us with the nothingness of space. I doubt he knew who was fighting or why.

It is folly to hate the locals and folly even to hate the enemy. You might as reasonably hate a rock, a waterfall. When the wind comes off the Karuq Tal and fills the night with frigid gusts, you could hate that chill before the old man who looks at you like a fruit fly—before him now, dead tomorrow. Some people's eyes move like they are watching not seconds but days. And your hatred has had its fill of cowardice, anyway, the cowardice of those like you who live in seconds and for petty wants. The wants of the body and most of all to live. Since power over others suggests that you will live, you delight in it. Who was it who said that the desire for safety stands against every great and noble enterprise?

I have smiled at sweat beading on the temples and foreheads of men we later killed. Two weeks ago, or perhaps longer, we caught an informant in a lie. He told us the rebels had not passed through M.—— at night, but farther to the north, when the signals chatter told us otherwise. He may have only wanted to spare the raids that would have followed, the firefights and mortars that would rain down on the outlying fields and slopes while we hunkered into another mortal stalemate over an irrelevant way station in an irrelevant war.

I say 'we' as though it were still in any sense my fight, as though I have a say in who lives or dies.

Once an informant turns, like a piece of rotting fruit, you must dispose of him. That's what Blaine tells us while we wait for HQ to radio back our instructions. To stake men's lives on the words of an informant who has lied is impossible. So is turning such a person loose. Fifty on liquidation, Blaine says, but no one takes his bet. It's a good thing too. You do it, he says, thrusting a SIG Sauer in my hand. But I'm not interested. He calls me a pussy, a hypocrite, but this is nothing new. And he is right, because what I felt, watching them chew out a man who knew we held his life in our hands, was an enlarging joy, and a hatred at his fear, which reminds me of my own.

In my mind, the truth is I have killed—and killed often. From the second on it is just a repetition of the first, the same man who goes on dying forever. His death lasts for as long as you continue to live. Someone said that to me at Camp Mercy. Beltrán or one of the Suicide Twins. Someone who had barely lived long enough to know the full confusion of puberty. But he was right, or I suspect he was.

There is beauty in death. The finality, the grandeur. It brings you close to the quickening spirit, the pulse, of life. I have sat in muddy boots, filthy clothes, caked in dust and dirt, and watched the bombs explode in concussive thuds, brilliant ignitions of fire and smoke—so encompassing to the senses it transfixes—and I have felt like a minor and forgotten god involved beautifully in a death I was safe from. I have seen the guns go cyclic, churning fire with such uncanny power I could have worshipped destruction for the force in it, like an earthquake, the force in our determination to destroy. I want to say it was my own preservation I worshipped—that viewed from a distance, everything is beautiful—or that war makes you hard, or turns you strange, but true as that may be, it discloses as well the endless fascination of death.

The fascination is with one's own, and one's own smallness before the forces that knit or rupture the ribbon of life. Others' deaths mingle in perverse intimacy with your own, not unlike love.

What these eyes have seen! What godless and cruel things . . . Religion in an exploding skull, emptying from the back. A man in repose, napping against a rock, who when the hat shading his eyes was removed proved to be a corpse. Rotting horses lying in the gullies where they fell. Putrefying cows and sheep. Broken families walking roads in torrential rains with their possessions on their backs, on rickety carts. Women digging through rancid garbage for food. Houses caved in like smashed boxes. Orchards, unexpected gardens, thriving near cadavers. Fruit hanging from branches, sweetening the air. Stars and bodies so bright the night sky howled with the intensity of life. Why was I brought before this scene? I have wondered that a thousand times . . .

It is to know that we are dust, motes of dust in an endless sparkling expanse. To know we are nothing. Not more than debts: on loan, borrowed, and coming due. We are the universe's lendings. And there is no meaning but enduring, fading into the moment or out. I cancel my debts. I retire gently into the unending moment itself . . .

How this too will be used against me, I don't know. Only that it will. And that I don't care. I cannot. I relinquish schemes and plans and plots. I put myself at the mercy of the moment. It is more important that I say what I think and reside within myself however briefly. In words I accompany my own body on this brief passage across the river. I stand before myself in the deferred judgment of silence and look inward at the face of God.

I laid the report aside, my blood not hot so much as replaced by a cold determination—anger at the eternal return of the expected, and at myself for guarding hope of anything else. How easy those edits prove that turn a story into its opposite. Blinkered eyes see one path forward. And what of the other turnoffs, other stops, along the way? Bruce was either a madman, gone rogue, or a pawn forced into the fray, severed from conscience by the dictates of a frame—and then another, and another, always clipping the truth at calculated points in its endless weave. Nested truths cheapen the name. Context stops nowhere. But stories do. And now I saw the authorship in Spearman's tale for what it was. Yes, I'd known not to trust him. It wasn't surprise at his connivance or at my gullibility that got me, but a feeling I associate with Brutus, the patriot led astray by his own principle. I'd been manipulated by a calculation that when asked to weigh duty against loyalty, the ethics of my work against allegiance to a friend, my vanity would prejudice me to the former. I mean something serious by this. Maybe it is only what the Greeks knew long ago: that the dispassionate ideals by which we overcome the bias in our hearts loop back around into the passions by an alternate circuit, the proud wiring of our self-regard, and that this love of self, disguised as nobility, means we seize rashly on chances to prove that we are who we say we are. Prove it to *ourselves*. How susceptible we turn out to be! How the journalist loves the mandate in his job forbidding the human element! The facts and nothing but them, wherever they may lead. But what about our self-conception, the stories that redound to our credit, our shabby heroism—what about the human element in that? Who won't we sell out to our benefit in the name of objectivity, professional ethics? We must answer for this. Those who see a way forward in loyalty to people or principle alone mistake how in isolation, absent their productive tension, each will bend imperceptibly to self-interest in time, to monstrosity. Bruce did need help: the rescue of his soul or psyche as much as of his person. My debt to him was real. It seemed to me far realer than I'd realized before. Thus my resolution ripened and took shape. I'd get him out, as quickly as possible, and I'd return to the capital and write the whole thing up. Whether or not James and Henry came around, whether or not the *Beacon* found its voice, I'd make it happen. I'd get the story told. And I would accept the consequences. If it meant war, then war it was. The misty horror of these dim plots would burn away in the fury of the truth.

I looked around the table. 'When do I go in?'

'Any time,' said Hunter. 'Now?'

'Just like that?'

'Just like that.'

'I don't need any prep, no fasting? Should I set an away message?'

'You won't be gone that long,' Nadia said. Ed was squinting at me as if by doing so he could peer into my skull. 'Time seems to pass more quickly inside . . .'

'Everything takes place within the brain,' Hunter said. 'Action at the speed of thought.'

'How long has Bruce been in?'

'More than a week,' Nadia said. 'In our time.'

'A week. But then . . .' I was churning through the ramifications. 'This isn't his first time.'

Ed regarded me with sparkling eyes. 'It's what makes Mr. Willrich special,' he said. 'He's the only one who wanted to go back!'

Was I blinded by rage? Is this what made me rush headlong into so reckless a venture? That's the charitable interpretation. And how long will I flatter myself with noble reasons? My sudden willingness to put myself in the hands of strangers bore the impress of desperation, even as I told myself that we could go on like this forever, getting nowhere, asking questions, receiving answers that were no answer. I had to *know*. Some part of me negotiated with that fateful inquisitiveness, the need to see firsthand, and my sense that I would always wonder and never forgive myself if I failed to take this journey.

For it is incredible, no? Another world inside our own. For how long have we dreamt of it, the realm that sits above or beyond the scrims of soulless matter and earthly life. The world of the mind, of pure form, where the contradictions of our partial sight become clear. Is this not a fever dream? How, you ask, are you hearing this now from me and not reading it in newsprint, that cheap paper we spent so many years filling with semblances of life? It must be a fantasy, a possibility tickling the imagination's skin, but thankfully beyond our practical and moral grasp.

Well, I can't explain except to say the long-awaited day had arrived. The brain is plastic, the varieties of experience greater than we think. Remembering how I felt on the eve of this immersion, I anticipate your skepticism. I still hadn't wrapped my head around the reappearance of Bruce after all these years, and I suspected at the heart of this some trick. I wasn't wrong, exactly, but what can I say? What other than that skepticism gripped me as the four of us got in Hunter's car and drove the lonely streets of Johnston to the office complex on the outskirts of the city. Nadia and Ed took turns explaining to me what would happen. They had an ID prepared for me, a fake name. How far in advance—how accurately—they had judged my acquiescence! Would I be confined? No. Merely sedated. Put under, paralyzed to a degree. 'Muscle relaxants,' Hunter said. And perhaps he told the truth. The procedure wouldn't hurt. It involved nothing more invasive than an IV, which was necessary to maintain hydration, nutrition, and the cocktail of sedatives in my blood.

I remember thinking for some reason, This won't work. It's a magician's trick, and I'll see through it, a hypnotist's vaudeville technique I will resist. At very least, the clarity of the moment will follow me inside. My heart thudded. It knew more than I could admit. It knew with the congenital wisdom of the species what it means to give control over to another person. To a substance. To be at the mercy of what you don't understand and can't resist.

Have you ever experienced real fear? I mean the kind that sets you trembling like pealing bell metal? It's amazing how the mind can enter a paralytic stupor, spiraling around a distilled terror, while the body carries on through its motions with detached ease. There are so many channels to this strange composite we call the self. Conscious life at times looks like no more than the filmstrip meant to distract us while deeper forces argue in a language of primal syntax. We watch the chess game but have no idea how far into counterconsideration each move goes. Nothing is hidden from us and still the meaning is opaque. The tinted glass doors, giving more light from inside in the dark, parted and we entered, breezing past the desk where the guard ran our IDs, confirmed them, and, after several clicks, opened the gates. No fanfare and no more than perfunctory security, in truth. Like everyone, I had been educated into an idea of the future's ornamental gloss: corridors of flawless white, smooth unblemished surfaces, doors that whoosh at your approach, rooms that softly light your passage as you move. An environment that anticipates and accommodates your desires like a womb, radial tunnels as pliant and soft as birth canals, which lead, it hardly need be said, to the next stage of our evolution.

But no. The hallways were as drab and dusty as a state-run technical university's. The flecked checkerboard flooring barely camouflaged the dirt. The doors each had a three-digit number and a letter identifying them. All were closed, and if any noise issued from within, it was only a deep thrum in the bowels of the building, a low frequency sinking beyond the threshold of audibility.

My memory is hazy. The drugs induced a twilight effect in the brain, a crown fizzing at the edge of memory and dissolving it through the filter of twinkling mist. Like a film that's been cut and spliced, the impression of continuity endures while many moments in the sequence have blinked out of existence. A thick bundle of cables ran along the top wall of the hallway in suspended rings held together by zip ties. I remember that distinctly: one of the lone indications that something in this shabby, unprepossessing building hooked into the great current of data-processing by which the streams and flows of evolving numbers, downriver from some event, learned to encode the world that contained them, and slowly replaced it . . .

I thought of the vast trial and error of an ant colony building to its unpredictable emergent patterns. Did I enter one of those rooms and lie down? Did I hear Ed's voice passing through me? I think so. But whether this was happening then or only the on-running echo of what he had told me before, I can't say. The most vivid elements would be those Bruce had touched and interacted with, as I knew, a consequence of building the simulation from our projections. I could use these to guide my search, but in time my own encounters with the world would adulterate its water with the dye of my idiosyncrasy, the system would learn my expectations, and I would suffuse the world with myself. It's impossible not to see what your mind expects, impossible not to end up chasing your shadow. A war between my reality and Bruce's would briefly rage, and then the cleavage would be complete, the two hemispheres distinct.

I remember laughing. I remember lights. Small lights blazing in a dimly lit room. Nadia's hand on my shoulder, or was it Hunter's? A last contact with the world outside, or the illusion and afterimage of a haptic pressure. 'Deep breaths,' someone said. I was laughing. Ed was laughing. Perhaps both of us.

IV

VI

QUENTIN STARED HYPNOTICALLY at nothing, lost to the ferocity of memory. Even in the dusky room his face looked pale. The yellowing, fraying books on the shelves, on seafaring and old wood yachts, watched us like kindhearted anachronisms. The caned chairs that creaked under shifting weight. We were there, in that uninsulated room whose walls let in the drafts like cotton—and we were somewhere else entirely.

Well? said Frank. He rose and knelt at the fireplace, arranging the split wood in a child's idea of a cabin. He didn't say it impatiently. From a pile by the andirons he took and balled some sheets of newspaper and stuffed them in with the kindling, took a long match from the box on the mantle, and lit this ephemera it had been our life's work to produce. Quentin rose and poured sour mash over ice. His hands shook with those small discontinuities that, like the needle of a seismograph, disclose a trembling beneath. A clear high note rang from the struck crystal. We started like fugitives at the sound of a patrol. What is this fear that springs from the recollection of things too far gone to harm us?

Quentin banked his breath with a sigh. What firmness we assigned the truth of all he told us was a question none of us, perhaps, felt prepared to answer. To doubt our friend, as maybe we would when all was at an end, would be a comfort, but one purchased at a price. We could believe what we liked—it was our human prerogative to trade in preferential illusion brokered by desire—but our attempt to penetrate the shadows of our solipsism, to hold ourselves to the standard of more than self-deceit, would suffer by our refusal to look squarely at what we didn't gladly face.

Quentin stood by a reading lamp whose warm glow swam up to the creases of his face. The fire snapped, the kindling sent torrents of sparks up the chimney. The logs relinquished their moisture, smoking and spitting, and the light and heat of the blaze spread into the chill room like the old fingers of a mesmeric guttering beginning.

He looked like an emissary from another world. And maybe he was. He made a noise as if to speak but fell quiet. I can only tell you what happened, he said finally. That's always the case, I know. What I mean is what happened, vivid as it was, comes back to me bound in a haze like a harbor in fog. I've heard of whiteouts that swallow mountaineers until all they see is an undifferentiated pallor. I'm no outdoorsman—he managed a grin—but I've read books, goddamn it, I've heard accounts of pilots lost in the mist and divers in the undersea dark who, with no frame of reference, not even the tug of gravity, lose all sense of up and down. Can you imagine? As if you had left the earth. Except this was a movement into an unknown dimension. A question of inner and outer, as though you could plunge into yourself like a body of water. How can any of this make sense?

The first thing I thought . . . He sipped the mash and closed his eyes. The first thing I thought on waking—though as I've said the haze and twilight kept the immediate reality remote, as if a glare were cutting my unadjusted eyes, or the afterimage of a blinding light prevented me from looking at anything directly—was that nothing had happened. I found myself in the same room, or a room just like it, reclined in that dentist's chair. I felt physically unchanged apart from a wooziness and the phenomenon of glare—not *light*, understand, but something like a naked exposure in your mind, a blinkering effect. This was purposeful, I came to see, for during the initial period of adjustment, as mind and machine learned to negotiate each other to their mutual satisfaction, certain limitations had to keep from spoiling the impression of a complete world.

But again, it seemed simply that I was in the same place, as if I'd fallen asleep, or fallen unconscious and awoken with no sense of time's passage. I considered the possibility that I'd passed through the ordeal already and brought none of it back with me, like a patient after surgery. I got out of the chair and fell to the floor. My legs, I realized too late, were asleep. I stood more slowly this time, holding myself against the chair arm, and waited as my extremities roused from their numbness. When I could stand I made my way to the door.

Have you gone out into the sun after an illness and found that everything looks washed-out? Your vision won't land with its usual focus. You feel not dizzy or off-balance, but unsure of the firmness of reality's anchors. A vague idea afflicts you that nothing is quite real, that you are not a thing in the world, but that one of you, you or the world, is the other's illusion? That's how I felt as I entered the hall. The throbbing glare receded and I could gaze around at last. I flipped the light switch and the light went on. I flicked it again: off. The corridors were as I remembered them, the check pattern of black and white scuffed with the passage of feet. I made my way down an empty stairwell, crossed the deserted halls, and left by the front door without passing a guard. The sun was shining in the lot.

I gather that 'entry' is as carefully managed an affair as 'departure.' If only the same could be said of life! The day was in full force outside, eerily still but otherwise as you'd expect. I noted a faint motion at the edge of my awareness, as if standing in a boat at sea. I guess that like an infant I was learning the terms of the world without realizing it, and I suppose that this time the world was learning me as well.

I'm piecing things together, you understand. I doubt any question of continuity entered my head at the time. I continued to exist as we do, waking up again and again. I had no doubt but that I was still in Johnston, in the parking lot before this strange building, and no closer to knowing anything that would release me from the responsibility—or curiosity—that obliged me to proceed.

And most peculiar of all, I think, looking back, I knew to find my car in the parking lot—as if returning to it after my first visit to the facility. Recalling this now, I am struck by how natural it seemed, how little I questioned any of it, how simply *given* the properties of the world were. But maybe there is no world we could awaken into that we would fail to find natural and familiar in time.

I felt within the normal contours of my life, in short, those effortless movements that carry us through the day. I had only the vaguest sense of another reality, another set of urgencies, beyond the present. The planes didn't call each other into question, much as a dream proceeds naturally, while we sleep, alongside a faint awareness of a life external to it. If something or someone from the world beyond had confronted me, I can't say I would have known to which reality it belonged.

I started the car and eased out of the complex. The light strobed gently in the trees. It was one of those exceedingly clear and bright days and the traffic on the rural highway beside me moved with its typical dull perseverance.

Thus it was that I passed in peaceful ignorance along a familiar sequence of connector roads and highways. The trees ended in a gathering of gas stations and retail stores; the forest became sparse, replaced by roadside bushes and tall grass, and as I drove, along the highway warehouses and factories appeared, refineries with dark smoke coming from their chimneys. The vegetation died off in the pallor and dead hay of a different season. I transferred from interstate to frontage road to bridge to overpass. The buildings now had a clustered urban feel, pawnshops and corner stores with foreign names, old busted sign lettering, metal grates before shut storefronts. In the distance, above the decorative and dark brick cornices of tenements, the skeletons of iron bridges stood out against the scrolled clouds. There was life in the streets. People stood, or lounged on stoops. A few kids shot hoops on a court immured in chainlink fence. Beside commercial pyramids of gravel and sand, a number of feeder roads converged in a multilane artery headed into the mouth of a tunnel. We rose above a plunging off-ramp, crested the artificial hill of the stilted road, and just then, briefly, I caught the silver top hats of skyscrapers peeking out over the lively chaos of the immediate surround.

What, a city? you'll say, but in the moment it didn't surprise me. Are you startled in a dream? I paid my toll fare, dipped beneath the river with the creeping traffic, and after several minutes emerged in the heart of a bustling vertical scene, a place I recognized at a glance. Without giving it the least thought I continued home, past crowded sidewalks and avenues of impatient beeping cars. Men hawked knockoff sunglasses and purses by the side of the road. Inert glass towers, old high-rises of granite, concrete, and yellow brick, and elsewhere bridges with rusted trusses and flaking paint claimed the sky. Antiquated water towers sat on rooftops next to old chimneys and the metal briars of antennae. Below these, lazy loops of graffiti knit and knotted. I didn't remember it having been cold earlier, but a snow flurry now fell through the canyons of the buildings in waltz-time. This seemed to glide or float above the earth, flocculating on sidewalks and benches and filling the air with levitant particles, great seas of soft visitation.

I made my way north through grinding traffic. The cars and delivery trucks were of an antique sort, though one that belonged within the matrix of memory. People on the sidewalks hunched into their collars, stopping briefly to glance up at the drifting spiral of snow. Buses with stainless steel fenders ran through the roadside slush, sending plumes of grimy water up along the curb like a tide. A ticker tape of trompe l'oeil rats paraded across a stretch of plywood. I'd lived here before, I knew. Rather, I lived here *now*—or somehow both were true and time, as it exists within us, occupied multiple points at once.

When I reached my street I had no trouble finding a place to park. It was a pleasant block—residential, though by no means fancy, lined with four- and five-story townhouses and slender leafless trees. I entered the building and climbed the two flights to my apartment, keys clinking in my pocket. The apartment was as I'd left it, which is to say, I suppose, as my mind was prepared to accept it. The answering machine blinked. I pressed the button, taking off my jacket and setting down my things.

The message was from Dave Taub at the *Stringer*, telling me to get my ass down to the office. He had a lead for me. That didn't sound like Dave—the lead, I mean. The imperiousness was spot-on.

You remember my time at the *Stringer*, that seedy gazette that came out once a week and did its brisk little business back in the halcyon days of the classified? I didn't bother showering, just splashed some water on my face, gave my hair a brush—I had hair to brush, you see—and threw on a wrinkled suit. Soon I was back out in the cold and down into the subway where the spray-painted cars swelled with riders in thick coats. They pressed against the windows like internees. On the platform destitute men lay sprawled on cardboard mattresses. Above one, a black-and-white enamel sign designed to resemble the transit authority's read, IT IS NATURAL NOT TO NOTICE THE PEOPLE TRAMPLED UNDERFOOT. That was indeed what it said; I looked twice. But by then my train had come and I had to get on.

Downstairs from the *Stringer*'s offices narrow ridges of snowfall lay over the sewer grate, protected from the breath of the city as it rose. The slush at the entry had a chocolate hue. Dave was behind his desk with his sleeves rolled up when I knocked on the door. 'There you are,' he said, patting his shirt pocket and peering at me over his glasses. 'We'll make a reporter out of you yet.' The sweet smell of cigar smoke lingered in the office.

'My lucky day.'

'Sure it is,' he said. 'You wouldn't know a story if it bit you.'

'*Story Bites Reporter*. The thing writes itself.'

A touch of sneer brought Dave's grin out of true. 'Good, because the only thing worse than your reporting is your writing.'

'They take away your punching bag again?'

'I prefer a more spirited target.'

'They're called employees.'

'Oh, please,' said Dave. 'You are *not* an employee.'

We smirked at each other. Stacks of papers littered the office. With the cigars it was remarkable you could insure the place.

He adopted a serious look and said, 'Hey, seriously, I need you to run something down. It's what we in the business call a lead. We call it a lead because it "leads" to a story.'

'Now you're going to tell me what a story is.'

'It's like a fairy tale,' he said. 'But it appears in a newspaper.'

'Once upon a time . . .'

'Yeah. Once upon a time you did what you were told. And this is that time.'

I shook my head. 'Doesn't sound credible.'

'You're telling me.'

Now, turning sober again, he proceeded to relate that he had made some calls, everything was shaping up *very* nicely, but he needed a sentient body down at the courthouse. 'Quasi-sentient,' he corrected himself.

'You want a favor?' I pointed at the window. 'Look at it out there. My frigid ass, my story.'

'Hey, Cervantes, we don't even know there *is* a story yet.'

'Leads lead to stories, remember?'

'He's already thinking about the award hardware,' Dave muttered to himself. '"Should I wear tails or a tux?" Do me a favor. Stop listening to me. You learn too much.'

'Don't forget there's vaudeville if this newspaper thing doesn't work out.'

'*I* have a job. It's you I'm worried about.'

'Said the coal miner to the canary.'

'Are you the canary in this metaphor? I've never seen such an ugly canary. Go see if there's breathable oxygen down at the courthouse, will you?'

Conversations with Dave always reminded me of the pleasure that could be snatched from the rigor mortis of a job. My tacit assent obtained, he motioned to the seat across from him to fill me in on the rest.

We had a guy, a name. Dex Chapman. Probably baptized Dexter, but he wasn't looking to sex up a book jacket. Had I heard of him? I hadn't. Good, said Dave. If I hadn't, maybe the other papers hadn't either. Chapman had been hauled in on some petty possession charge. This was laughable and no one believed the official line. Concerned citizens didn't call in tips on guys like Dex. He wasn't that threatening, or that stupid. Which didn't mean entirely unstupid, either. He was an entrepreneur. Taub had this from a gallerist he knew named Ida Franks. The theory was she sourced recreational substances from Chapman for her artists and sometimes the two collaborated on finding buyers for their work. Dex, after all, knew a lot of people with cash they hoped to turn into the sort you could deposit in a bank. A back-scratching arrangement. Chapman had been doing a nice business until he stopped wanting to carry water for certain low-empathy individuals with unusual ideas about professional obligation. He possessed zero ambition when it came to the compulsory side of crime. He wanted to make money, that was it. Franks too. And suddenly there *was* money to be made in the downtown scene. The harvest ripened. Not long before, it had been crap musicianship, junk, and graffiti in the sunset of a golden age just missed. Some pretty excellent parties. Now the market had caught the scent. Anything cool enough *not* to sell itself was cool enough to sell.

Chapman had balked at a bit of wet work, that was the upshot. His unofficial employers had asked politely. The asking *was* the politeness, since the extracurricular was not strictly speaking elective. So Dex got spooked and started talking to the cops. And he knew cops. Thanks to networking serendipities over the years he'd made the acquaintance of not a few city detectives. Now he wanted to know whether what he knew meant enough to the aims of justice to earn himself legal absolution under the state's protection. Alas, the cops were little aroused by fraud. There were two thousand murders in the city a year; nobody made a career going after money laundering. And this was still a half decade before everything down to punk scrawlings became a high-ceiling investment vehicle. The scope of what Dex was involved in dampened police interest. We should be so lucky that our gangsters had turned to art, was their way of seeing things. We already plied them with painting classes in prison to sublimate their vicious tendencies through still lifes and pastels. Extortion, by this theory, was mostly a problem of misplaced self-expression.

But anyway, Dave continued, Chapman had been indiscreet enough that it might have caused certain people problems if he showed up to work dead. He'd spent the past months peddling plausible conspiracy theories to every second beat cop who'd listen and at the center of these was his own untimely demise. Murder would get a detective engaged. So they figured it made more sense to set him up than bump him off.

He'd cool it upstate while his handle on current events went stale. Maybe they'd get him on the inside.

Unfortunately for the guardians of the status quo, Chapman had cleaned out his holdings ahead of time and wound up, to everyone's significant surprise, with a public defender who was neither incompetent nor indifferent. She put a few uncomfortable issues before the judge, including Chapman's spurned desire to turn state's evidence and the stink of mystery around the tip-off. The prosecution, unable to pry anything more creative out of their detectives, called it an anonymous lead and played the privacy card till the edges wore soft. But there were reasonable questions about Chapman's privacy too. He was entitled to the punctilios of search and seizure. His lawyer managed to emphasize the point without appearing to lecture. (The prosecutors were downright pharisaical by comparison.) Chapman's bail was set substantially below what the attorney's office wanted, he posted, and after laying low for several weeks, he was due in court for a sentencing hearing that afternoon. Dave even knew when to expect him.

I made a show of turning all this over and asked Dave how he'd come to know so much. You didn't go this deep into reporting a story only to hand it over to someone else.

'There's, uh, what do you call it? A personal angle.' Something like chagrin convoluted his face. 'My sister-in-law, Staci—the artist? She's friends with Franks.'

The women had known each other since high school, it turned out. Dave was too close to the story for even his own liberal idea of ethics. He'd also gotten Ida to spill her guts on the tacit suggestion that he could help her. '*We*,' he corrected. 'That *we* could help her.' He meant the paper. Ida, for her part, was understandably freaked out by the turn things had taken. 'People in the arts love crime,' Dave reflected. 'In the abstract, from a distance, it resembles art. But they're not disposed to the consequences, which often involve grievous personal injury and prison.' No doubt Franks was guilty of some low-level fraud. She was in a unique position to help cash-rich, credibility-poor investors, by arranging, for instance, records that showed depressed prices at point of sale. Also by not asking tough questions about whether, when you got all the middle-men sorted out, buyer and seller weren't one and the same. Dave of course didn't want us to land too hard on Staci's friend. What did she know about these schemes? It was hard enough making a living. Buyers show up, you don't ask questions. I thought she probably knew plenty, but Dave said it was just how things worked in her industry. He thought Chapman was a lively enough protagonist to carry the story himself. Once the farce came out in the papers, making its tiny pebble-drop in a roiling pond, there'd be no sense silencing a bit player like Franks. Plus, it wasn't a bad little scoop for the *Stringer*.

Dave was a good enough sort but the scale of his operation, the hus-tling it entailed, and his intimacy with the seedier side of city life meant he'd developed a comfort and even a fascination with the grayer aspects of moral existence. His professional scruples had gone salt-and-pepper. I liked him anyway. And the story sounded juicy. If I disagreed with his sense of where the beats and stresses fell and who got hero's billing, I could argue my case later when I had the facts at my disposal. First thing first: I needed to make my overture to Dex and see whether he talked to strang-ers. Was he the kind of colorful character who could hold the stage for a thousand words, or a buck-twenty? Maybe even a longer feature? I left for the courthouse on foot, blowing into my hands to keep them warm.

The snow had mostly stopped. A few stray flakes chased through the air like tinsel in a dance hall after everyone's gone home. Graffiti, plas-tered to the sides of buildings, showed through the snow and frost like pentimenti, recalling the paintings ancient humans had once drawn on rockfaces and cave walls. Lost messages, dreams. The simple defiant as-sertion of being. *I was here. I left my mark in powder blown around my hand. Fit yours to the deathless stencil.* There were repetitive motifs—names with three-digit numbers and words twisted in on themselves in kaleidoscopic contortions. The outline of a crawling infant tossing off sparks. Above a handball court, the spray-painted words: IF ART IS A CRIME, LET GOD FORGIVE US ALL. The snow collected like cobwebs in the corners where brick and concrete met. I moved on quickly.

Did these communiqués recall something more, an echo of the past? Maybe even the past in which I found myself? I was awaking to this world and my place in it. My *new* place, I suppose I mean, half fitted to the rails of a preceding time, half coming in at an angle like a train car from some dim future to meet and join this course. The drab sky stole color from the city. In doorways on stone stoops junkies lay bundled in jackets, motionless in their coffins of eiderdown. I didn't fully recall my purpose here, my mission, if you want to put it that way, but nagging thoughts and memories surfaced inside me like the wisps of steam rising from the manholes to meet the snow the wind kicked off the cornices.

It wasn't long before I reached the courthouse. The old stone building, fronted in volute columns, bore chiseled Latin inscriptions on its face. On the pediment a frieze of lady justice weighed culpability and punishment—an extravagant idea that blind process, codified in words, could act on any human matter to return the violated order to equilibrium. We glimpse our longing in our ideals. But then it turned out this august structure was *not* the building I was looking for. A taciturn guard housed in a cubicle of security glass directed me to an annex across the street, where I milled around the downstairs lobby, drinking a coffee purchased from one of the vending machines, and watched the traffic of guards and attorneys, cops and court officials—the daily routine of justice so familiar to those who oversee it, so alien to everyone else.

Discreetly I checked the passing faces against the photo of Dex that Dave had given me. It was during this period of waiting that I noticed a curious enamel sign on the wall, just like the one I'd seen in the subway. YOU NEVER KNOW WHAT IS ENOUGH UNLESS YOU KNOW WHAT IS MORE THAN ENOUGH, it said. At first it seemed to be a peculiar statement of principle put up by the court authorities themselves. It struck just the note of public-service pablum that municipal spaces are rotten with. But the longer I stared at it, the odder it seemed. Then, in the shadows of a hallway where no one would notice, I found another sign that read, WHAT LOOKS LIKE AN OPEN DOOR MAY BE THE ENTRANCE TO A CAGE.

Whoever had put up these signs had chosen their locations well. Your eye passed over them. Next to a fire alarm, in the red-and-white lettering of a safety placard, a third sign declared, EMERGENCIES ARE RELATIVE. I had just found my fourth on the doorframe above a janitor's closet—PRISONS ARE BUILT WITH STONES OF LAW, BROTHELS WITH BRICKS OF RELIGION—when a man in an off-the-rack suit, which put mine to shame (or glory, depending), bumped into me. 'Excuse you,' I said, and only a second later did I realize that it was Chapman in the flesh. I looked again and the man flinched. A minor spasm, but he didn't master himself quickly enough to look casual. He must have been seeing ghosts.

'Mr. Chapman,' I said in a new tone of voice. Beside him was a petite woman with short hair and a nicer make of suit. She blinked at me, a bright look of mystification.

'Who's this creep?' Dex muttered, canting himself partway back to her like maybe she knew what my game was.

'I take it you had a good day,' I said, offering him my hand and rattling off the boilerplate like the voice at the end of a drug commercial. *Quentin Jones . . . a reporter with . . .* I spoke on autopilot, all at once— utterly—distracted by the woman at Chapman's side. I'd finally taken her in, looked her carefully in the eye. And I *knew* her. I was certain of it. This sense deepened with the passing seconds as I dwelled on the surface and proportions of her face. The recognition stirred me, cutting like salt into the ice of my oblivion. 'My editor's pals with Ida Franks,' I was saying. The words cascaded from me unbidden while I clawed for the solid ground of memory. 'Thought you and I should . . .'

It became impossible to go on. I was staring at this woman, Chapman's lawyer, with amused bewilderment.

She was grinning back at me and frowned slightly. 'Do I know you?' she said.

'That's just what I was wondering.' I laughed. Dex, so guarded a moment before, now seemed upset that the action had shifted away from him.

'Ms. Freeman?' he said, half with the proprietary air of a client, half like a child who's just seen his mother kissing the milkman.

'Yes?' She didn't turn and instead held out a hand to me. 'Jada Freeman,' she said. 'And you said . . . Quentin? Quentin Jones?'

I told her she had it exactly right and asked whether I could take her and her client out for a drink to celebrate.

'You got to be out of your damn mind,' said Dex. He was making a play for relevance, and when neither of us looked his way, he added, mostly to himself, 'What makes you think I want to get mixed up with the papers?'

'I don't think you want to,' I said, turning back to him at last. 'I think it's your best chance.'

'Chance of what?'

'Surviving probation.'

He stared at me. 'Who says I'm on probation?'

'You weren't remanded, right? This isn't the clemency committee.'

Jada didn't say anything. Dex folded his arms and looked away, annoyed that I'd guessed correctly. 'I talk to you, maybe it's good for you. It's only trouble for me.'

'Possibly,' I said. 'Or maybe it only makes sense to shut up someone who *hasn't* talked.'

He'd had enough. 'Look, buddy . . .'

'Hey, weren't you just trying to sell your story to the cops?' I said. 'How well'd they listen?'

He shook his head in amazement. 'Just 'cause I don't get along with cops doesn't mean I get along with you.'

'What about bourbon. You get along with bourbon?'

'What do you think, Ms. Freeman. Should I tell this guy to go fuck himself?' Her eyebrows were raised. It was impossible to tell whether she found this amusing or embarrassing. 'Well?' said Dex.

She shrugged and the motion freed a few papers from the top of her overflowing bag. These somersaulted to the marble floor. I bent to retrieve them and picked up a flyer for a talk being given that evening at St. Martin's church. Professor Jacques Turquet on 'Criminal States of Mind.' Six p.m. I stared at it for a moment before handing it back to Jada. 'Thank you,' she said with an apologetic smile. To Dex she said, 'You're a free man. Be smart, though, OK?'

Dex made a show of looking at his watch. 'Buy me a drink and I'll give you ten minutes.'

I turned to his lawyer. 'Care to join us, Mrs. Freeman?'

'Ms.,' she said. 'No, I'd better not.'

I didn't want to see her go but could think of nothing to make her stay. I consoled myself that I knew where to find her later that night, assuming she meant to attend the talk. Jada Freeman, I repeated inwardly, and as I did, the name struck a deep echo in the well of memory. I'd once been close to a woman named Jada. Her hair had been different, perhaps her face. Why did I fail to place her just then? I can't tell you, not for certain; only that whereas a figure like Dave Taub lived organically within this past, Jada had been transported here from a time yet to come, by my own act of dreaming—or someone else's.

It may have been this premonition, or perhaps simply what Jada awakened, that primed me to start remembering that other figure from my past, or from the future: the one I was meant to find. Across a street of stalled cars, horns blaring at the gridlock, Dex and I found a grubby dive with a lit sign pressing its glow into the foggy window. It was the sort of place that looks darker by day, the weak glare of its sallow lights spread over the lacquer of the chipped wooden bar. We were the only customers. Dex ordered a shot and a beer. I asked for a ginger ale, but Dex insisted on a toast, so I got a shot and we clinked glasses to his release.

'And to your lawyer. She did all right by you, huh?'

He was smiling. 'You got a crush on her or something?' It was no longer an accusatory look. 'Yeah, she's OK.' He raised his beer and took a swig.

Later I learned that Jada had done a number filing pretrial motions and nearly destroyed the entire case when she crossed the prosecution's main witness, a police officer, in the suppression hearing. Dex initially wanted to cut a deal, and when he didn't get it the attorney's office expected him to plead straight up. But this wasn't going to happen on Jada's watch, not with so many irregularities dogging the government's evidence. It was simply too uncomfortable for the police to divulge how they knew what they knew. When this became clear, the prosecution reevaluated and decided they wanted to cut a deal after all. But now Jada had seen enough of the government's case to know how it would play in trial and she advised against pleading. The prosecution had badly misplayed its hand. She got most of the evidence tossed with motions in limine. After lengthy, testy wrangling over the presentence report, the judge couldn't see her way to incarceration; she seemed more upset about the government's ham-fistedness than Chapman's alleged crimes. None of this mattered to me. I even felt some sympathy for Dex, and my intuition vindicated Dave's: he'd been set up to protect the privacy of distinctly shadier legal entities. I was there to figure out what I could about them.

We were sipping our drinks, holding counsel with our own thoughts, when I asked, 'So how does a guy like you get mixed up in the art scene?'

'Guy like me?' He laughed. 'I'd almost think you meant something by that.'

'All right, you studied at the Courtauld.'

'Not there. Madame Penetralia's.'

'*Penetralia?*'

'Busy little downtown joint, messy as hell. Stays open till dawn sometimes. Popular with my clientele.'

'I see. We're talking artists or junkies?'

'No "or" about it.' He motioned with a finger for the bartender to refill his glass. 'They call them artists now. When I first knew them, they mostly defaced property.'

'Doesn't sound like a promising customer base, but what do I know.'

'They're loyal. They just got cash-flow problems, is all.' Dex stared at the twinkling bottles behind the bar, lost, I thought, to memories of other nights, other angles.

'You got to know Franks through them,' I suggested.

'Frank who?' said Dex. 'Oh, Ida? Yeah. Eventually. *Sort of* . . . Hey, this is between us, right? What do you call it? Off the record and nowhere even near the fucking stereo.' I held up my hands in assent. 'These customers—look,' he said. 'They either owed me money, or they were desperate for money.'

'Pretend I'm simple.'

'I had them do jobs.'

'*Right.*'

'Easy stuff. Courier work. They broke the law from the moment they got up in the morning, but they didn't look the part, see. Cops don't bother with punks like that. Small potatoes and a headache to boot. The ones I could clean up I ran as casino smurfs for a friend . . .'

'Smurfs?'

'Yeah, smurfs.' I could tell he enjoyed having me on the back foot. 'Casinos are like banks. At a certain echelon of transaction, they have to start asking questions. Monetary threshold, you follow? So you want to clean some dough at the tables, you walk with the chips. Then get a whole bunch of smurfs to take it back and cash it out in small batches, below the threshold, see?'

'You never worried they might run off with the take?'

'You worry, sure. I worry about stepped-on junk . . . But c'mon. These guys? If they inherited two grand, I'm the first person they'd come looking for.'

'And this was worth the hassle?'

'Not so much hassle. And I got paid twice. Once by my friend for the work. Second time when our gophers had a chunk of change burning a hole their pocket.'

The lights glittered behind the volatile liquids. 'You got it all figured out.'

'Never was a barter economy, nowhere in history. But the scene here, downtown . . .' He whistled. 'We had them run errands too. Some private individuals don't want anything to do with the banking system. I had one guy taking cash out east to the coast.'

'These were artists?'

'Sure. Musicians, painters, DJs . . . They had a finger in everything, and usually substances you couldn't buy at the bodega. Even after the jobs they always owed me. So on a lark one day I took a painting. Not payment—more like collateral on a loan. I got along with the kid. I wasn't trying to fuck him, but he told me the piece of shit was worth eight hundred bucks, and I thought he was nuts. I had to find out.'

'And?'

'I took it to a few galleries. Ida paid cash for it on the spot.'

'That's how you met?'

'Thing about a lady like Ida,' said Dex contemplatively, 'she's a hustler, just like me. We're not criminals the way people mean it. We're small-businesspeople. Do we operate on the fringes of the respectable market? Maybe. Can I stop you if you want to call that a crime? No, I can't. But the market exists. The margins are there, and we satisfy a demand. We facilitate the transaction and take our small cut. If that's a crime, so's half the things we call business in this city.'

'Yeah, well. The mother of some kid who OD'd doesn't agree.'

'You never did a line?' Dex smiled, narrowing his eyes. 'This guy'—he pointed to the bartender wiping a pint glass with a rag—'he's in the same business. He's just got a license.'

'Ida's got a license too,' I said. 'Or the equivalent. Say what you will, her business wasn't breaking the law.'

'It's all a matter of perspective, I guess. It wasn't such a bad gig for her, having these punk Picassos around hooked on smack.'

'I think there's an imputation in there that she might resent.'

'Yeah, yeah, and we've got to be real sensitive to her feelings, huh? Back in the day they had something called a company store. You know what that is? Ida's business model, top to bottom.'

'I'm talking about the law, as it exists. You don't just get to follow the ones that make sense.'

Dex sighed as if to say, *If you think I don't know that better than you, what the fuck are we talking about?* He tapped the wood counter for an-other pour. 'I'm tired of the idea that there's some big difference between you and me, Ida and me . . . Like the "legal" economy isn't exploitation up and down the line. Half of what's sold is poison. But some hustles occupy the light and some crouch in the shadows.'

'It's not fair. But it's how it goes.'

Dex nodded and sipped his beer. 'Look, Ida's all right. But she's after the money, like the rest of them.'

'You exclude yourself?'

'Usually, no.' He grinned. 'But currently I'm on sabbatical.'

We talked awhile longer. Dex had settled on a liberal interpretation of

my offer to buy him a drink and he kept the rounds coming. I eased into
the question of who these friends of his were. We didn't get into Christian
names, but he left me with a vivid enough impression. They were the sort
of people you didn't want to owe too many outstanding favors to. Someone had planted interesting ideas in Chapman's head about the business
environment we were headed for and the opportunities for profit therein.
An economy of debt, he confided after a third shot and a beer chaser.
He'd clearly devoted some thought to this. The future of moneymak-
ing, he told me, was all in debt. By this he meant the careful calibration
of usury to bleed the host within an inch of his life. Extract maximum
blood without killing the golden goose. It was the only way in a time
of plenty and legal freedom to keep servitude alive. *Peonage.* He pronounced the word with evident satisfaction. I asked whether it wasn't all
a Jewish conspiracy to keep the cisterns full of youthful Christian plasma,
but he didn't find this funny. 'That's got nothing to do with it,' he said. It
was a matter of who staked their claims first, tucked away their principal early enough to get in on the long-running miracle of compounding
interest. He meant those who had title, deed, and capital to invest when
the cement dried on the modern liberal order. When free enterprise said:
Ready. Take your mark . . . Pun intended. The origins of so much seed-
funding lay buried too deep in history to investigate. Certain people got
lucky. A lot of worthless land turns around in a century and some winds
up with residential towers on it. But luck was not the rule. The tributaries of historical privilege mostly flowed back to a rarefied source. Then
it became a matter of preserving this privilege, by any means necessary.

'We're done with the era of risk,' he said. Reward was being decoupled
from its partner as we spoke. Profitable lending was where the action was.
Rents. Schmucks needed to live. Keep them poor enough and life dicey
enough and they'll take your loans. They'll have to. It doesn't matter if
they can never pay it back. They'll pay and pay, far more than the loan
was ever worth, and when they default the politicians will step in and pay
the creditors from the federal purse. A perfect business. Risk free. So too
with investment. Keep upward pressure on asset values. When the crash
comes the affluent ride it out. Hell, they'll buy what gets sold in the fire

sale for pennies and wait for prices to recover. It's the suckers, the little guys, who get wiped clean.

I asked where he was going with all this. Dex stretched his neck, twisting this way and that to unkink it.

'Where you finish the race is a matter of where you start,' he said. It'd been this way throughout history, but now the game was wrapped in the invisible garments of justice, and the legacy of privilege would be stronger for going unseen. The only way to make up the lost ground was crime, on a significant scale. Legally hazy fraud. No one was breaking patellas anymore. Extortion and racketeering were out. Kneecaps were small-caps. People had to think more creatively. Playing within the bounds of regulation and fair competition didn't offer the margins. To catch up to the wealthy, you had to strike out beyond the boundary of the law. And you had to avoid getting caught. Then you had to bring your gains back into the system clean.

That's where he came in. Dex wanted to position himself at the vanguard of a new industry. This wasn't your first-generation immigrant parents' laundromat; he was talking about modern-day alchemy: turning corrupt metal into legit gold.

'It's going to change the world,' he confided. 'I'd have to be an idiot to think selling horse to a few broke kids was a growth sector.' He saw potential in big-ticket items that held their value, appreciated, and didn't attract strict scrutiny at point of sale. 'Homegrown criminals everywhere want to go legitimate,' he said. 'They all want to get into the aboveboard economy. They want their kids in fancy colleges. You watch.'

I left him to enjoy the rest of his celebration. His conversation tended to the conspiratorial as he drank, but it wasn't all nonsense. In fact, the more I thought about what he'd said, making my way uptown to Ida Franks's place, the more it sounded like the words of another figure, one estranged from the present moment by a new geometry of time. Much as Jada had, Bruce now appeared to me like an image reflected in a storefront window: a ghostly impression I could call into focus or see through by adjusting the depth of my gaze. Indeed, he was the only person I ever knew to use the word *peonage* as Dex had. Debt fascinated Bruce. He had an idea that there was an inherent connection between the rise of finance and the rise of criminality. An economy dominated by rent-seeking held the hierarchy steady. It kept pecuniary success zero-sum, incentivizing shortcuts, work-arounds, playing outside the rules of the game. The platonic market worked by yoking risk and reward, and it understood that risk was inherent to freedom. But finance sought to corral the market, to limit rather than encourage risk. As a consequence it constricted freedom and allied itself with those criminal acts that could hide in the legal recesses, wringing profit, like a tax, from the simple necessary movements of life. Human flourishing threatened to disrupt its take. Better to profit on food, shelter, medicine—the things people required to live.

Did I agree with Bruce? You could hardly work the beat and fail to see the sense in his indictment. But what was the rule and what the exception? How much of profit's churn existed in shadow and how much in light? What was the *scope*? It is simply very hard to conceptualize the largest systems we have words for and thus believe ourselves the masters of—abstract systems like governance, economy, or law, which bind our actions in their inscrutable unities but exceed and overwhelm the mind. How is it that we create and live in structures we cannot comprehend, and what mistakes do we invite by reducing vast, anarchic circuits to the scale of contemplation, thereby imposing on them our mortal errors and hopes?

Ida's gallery sat on a pretty side street in a charming, scruffy set of downtown blocks. In places the pavement broke out in rashes of cobblestone, bulbous rock polished by traffic. Light from the gallery spilled into the road. The scene lay charcoaled in the early dusk, so that, against the lifelessness of the block, the gallery had the air of a stage-set storefront, intensely, surreally lit. A taxi rattled down the street, chassis shuddering on the washboard of stone. Its brakes squealed, and then it lurched back onto the pavement and sped up. A falcate moon carved the pale blue above the roofs and showed a trail of smoke rising to meet the night.

No one was in the front room of the gallery when I entered. The canvases made their silent statement from the whitewashed walls. They formed a series. Each painting showed the same marshland, a landscape of retreating drab and olive lines, puddled in a luminous gray ether, and sitting above the marsh in each picture was a giant white duck. I was chuckling to myself when I heard heels ring out on the hard floor. The woman coming toward me walked purposefully. She wore a loose black sweater that revealed more of one shoulder than the other, tight high-waisted jeans, and thick-rimmed glasses. She looked slightly older than the ensemble might have suggested.

'Can I help you?'

'Yes,' I said. 'I'm looking for a painting with a duck in it.'

She let this pass without a smile. 'Are you a collector?'

'Why not?'

We regarded the painting before us silently. In the upper part of the canvas—the sky portion of the landscape—a tool had been used to cut down to deeper layers of paint, a violent, abstract effect, reminiscent of the cobblestone écorché outside.

'Striking, isn't it.'

'Mm,' I murmured in what I took for seasoned discernment.

'I have a lot more that isn't on display, of course.'

She hung just behind me as I moved to the next painting, attentive, skeptical. 'You didn't tell me who the artist is,' I said.

She followed my eyes to the canvas. 'Alfonse Ricard. He's playful, but his technique is excellent, as you see.' The white duck stared at us: black beady eyes, carrot-like beak. 'Before you know it he'll be a name.'

'Yes, I've heard of him.'

She gazed at me and said softly, 'I doubt that very much.'

'I'm good with names,' I said. 'I'm almost never wrong.'

She opened her mouth to argue but decided against it and smiled. 'This is Alfonse's first show. It opened last week.'

'What's the show called?'

'*Quack.*'

'Bless you,' I said.

'Funny.'

'What's this one?' I pointed to the painting in front of us.

'This? This is *Canard 7, Anchoret*, I believe.'

'He has a sense of humor.'

'Yes.'

'What's Anchoret?'

'A town. Out east of here on the coast. Alfonse had a job there for a while. I guess it made an impression on him.'

This called to mind something Dex had said. 'What kind of job?'

I didn't look at her but I could feel her gaze on me. 'That's an odd question,' she said.

'Is it? I thought maybe he was a boat painter or something.'

'Alfonse?' She smiled. 'No, I don't think so.'

'What does one do in Anchoret?' I mused. 'Maybe he hunts duck . . .'

'I'm sorry, I didn't get your name.'

'Quentin.' I watched the light wrinkles and lashes around her eyes dance with her focus. 'Ida, I presume.'

'Yes.' She stared at me intently. 'I'm starting to think you didn't come here to decorate your parlor.'

'You have a natural feel for your clientele.'

'I'm starting to think you aren't clientele.' She paused. 'What line of work are you in, Quentin?'

'I ask questions.'

Ida spun her foot on her shoe's slender heel. 'You're a philosopher,' she joked.

'Only when I've been drinking.'

'Don't make me guess.'

'I write newspaper articles.'

'A reporter.'

'That's what it says on my card.'

'I'd like one of those,' she said.

'It was more a figure of speech.'

We'd moved to the threshold of the gallery's back rooms. The air smelled of paint and plaster, a pleasant smell like a garage. In one corner, beyond several tall windows, was an enclosed office and along the other wall a storage unit for work that wasn't on display.

'So what can I do for you?' A faint tightness had entered her voice.

'You're not going to tell me what our friend got up to in Anchorage?'

'Anchoret.' The phone rang in the back, muted through the interior wall. 'That wasn't why you came.'

'Stuff changes.'

'You should ask Alfonse if you're so interested.'

'I'd like to.' I leaned against a whitewashed drainage pipe, pen and notepad in hand. 'You have a number for him?'

She sort of smiled at this. 'I assure you, there's no phone where Alfonse lives.'

'No?'

'It's a live/work space, you know. The kind you're not really supposed to do either in.'

'I won't tell.'

She gave me the address after I took pains to convince her I meant Alfonse no harm. I also told her I knew Dave Taub, that she and I had friends in common, and that I'd just had an interesting talk with a fellow named Dex Chapman. She must have been expecting this because she didn't say anything. She wanted me to get to the point, I could tell, but first I made a show of understanding her perspective: the challenges of bookkeeping, the vicissitudes of pricing.

She tapped her foot. 'You must really want something if you're going to be as nice as all that,' she said.

'I didn't come to pick a scab.'

'And yet you seem to know where it hurts.'

'Life's not fair, huh?'

'That's an annoying thing to say.'

'Yeah, you're right.'

She walked abruptly to one side of the room and pulled back a hanging sheet of vinyl to reveal a small plaque like the ones I'd seen earlier in the day. This one read, STEP ONE IS FUCKING YOU. STEP TWO IS CONVINCING YOU YOU LIKE IT. 'That's my feeling on life and fairness,' she said.

'Someone has a future in the fortune-cookie business.' I glanced at my watch. I still had time if I wanted to make the end of the talk at St. Martin's.

'*Are* you going to tell me what you came for?' asked Ida. 'Or just dance me till I'm dizzy?'

'My parlor, like you said.'

'Let's stop joking for a minute.'

'I thought humor was in. *L'absurdité*.' I was poking idly through the work housed in the storage unit. 'I don't want to sound melodramatic, but some pretty stolid burghers are worried your friend Dex might fall off a balcony or something.'

'Really?' She said this in a blasé tone, but there was little conviction in her voice. She was suddenly far away.

'Things might get hot for Dex,' I continued. 'I wouldn't stand too close.'

She watched me move through the paintings. 'And I'm supposed to believe you're here to help.'

'I'm not here to hurt.'

'Should I be grateful?'

'Honest's good enough.'

'I've been honest.'

'Alfonse Ricard?'

She sighed with frustration. '*Nobody* uses his real name.'

'Yeah, exactly. Let's not argue like this game has rules.'

'All right, Tristan Tzara. Now tell me you care. I dare you.' She'd recovered some of her swagger and the blood had come back to her face.

'You're fun, you know that?'

'Don't mock me.' I felt bad to think I had. The stakes were higher for her than for me. From her perspective I knew it wasn't funny. 'You must think I'm a complete moron,' she said.

'Far from it.'

'You make a deal. You earn some cash. You start thinking you're pretty clever.' The phone was trilling again in the back, but Ida let it ring. 'Before you know it you're in something it's not easy to get out of.'

'You'll get out.'

'Maybe.'

'Tell the little you know. Then there's no one to shut up.'

'I'm not sure Dex's friends take such a bloodless angle.'

'What are you imagining?'

'Sometimes you prove a point.'

'You're not the kind of point they prove.'

I could see the depth of night taking shape beyond the barred windows to the back. A floodlight ran amber threads through the dusk.

'So you found some new clients through Dex,' I said. 'What were they buying?'

'They didn't care. It couldn't be A-list stuff. The prices had to be low enough for modest but meaningful appreciation. Otherwise they were open-minded.'

'No bourgeois hang-ups, I guess.'

'Right.'

'What did they do with them?'

'The paintings?' She had a funny look on her face and touched the storage rack without much thought. 'Most of the time they just left them with me.'

Suddenly I understood. All these paintings in these racks were someone else's property. When the time came to sell them at a higher price, you cleared the difference as a legitimate gain.

'Who was the end buyer?'

'In the secondary market?' She held my eye for a while, gauging me. 'Sometimes I found a buyer. A lot of them I bought myself.'

'Bought's figurative, I assume. It wasn't your money, was it?' The shape of the hustle was becoming clear. Ida could sell her artists' work, take her cut, and when a sufficient period had passed, 'buy' the work back at an inflated price. The artwork didn't have to move and no more than a fraction of the initial purchase price had to change hands. The 'collector's' money came out clean in the end and Ida came out owning the work, the value of which had now risen.

She didn't respond but pulled out a painting and regarded it. The canvas bore the menacing figurations of an angry teenager's marginalia.

'Who's this?'

'Arto Cras,' she said. 'They'll be worth a lot one day. Millions maybe.'

'Millions?'

She shrugged. 'Stranger things have happened.'

'I take it Arto's not his given name, either.'

'What do you think?' She took a few more paintings from the rack. They were large canvases, wild and primitive in their representations—colorful, unsettling. She pulled out an orange-and-red one and I stopped in my tracks.

'You're joking.'

'What?' She didn't look like she was joking, and I felt a weakness pass into my legs. The painting was the one Rob Spearman had purchased from Cy's gallery several years earlier. Perhaps I mean years hence. Words fail at a certain point . . . This intrusion from another world in any case broke my sense of an operative naturalness, whereby the levels of aware-ness hung together peacefully. I had the impression, as one might have in the face of extraordinary coincidence, that this had been orchestrated for me, or more metaphysically *by* me. Except now, glittering with the throb of dread, this sense came without the comfort of discounting paranoia. Here, in this place, paranoia morphed into something unlike itself—an elemental facet of reality. The strands of implication were too knotted to sort out.

The light beyond the windows had gone completely. The luminous gallery felt harsher, more exposed in response. I remembered for an in-stant the glare I'd experienced on awaking. *Had* I awoken, or had I merely stumbled outside, or inside, to a dark place brightly lit, or a bright place entombed in darkness?

I took a shot into this darkness. 'You know a guy named Bruce Willrich?'

'No, who's that?'

'Someone I guess is mixed up in this.' I turned away from the paint-ings. 'You really don't know what Alfonse was up to in Anchoret?'

She hesitated. 'Listen, you didn't hear it from me, but a lot of the jobs Dex got for Billy came from this lawyer Olive.'

'Billy?'

'Alfonse. That's his real name. The lawyer's called Tom Olive. And that *is* his real name as far as I know. He's in banking. I'd give you his number, but it's better if you just find it.'

'Can a guy named Tom Olive be as scary as all that?'

'You know, I go back and forth between thinking you know what you're doing and thinking you don't.'

'Maybe we're still dancing.'

'No,' she said, 'I don't think we are.'

It was true. The music was now faint above the cold din and rattle of industrial plumbing systems in the bowels of the building, ominous, environing. Ida had turned with the upright grace of a skater, the way women in heels sometimes do, and clipped a metronomic path to her office, finally answering the ringing phone.

I figured it was time to go. She glanced at me through the office window and I made a motion to say I was leaving. Hold on, I saw her mouth, and she put down the receiver, stepping out into the room. She held out her hand.

'I'm taking a risk here, Quentin, trusting you.'

I took her hand and held it. 'And now *I'm* supposed to think you just want to help.' It seemed more understanding passed between our hands than in our words.

'It's 'cause I care,' she said sarcastically, smiling, arch. 'Hey, do me a favor. Don't get Billy in trouble. He's a good kid.'

When I made it into the street I had just thirty minutes before the lecture was set to conclude. I hailed a taxi—Ferryman Cabs, it said on the door—and we cut over, crosstown, but when we turned north the avenue was lousy with traffic. Our progress came in fits and starts as we waited for the gridlock to clear. Steam rose from the hoods of stalled cars.

Five blocks more and I saw it would be faster to walk. I paid the cabbie, who had the air of a girl left at the altar. I apologized. I was late.

Just beyond the busy avenue, hurrying east, I mistook a dark silhouette on the flank of a building for a person lurking in the shadows. The figure's hair stood up in a static, tousled spray. But it was only a likeness, I saw, applied in flat black paint. People in overcoats bent forward, moving stiffly. Eight or ten blocks on, walking fast, almost at a trot, I came to the church gate housing a fenced-in yard. Its rows and plots lay gently fitted with snow. No time to linger, I pushed through the heavy wood doors and the voice of a speaker met me, accented with a wry inflection and pompous surety of rhetorical purpose.

'Soon though,' this voice was saying, 'so fast that we must scour the record like detectives to find evidence of this monumental swerve, motive becomes the sine qua non of justice. And now we must consider crime the *symptom* of the criminal mind and the criminal himself to be the proper object of the judicial system. Not his body, but his *mind*. Thus begins the long and ever more complete articulation of punishment as something enacted continuously on the person, most often in the guise of reformation or rehabilitation. Like religion, the judicial system is concerned with the state of the criminal's soul. His inner, moral health.'

The audience sat in reverent silence. No one had noticed my entrance but the severe young man minding the door, whose glance told me what he thought of this tardiness. Professor Turquet, grinning with the obscure mischief of a fox, perspired under the stage lights. The effort of his inquiry had left his bald head dotted with reflective pearls.

'This appears to commit the better part of justice, of legal punishment, to the discipline of psychiatry,' he was saying. 'But for psychiatrists too, at the base of this question—"How are we to judge sanity and fitness?"—lies the fundament of legible motive. What impulses to action reflect the operation of a sane mind? The set of legible motives that provide an answer do not derive from any empirical inventory. No. This is critical to emphasize. They derive very simply—and peculiarly, the longer you sit with it—from a sense of the purposes to which society can put a human life.'

The professor picked up the glass of water provided him and held it so that our anticipation stayed with the glass and his hand, even while he grinned at us, appraising the sea of faces before him. He held the glass but did not drink from it and began anew before putting it down.

'At first blush this seems not so strange perhaps, and yet consider: What does it mean for society to have ends of its own that do not reflect the ends of the individuals within it? This possibility stands at odds with our intuitions. We believe government permits our freedom and thereby the realization of our selves, and we believe it does this by attending to our dignity, our rights. When I say, "We believe," I mean that these are assumptions our language perpetuates and encodes. Maybe no one believes such things at heart. Regardless, we encounter once again the distinction between illusion and practice, for while the *story* of our rights and dignity may be necessary for society's functioning, this does not entail the reality of our rights and dignity as ends themselves. They may be no more than impalpable and occasionally useful means. The story may be most useful as a lie.'

I glanced around while the professor spoke, conducting an impressionistic sociology of the audience. It was young and outwardly serious and it laughed with a performative air. Several rows ahead, as if sensing the pressure of my gaze, a woman looked back over her shoulder, and it was somehow not surprising at all to see the very person I had come to find: Dex Chapman's lawyer, Jada Freeman. Her perplexity shifted quickly into an echo of my own grin.

'And so this leaves us in a peculiar state . . . I do intend the pun,' Turquet said, setting off a murmur of laughter in the crowd. 'Society is composed of individuals, but its aims and purposes may be its own. To make sense of this larger structure, which governs our lives, quite literally, we must fight through the stories society elevates to make us tractable to its ends. We must escape the comfortable illusions that take up residence in our head and which society teaches us it is folly to abandon. The state on the other hand is concerned with getting inside our heads to apprise motive. To confirm it is of the normal sort—the sort already installed with the state's own motives.

'In short, we must be desperate to get out of our own heads, while the state is desperate to get in.'

Turquet's voice had grown hoarse and now he did sip his water. 'Add to what I have said the fact that the state does not exist in nature and is therefore the product of our distributed consciousness—a communal story about what a state is and does. The state thus exists wholly within

the very minds it seeks to penetrate. Is that not odd? It persists as a powerful mass illusion, realized partway—but only partway—in institutions,
behaviors, and specialized bodies of knowledge like the law.

   'And yet insofar as the state is not unchanging but evolves over time,
and responds in some way to our imagining what it could be and how it
could be different, we see that for its survival—to be anything *but* a totalitarian system to which the individual is subjected and sacrificed—it
requires the sanctity of the privacy it seeks to destroy. It requires perversity, even deviancy, because it requires people to expand the boundaries
of what legible motives we recognize and accept. Only in so doing do we
broaden the scope of what it can mean to be a human, a scope that the
state, in the deepest recesses of its nature, seeks always to constrain!'

   These words seemed to crescendo and a smattering of applause broke
out, until Turquet held up a hand and ran the other across his bald, still-
perspiring head.

   'The state has one goal,' he said. 'To make thought a crime. In its
innocence it doesn't even know this is its goal. But eradicating privacy,
penetrating this sanctum sanctorum, is the objective to which it finds
itself helplessly drawn. The most consequential battles of the dawning
age will center on the endurance or eradication of privacy. But the fight
may not play out as we expect. The victory for the state may not come, if
at all, as we envision: by penetrating our minds against our will. It may
instead arrive by our eager relinquishing of our own privacy, a cult of
self-revelation, of exhibitionism. And we will see these activities as self-
directed. This is the key. We will believe they are our own decisions and
instances of our own empowerment. But we will be working for the state.
We will betray ourselves, as ever, for little more than the reassurance that
we are normal, that we will be welcomed unobtrusively into the social
body—a healthy man or woman, inside and out.

   'That is all I have to say to you this evening,' he concluded mildly. 'My
regards, and my thanks.'

   The applause returned more confidently this time, redoubling with
a percussive rhythm that seemed eager to announce the sobriety of its
approval. I wondered if such collective approval and all it represented

was not exactly what we had just been warned against, but I clapped too. The tide of the crowd began to turn. People gathered their things and started for the door. I found myself pushing against this movement, past companions pivoting to wrangle over doctrinal disagreements. Above the milling crowd, electric bulbs blazed in chandeliers fashioned from cart wheels. I thought I'd lost Jada completely when someone behind me coughed lightly and said, 'If you were going to follow me around, you might have been more discreet.'

She had mischief in her eyes and I set innocence against this. 'I don't know what you're talking about. I never miss Turquet.'

'Uh-huh.'

'You too then?'

She rocked slightly forward on her toes. 'Actually, I studied with him—in Paris, believe it or not.'

'I have no reason not to.'

'Me and two hundred other worshipful fanatics,' she said to soften what might have sounded proprietary.

'Don't let me keep you. You should go say hi.'

'I did.' She paused like a diver before the leap. 'That's what I wanted to tell you. We're throwing a little party for him next door. A reception for the talk. You're welcome to join.'

I said I'd be glad to and she told me the address. 'It's just around the corner,' she said.

The temperature had dipped when I stepped outside. Wisps of steam garlanded the streets, filtering up through the fire escapes, and for once the city smelled crisp, like burnt leaves and car oil. Pedestrians brought mittened hands to their faces. I could hardly have explained the elemental magnetism that drew me to Jada. I had the sense that I had known her in another life—and of course it was true, although did I know it then? The night seethed with motley light, possibility, disorder—her aura bled its glow into the charged air, infecting me powerfully with the thought of her proximity.

I got a coffee and walked north to the address she had given me. The building put out little light into the street. It was only the din of voices

in the unheated stairway that told me I had the right place. The banister
listed under pressure and decomposing wallpaper peeled at the edges. The
door wasn't locked. Bodies pressed together in the room, their warmth
fogging the windows. At a certain height like a still layer of cloud hung
bluish smoke. I pushed through the crowd to the kitchen and took a beer
from the fridge. There wasn't much more to the place. I passed through a
room with a bed full of coats and found Jada in the study, where Turquet
and a band of acolytes sat on cushions talking.

'Quentin,' she said and took me by the hand. 'I want you to meet
Jacques.'

She led me to Turquet, who had a small leather case of works open
next to him. His left sleeve was rolled up, a rubber tube affixed loosely
around his arm.

'Jacques, this is my friend Quentin.'

Turquet held out his unengaged hand to mine. 'A pleasure,' he said.
He had the toothy smile of a person who grins more often than he laughs.
His glasses glinted in the faint light. 'You will forgive my'—he gestured at
the drug kit—'What shall we call it? My "deviancy."' He laughed and the
others joined him. He'd melted the powder and now drew the solution
into the syringe, tightening the band around his arm with his free hand
and his teeth, a practiced motion, as the needle found the vein.

I met Jada's eyes. They offered no apology.

'Quentin's a journalist,' she said.

'Ah,' said the professor—whether an 'ah' of comprehension or of release I couldn't tell. After a pause he seemed to reencounter the information. 'Dear lord, a journalist! Do not tell me you report the facts.'

'Only as a last resort,' I assured him.

He snorted at this. 'I am . . . *Comment dit-on?*—*aggrieved* by this idea,
the facts.'

'There's always lies. Falsehood, spurious allegation,' I said. 'No sense
limiting yourself.'

He smiled with Cheshire teeth. 'I am not against truth, Quin*ton*. The
fact is—how to say—unimpeachable. It is this idea—*the facts*—I don't
understand. Whose? Which?'

The room buzzed expectantly. 'You don't think we cover what's important,' I suggested.

'Ah, important, unimportant—this is the point,' he said. 'The question lies beyond the reach of facts. When we say "Here are the facts," we do not distinguish truth from lie. We say instead, "Here is the proper object of your consideration." But proper for whom? Perhaps for profiteers? Or for the state? Or for the entrepreneurs of scandal who hijack our anger and fear?'

Though tempted to argue I preferred to hear the professor out. 'I don't disagree,' I said. 'I just don't see an alternative.'

'You cannot. You are the *bearer* of facts. You believe that since you expose the secrets of the powerful and the merciless, if indeed you do, you are an insurgent at the root of power. And perhaps where individual power is concerned this is the case.' He sat up in his chair and someone arranged a pillow behind his back. 'Thank you,' he said. The twinkling clarity had resurfaced in his eyes. 'The facts are a technology,' he went on. 'A bid for power. The incremental transformation not of truth into power, but of power into truth. The slow dissolution of experience until we live in a realm of pure symbol. And you, doing the best you can, I am sorry to say, you can only reinforce this regency of fact—its sovereignty and tyranny—until one day the forces of despotism come and seize power from you, the very power you have helped build up. And there will be nothing to fight them with because the facts demand that they alone are truth. They stake their claim to power not on superiority to other ways of knowing, but on the thoroughgoing *irrelevance* of anything else.'

I considered this before replying. 'Are those the facts?'

'No.' Turquet laughed. 'No. Thank goodness. But it is what I believe all the same.'

The gathering had enjoyed this disquisition. I summarized diplomatically: 'So you don't read the news.'

'I do not,' he agreed. 'I much preferred the cartoons. What do you call them? The funnies.' Here was the deeper truth, he explained. The news was so much strange, improbable event, culled from across the world and made to seem typical when it was in every sense exceptional. Like uranium, very rare but dangerous when collected in a small place. The comic was truly typical. *Arche*typical. Concerned with the naked elements of human life—repetitive, reiterative, drawn from memory, experience, often dramatizing the position of the individual in confrontation with the news, which was to say ideology and social forms posed against the reality of the body, collapsing on the shoals of daily life. The cat pursues the mouse, the dog barks at the cat. The wife rolls her eyes at the husband's pride, the husband dreams of a freedom he's renounced. The child wants love, hates the prison that is wanting love. The neighbor meddles. The politician lies. The bureaucracy crushes the human spirit in cubicles, meetings. Stereotypes, yes, but endless variations of the real encounter. Here was the truth of existence, stripped of sociological, journalistic pretense. A literature of the absurdity of our predicament: our confinement within repetitive formulae. 'It's Kafka,' said Turquet, 'the pinnacle of the comic form. So pure he needed no drawings.'

A young woman summoned the courage to ask who then decided, or should decide, what was worthy of our attention, our devotion.

'I don't know.' Turquet sighed. 'It is not the church today. Maybe Quin*ton*'s paper decides. Or maybe it is only the henchman of a secret principle, an institution so powerful it has used its potency to disappear from view, to recede from material existence altogether. It is my work, I hope, to catch a glimpse of the faint edge or outline of this departing ghost . . . the immaterial machine, which writes itself out of perceptibility by suggesting it is only the transparent, ineffable medium of our lives. Reality, fact, truth . . . What I suspect will govern us will be the parts of ourselves we cannot see, don't you think? The parts we have exiled from our words and cannot talk about; the parts of us our description of reality omits. Not repression, but those things we cannot talk about in newspapers, that when you mention them, other people look at you funny and cross the street . . . This part operates with impunity. Even the greatest dictator in the world can't control it. We don't see it as it operates. We don't feel it as a force on us because we feel it *is* us: our natural movement, our inclination . . . This will be our master in the end. The thing that hides behind its inexpressibility. The shaky foundation, the quicksand, all this rests on. Everything.

Perhaps you will conclude it is better not to know, better to remain in the embrace of comprehensible illusion, than to aspire to see the chaos of the truth. Perhaps you are right.'

He tapped his works, maybe unconsciously, but it seemed to me to say something about the burden of living in occasional contact with this truth. The group splintered at Turquet's words, conversations or disputes rising up among the audience. I suspected Jacques knew more than he was letting on, that he had, in a way perhaps incompatible with speech, grasped some inkling or fleeting vision of the imperishable form. I hardly know what to call it. A vision so brief and amorphous that it darts away upon apprehension and stays, like an eccentric imprint on your eye, just out of sight as you move to catch it. I mean the depth of that rock quarry within us, next to which everything we say and believe is a kind of lie. We stand along the rim, whispering bloodless expediencies in a language of fake cheer, as if the abyss didn't lie at our feet ever ready to claim us. Have you sensed its presence? If you haven't felt this vagrant proximity, I am not sure I can describe it. It is a species of awareness and sentiment foreign to naive experience. A perception that lies in store for us and may pass us through, if we're lucky, without our registering more than a shiver. I can't name it. Before the blinding aspect of the unmediated, words grow weak.

By posture and movement Jada had separated us from the group. We spoke privately. 'I'm worried I'm imagining things,' she said, 'but I have the most vivid impression that I know you from somewhere.' She blushed. 'I know that sounds like a pickup line.'

'It does,' I said. 'But I feel it too.'

'I felt it the second I saw you. I keep expecting it to fade.'

We stood very close. 'You're not crazy, or we both are.'

'Then we must have met, is it as simple as that?' I shook my head, I didn't know. 'Where could we have met?' she said to herself, as if invoking a prompting formula. In it I felt her desire for the sweetness of an answer, a simpler explanation than space shifting around us, inverted by the gravity of feeling, the day's dull register drifting into poetry. We were alone in the world, the night.

We knew this feeling without naming it and an understanding now coordinated our movement. Jada retrieved her jacket and I got my scarf around my neck. The evening had taken on a drunk, dreaming logic. Jada led me across the threshold and out into the night. We must have walked, but it seemed later that we had moved only by internal displacements, arriving at her apartment as if leaping across a collapsed region of space. I backfill the memory with the flash of headlights, the city's bright bedlam, another outline of a figure splashed in black paint on a building, lurking, watching us . . . and then we were alone. A wood floor. Open curtains before high windows. Connected by life's impossible architecture to all the instants of previous being, in mystical sequence, we found ourselves—*there*. Dim luster strained by the window lay on the ceiling in oblique forms. Darkness held us, and would until morning, with its patient light, rose to undress our privacy. Later, I had the urge to ask her how we had gotten there, but I knew the look I would get, the answer. *How do you think?* Explaining this now is like adding syntax to a dream. And to hear some tell it that is all we ever do, conjuring a world from the suite of fragments. Knitting chaos into continuities, stilling it in language, to look at it ourselves. To pour ourselves into other minds.

By this logic it did not seem I had forsaken Cy. Do you betray a lover in a dream? And yet the vividness of this dream unnerves me. The coarseness of Jada's winterworn lips. The fullness of her tongue. The chattering aroma of herbs growing in tidy vessels beneath the window. A different hunger got mixed up in this. The intensity of her body startled me— the life in it. Its pliancy and animation. Hair, flesh, sinew, breath. Scents like coffee, closets, woods. I longed for what had already been given me, the boundless permissions of common lust. The notches in her back lay as still as frozen waves. She smelled like burnt cinnamon, sharp and bitter, tannic, vaguely sweet.

Is it the cliché in sex that unearths my shyness, a want so crude and formulaic it reveals the shallow beast in us? How can simple words penetrate the marrow of a feeling, a voracity as soon to fall in on itself as hunger, thirst? If there is truth in such a hunger it is the consuming desperation that points us back to our wholeness, disclosing us as instruments of a higher power, and for this bondage we get the dumb creaturely abandon of fucking. Sex is love for everyone in that case. For the ecology, the brute. For the newborn and the dying. Perhaps we are afraid of this love. That is our bashfulness and our prudery, how much it *involves* everyone. They might as well be there with us in the room. Such a dissolution of self troubles us. The eminent domain of heritage. We abandon our bodies as property in sex, and we return them to one another like borrowed charms.

It took us a long time to spend what we had stored up. The night returns to me in strobed stills. I can't recover that intricate electricity networking through my body, but sometimes the character of a room and its shifting forms amalgamate in an indestructible mood, an impression that stays with us much longer than the fragile, expiring moment and becomes a talisman of memory far more potent for pulsing in the antres of the soul. We lay there exhausted as the kettle rose to a whistle on the stove, amid the tumult of Jada's apartment, clothes draped everywhere on chairs and cabinet doors. For Jada this sudden intimacy was uncanny, like déjà vu cooled and made solid as glass. For my part I had begun to recall a background to our romance, faint forms revealing themselves in outline. Did I understand that Jada had an original? Yes, I think so. I think she even began to understand it as well. And still she was as solid as the hand I see before me . . . but I get nowhere troublesome doubting a hand! A human being though! How unprepared I was to recognize, much less explain, a person's immateriality, her nonbeing—*explain it to her*. How do you tell someone they don't exist?

The day rose and wrapped us in the languors of a still-warm bed, that pale high light that gathers at the roofs of buildings on clear winter mornings. Jagged shadows lay beneath the cornices. The city had a feeling of newness, as if purified of its tawdry accretions, litter, hustles—a Luna Park chained and unelectrified in the daylight. People called out in the street. Quickening motorcycles shredded the fabric of the air. In the distance church bells cluttered melodically. The weekend began, announced by the straining notes of opera on a record player, sharp and tinny like the PA above a prison yard.

We were learning each other from the beginning. Jada talked of Paris and studying with Jacques. She spoke of the ubiquitous pale beige stone, the sooted aprons of buildings, air choked with car exhaust, caporal smoke, saxophone music in the evening, and the carnival blaze of the boulevards. It collected like water in a marble basin, the memory of this place, so brimming with its shabby beauty, effortless order fronted by disarray, that in the halls of the grandes écoles they could discuss arid theory with no worry that it threatened the vitality of the streets. She walked the banks of the Seine under gravel skies. Drunkards, passed out on cheap wine, lay beneath the bridges. The day toyed with the idea of cold rain and the louche bars and bistros extended their offer of refuge with dirty yellow lights, waiters peering into the drizzle like defeated poets.

She had had her romances, the young men licentious dissemblers who spoke earnestly only of ideas; the older ones cynical and direct, unhappy to have received what they wanted in life, as if they should have asked for more, or different things. The women she knew seemed to couple out of principle more than desire. A place where romance came more easily than friendship. She was not unhappy there, but in the grapple of daily existence, bleached by a stale and inadequate theorizing, the mental life she had come to Paris to pursue appeared a game to her. The words she heard spoken in class described matters so abstract that belief rested on nothing more tangible than the givens of the argument itself, manipulated like tokens on a board. She had been led to believe that striking a note for good meant understanding and then unwinding power. This was Jacques's goal: to catch the internalized power at play in everything we embodied, everything we believed naively was *us*. But out in the streets of this old city, composed of the chaos of the ages, the organic order of people living in proximity, conflict, and compromise with one another, a rookery of accommodation resisting even the enlightened attempts to modernize it and force organization on the gnarl, it didn't seem that one should fear the tentacles of secret power so much as the overpure and tooneat ideas of abstract thinkers who meant to decide what was right—the full scope of the good—and then impose it on people who had already found their balances within this confusion.

'Jacques is afraid that we live caught up in stories we didn't invent,' said Jada. 'Stories not remotely our own and that, for how common and vast the delusion is, we have no faculty to probe.' I told her I shared his fear. 'It *is* a worry,' she allowed, 'but the way out of it is far from clear.'

We were lounging in her apartment, drinking Ceylon tea from bone china mugs. I held her foot, moving through the toes like prayer beads. 'Academics,' she said, 'like politicians, like activists, like *all* of us, have ideas about how people should live. But do we really consider how people *want* to live? I mean day to day, minute to minute.' She cupped the tea for warmth. 'I abominated injustice, but I started to see that it was never as simple as undoing injustice, because you couldn't *undo* a human life to a neutral point. You needed a positive vision, a theory of happiness, goodness, freedom. And to develop one you had to know people as they truly were.'

I smiled. 'Warts and all.'

'Warts *especially*,' she said, pressing a hallux to the mole on my collarbone. She sat on the bed, knees up, legs lazily splayed. She had nothing on below but underwear and I could see the hair beneath it pressing into the cloth and kinking out the sides. 'I wanted a kind of adulthood,' she said. 'I felt trapped in a child's world, an infantilized culture.'

'What was childish about it?'

'Take this question of power,' she said. 'At the far point of deconstructing the world with power as your skeleton key, what you mean by it is simply the capacity to act. To change something. It lies then equally behind everything positive. Power isn't good or bad in itself. Only a child, habituated to powerlessness, would view the world this way, as little more than coercion and injustice.

'I began to wonder,' she continued, 'where the impulse to seek justice comes from. I don't mean the instinct for fairness, but the adoption of justice as a cause. Children learn a cosmic order from their parents, whether they understand it that way or not. And does that not raise the question of whether our longing for justice isn't really a longing for childhood: not the values of our parents, but the coherent moral order that is only possible in childhood and within a family? Might we say that our fixation on the plight of the weak holds within it a primordial memory of our own smallness and vulnerability as children, and the comforting idea that an inviolate set of rules might compensate for this weakness? I don't say this to disparage the instinct, but to achieve a certain distance from it by offering one of Jacques's genealogical explanations. I didn't want to be ruled by childish rage—the rage of having been made to believe in a cosmic order that did not in fact govern our lives.'

'What did you want?'

'To be happy.' She fixed her twinkling gaze on me. 'If I was going to help people, I'd do it for the world I wanted to live in, I decided—not to engender this world by some unfathomable chain reaction, but simply to create it, to instantiate it, in the act.'

I sat facing her, a woven blanket around my shoulders. Winter moved easily through the windows. The hissing radiators gave only a thin trickle of heat. 'So you became a lawyer,' I said.

She laughed, throwing her head back and letting the delight peal richly in the still room. 'I did,' she said. 'You might say I decided to claim a small power of my own. I had a strange idea of the law as something like the hard, flexible tendon between the bone of violence and the soft tissue of belief. We all look for our points of leverage, of course. As a lawyer your goal is often simply to frame an argument in language that permits a judge to certify what he or she already believes. Does the law ordain outcomes, in that case, or only formalize the convictions of a culture? It was studying with Jacques that prepared me to see these paradoxes, but escaping them is another matter entirely. Defending my clients gives me a modest way to act meaningfully.'

I waited until she was done. It had worn on into afternoon and the winter's acrid glare fell at a melancholic angle, naked and weak. I touched her cheek with the back of my hand. She felt as cool as marble, as real as any matter coaxed to life.

'I knew a young woman like you once,' I said. 'You could even say she was your secret twin, only she took a turn into the self-seriousness and melancholy you describe.'

Jada looked at me closely. 'Don't think it couldn't have been me.'

'And why wasn't it?'

She shook her head. 'I don't know.' She seemed to think about it. Fine dark lashes curled up candidly from her eyes. 'What breathes its spirit into any of us?'

'Passion? Love?'

She chuckled lightly. 'Maybe.' She put her hand to her temple and rested her head on it, regarding me for a long time, as if to say, *Is that what this is?*—as if, I thought, to ask whether we ever have experiences with another person, or only inside the locked box of our minds and therefore with ourselves. But I was too far down the path of finding everything in her compass precious to stop and wonder, or care, whether love emerged from a recognition of oneself in another, or represented the closest contact or intoxication we could achieve with the foreign element.

She got up, stretched briefly, short legs rising on tiptoes and dimpling faintly in bands of muscle. She went into the kitchen, where she retrieved a bottle of cheap red wine and two glasses mottled with mineral residue. She picked her way through the cluttered room like a tipsy dancer and set the items down on a small table. I watched her pour the wine, a slight wobble in the bottleneck, a rush of liquid. The sense that she was two people, that this original had an original, twinned her image like a person regarded with tired, unfocused eyes. I didn't dwell on this. I pushed it from my mind, in fact, drinking the wine to blunt a twinge of conscience that told me I now flirted with a dangerous indulgence, far from my proper course. 'Here you say you knew a woman who might be my secret double,' she remarked, holding the wineglass contemplatively and speaking as if apprised of my unarticulated thoughts. 'And if this woman and I could live our lives in parallel, perhaps where our path branched we would discover the true dimensions within us—how expansive or narrow our possibilities of being really are. But we write a story alongside our life as we live it, and in time we live partly, even mainly, perhaps, to affirm the story we've written to that point.'

I asked what she meant. She leaned back on the pillow before she spoke. 'We grow committed to our story. The story takes on a life of its own. But if someone came and erased it—erased it so completely that you didn't even recall the identity you had worked so hard over the years to turn into a prophecy of itself—would you proceed along the same arc? Or would you turn out to be someone else altogether?'

Quentin paused here, long enough that we sat in a peculiar silence, the four of us, afraid, it was clear, to break the spell that gripped our friend. It was getting late. The night's quiet assumed a permanent and depthless quality. The fire, burnt out long ago, had turned to white ash that fluttered in faint drafts like desiccated moths.

At last he resumed his tale. I wonder, he said, whether what Jada said was right. There are so many points when I might have turned from the path I took, taken another, and never have come to the end I did. Did I have a choice? This is what I have wondered, lying awake long nights. Was the story *mine*? Did alternatives exist, in a world of parallel possibility? Or had I chosen differently, would an unknowable force have corralled me back onto the same track? We only run the experiment once.

Jada and I spent the rest of the weekend talking our way into the warm black corridors of night, he went on. Gatherings of stars pressed into the slate above. Our conversation coursed around stonelike ideas; we were the river, the flux. We conjured past moments; told each other, spurred on by liquor, what we hoped to accomplish in our short time to breathe and roam this crust of earth. We shouldered out into the street, a revelry of discordant harmonies as organic as the slums and warrens of Paris Jada had described. Traffic shuddered over sunken grates. Prostitutes in leggings and leather jackets, bras, short skirts shivered on the corners, smoking. Noise from the clubs lit up the blocks, the weft of music's lower registers stitching the fabric of the night. From packed bars came the dull ocean sound of voices; a squalid exultation pocketed the raw air. We moved along demolished roadways, buildings knocked out of their rows like hockey players' teeth. Trucks downshifted, trembled, rumbling into depressions. Tires squealed, far away. Engines purred and revved above the jaillissant funk emanating from car stereos. Abandoned chassis rusted in the shadows of tenements. We watched a sedan with an endless prow of a hood drive onto the sidewalk, nudging galvanized garbage pails out of the way and sending them rolling to the stoops. Celebrants choked the grid and we slipped into their stream, satisfied with each other as the destination. We patched into bars without much discrimination, joining the noise, the damp warmth of breath and spilled beer. We had to keep our heads close to be heard. Jada's tight-cropped hair caught the light, a pebbled texture, red from the glow that spilled over it. A faint patch of effervescing foam lingered on her lip when she put down her beer, eyes bright, smile broad and easy. No wonder I hadn't recognized her at first— the short hair, the courtroom attire—but also: she seemed *happy*. Not like the woman I had known, the woman I would *come* to know . . . No, there was an alien lightness to her. She spoke as if by speaking you might illuminate the sky; and I felt an indescribable affection for her, reaching out of me, bodily, like helpless limbs falling on what they adored, to grasp and hold dumbly what they wanted not to be separate from, and could do no more than touch, and touch again, like a bell that held within it one clear, cherished note. We became intoxicated in a slow, tidal way and didn't realize how drunk we were until we found ourselves stumbling home through the pallid, barren streets. The occasional taxi or huddled couple or stray roisterer performing inadvertent tango steps on the empty sidewalk only accented the desolation. The city seemed to belong to us, to us and a few other shuffling souls, awake to the brightening sky of the cold morning.

No, I never forgot the rest. I knew where I'd left off in my reporting. I knew implicitly that two spheres of reality arced over each other. But I felt released just then, cut off from the past, even as Jada—through Dex—led inexorably back to my investigation and the figure I was meant to find. Somehow it didn't matter, not that weekend. I felt free to shrug off responsibility. And maybe this is the promise, and the danger, of a technology that turns reality ambivalent and unmoors consequence from the ramifying impingements of history. Life takes on the character, and the insignificance, of a dream.

We watched from the roof of Jada's building as the weekend came to an end. Sunday's light became one dying coal to the west, beyond the ragged edge of high-rises and silhouetted water towers with their rice-hat tops. The leaden air grew chill. We held each other against the cold. Silences formed in our conversation like puddles becoming ice. The contrast in the city grew as daylight bled from the sky, turned watery blue then faintly violet, a color like a withering flower. Graffiti lay on the face of the metropolis like a veil. We slept together and woke to a sky as flat and bright as tin.

Monday had returned and now the city roused itself in sober bustle. I left with plans to see Jada again that night. Stopping briefly at my apartment, I changed, checked my messages, and rejoined the streaming, spinning cogs on the subway downtown. The train screamed, banking against the rails. Straphangers listed like morning lushes. We crossed south and east. When I exited into the cold shining day the streets were vacant, full of windblown garbage. I checked building numbers against the address I had and at last found myself in front of a chestnut facade. The tall stories had ornamental arches before the setback that held the windows. The paint calved in significant flakes, and across half its face the building wore a filigree of fire escape like a mantilla. It seemed to have been a showroom once, though clearly long decades had passed since the decorative stone fruit carved into its columns read as more than an anachronism. Above a fallout-shelter decal by the entry an ARTISTS-IN-RESIDENCE sign hung by a single screw.

I saw now why Ida had laughed when I'd asked for Alfonse's phone number. The place was a dump, the vestibule encased in cracked glass held together by its reinforcing wire. None of the buzzers worked, and the names listed by the apartment numbers on the tenant directory were all jokes: The Voluptuous Horror, Dense Franklin, Calefactory Lunch, Vito Sleaze. Apartment 4C listed NeedLess NeedLes as its occupant. Luckily nothing was locked. A long triangular shadow cleft the ground-floor hall when I pushed in and the sun lit an enamel sign: TRUE FRIENDS STAB YOU IN THE FRONT.

It took a while wandering through the scuffed and scraped building to find Billy's apartment. The corridors were filled with junk. It was impossible to tell what was trash and what the materials for an artwork or props for a show. Five of those stories were enough to wind you, and I was breathing hard by the time I made the top. Light streamed down the hall. The door at the far end was open and music fluttered into the corridor.

I knocked on the doorframe. 'Hello?'

'Who's there?' someone called from inside. Then, 'Company, Artie.'
I peered in. A skinny man in tight pants wearing a scarf sat reading on a
couch. He regarded me warily, rose, and walked over to the door. 'Yes?'

'Who is it?' a heavy voice deeper in the apartment called back.

'I don't know. Who is it?' asked the man in front of me.

'I'm Quentin Jones. I'm a reporter and a friend of Ida Franks's twice
removed.'

'A reporter?' He took a while processing this. 'This is about the
building?'

'The building? I don't think so.'

'*Fuck.*' His relief was palpable. 'You show up at people's residences
looking like a loan shark. I thought you were going to break my knees.'

I glanced down at my clothes, my skinniness inside my suit. 'I look
like a loan shark?'

'It's just some fag reporter, Artie,' he said. A shorter man, balding, in
a lumberjack jacket, leaned against an interior wall, watching us.

'What kind of a reporter?' said Artie.

'Yeah, what kind of reporter?' asked the first man.

'What kinds are there?'

He folded his arms across his chest. 'We're not the experts.'

'You're definitely sure this isn't about the building?' said Artie.

I eased into the room gingerly. I hadn't been invited. The high-
ceilinged apartment had tall close-set windows on one side and was open
but for a few unpainted supporting columns. In the back corner were the
rudiments of a kitchen with a hot plate and deep-basined utility sink.
A few dishes rested in a drying rack. The most interior space had been
walled off and a couple of fans sat idle in the patterned ceiling. By the
windows an assembly of beat-up chairs and a couch made a small living
room. Artie perched on the sofa arm.

'What's going on with your building?' I asked.

'We're not telling you what's going on with the building until you tell
us what kind of reporter you are,' said the man I guessed was Billy.

He looked to Artie for support in this, but Artie's face was inscrutable.

'I work for a paper called the *Stringer*,' I said. 'I haven't written a

word about artists' lofts and I don't plan on starting. I promised Ida I'd
be friendly. She showed me your duck paintings.'

'This is about my paintings?' Despite some skepticism Billy seemed
touched.

'You could say so. I'm interested in what inspired them.'

'Canard,' Artie remarked.

'Yes, the duck inspired them.'

Artie didn't move a muscle or change his expression. 'Quack, quack,'
he said.

'What *is* the duck?'

Billy didn't answer and led me instead to a corner of the loft he
seemed to use as his studio. Mounted on a makeshift easel was a painting
of the same landscape with the same ivory duck in the distance. The scene
was dusk. The painting's greens, blues, and browns were dark, nearly
black, but inlaid in them were faint seams of luminosity. On one edge of
the painting a white shape, the side of a building, glowed brightly. A few
letters—*B l o*—were visible on its face, trailing out of view.

'What's this?' I asked.

'The mall.'

'The mall?'

'The Elysium,' said Billy.

'And this is in Anchoret?'

He smiled. 'You know Anchoret?'

I shook my head. 'Ida told me.'

'Quack, quack,' called Artie from the couch. 'So says the canard.'

'He's very proud of that,' Billy said. 'He gave me the name.' We looked
together at the canvas before us. 'I'm calling this one *Anchoret Blo's*.'

'What brought you out there?'

'Oh, just this job,' said Billy. Then he turned and looked at me more
carefully. 'Is that what this is about?'

'Could be.'

He made a reproving face and turned from the painting. 'I'm not supposed to talk about it, actually.'

'Your friend Dex was more forthcoming. He said he had gophers—smurfs? elves? something like that—running dough out to the coast.'

Billy blinked at me and a cloud passed over his face. 'Dex's a fucking idiot,' he said. 'Did he tell you he sold a painting I lent him back to my own gallerist?'

'He did say something like that.'

'I don't do errands for Dex. Not anymore. I'm quitting. Anyway, I only did it to pay the lawyers' fees.'

'Lawyers,' said Artie, 'are the plumbers of corporate society.'

'You have a lot of dealings with corporate society?' I asked.

'We're part of a tenant's association,' Artie said.

'They're trying to kick us out,' explained Billy.

'And buy us out.'

'Yeah, and buy us out too. Whichever they can get away with first.'

'Who's "they"?'

'On paper? Elegant Ventures Inc., LLP,' said Billy. 'But nobody really knows.'

'It's a shell company,' Artie mused. 'As brittle as a shell . . .'

'We don't know what's inside the shell.'

'It could be a chicken. It could be a lizard. It could be a dildo. It could be a wizard.' Artie sort of sang this.

'It's probably not a wizard,' Billy confided. He passed me an envelope with an official notice on the letterhead for a law firm called Youck & Suchman-Dieke. The letter offered a cash payment to the tenants of apartment 5E (William and Arthur were named) if they agreed to renounce their lease and move out.

'So you have a lease.'

'Yeah.' Billy sighed. 'Though you're not really supposed to *inhabit* this building.'

'You're supposed to sew dolls in it,' said Artie.

'What does that mean?'

'It was a doll factory,' said Billy. 'The creepy little sort.'

'And they're trying to evict you . . . because you're not sewing dolls?'

'Yes. And they're offering us money to vacate.'

'A pincer movement,' said Artie. 'Carrot or stick? Carrot or stick? Elegant Ventures, Youck & Suchman-Dieke.'

'Artie has a thing for rhyming,' Billy said.

'I noticed.'

'We applied for a certificate of occupancy, what, two years ago? There keep being problems.'

'They're against occupancy,' said Artie. 'Occupancy of every sort.'

'A few years back landlords couldn't get tenants in these buildings to save their lives. Now we've made it cool and they want us gone.'

'Artists are the engine of prosperity at the heart of your vile machine,' whispered Artie.

'Hey, write a piece about this,' Billy said. 'Bullshit companies evicting artists. Drag these fuckers through the mud.'

'Pigs like mud,' said Artie.

'And shit,' said Billy.

'We've been taking your shit for so long. Now we're selling it back to you at highly inflated prices.'

'Except we don't want to sell. Or move.'

'If you want to fuck us in the ass, have the decency to do it where we live.'

'Yeah, fuck us here,' said Billy.

'In the ass,' said Artie.

'Metaphorically,' I suggested.

'For every avant-garde, there's a *rear* guard,' said Artie. He looked at Billy and they started laughing.

A yellow-white glare sparkled in the windows. 'So what's holding up the C of O?'

Billy, still giggling, shrugged. 'What is it this time, Arthur? They keep finding new problems. Sprinklers, gas lines. Railings . . .'

'*Railings*,' Artie repeated in a whisper.

Billy pointed to a water-damaged patch of ceiling, laureled in dangling flakes of plaster. '*Of course* this place is a disaster. *Of course* it isn't safe. But we were living here for years before they cared. So what are they actually concerned about?'

'Their pocketbooks,' said Artie. 'Like us, they are defending colored paper with drawings on it.'

'Not exactly like us.' Billy turned to me. 'First we had to fight not to get rezoned. If it were legal to live here, the uptown dentists would move in tomorrow.'

'Bankers, lawyers . . . ,' said Artie. 'The kind who like it a little slummy. You dig? Like to dip their white shoes in the dirty gutter, mix it up with the unwashed.'

'We're the unwashed,' said Billy. 'We literally don't have a shower.'

'So you're fighting not to get evicted by the landlord, and not to get displaced by new tenants?'

'We're fighting for our little world where everything is just so.'

'And nothing makes sense.'

'Yes,' said Billy. 'And surprisingly that requires lawyers.'

Artie sighed. 'Even nonsense requires lawyers these days.'

'But you stopped making runs for Dex.'

'I'm stopping,' said Billy. 'And they weren't really for Dex.'

'You don't need the money?'

'Who stops needing money?' Artie mused. 'Bugs Bunny? I don't think so.'

'It's odd,' Billy said. 'All those trips to Anchoret to earn a little cash and it's my duck paintings that finally started selling.' I must have looked like I had an unvoiced question on my lips because he added, 'And if you must know I got curious.'

'We all get curious.' Artie stared at me. 'You would not believe the extent of my curiosity.'

I gave Billy a smile. 'No harm taking a peek.'

Billy put a hand to his chest. 'I'd never. The zipper was open, just a crack. I tried to close it but it was one of those jammed zippers where you have to open it all the way to get it closed?' A twinkle lit his eye.

'I'm guessing it wasn't leaflets for the church social.'

'Lots and lots of little drawings,' said Artie. 'In an unlimited edition.'

'By a government artist?' I suggested.

'Every one of them signed,' Artie averred.

I turned to Billy. 'And this spooked you?'

'We have cockroaches crawling out of the Chinese take-out cartons. It takes a little more to spook us.'

'What then?'

'Different sort of cockroach,' said Artie.

'We stopped trusting Mr. Olive. You know, that gross banker? We think he's playing both sides.'

'Sides of what?' I asked.

'Tom's bank, DeBere Fleisch? They retain Suchman-Dieke,' said Billy. 'Or so we're told.'

'We've got a man on the inside,' Artie said. 'Inside the shell.'

'*Well.* Sort of.' Billy turned to me. 'Tom's one those guys who likes to dip his white shoes in the mud.'

'Except instead of mud in this case,' said Artie, 'it's someone's twat.'

'I'm guessing it's not his shoes either.'

'You never know.'

'What's in it for the lucky lady?'

'Money?' mused Billy. 'It's not like Tom's so hard on the eyes once you get past the glare from all that oil.'

'But he's indiscreet.'

'It's hard to believe you can't trust someone who's got your dick in their mouth,' said Artie. 'But you can't.'

'I'll keep it in mind.'

'You wouldn't know it to look at us,' said Billy, 'but we're not criminal masterminds.' Artie nodded. His sweater was bursting with moth holes. I asked what the plan was and Billy said they were organizing.

Artie raised a fist. 'Cocksuckers of the world unite.'

'Artists,' said Billy. 'An artists' strike. They play the lawyer game better than we do, but they need us.'

I asked what sort of strike he had in mind. Billy explained that they planned to pull their work. 'Galleries, museums—everything. Just wait till the walls are empty.'

'Yeah.' Artie grinned. 'Your parasitic metropolis runs on the fuel of our dreams.'

'You should get in the placard game yourself,' I said. Then: 'You really think your strike will work?'

Billy had a foot up on the windowsill and leaned forward toward the city, staring out. Daylight drenched him in a bright, thin wash. 'Win, lose—whatever. If we win, it'll only be for a short time. Either we sell before too long, or we sell out. There's too much money in this dump.'

'Sell out first,' I advised.

Artie started laughing. '*Ha ha ha!* You think we don't try? Tom bought Billy's paintings.'

'That's true. He bought one of my canards.' Billy didn't sound overly concerned. 'Even our battles are incestuous.'

'Everyone's got a hustle, Quilbert. Just because we're getting scammed doesn't mean we're not scamming.'

'Quentin,' I said. 'So who's the lonely widow in Anchoret with the fancy taste?'

Billy glanced at his counterpart, who was now toying with his mustache. 'I don't know the guy's name.'

'Then what's his gig with Olive?'

'They're in love,' said Artie. 'An affair of the wallet.'

'You must have noticed something,' I pursued.

Billy stepped from the window, unwound his scarf, and tossed it on a chair. He appraised me, his lips set in a thin line. 'The job was kind of *not* to notice a whole lot.'

It wasn't the time to press him, I thought. I needed something to offer and I had an idea. 'I'm going to ask some friends about your building,' I said. 'How do I get in touch with you?'

'We're often in,' said Artie.

Billy threw an idle hand around the loft. 'The phone is at the shop, as you can see.'

'All right,' I said. I gave Billy some change and my number at the *Stringer*. I told him to call me at six from a pay phone and left with a last glance at the glowing white duck.

Midday had crested outside. The temperature was tolerable in the sun, but in the shade the day's crispness had liberated an iron chill. Shopowners in shirtsleeves squinted up at the sky, smoking from the doorways of their bright, steaming stores, the windows fogged with indoor heat. Kids in down coats threw rocks at a stop sign, hitting the windshield of a parked car and dusting it in a tracery of cracks. At the end of the block I found a bank of pay phones outside a bodega and called Brooke.

Brooke was an ex of mine, a smart girl, morally sound if a touch sober. She worked for the mayor, advising his office on housing and land use. Once upon a time she'd done a degree in urban planning, but several years in city government had cured her of her idealism. Still, she sided with tenants, ordinary city dwellers, and other entities without limited liability. It was the losing side in a city run by developers, but she waged her urban warfare, block by block, to stall the monied reaper from making hay of old buildings.

'Hi,' I said. 'It's Quentin. Got a minute?'

There was a rustling sound and then she came back on. 'Can we talk later, Quentin? I'm on the taxpayers' dime.'

'I'm a taxpayer,' I reminded her.

She sighed. 'Barely.'

Across the street punks and dogwalkers passed into and out of a park. A man in a suede jacket was yelling at an unimpressed young woman.

'It's about work. I'm calling on behalf of some of your constituents.'

She considered this with a certain mordancy. 'Are *they* taxpayers?'

'Unlikely.'

'Well?'

'You know those hope zones you told me about?'

She might have been scarred by my habitual sarcasm because she said, 'Fuck you.'

'I'm actually not joking.'

It took her a moment to fortify her trust. 'Well, what about them?'

Hope zones were a boondoggle the real-estate lobby had cooked up with the governor's office. The idea was to get development money into poor neighborhoods; in practice it meant lavish tax write-offs for projects the builders already wanted to do, or had underway, on the city's gentrifying fringe. These were those hotbeds of creative ferment which had begun to emerge from poverty and neglect on their own—artistic enclaves that, having revitalized organically, landlords and building moguls salivated over. The demolition of old buildings accelerated. Factories and lofts were torn down to make way for luxury high-rises and hotels—that is, when developers didn't simply buy out or evict tenants to gut-renovate what ten years before mortgage lenders wouldn't have accepted as collateral.

Where hope zones came, hope fled. The mayor, who may have shared Brooke's skepticism, had too much political interest in the development sector and the trades to sanction more than a piecemeal defense. The creative class gave the derelict, busted-up downtown new life, only for the palm-anointing power brokers with friends in the governor's mansion to descend like Midas and transmute deviancy into condos. An old story.

I explained Billy's situation to Brooke, the efforts to deny his building a C of O and to bribe the residents out of their leases. I asked whether his address didn't happen to fall within the latest hope-zone boundaries the governor had approved. Brooke didn't know off the top of her head but said to call her back in ten. 'This isn't a joke, right?' she said. I promised it wasn't and we hung up.

My hands had grown numb. I bought a coffee at the corner store and loitered inside. Flyers lay as thick as feathers on the noticeboard up front, ads for lessons and services and an endless number of showbills. The Obstetricians were playing Paradise Alley that week; Theoretical Mischief and Gallstone Galore the week after. Level 103 had a gig coming up with Sancho Pancho. Same Old Beige with a group—a trio?—called Fem, Gnome & Oli G. de Spiritus. The notices imbricated to a significant depth. Peeling them back I found more of the same, and underneath everything another placard in its public-service type: WE USE ART TO RE-FABRICATE A BASIS FOR INDIVIDUALITY IN THE FACE OF THE STRUCTURAL DETERMINATION OF OUR LIVES.

Back on the street, my coffee steaming atop the pay phone, I dialed Brooke again. 'Bingo,' she said before I'd even spoken. 'Tucked inside the latest boundary proposal.'

'From the statehouse?'

'You make it sound like a democratic institution.'

'What about the C of O?'

'What about it?'

'You don't know if anyone's taken an interest in stalling it?'

'*It?*'

'All right, it's an epidemic,' I said.

'You know Leo Lazarus?'

'The comptroller?'

'Our onetime comptroller, yes. He's a lobbyist now, he just won't die. He's been making the rounds to council members. Some ludicrous campaign about fire risk in industrially zoned buildings.'

'Good honest work in the public interest.'

'I'm sure they'll write it off.'

'You don't know who hired him?'

'It's a holding company. One of those faceless phantoms, you know? Fancy representation in the city and some bogus address in the sticks.'

I asked what it was called.

'Let me see . . .' I fed more change into the machine while Brooke looked up the name. 'Chinvat Enterprises,' she said. 'Whatever that means. An LLP. They're using Suchman-Dieke.'

'Spell *Chinvat* . . . ,' I heard myself say, but I had made the leap, pricked by an otherworldly awareness, the memory of Bruce's old joke and term of abuse for his father's company. Chinvat Bridge Co., he called it, meaning, it seemed to me, that his father, for his pains, would no more achieve the far shore of paradise on that attenuating roadway than a camel would trespass the eye of a needle. Maybe Bruce included himself, I don't know. But this could be no coincidence. Perhaps in real life, not here. Not after my encounter with Dex, and with Jada, and my growing certainty of what—*who*—lay at the center of this web. Was it a joke then? A secret message? I'd known to expect Bruce, yet this confirmation of what I already dimly understood broke into my peace, dented or disfigured something. Its implication ran through *everything*, down to the taproots of ardor. The seamlessness of life splintered like an ice-skin on asphalt, revealing the grooves in fate.

I was still on the line with Brooke, the fog of my breath releasing gently in the air. I thought of Bruce, that gravitational nub around which my life seemed to orbit and, in circling, draw back to when I felt this motion as the possibility of escape. The pale avenue blanketed in winter's faintness, in a dissolution in color like age, startled me with its reality. For I was *here*, and not here—as if a telescope had collapsed and I were left inhabiting the sudden condensation, dimensions pushed together as though, for a brief moment, time had been made to overlap in space as it does in memory. 'Hello?' I heard Brooke say. I murmured, 'I'm here,' though I was far away. 'What are you thinking?' she said, and to answer honestly, I saw, to mention my old friend, would be to play the lunatic. 'I'm thinking . . .' I picked through my words slowly, prying my mind from the figure it attached to. 'I'm thinking Billy and his friends are getting screwed.'

Whoever had organized the lobbying effort to ensure their building was considered legally uninhabitable had had a hand in drawing up the latest hope zone. Tom Olive's bank was involved and now, it seemed, so was Bruce. I couldn't tell Brooke that my mind had drifted again to that lonely figure in Anchoret, the one Billy had done his courier runs for. I had no doubt that whatever loyal discretion Billy maintained for his one-time paymaster would collapse upon learning that this figure had quite likely been working to evict him from his shabby paradise. But having thanked Brooke and let her return to work, I decided against returning to Billy's loft and found myself walking instead, walking with no destination in mind but simply to locate the rhythm of my thoughts.

Strands of speculation swirled like ribbons at the edge of sight. Of course it had been Bruce all along, crouched like a morphing virus in the code. We say 'of course' to gesture at a hidden center. I had little doubt now who my coauthor really was, but to what end he strove remained a mystery. What business did Bruce have with Tom Olive? Why spend time speculating on real estate, driving artists from their lofts? These were the big-city machinations, the development politics, he abhorred. I called my friend to mind. I tried to picture him. This was harder than I expected. There is something assaultively plain about Bruce, not homely but unremarkable, and it feeds the force of him, his iron drive. What he was doing here, what moral boundaries he had strayed, and what I had to give or gain by intruding, I couldn't say.

I walked several miles, turning over these thoughts, and sat for a time on a bench in the sun. When it fell behind the towers to the west I rose and moved south. The air was icy. I passed diners advertising dinner specials, cuts of marbled meat in the butcher's vitrine. Junkies and musicians pulled rag jackets taut against the wind. Weak threads of steam drifted at our feet. In a gallery canvases were lined up on coat hangers like dresses on a rack. Flags hung limply beneath apartment windows. I kept marching through this sprung mechanism, as clatteringly cold and alive as a dancing skeleton. I no longer had the comforting illusion of arbitrariness, that refuge for meaning free from the impress of human design. Bruce had banished it at a stroke, and with it any chance I had of indulging this fantasy, this lucid dream. Driving toward or away from one's goal in a universe that folds in on itself makes as little sense as walking to the end of the earth. But what was hardest to accept, and what I now understood, was that if Bruce lay everywhere in my path like the grain in the wood this world was built of, Jada was no chance reoccurrence either, nor even the private reverie of my own twitching past buried in its shallow grave. Here the truths of mental life bodied forth concretely, reminding us we are only temporary, provisional vessels in an ongoing communication.

Chinese take-out joints began dotting the storefronts, venting heat from their kitchens. Despite the weather their side doors stood open, oil sizzling in deep fryers. The grid kinked and went crooked, streets attenuating like capillaries. Above the dry cleaners, tenants blew smoke from cracked windows. The tall, narrow streets rested in an early dusk, the sky mostly blotted out. I emerged into the plaza facing the courthouse where I had met Jada just days before. It stood like a proud brow in the dissipating, angular light. Workers trickled out. Dendritic shadows stretched across the square, and pigeons wheeled through the day's last breath. I stopped beneath a denuded tree whose branches swiped at one another in the wind. The clouds broke at the final instant and a canary blush shone above the rooflines. I drifted off, daydreaming, until soft hands covered my eyes and the light found gemmy pockets in the wool.

'Guess who?' I turned to find her laughing and we kissed. 'What is it?' she said when we pulled away.

'What?'

She ran a finger down the crease that went from my eye to my mouth. 'A touch of sorrow,' she said. 'Like you'd seen a ghost.'

She wasn't far off. I told her I'd heard from an old friend, someone I hadn't been in touch with in a long time. 'Walk with me to the office,' I said. 'I'm expecting a work call at six.'

A block or two into our walk she asked, 'So who is it?'

The small stone church we were passing, set in a triangle of streets, looked like it belonged to a rural village, not a city. 'An old colleague,' I said. 'We worked together ages ago. Bruce.' I meant to elaborate but, having uttered this, the impossibility of explaining further brought me up short. When exactly had I worked with Bruce? Where? Jada didn't press me, but I could see down the barrel of these irreconcilable facts. I saw too late what a tangle of lies it would take to tousle the contradictions sufficiently. She already had the scent. 'It couldn't have been *that* long ago,' she muttered. And it seemed that beneath the sovereignty of cyclic time these stars were destined to crash into each other forever: me, Jada, Bruce.

We walked north in silence. I could feel a mood growing in her, an annoyance as, against her own desire, she found reason to doubt me. Perhaps a sorrow too. At the office I held the door and we climbed the stairs to the second floor, where Frances, the nighttime receptionist, greeted us.

'Dave in?' I asked.

'Just left.'

'Perfect timing.'

She rolled her eyes and shot Jada a look. 'Watch out for this one,' she said. 'He's sneaky.'

I thanked her for the vote of confidence and we went in. The newsroom was nearly empty. A few people hunched over their desks on deadline. The phone rang at intervals and we heard Frances answer curtly. Not long before I would have killed for this job, but looking around I found the place grim, grungy in the sallow light. The cheap, threadbare carpet. The desks piled with yellowed, decaying newsprint. The glare of streetlights simmered in dark windows on the south wall.

Jada leaned against my desk. 'So why did this friend of yours pop up now?'

I shook my head. 'Would you believe he's mixed up with Dex.'

'Mixed up how?'

'They take salsa classes together.' She stared at me. 'They have a common passion,' I said. 'Neither of them likes banks.'

The absurdity of the situation must have struck her. 'And you met Bruce working at a paper?'

'In a sense, yes.'

'What *sense*?'

With anyone else I would have dodged the question or made a joke, chided my interrogator for nosiness. But this wouldn't work with her, I knew.

'That's a hard question to answer.'

'Try.' Already it was breaking: the perfection of this reality, sealed off from the deteriorations of lesser worlds, less pristine sentiments.

'I don't want to lie.'

'That's easy, tell the truth.'

'It's not that simple.'

She must have noticed my anguish. '*When* did you know him?' she said.

'It was a long time ago . . . and also not a long time ago.'

'You're not making sense.' She looked at me. I thought she was angry, but in retrospect I wonder whether she might not have begun to understand. How that's possible I can't explain. We held each other's gaze; she wouldn't let mine go. I was about to speak when Frances called from the front, 'Quentin, phone. I'm putting you through on line four.'

I held up a finger to Jada, picked up the receiver, and pressed the blinking button. 'Hello?' I said. She turned and walked over to the bank of dim, glowing windows.

'It's Alfonse,' said the voice. 'You asked me to call you. Artie, needless to say, is in a fit of jealousy.'

'Hey, Billy.'

'Alfonse,' said the voice. 'It's Alfonse for business, journalistic or otherwise. I could have spent your money on wine, you know.'

'All right, thank you,' I said. 'I held up my end of the bargain too.' I explained to Billy that I'd talked to a friend in the mayor's office and I sketched for him what I'd learned about the web of interests connecting DeBere Fleisch and his friend in Anchoret to the governor's hope zones and his loft. Forces were at work to deny his building and others like it C of Os. 'They won't stop with the sticks until you eat their carrots,' I said. 'That'll make sense to Artie. And when you do,' I added, 'the state will do everything but pay the developers to turn your block into luxury apartments.'

'Forgive me if I'm not falling out of my chair in shock,' said Billy.

'Fair enough.' I gently underscored the perversity of his couriering work in light of what we now knew. What I couldn't figure was why Tom involved him at all.

Billy laughed ruefully. 'Olive lives for the scene. The seamier the better. He's not giving up his gold watch, but if he can rub elbows with us lowlifes, he's there. The only sorts he likes more than artists are prostitutes and criminals.'

'Your uninhibited life arouses him.'

'Arousal's not his problem.'

'So Tom wanted you around.'

'The sleazeball owns my paintings. Calls it arbitrage when he's drunk. Get them coming and going, he says.'

'How'd you feel about playing a joke on Tom?'

'What kind of joke?'

I told Billy to arrange one last handoff. I would do the run for him and he could pocket the cash. And I'd get him out of this once and for all.

'That's a promise you can make?'

'Yes.'

He seemed skeptical of my assurance, but he agreed to get in touch with Tom. He said they usually met in the lounge at DisPater. 'We used to do the Sludge Factory,' he explained, 'before they got shut down.' I said I'd drop by the next night. 'Hey, don't spook Tom,' he said.

'How would I do that?'

'I don't know,' he said. 'I just get a feeling you might.'

I was telling him not to worry when he ran out of coins and the call dropped. Jada was still staring out the window. I could just make out her pensive reflection in the glass. She watched the traffic crawl in the street below. We got our coats and headed out. A wind had come up, a softer element entering the air. The headlong breeze, with its damper, warmer air, barreled down the broad avenues. We clutched our collars at the neck.

A change had come over Jada. Her mood had slipped out of reach. She no longer pressed me about Bruce, and I found myself as a result talking about him, the young man I'd known, so uncompromising in his judgments, so impossible and naive. He wasn't a figure of this world but a misplaced traveler from a realm of unearthly purity. A place where anger was the life in one's veins. His refusal to indulge our little dishonesties amounted to a kind of holy wisdom. I described his fights with his father, his guilt about the fortune of his birth, and his early foray into journalism. I told her about his break with his family. His obsession with debt—a strange, narrow fixation, and yet a proxy for a metaphysics of responsibility, the impossible question of what we owe one another and are owed. I didn't mention Bruce's war years. The war hadn't yet occurred.

And now Bruce, I continued, rounding the corner onto Jada's block, where the wind tore at awnings and dragged garbage cans in their enclosures, now Bruce had turned to some other life entirely. A criminal life? I didn't know what else to call it. He'd seized the very harrow of exploitation he reviled. There was no making sense of it. Did people change so much? Did they possess these possibilities inside them all along?

In Jada's building, voices, music pressed through the walls of the apartments on different floors. Dirt lined the stairway. The lights were out on the landings. She let me talk. In that instant, recalling Bruce, I could find no firm dimension to separate moralism from evil, the fanaticism of the one from the selfishness of the other. Each liberated itself to act by an autonomous judgment. Each disdained half measures as the imperfection in life. Maybe this explained what knit together the iterations of my friend.

Jada unlocked the door, tossing her keys in a bowl and flipping on the lights. She took off her coat, filled the kettle with water, and put it on the stove. We settled opposite each other on the couch. Though poorly heated, the room was warm after the cold. A dim light bathed it in the color of strong tea. She looked at me. 'Maybe you saw who you wanted to see in Bruce. We all displace our conscience onto others. We look inside, we're revolted by what we see. How far short of our expectations we fall. We imagine it's different for others. Maybe Bruce was never who you thought.'

'He was young,' I admitted. 'He could have reflected back to me the person he thought I wanted him to be.'

'Maybe he was unknown to himself,' she said, bringing up her legs and tucking them under her. 'We place the burden of living without contradiction on the young. We ask them to embody the simpler moral world we wish we lived in and leave them unprepared for life.' I didn't say anything. 'When I first saw you, I had the feeling I knew you, that I'd known you before, and I took this recognition for love. I wasn't exactly wrong, but now I don't know that I was exactly right, either. I can feel something moving beneath this. The improbability of too many coincidences in too tight a space, a time . . . Now your friend Bruce mixed up with my client Dex. I can't shake the sense that this somehow *involves* me. Don't ask me what that means. Either you know or you don't.'

What could I say? I said nothing. I went to the bathroom and ran the water until it turned warm and splashed it on my face. Only then did I realize how cold I was, clenched into myself as if absorbing a punch that had been landing for days, or much longer still. I turned on the shower and let the room fill with steam, stepped out of my clothes and into the water. The hot liquid ran over me in an annihilating torrent. The sensation gathered me into it, leaving no room for anything else. We are just poor stupid creatures, I thought, creatures of the earth, not meant for the godly knowing we clutch at like blind drunks. The water fell from my cheeks like tears.

After a time I emerged. Jada was still sitting on the couch, gazing out the window. The first raindrops appeared on the glass the way the first stars emerge at night. The books along the wall showed glimmers of gilt lettering on their spines. Jada turned as I came near. I had the urge to confess to her every privacy I had wasted my life protecting. To her encompassing heart I knew my badness wouldn't be enough. I knew she would walk me to the end of myself and say, 'This? Only this?' But in this intuition that she surpassed me, and might therefore coach me past the crossroads of primitive horror in myself, I couldn't fail to hear the voice of inconvenient wisdom whispering that I alone was capable of such a journey. I would be my own guide—and is this not the true promise and enormity of a cave, worse and deeper than anything I could discover in Bruce's acts, or rather what lay behind them? The madness of self-knowledge. How unequipped we are for the glare that lives in the raw outdoors. And how we would suffer for embarking on this program of liberation without first locating a proper self-love for our own rottenness. Without this peculiar love we would tear ourselves apart for finding, at the end of our quest for angels, our self.

'You intend to find him,' she said. It wasn't a question. And I did intend that foolishness. 'And this will end,' she said. I didn't answer. Heavy drops now hit the window with the patternless noise of corn kernels popping in a pan. I wanted to tell her I would return to her when this was over, but it wasn't the truth. I couldn't remain in this tomb as Bruce had attempted to do, this endless lucid dream. I had no interest in the imperium of solipsism, the loneliness of a god.

I reached out to touch Jada and felt her refuse me. She was done with so much playacting. It is tempting now to dismiss her somehow—as a symbol in an inner drama—but she was as real as you are sitting there before me, her legs drawn up, her eyes shining and alive. The hair at her temple had a fine definition, follicles clinging to her skin with the grip of life. Her lips curled with their precise inflection, all that makes us particular in the brushstrokes and sinusoids of love. The mole by her mouth—a goddamn mole!—pierced me. But have you truly dwelt on the reality of another person, the odd beauty of asymmetry, deformation, and felt even rescued by this foundational realness, which means nothing, with which there is nothing to do but recognize that life comes to its irreducible points, that the deepest part of us lives in these cul-de-sacs, these imperfections? They are the rock we cling to in the seas of mutability. Was I then responding to the sharpness of feeling that breaks us open in a manner we partway like? Or was sorrow's approach only a symptomatic perception of a deeper structure moving inside me, reorganizing an amplitude that represented, constellated in form, an attitude toward the future?

A long pause had bled out since Jada last spoke. Now she said, 'And if you can't?'

'I'll find him anyway,' I said.

'Why?' It wasn't angry, the way she said it. The rain rapped against the screen.

'It's who I am. What I do.'

'And we have these natures, you're sure?'

'Never sure.' I tried to smile. 'We're flies caught in webs. We didn't make the webs.'

She nodded. 'What are they?'

'Fairy tales,' I said. 'The gossamer of belief.' The rain was really coming down.

'And the spider?'

'There is no spider.'

She said nothing. The radiators rattled to life. I dressed. We opened a bottle of wine and sat watching the downpour, each with our own thoughts, until the window fogged over completely and we only knew the storm by the sound.

Somewhere time ticked on in the deep machinery of the universe.

Somewhere insects caught, struggled, and hung from silken tombs.

We made love.

The rain had stopped when I awoke.

I woke abruptly. We had fallen asleep without meaning to and lay entwined. In my disorientation I didn't immediately know where I was. The darkness you encounter at such moments is sometimes so complete that you can't help wondering whether day hasn't extinguished permanently and you won't sleep and wake forever in the haunted city of the night. A vintage lamp with a clunky metal shade cast a glow just weak enough not to disturb the room's underwater stillness. I sat, gathering my wits. Jada slept peacefully, I listened to her breathe, so soft a trickle it hardly seemed adequate to the preservation of life.

I had been dreaming of my grandparents' farm, the stirring beasts, watching the land emerge in the watery light of the rousing sun, pallid against the milk-pink embroidery of the sky. The rolling bluegrass lay in the shadow of the barn, stately red with white trim, and rocks rose in the distant meadow like the backs of breaching whales. This returned to me with an unusual clarity. The honeyed light swollen with dust and pollen. The copse of trees set jauntily against the sky. Toads the color of wet sand struggling up the bank of the reed gully that sat muddy and dry in summer. The scene was so luxuriant it might have been a painting, only now transposed across the axis of memory, like a mirror image, as crystal clear as the sun that settled dew-like in the horses' eyes; and yet only a reflection, a magical vision of a vanished past, so real I could run my hands through the fountain grass and throw the latch on the barn door, drawing a grudging creak from the hinges—could almost hear my grandmother calling us in to eat, while the cows turned their heads to us idly behind the fence, or lay under shade trees in the midday heat. The warped windows of the farmhouse caught the light, old and imperfect so that the sun's rays puddled on them in bulbous forms. In this fading breath of dream I felt the coincident sense-form of so many departures—unrecoverable moments, lost people, the caustic of life's first bitter lessons—and I understood in the dim way we understand such things that all our experiences, our entire lives, rhyme on the tonality of these emotions, this iterative formulary, at once dull in its repetition and nuanced, layered even, in all the pleated crosscurrents of its ambivalence.

This was my benediction, then, to pass my hand over once again, memories we never fully return to, having lost the innocence in which they were forged; intimations we can't later recall as more than the afterglow of an emotion that pulses briefly to life, a fulgurant residue cut off from an ecology of feeling. These are memories not of how things once were but of what it once felt like inside us. And indeed, in this dream, as if called further into myself, I felt the forest beckon me and, after a time, I entered it to find a figure standing at some distance, turned away. The high canopy strained the light as I approached, the warmth of this glow landing everywhere on moss, on gnarled roots running through and over knuckles of rock, the rufous pallor of downed pine needles, rotting leaves and veiny webs patching the divots and hollows. The embowering profluence assembled from nature's motley dazzled me as I stumbled forward. Who was this figure, silhouetted before me? A primordial temper ran through the trees, an inkling of containment and infinity, and I had a sudden sense that I could choose the face on this figure, could compel its being when it turned, but to do so would surrender a knowledge that lay beyond me, a message from without. Thus only by willed oblivion or inattention could I, as I neared, keep this fragile mystery intact. This horrid mystery. What is the thing the mind anticipates, and hopes, and fears to see? I had my hand on the figure's shoulder when, still turned from me, with unexpected clarity in the sylvan hush, I heard it say, 'Wait—not yet.' And I awoke.

There I sat in the night's cold-blooded stillness. The city might have been dead beyond the windows. No sound rose from it, no more than a weeping glow of inhuman light. The apartment was frigid, the radiators long past rattling and cool to the touch. How did I know I was awake? How do I know now that I was then? It is only an undefinable sense of wakefulness that stands between us and disregarding our experience. And what is this gauge of alertness, of being awake to life? And who can say when, as time passes, the categorical distance between dream and memory attenuates until the two are no different at all, neither real nor unreal, but subjective and imbued with both possibilities at once?

Jada was still sleeping. I lay back down. The warmth under the blankets stilled my thoughts. I didn't believe I would sleep and didn't realize I had drifted off until I woke to the timelessness of a gray sky and saw Jada in a chair. She held a mug in her hands and didn't immediately respond when I sat up. For a moment I had no memory that anything had changed between us; I was still somewhere else. She turned to me at last like a sculpture animating at a magician's word. I must have reflected the undimmed ardor of an expired moment. It was only her look that jarred me into remembering the previous day. She wasn't cruel. Her coldness wasn't meant for me, but she had hardened herself against the disappointment I represented.

After a moment she spoke. 'I had a dream,' she said. 'A strange dream. Strangely vivid, I suppose.' She stared straight ahead and seemed to speak from still within the vision. 'You were there, and so was I, and your friend Bruce. Yes, Bruce. And I was in love with Bruce. And you were his best friend. Or, well, "friend" . . . You were his hero, his mentor—and I loved him because he was pure the way young people sometimes are.'

She rose and came and sat with me on the bed, looking beyond me as she spoke. 'Well, I was young and naive in this dream too. And Bruce and I lived together in an apartment with a view of a shabby park and a garden. Rioting vines and weeds and stubborn wildflowers threaded the chain-link fencing and the concrete. I worked as a lawyer'—she smiled—'and Bruce worked as a journalist like you. And we lived in a chaos of chipped dishes and unwashed plates, dried-out tea bags, crusts of bread and fruit peelings on the counter.

'Just beyond the buildings facing us we caught snatches of the elevated train. The cars rumbled on, day and night—a comforting sound whose absence we noticed more than the grumble and screech of the wheels. We slept on the floor on a simple mattress. Bruce refused to spend money on anything and this meant senseless cost cutting. Penny-wise, pound-foolish: that was him in a nutshell, fixated on his battles to the exclusion of all else. Maybe a trace of something impure burned in him alongside his passion, a contaminant sparking chemical green in the flame. His moral impulse seemed at times less about goodness than his great desire to punish badness. He wanted to afflict the comfortable—men like his father, whose compromises he knew too intimately. He intuited that his moral sense had been purchased from the spoils of his father's self-serving efforts. Every cent negotiated out of an employee's paycheck ran together into the river of plenty that nourished him, the expiating child, who would atone for the sins that had created him. No, his father's sins weren't so bad; Bruce had his sights on the dark-winged angel that enfolded men like him in its wings. They hadn't sold the controlling interest in their souls, but only a portion in hope that the full organ would grow back. They meant to have it both ways, and this seemed almost worse to him. It asked less courage than true evil and so it blossomed pervasively. Everyday corruption required nothing special of its human host beyond weakness and cowardice. It meant to cheat fate.

'A contradiction in terms, no? And when the bill came due, could you carve the rotten part from the pure? Funny how a dream can give you a story and the story's shadow at the same time. I don't think I've ever had a dream so detailed or particular. So vivid, as I say. It wasn't a dream at all but a prophecy. A prophecy of the past . . . I say that, and you should laugh. But you're not laughing. And I'm not entirely joking.

'Well, Bruce loved you. Worshipped you. He went to work each morning in his cheap collared shirts, the strap of a satchel around his neck, a piece of toast in his mouth. In his affectations he tried to follow your lead, but the light smoldering in his eye was his own. An anger that at times bordered on pleasure. You were immune from this and more effective for it. Bruce admired that too, the coolness of your fury. The humor that ran at ironic angles to self-importance. I wonder now whether you really were immune, or whether you were simply stronger than Bruce, more fortified in spirit, less sickly pure. Maybe the fat in your soul could trap and isolate that illness. It doesn't really matter. I watched Bruce watching you. Studying you, idolizing . . . I could pick it out in the way he spoke. And he spoke of you often, ran after you, downstream from your shadow. You must have known. Yes, I see it now. Bruce meant to study what he found great in you and graft it onto himself. But you can never catch a shadow. Aiming for the stars, you strike out into cold, dark space.

'I shared Bruce's intensity and severity in this dream. I was, you see, myself and not myself. I recognized this character as "me," but I would never have become such a person, not in this life. I have too much wickedness in me, too much irony. Posed against this alter ego I am practically bourgeois. My dream double frightened me. She could make life unlivable in attempting to fix it . . .

'But can you see then how much not just Bruce, but *Bruce and I* needed you? You were a different answer. Your solvent cut our zealotry. That's what I thought. You'd fortified yourself with enough humor to keep hope from curdling into hate. How had you done this? I don't know. A twinkle in your eye when anger seemed more appropriate. And still Bruce must have meant something to you. You undertook more of the stories he cared about. It didn't always work out. When you couldn't nail a story down, you'd say, "We'll get 'em next time," while Bruce ranted and raged. He broke his wrist punching a chair at home. Lawyers had strong-armed the paper into killing a piece. Bruce refused to go to the doctor—like he was punishing *his enemies* by doing so. He winced when I held him down in bed. That wincing seemed to be his consolation. What's in a man like that? Part of it must be the primordial memory of an age made whole by gods. You laugh, but I'm serious. When we weren't forced to choose between chaos, which kills meaning, and pattern, which kills free will. He meant to see order up and down the scales.

'But I am speaking too much of Bruce when you are the figure peeking discreetly from behind the hedge in this garden scene. It's you I'm interested in. Your motive. Your nature. The crushed rock ground to liquid in the earth's depths that flowed into your mold. I thought Bruce was the martyr. We all did. He looked—acted—the part. But I wonder whether you weren't the one who meant to give yourself for our sins. Maybe because you had more to give, and for this bounty giving seemed natural. You'd made your peace with the good. And you were right to fear that fanaticism in the perfect. To be scared of what's frightening is no failing.'

Jada looked at me, weighing a thought I couldn't anticipate. A breeze shook drops of water from the fire escape. 'Bruce brought you around,' she said. 'Maybe it flattered you, this idolatry of youth. For so long he had simply wanted me to appreciate you the way he did that he failed to see how esteem passes into love. You didn't know it. I didn't show you. When I was a girl I had a tutor, oh much older than me. He seemed old at the time, in any case, and I loved him as you love certain adults when you're young, people who know so much more of the world and life and who show you what it is to be grown in the gentle, forgiving way they don't dismiss your inexperience. I yearned for him. What did I want: His body? His lips? I don't know. Let's not discount any of it. I wrote about him in my journal in those terms of adolescent anguish as a way to think about him when he wasn't there. I yearned for some form of passion by one turn more abstract than sex. I wanted to be swallowed by his confidence, his ease, carried inside the bubble of his maturity like a womb. It was sexual and filial at once. It flowed in the wrong direction from what our conventions understand. Desire strains against every barrier soldered to the soul . . .

'But I was a grown-up in my dream and you were only a little older. I felt the second stirring of this longing, its echo. Maybe you knew, after all. I only partly hid it from you. And Bruce and I had grown stiff in our interactions by then. We made dinner and talked about work. We swore on the principles that united us and grew apart as the shell around us started to crack. You could scarcely breathe in our apartment, the claustrophobia had set in so tight. Bruce was scared, I think, that what drove him would never be satisfied, would only recycle upward, feeding on itself. You can't put out a blaze by dousing it in fuel. But what else was there? What did he know to do but give more of himself, work harder, sacrifice more.

'It was obscene—yes, I mean that—how chipper and oblivious you remained through it all. Oh, yes, you *knew*. The great undeceived roving eyes arrested briefly enough in their pilgrimage to tell their secrets. Your banter is a cultivated trait, a distraction from the gearwork of whatever calculation takes place behind the facade . . . Yes, I *get* it. You were all too conscious. And you and I fell into the habit of getting drinks after work. First Bruce invited me to join you and your pals. You liked this grotty dive, a truly terrible place. A pub so without pretension that *was* its pretension. Bruce included me one evening and then, just like that, I kept showing up—even when Bruce stayed on in the office after you and the others had called it quits. You and I would grab a bite, and sometimes another drink after dinner, growing more intimate in spite of, or perhaps because of, what stood between us. Did you have a responsibility to see what was happening? I'm not particularly interested in that question, but it hangs there.

'Of course Bruce left . . . Not me, I mean. He left to report from the war. Which war is that? Well, you tell me. Maybe the intensity of combat would soothe his spirit, banish whatever sense of undeservingness haunted him. When people go to war by choice it's always about what is insatiable in them, or what feels unforgivable.

'But did you *encourage* him to go? That's the question I'm interested in. Yes, you told him it was a smart move professionally. But was there more? On some level did you want him to leave, and were you worried when he did? Did I, in short, have something to do with your advice? Because if so, then you would have something to answer for, since, well, you can imagine: Bruce got killed. Got himself good and shot. Or blown up, I don't know. Got made unwhole at any rate, disintegrated when he was always trying to integrate everything more profoundly.'

'In the dream,' I said.

She looked at me strangely.

'This happened in your dream,' I repeated.

'Yes,' she said. 'In my dream.'

'And before Bruce died?'

'You and I were in love.'

'Like this?'

'No. Of course not.'

'Why of course?'

'Are you listening to me?' There was frustration in her voice. 'I was a different person. So different, in fact, it's as if you took this double and molded her with a sculptor's hands into the version of me you liked best. The version I am now. More suitable to your desires. In the dream our love wasn't easy or light. It wasn't *fun*. Not carefree. It bore the weight of another person's absence, the millstone of guilt. But more than that, it wasn't real. Oh, we felt it. But not for whom we thought. We were screens for each other onto which we projected a necessary idea, a flat image that looked full because it clung to a body. We were each other's promise of escape—from all we had been, all that had come before—flight from the choked atmosphere of disappointment in seeing the grand illusion and charlatanism of our ideals like idols unmasked. No, we thought—we can push through and by self-delusion shape reality to our needs. But your need wasn't mine and mine wasn't yours. In silence we let each other believe it was a delusion we shared. But as the distance between the idea of a person and his reality grows, it is with the feeling of drifting on a raft at sea that you look up one day and notice you are far from shore. The land is gone. And land is better.'

We met each other with quiet eyes. I thought, glancing out at the skeins of moving fog and crushed marble of cloud, that I might have been gazing out over the sea she described, that our bearing was a return and a venturing forth, a home unto itself, that it was the companionability of the unfinished, which is the companionability of the sea, and I hoped—I don't know how to say it—that we should live forever in the safekeeping of this passage, in this mood trembling and rolling with the waves, a motion that grew from such subtle, unknown reaches in the depths that we felt cradled by secret hands. It was a glorious day, dark glowering and glorious, and full of a conversation that like the rain was everywhere and purifying, with a lament that protects the embers of such necessary light against the cold and damp of what is only actual, passing, real.

'It happened,' I said. 'But I suppose you know that.'

She nodded. 'But *how*?'

'In another time, another place.'

'Another world, you mean.'

'I guess I do.'

'And what am I supposed to do with that?' A note of anger glinted in her words.

'Do you doubt it?'

She considered this and shook her head. 'No. I know the dream was real. The way our ancestors knew that dreams are real. That life happens many times. But I can't accept it as easily as they did. I'll have to forget it in time.'

'How do you forget such a thing?'

She smiled at me sadly. 'It's not so hard. I'm already working to make sense of it, dulling its edges and the bite of its disappointment. Eventually it will settle where it rests most easily and fold into an intuitive understanding where it won't trouble me. This will be a kind of forgetting. We do this all the time.'

'Chalk it up to a religious experience.'

'Why not? Many people do.'

'How will you explain me?'

'To myself? I don't know. It's too soon to say. Maybe you will be the dream. Or maybe you'll dangle like a thread.'

'What if I told you that you were the dream?'

Her dark eyes pooled with light. 'From my own perspective, it makes little difference,' she said. 'A person is just a feeling to herself. And that feeling is the only thing that has a chance of being more than the dream, wouldn't you say?'

'I don't know.' I didn't have it in me to tell her what I felt—that I had jurisdiction over her existence, her very sensation of herself, blinking into existence, and blinking out. It made me think of Nino and Hassie—the thirty-second delay, the do-over. I didn't doubt that so many seconds would save untold lives. With a further moment's reflection, how many fingers wouldn't find triggers, how many headlong leaps into permanence would we recant? Death was one thing. But a person? Our past? Love? Where did the instinct for revision, for perfection end?

I looked at her. 'But Bruce isn't dead.'

She shrugged. 'Does it matter? It was just a dream, right?'

'You know that isn't true.'

'Maybe things happened differently the second time.' She seemed angry when she said this, and only later did I understand that she was talking about us. 'Anyway, for all I know he never died. I didn't see it myself. It was only the sort of thing you know in a dream.'

The morning had run late. The rain was returning. I wanted to take her in my arms, but this desire to comfort her in a sorrow I had caused was perverse. Who would I be comforting in the end? It would have been an apt question in any circumstance, but when so much of me had seeped into her that I could not discount, entirely, the possibility that I had willed her into being, it assumed a metaphysical weight.

'When you look at me like that,' she said, 'I feel like you're trying to peer beneath my skin.'

'What would I find?'

'I've never looked. Flesh, blood, veins, ribs? That's what they tell us, but can we trust them?'

'I'm not getting a knife.'

She laughed lightly and rubbed the skin on her forearm as if to confirm its flesh. 'And Bruce,' she said, 'will you take a knife to him?' Sadness touched her smile. 'We have the choice to insist on knowing, to penetrate mystery indefinitely until we've killed life's beauty and innocence, or to stop and live. Have you considered that you might stay here instead and be happy?'

'You don't really believe I have a choice?'

'I don't think you believe you do,' she said. 'But I have to believe it.'

I couldn't tell her that the ignorance she recommended, in light of what I knew, amounted to a species of aloneness, a way of retiring from the world. This would have engraved more deeply what she was trying to forget. And maybe she understood my thoughts and shared them because she opened her mouth to speak but thought better of it. And in that moment of self-correction I heard everything that lay behind the dam of caution and pride. It was futile to ask me to stay. To desist. This knowledge passed between us in a transaction too subtle to name.

And so I'd give up this garden. I had no choice. It wasn't knowledge that exiled us from Eden but that, in possessing knowledge, paradise was no longer paradise. We could only find it in each other then, by shared dreaming. But it had to *be*, in fact, another—a person who could surprise you and force compromise on your reveries and myths. And in this twilight world I felt certain only of Bruce's ability to tell me what I didn't already know. Though leaving Jada pained me, these thoughts gave me comfort. Steeled my resolve. Only now do I wonder how certain I should have been of the privileged subjecthood I kept for myself and denied her.

I left that afternoon. We barely said a word. An understanding had annealed and we no longer spoke of reconnecting. I knew it wouldn't happen. I have to think Jada knew it too. To what extent I had complicated her reality I can't say. Your guess is as good as mine.

Looking back, I hear Ed Yang's warning more clearly. He had suggested an untethering from the ballast of external truth and a subsequent madness that took hold as one spent time inside this place, this sphere of ambiguous and liminal existence, where outer and inner reality coincided. If I could bushwhack my way to Bruce, I thought, there I would find a freestanding soul against whose reality I could judge my own. And yet I knew Jada's words for their prophecy of regret. I would turn back more layers of the onion to find that one could go ever further into subsequent truths without getting closer to *truth* itself. I'd find instead that the onion is only skin, the network only unpatterned numbers, which at best hold a warped mirror's correlation to the composition of the world beyond. Some regrets one must taste for oneself. Certain mistakes. A true loss of perspective implies the absence of perspective on this very loss.

Out in the street I recovered myself, the drizzling unguent cooling my face. Though drops of rain still fell, intimations of blue had begun to emerge in the cloud finish. The cloacal smell of wet city and the noisy streets carried me clear of remorse. A lightness played at the sutures of the day. At a thrift store I bought a camel-hued suede jacket for the night ahead. It seemed like something Billy and his friends would wear. THE FUN IS GONE, spray-painted in orange-and-magenta letters on the wall outside, announced the melancholy of my freedom. I savored this mood, walking the avenues idly, steeping in the urban fug. Jada was already disappearing from my thoughts. At my apartment I drifted into a deep, dreamless sleep, and by the time I made it back downtown the sky was a darkling ultramarine and the circus lights of the city had come on.

I prowled the boulevards, watching the metropolis take on its night-time aura, the illuminated signs, the human pageant stumbling up and down the avenues, campy, drunk, destitute, preening. Trucks rattled and huffed. Taxis choked the roadway, moving in the lanes like orange sleds on gliding runners. I stopped for a drink. Amid hedgerows of elbows and shoulders combusting sirens in the distance recalled us to the deep processes of life continuing on in the surround. Jostling drinkers. Traffic. Music, voices. A fibril of kinking salsa, shuddering bass. The noise—shouts, laughter, squealing rubber—compounded in a substance more physical than sound has any right to be. I didn't know when Billy's handoff would take place, but I knew I was still early when I spotted the grand art deco building with the mural above its marquee. DisPater commanded the street like an iniquitous temple. The crowd outside milled with the baleful air of doped sentries, too narcotized to do more than glare. As I passed through the heavy doors, the intensity of color and noise immediately severed my connection to the world outside. Bright stage lights poured down in a variegated psychedelia. This iridescence dressed the exotically coifed crowd in hued blotches that fell equally on the walls' palm-frond motif. Despite the garish eccentricity of the assembled, the scene fizzed in the mind's eye without any element settling in memory. I pushed farther in. On the main stage a performance was underway. A horrent-haired woman toting a suitcase and a large kitchen knife strutted back and forth across the papier-mâché set, stabbing walls to punctuate the monologue she delivered. She wore a cheap powder-blue business suit and had a ruddy, hemic substance smeared over her mouth. The audience cheered her on. She acknowledged their shouted comments with grins and glares. Above us, banks of canted TV sets showed a flow of soundless video, smiling faces from advertisements intermingled with clips of devastation, violence, sex. Every so often a clown appeared in the sequence, hesitant, apologetic, smiling as if it had wandered into the frame by accident. Music played, a calliope cartoon-organ theme interrupted at points by the noise of crashing machinery. I ordered a whiskey, shouting to be heard, and wandered into a room blocked off from the rest by a heavy curtain where people reclined on large carpeted risers, watching a film. It took a minute to understand what I was seeing. A series of scenes resembling TV shows and commercials came and went, recurring at intervals, all with the same actress. The image cut with the sound and static of flipping channels. There was a talk show, an exercise show, an ad for coffee with a peculiar Russian spokeswoman, a televangelist in a platinum-blond wig with a gold braided headband and a silver lamé jumpsuit, a troubadour strumming a lute, the confessional tale of a starlet manquée, public-access shows with exiguous production budgets, Dutch-tilt angles, off-plumb cameras, midday news shows, telenovelas, music videos, ads for grocery stores and laundry detergent. As the film progressed the cutting between channels accelerated, a cascade of images, words, screams, snippets, like the condensed matter of the technology's own unconscious.

The audience roared. I glanced around and saw, on the top riser, touched by a faint illumination from the projected light, the actress from the film. She watched with a quiet, wry look—a smaller, more demure person than you would have expected. When the screening concluded the audience whistled and applauded, and I drifted back into the main room where the knife-wielding woman's performance had also ended. A stage crew disassembled her set and carted out amps, arranging microphone stands and unfurling cables in its place. Each TV screen in the hovering banks now showed the image of a daisy on a white background with long capsule-shaped white petals and a pointillist yellow center. The sea of identical flowers trembled in an unseen wind.

I placed my empty glass at the end of the bar and wandered into the lounge. It was dark and relatively quiet inside. Subtle lights illuminated the area behind the bar, and on the wall opposite a banquette was lined with small round tables, lit dimly from above. I took up an empty barstool and signaled for a drink. Inset TV monitors played staticky images above the glinting skyline of liquor bottles. I watched a woman in a pink skirt suit page through titles on a blinking jukebox. From the main room,

I could just make out the first experimental licks of guitar chords, heavy with distortion.

The bartender, dancing lightly on his toes, poured my drink without a word and held up two fingers. I paid him and the woman from the jukebox came and retook her seat, two stools down. 'Then we sublet a place on Waters,' she told the bartender, picking up a story where she'd left off. '"Sublet," right? Turns out there was no lease and the building's condemned. Twenty Chinese bunking in the apartment below ours and they're cutting drugs on the second floor.'

'The Chinese?'

'No, someone called Rodney.'

'I'm called Rodney,' the bartender said.

'Really? Why have I been calling you Olivier?'

'I go by Olivier.'

'Well, I don't think this Rodney was you.' She sipped her drink. 'You haven't been cutting drugs on Waters, have you?'

He dissembled innocence. 'Not to *sell*.'

I had my back to the room and glanced around casually. A group standing at one end of the bar had shifted and I could now see a man in a pinstripe suit, sitting by himself in the far corner. He had wavy hair falling over his brow and held himself stiffly upright. A martini glass sat on the table in front of him. He looked strangely, privately pleased with himself, as if he had just received extraordinary news that could mean nothing to anyone else.

I knew it was Tom Olive. He looked ahead almost dumbly, grinning in my general direction like a secret spectacle were taking place in the air between us. He didn't register my gaze. Then I understood. On the other side of me, down the bar, a pretty, sneering woman was giving him the finger. He smiled placidly at her, his teeth gleaming between his parted lips.

'What's your story?' I didn't realize these words were addressed to me until the woman in the pink skirt suit said, 'Hello?' and waved a hand to get my attention. 'I haven't seen you before. Who are you?'

'Quentin,' I said and gave her my hand, which she glanced at briefly and didn't take. She squinted at me.

'Isolde,' she said. 'Where are you from?'

'Around.'

She sighed. 'It's the same losers in here every night.'

'And yet you keep showing up.'

'Looks like I'm one of them.' She sipped her drink from a straw. 'We're sick of fucking each other, but we're all in each other's bands. So what are you going to do?'

I gestured at Tom Olive. 'What band's that guy in?'

'That creep? He's in no one's band. He's just here in case some drunk chick loses her keys.'

'I thought maybe there was a board meeting.'

'Room and board. Tit for twat.' I laughed at this. 'Oh, thank you for laughing. How generous.' Her eyes were rimmed with kohl, the lids moving as if under a certain weight.

'What's your band called?'

'We used to be the Hopefuls,' she said. 'Now we're Lush Whore.'

'Why the switch?'

'We're big on honesty.' She took a drink. 'And what are you supposed to be? Another bond trader with a vintage jacket?'

'Why not? Now I guess you're going to tell me you didn't grow up middle-class.'

'Upper, you pervert. Skiing lessons, trombone, Catholic school . . . They gave me the deluxe package. Your shirt's full of holes, you know.'

'I know. It didn't come that way.'

'How'd it come?'

'Hopeful.'

She smirked. 'Don't misunderstand. We're all whores here. We're just waiting for our stock to peak.'

'When's that?'

'Didn't they teach you anything in bank school? Only dummies think they can time the market.'

'Then what's plan B?'

She shrugged, shook the ice in her glass, and downed what was left of her drink. 'Hang on for the ride. Try to get out before the fun stops.' She inclined her empty glass toward me, offering, it seemed, to let me buy her a drink. 'You're not really a banker, are you?'

'No.' I tried to flag down the bartender. 'Journalist.'

'What's that, like a failed poet?'

'Sounds about right.'

'You in a band?'

'Uh-uh. Why?'

'Most failed poets I know are in bands.' Rodney, the bartender, was waiting to take our order. 'This is Quentin,' Isolde told him. 'He's getting a band together.'

'Right on,' said Rodney and poured our drinks. I glanced down the bar. Billy was at the entrance to the lounge, greeting friends.

'Tell me something, Isolde.' We had our drinks—whiskey for me, something fluorescent pink in her glass.

'Where's Tristan? I've heard it.'

I didn't see exactly how to ask what I meant to ask. 'I like the scene,' I said. 'The shows, the pageant. Everyone's an artist, and too hip to get caught trying. But what part's the joke and what part's serious?'

She looked at me, an arch remark on her tongue, but she turned and in a soft voice she murmured, 'Nobody's sure.' This earnestness seemed to spring something in her, a cloaked ardency. 'Maybe we don't recognize the distinction,' she said. It was in fast, whispered words that she spoke. She explained that they'd all grown up in vulgar suburbs: sprinklers on the lawn, shiny cars in the driveways. One minute they were watching the news—missiles to level cities and melt off skin, daddy figures in suits telling them why we had to burn Asian thatch villages. Next minute ads for cereal, swimming pools. Flags waving and stirring music. Diets to make you thin enough that your husband might fuck you. If it wasn't all a dark joke, what was? All those voices saying to trust them. *We'll take care of you, tell you the truth.* Just another commercial. Except they were selling reality: an all-inclusive shimmering reality that was yours if you'd just credulously believe. But there were cracks in it, and they could see partly through the cracks. Unless you closed your eyes, the figures started to look like bad actors. Not that there was some other reality waiting for them. It was fracture and make-believe the whole way down. The whole culture, drifts of steaming garbage. No, they weren't going to turn off the show, but they'd seen it was a farce. A spectacle. Reality was a performance filmed in a sound studio on the far coast. On a parking lot. It was *acting the part*. Leaders mimicked B-list actors until they *became* B-list actors. There wasn't a difference any longer between playing the thing and being the thing. 'We cracked the code,' she said, sweeping a hand over the scene. 'All of us here. It's not like we're getting a turn at the controls. But we're onto them. Onto the game. Culture's a con. And so's the power that emerges from it. *How long can you believe your own bullshit?* That's the standard. The future is shamelessness, and pretend.'

She looked like she might say more, but she didn't. She blushed when she finally lowered her eyes. Her voice was quiet. 'That's all to say, Quentin . . . I don't really know how to answer your question.'

The music in the lounge continued its upbeat patter. 'We're doomed to bullshit and jokes?' I said.

'We're doomed to commercials,' she said. 'Pretty soon the commercial's going to be the thing itself. And vice versa. Everything will be its own ad.'

The sound of the guitars was coming through from the main room, a gravelly noise like subway cars passing beneath us. I spun my drink around in the glass and glanced over my shoulder to see if Billy was sitting with Olive.

'A friend of mine just came in. I need to go say hi,' I said. 'But I enjoyed talking.'

'I scared you away?'

'It takes more than that.'

She shrugged. 'Buy me another drink sometime and we'll talk about *your* childhood.'

I rose from the stool. 'There's not much to talk about.'

She snorted. 'That's what the really fucked-up ones say.'

I made my way to the table where Billy and Tom were seated, edging through the crowd that stood talking into one another's ears, laughing.

'Alfonse.' I sat without waiting to be asked. 'I saw you come in, you gorgeous creature.' I gave Tom the once-over. 'Who's this freak?'

Billy looked startled to see me. He may have forgotten the plan because he said, 'What are you doing here?'

'Same thing you are.'

'What's that?'

'Partying.' I could feel his apprehension settle into crossness as he realized that pressing the point would only engage Tom's suspicion. '*Partying*'s a funny word, isn't it?' I said and lightly flicked Tom's lapel. 'I didn't realize it was Halloween.'

'This is Quentin,' Billy said irritably. 'Tom's fashion sense is . . . unusual.'

'Call it avant-garde,' said Tom.

'I think it's lapped the garde,' I said. 'Now it's back in the rear.'

Olive sat with a fixed, imperturbable grin on his face.

'Consider him well,' he remarked suddenly. 'Unaccommodated man is no more but such a poor, bare, forked animal as thou.'

'Your friend talks funny,' I said to Billy.

'We were discussing the future of art,' Tom informed me, apparently oblivious to how these words would strike a normal person.

'I'm glad to hear it has one.'

'Yes, art is irrepressible.'

Billy rolled his eyes. 'Yeah. Tom would know.'

'You're an artist then,' I said. 'What's your medium?'

He grinned. 'Money.'

'That one seems always in vogue.'

'I'm a traffic cop,' he said. 'I tell people when to go and when to stop. You could say time is my true medium, like a composer.' The concert was gathering force in the other room. The wall between us fizzed with overtone. 'Classical music for loud guitars,' Tom remarked idly. 'We're working these days to exhaust the possibilities.'

'Who's "we"?'

He turned to look at me. He had surprisingly gentle eyes. 'You're right.

I like to pretend I belong, but I'm not really part of the scene. They're nice enough to let me hang around.'

'It's not like we put it to a vote,' Billy said.

'You tolerate my presence.'

'Tom's got a finger in real estate. It's actually more like his whole hand.' This was directed at me. 'Half of us live in buildings his firm's involved with.'

'These artists just make so much damn money.' He laughed. 'Wherever you set up your little dream factories. It'd be malpractice to ignore it.'

'And someone put a gun to your head and forced you to work for a bank.'

'No, no. I love what I do. I love money. Money means choices, freedom. Artists just want freedom too.'

'Our freedom doesn't charge rent,' said Billy.

'We have different theories of the long term.' He had such an easy, unrepentant way about him that you found it hard to dislike him entirely. From time to time he straightened his cuffs, freeing his watch from his sleeve without checking the time—a tic that communicated neither anxiety nor impatience. He fit in his suit like a second skin. To imagine him in anything else diminished his power considerably.

'I know this view won't win me any friends here,' he said, 'but the truth is art grows in shit. It needs shit. Marginality. Dispossession. Everyone's going to bitch and moan for years about getting priced out of their lofts. But once the tide shifts, the soil for art goes barren, fallow. This scene has another year or two tops before it gets fat on its own decadence. The ones who bought in when you could buy six stories for pocket change are going to make a killing. But they won't make art after that. Not the good kind.'

Billy pursed his lips skeptically, but I got the sense he didn't entirely disagree. 'Either way,' he said, 'it's an awfully convenient view for someone in your position.'

'That's true,' replied Tom judiciously. 'But that's not why I think it.' He rearranged his cuffs. 'We're part of an ecosystem, you and me. Space and time, property, credit: these are the dimensions of our lives. Everyone thinks banks are evil, but they're dispassionate. A tollbooth at a bottle-neck. Where the dimensionality of people's lives is decided, we run the meter. Businesses make stuff, people consume it. Artists rummage in the excrement of this consumption, recycle it into something we can use again and value. It's all necessary. Without microbes nothing would re-generate, nothing would flower.'

'Microbes?'

'Don't take it the wrong way. Microbes are remarkable creatures.'

'Keeping us in the shit is your role in the ecosystem, that's what you're saying?'

'Yes,' said Tom, nodding as if confirming for himself that this was precisely what he meant. 'I'm not trying to say I'm doing you a favor. I'm just saying that cutting you a break wouldn't do you a favor either.' His cheeks were immaculately shaved, the skin of an adolescent. 'All this'—he gestured around us—'is the product of suffering.'

Billy gave him an incredulous look. The music was somehow (it seemed impossible) getting louder. It built on itself, deepening, crowd-ing the air, removing us further from reality's grip. The bright sphere of our table sealed our conversation in a golden membrane. The pale illumi-nation ran down Billy's and Tom's faces and glinted on the laminate table.

'What's your medium, Quentin?' Tom asked. I was startled to hear that he recalled my name.

'Information,' I said.

'The science of arrangement, of forms.'

'Is it?'

'I have no idea. A physicist I work with said that. He's applying partial differential equations to the annihilation of risk. He said information describes how a system is organized.'

'Like a criminal enterprise,' I suggested.

'Yes . . .' Tom glanced at me with more alertness than I was expecting. 'There's this don I've heard of,' he remarked, 'a crime boss, who spends his days in a bookstore on Eighth Street reading Camus.'

I swirled the whiskey in my glass. 'Your point?'

'He's an existentialist. He believes in action and he believes in the moment. But the fact that he's looking for consolation in books means he has his doubts.'

'What sort of doubts?'

Tom's upturned bottle-green eyes caught the light. 'Doubts about our condition. Our impermanence. The chaos of the street is exciting, but we prefer it in a photograph. He's started to wonder what it all means. What the moments are adding up to.'

'That's quite a speculation.'

Tom smiled. 'Well, maybe he's just killing time.'

'As long as it's only time.'

'Back in the day there was a gangster with a passion for Yeats. Maybe he was Irish. Anyway,' said Tom, 'I have to believe Camus is significant.'

'How's that?'

'The man of action is interested in other men grappling with action. Lives that have no meaning beyond themselves. Can they get there? Can they accept that bleak standard in a world that wants them to believe in higher, hidden meanings?'

'I'm guessing you have feelings on the matter.'

When Tom laughed, he shook with an unselfconscious pleasure. 'It may surprise you to hear that I'm not a churchgoing man. Will we be punished for our sins? I doubt it. Not unless we do the punishing our-selves. But the unexamined life is no life. The unadorned life. I couldn't live without art.'

'What about artists?' asked Billy. 'The kind with skirts and pussies.'

'I'm a man,' said Tom, 'and anyway, art and sex have many similari-ties. Both arise in longing and incompleteness.'

'In what way are you incomplete?' I asked with no little interest.

Tom stared at the small TVs in the wall behind the bar. They all showed the same scene, a beach late in the day, palms faltering in the wind and surf crashing on the sand. 'The moment isn't enough,' he said. 'Our life, wherever we happen to be, it isn't enough. Somewhere out there real life is taking place. Somewhere there's a center. That's what we've been taught. And the same thing that taught it to us promises to save us—by taking us to the center. By collapsing the stray, incoherent meaning into one saturated, glowing image.'

Neither Billy nor I spoke. I don't know what he was thinking but maybe, despite himself, he was as strangely moved by this oracular fugue as I was. The noise and liquor condensed my awareness to a sheltered radius. But in the eye of this storm, a momentary breath of truth seemed to float free of bondage. Everything was still.

'Go on,' I murmured.

Tom's face appeared to age a decade in the time it took for him to turn to me. Under the glare, suddenly pallid and primitive in timbre, his skin looked mottled, weary. Maybe it was only the angle of light which brought the surface into relief, revealing a reservoir of fatigue and unctuous luster.

'We're drawing closer to the surface,' he said softly. 'To the fantasy. For now we content ourselves with the image growing larger and clearer. But at some point our longing to penetrate the image will overwhelm us. We won't abide separateness. We'll pass into it—through the glass. Don't ask me how. Maybe we'll enter it so slowly it takes generations, and we won't know we're inside until it's too late. Too late! I say it like it's a bad thing, but won't it be marvelous? Won't our dreams come true? Our memories return? Our fantasies take place? Then the limits of our life— the inadequacy of moments, our insignificance—will be no more.'

'And we'll be lost,' I said.

He looked momentarily shocked to see that Billy and I were still there. 'Lost?'

'Lost in the labyrinth of ourselves. It's the only one we can't escape from. Not on our own. It knows just how to trick us. How to seduce us. We'll hear our own resounding heartbeats and we'll mistake these for the truth.'

'We won't care.'

'Maybe,' I conceded, 'but then we'll die. We'll begin to die.'

His eyes flickered with reflections. 'What do you mean?'

'The fantasy will suffocate us in time. No one can live shut off from the world forever.'

There was a period in which we all seemed to retreat into our thoughts, and I wondered what it would truly mean to pass into the image—what would happen if, for instance, I abandoned my quest and returned to Jada and the love she offered. What if, like Bruce, I decided not to leave? I didn't know what this would entail exactly, but I wondered whether my conviction that it would mean a kind of death, a slow suffocation in a sealed jar, was the final word, or partly a hope—that something would make this inverted paradise impossible, this horror of coming to rest within oneself.

Billy was kicking me under the table; it was time to go. 'Right,' I said. I put my hands on the table's edge and Tom glanced up. 'I have to urinate,' I announced. 'It was nice meeting you.'

His eyes made small precise movements, looking me over as if conducting a forensic survey. 'You're not from here,' he said.

'No? What makes you say that.'

He smiled, staring off. 'I met another one like you. It was the same feeling—my body, my mind flooded with a certain . . . light. A clarity. *Thoughts.* The presence of a different time and place altogether.' He laughed suddenly. 'You'll find him if that's what you're after.'

'Him?' I whispered.

He didn't respond. He gave a half-wave farewell, and I rose, replacing my chair under the table. I turned from Billy's troubled eyes. Tom just sat there grinning with the vacant, drifting intensity of a cracked Buddha.

The bathroom, where I waited for Billy, was wretched, the floor covered with beer, urine, ribbons of toilet paper. The stall doors either were falling off their hinges or had been removed altogether. A cavalcade of people shouldered into the tiny space, the concert's noise rising and falling as the door swung. The script of inked and carved characters on the walls had been applied so densely it made a gestalt motif, like thickset crewel. Mostly this was illegible, but occasionally one could make out scabrous insults attached to certain Mollys and Jeffs, vendettas registered in blue ink, phone numbers listed of those available for unnatural acts.

Billy arrived out of breath and shoved the package Tom had given him into my hands. 'What the *fuck* was that?'

'What was what?' I asked.

He looked at me with incredulity. 'You weren't supposed to *ambush* us. Tom saw right through our little act.'

'Did he?'

'He said as much.'

'Tom saw that he's dealing with something he doesn't understand. That's all.'

The lids on Billy's bloodshot eyes twitched. Their delicate lashes curled over his pale, handsome face. 'Well, I don't understand it either.'

I handed Billy back the package. 'I don't need this. You do.' He took it reluctantly. 'No one's going to come looking for it.'

'How do you know that?'

I shook my head. 'You have to trust me.' We were quiet a moment. 'The food court at the Elysium Mall? Nine a.m.?' This was where Billy had told me the meetups took place.

He nodded. 'He's usually the only one there.'

I took out a slip of paper and wrote down Jada's name and number and handed it to him. 'You need a better lawyer,' I said. 'Tell her every-thing.' I squeezed his shoulder. 'You'll be all right.' We locked eyes briefly and I left.

The streets, which had seemed so loud before, were almost silent when I emerged from the club. They hummed with a low, echoic purr, as if everything were taking place behind a thick pane of glass. I had time to spare. The morning was a long way off, even taking the train journey to the coast into account.

I made the forty blocks to the station on foot. It was cold out but the walk roused me. My thoughts drifted without alighting, and before I knew it I was pushing through the terminal's heavy doors. Golden stars and constellations embroidered a mythic iconography on the vast ocean-green ceiling high above. It was nearing three. In that cavernous space the only other people were indigents and a few tired cops nudging them awake. I looked over the schedule. The next train to Anchoret didn't leave until half past four.

The lights were on in the all-night café, but no one seemed to be work-ing there. I drummed lightly on the countertop, peering at the swinging doors to the back, where a light shone through oval windows. A short man in the far booth, mostly hidden by the seatback, was the only other customer. Absorbed in reading, he didn't look up. He was balding with gray hair swept back in two waves on either side of his head. He wore a dusty slate-hued suit and perfectly round glasses. A cup of coffee in a stained saucer rested on the table beside him.

'Do I need to ring a bell or something?' I asked after a few minutes of waiting. He looked at me, startled, staring at my mouth as though it might disclose some further meaning. At last he said, 'I don't know,' with a little shrug. 'Sometimes they come.'

'You're here often?'

He raised his eyebrows and nodded. 'Yes. I read here.' He lifted the book in his hands ever so slightly from the table.

'Late for reading.'

The skin on his forehead furrowed and went smooth more often than any mood required. 'Yes . . . Is it? I suppose so.'

I pointed at the bench across from him. 'May I?' He gazed at it blankly before gesturing in assent. I asked what he was reading and he hesitantly turned over a worn copy of *Timon of Athens*. He tapped a cigarette from the soft body of a pack and rolled it in his fingers. The wall lamp spread a glade of illumination on the table. He lit the cigarette.

'What's it about?'

'Money.' I motioned for him to say more. 'It's about the flimsiness of relationships built on transaction. Also the foolishness of denying that relationships involve transaction.' He tapped the book absently on the table. 'It's an argument between the person who doubts human goodness and the person who believes in it to a fault.'

'Which view wins?'

'Both lose.' He grinned. 'The cynic Apemantus says of Timon, "The middle of humanity thou never knewest, but the extremity of both ends." This is disappointing. That humanity occupies this middle ground is unsatisfying to purists, but it's the truth. Take the measure of man and you find a mongrel cobbled from nobility and avarice, dissembling even to himself.'

I said it sounded like a sensible piece of work. A finger of ash hung at a slight angle from his cigarette; he didn't notice when it fell soundlessly and intact on the table. I followed his eyes. They swam behind lenses that caught the light. A trace of a smile bled through his features. His bony fingers ran aimlessly over the phrases carved into the table's laminate. 'It's a disappointing play,' he said. 'Almost certainly unfinished and probably a trial run for *Lear*. Their themes are the same: whether loyalty and love ever rest on more than self-interest; how to recognize genuine sentiment when it is by nature quieter than flattery. Both plays take up the distinction between appearance and reality, and both Timon and Lear, disgusted by society's pretense, abandon it. Timon takes up residence in a wilderness cave. Lear turns himself loose on the heath where, by stripping naked, he hopes to approach truth. Adam and Eve, once they have eaten from the tree of knowledge of good and evil, become ashamed of their nakedness. Lear hopes to recover the clarity of their primitive state by shedding the garments that cloak our true selves. But there's no going back. Lear and Timon hope to reverse the Fall by returning to nature; each discovers he can't. There's no return once self-awareness has distinguished appearance from reality, our words from the motives underlying them. This is the meaning of the expulsion from paradise, our departure from the state of nature with its innocence and violence, to something far more ambivalent: it is the parable of our guilt, of inward shame, in moving from awareness to self-awareness, acquiring the ability and inclination to see the self, where all the necessary and corrosive second-order emotions derive, envy and resentment, regret and guilt—the crown-jewel neuroses that make us creatures bound to one another, and exploitative of one another, since in self-knowledge arises the possibility of deceit, covenants as bondage and covenants as language to be slipped from legalistically. Guilt is the price we must pay for this power—guilt, which is two sides of the same person at war with himself—one part horrified at the shameless self-servingness that in animals we find innocent. And why innocent? Because to bear responsibility for an act one must not merely *commit* it but understand and intend it. Thus our knowledge of good and evil is identical to our loss of innocence—one and the same—the instant when responsibility arises, when guilt as the inner property of a psyche coiled back on itself shakes off from mere agency and we lift up a meta-physical burden of past actions to carry with us on our shoulders forever as culpability, sin. The fork in the road where we start walking alone, after which we decide for ourselves and face the consequences without help.'

He had been talking with a possessed fluency and suddenly stopped. He looked at me, embarrassed, even surprised, it seemed, by my presence. A tendril of smoke curled from a tiny ember in the ashtray. 'I'm not used to company,' he said apologetically. He explained that he had been a scholar once, or so it seemed he would be, but it had been many years since he held the sort of position that permitted one to claim the title. He stirred the dregs of his coffee with a tiny spoon. 'My project,' he said, 'is now strictly my own.'

I asked what this project was and he touched the pages of the paper-back and let them fall from his fingers. He said he was no longer confident it made sense to anyone but him. He sought, he explained, to trace the moment of our species' awakening into the full flower of consciousness. Had this occurred precipitously, in a sudden epiphanic flash, or had it dawned gradually over millennia like an auroral creep upon the plain? One part of his study examined those fitful and fruitless attempts to re-turn to nature and recover the prelapsarian state, the dream of so many recluses and ascetics. This proved an ironic literature, since it was the very stilling and subduing of the dynamic world in words that marked the critical leap, freeing experience from time and the possible from the actual. This brought us from awareness into self-awareness, a state more profound than simple wakefulness or sensation. 'But as the world ac-cretes names,' he continued, 'as words start falling from our lips, as they link up in stories of primitive grammar—in whatever manner this supple fabric of proposition comes to rest over life—the flux of the world now has a resting place, which obscurely falsifies it to permit its contempla-tion. Aliveness is no longer just something to *feel* but something to speak of and consider separately from any instance of life. Soon we begin by unseen increments to treat this abstracted world as real, as more than a convenient fiction drawn from life. And this shadow realm, virtual and ever more replete, displaces the world it arose to represent. The means of escaping contingency, of developing knowledge of what lies outside our head, become equally the means of fantasy, paranoia, and self-deceit.'

He looked at me with a slight air of self-mockery. He had a way of suggesting humor very faintly and a distant mirth rippled across his gaze like a breeze trembling a lake. I asked whether that was the sum of it, and his laughter tangled in the phlegm of his throat and turned to coughing. 'Almost,' he said. He spun his coffee cup idly on its saucer. 'It is the nature of this second life, this shadow realm of concepts, to diverge from the first, until a world of pure representation, pure mind, can be inhabited as naturally as the first. When we have achieved this, we will have completed the evolutionary process of our apotheosis: the long journey from departing the garden, where we were creatures of God, to at last *creating* the garden and inhabiting a world where we *are* God. The circle will be complete.'

He tore his glasses suddenly from his face and pinched tightly the bridge of his nose. 'These headaches . . . ,' he said. His eyes were firmly shut. 'Do you ever get this feeling, as if you are living in someone else's dream?'

'More and more.'

He didn't return my smile. He blinked, opening light-pained eyes to the sallow illumination that swam like a fluid through the station. In the distance came the sharp hiss of air brakes unclenching and the garbled, harsh announcement of trains arriving and departing. 'Most people believe they live their own lives, of course,' he said. 'But our language is a hand-me-down, our imagination forged in a borrowed mold. *Cast of mind* may be a literal description. Is it not fair, then, to suggest we were always figments in another's dream, or a collective dream, past the wit of man to say what dream it was?'

I told him I thought I understood. He raised his eyes to mine and began laughing. 'In that case, perhaps you are as crazy as I am.' He coughed wetly into his fist. 'But here you have got me talking nonsense again. Why don't you call the waiter?'

I took his advice and rapped on the swinging door to the kitchen.

A young man in a white apron emerged a moment later with the sour look of someone roused from pleasant dreams. The leftover coffee had cooled, and by the time he reheated it the man in the booth was absorbed again in his old copy of *Timon*. I sipped the burnt liquid, sitting at the counter before the brass fixtures and shelves that held the dishes and cups.

The hour had nearly come. I left the café and stepped out into the depths of the night to find the streets bathed in a drizzle so fine it was nearly mist. Lamplight inspirited these drifts with luminous breath. Halos of bright fizz pollinated the glowing bulbs. There were few cars in the street, just a couple of ferrying taxis far off down the avenue. I turned to the sky and let the particles accumulate on my face. It was time. I rubbed my eyes to dry them and returned to the station to take a seat on the empty train.

V

THE NIGHT INTO which Quentin spoke was as fathomless and black as the night of the journey he described. The car started with a jolt, he said, and for several minutes we passed underground. We moved through dim tunnels where shades of graffiti tattooed the columns and girders like cryptic ruins of a lost civilization. The concrete caverns echoed dully with the clanging of the train. Then the tunnel rose to the surface and the ash-brown sky sealed us in its lambent skin.

Leaving the city on a bright day often has a hopeful air, but at that hour of night, crossing that circuitry of serpentine roads, raised roadbeds and bridges, tracing alongside buildings concealing their cagelike and unknowable purpose, you might have thought yourself transported to a mining colony on a distant planet, he went on. So peculiar was the color and quality of light, the city's mechanism bristling electrically beneath the irradiated puddle of the heavens, that it seemed possible this wasn't night at all but the regular condition of our cursed preterition. Brick facades streamed past, gas stations, flophouses, cut-rate hotels. Stoplights blinked above the rutted, scarred street. A broken flood lamp flickered over a desolate athletic field. The scope of the world stupefies. What a massive arrangement each building represented, not just its structure but the interlocking human agreements from which it was knit. And here were hundreds flowing past, thousands if one counted all the eye took in from the prospect of a gentle rise. The city extended in an endless glowing carpet, dwarfing the mind's reach and offering, as consolation perhaps, a sense of liberated insignificance beside the massive improbability of human plans. And yet an atlas, I knew, would house this infinite and involute architecture in no more than a pinpoint . . . Yes, I was thinking of Bruce—of how insufficient he liked to remind you a map was to imagining a place, how much more complicated he always believed the world was than our abstractions allowed. I remember him in those last months before he left for the war, when his convictions began to spill over into rage. I recall him at the windows in the newsroom, gazing out at the city. How infuriated he became at the hubris in our fantasy of control. The impulse that looks at a map and concludes that what the mind can comprehend in schematic it can master in full. He saw the seduction everywhere, this fatal mistake. Any state of idle dreaming in which you believed the world would bow down to your simplicities and grand intentions. And was he wrong? The spatial world has three dimensions, the map has two; the three-dimensional body rises out of flat simplicity in all its manifolds— and how many shortcuts do we take to entrap this world beyond our heads, to make its vast plane amenable to comprehension? How many do we project back out, mistaking our software, our dreams for the world? And how many of us, in our search for truth, resort to a vocabulary of common understandings that points back mostly to itself? This insubstantial foundation becomes our speech, and then our thought, and from there spreads out to texture every moment of experience—lightly, it only takes a little . . . And so like marionettes with tangled lines, we create one another in each tiny movement we make, each tug, determining thereby the ambit and form of potential being.

And we chroniclers play a special role in this, Quentin continued, we archivists of grand event, for there is a twofold nature to our work, as people turn to us to learn what they do not know, but also to hear what they already believe. No speaker of truth ever succeeded without honoring both. And as time goes on, as the day of retrospection dawns, no teller of tales ever fails to look foolish for that inevitable deference to common belief, the full historical prejudice of accepted truth.

Bruce was more sensitive to this than most. You could even say that his preoccupation with the quotient of lying that passed for civil discourse had become perverse. He didn't see these casual lapses as malevolent but as the origin of our worst errors, the little deceits we permitted in the name of ambition and good taste. It was through these chinks in the social edifice that the infection of a more malign agent found the corridors to spread. Encouraging a person who believed this to go off to war was madness. It appears much clearer looking back. But Bruce wasn't wrong. Not in kind, if possibly in degree. And did I think the war would balance the disproportions in his soul? Or did I believe we needed him, his stubbornness before expediency, right where we forged our most consequential and pernicious lies? All of the above—and none of it. Most likely I *wasn't* thinking, or merely sensed these fortuities like an improvisationalist plucking notes from the possibilities in an expiring moment. That is roughly how careless and brash, how drunk on my own enthusiasm, I was at the time, or how I felt I had been, looking at the past through the lens of guilt.

Maybe it only matters to me. Cy has told me, with her clear, uncompromising stance on the penance we owe the past, that I can't shoulder the burden of anyone else's decisions without indulging a maudlin idea of our indebtedness to one another and therefore the world's indebtedness to us. Oh, Cy! Your wisdom is too austere in its severity even for you. She was right, of course. But did she tell me this because it was true, or because, as the story of our regrets took clearer shape in each other's eyes, she saw that I needed to hear it to patch a wound that might bleed out? There are limits to how much truth is good for a person. I've known this and had the perversity not to respect my knowledge of it. Maybe Cy didn't want to see me dragged out to sea by my incaution. Because she had the bug herself. But if I wanted to feel she was right, I couldn't get there. Intellectually, I agreed. But emotionally? . . . I had a burden to offload. A balance to expiate. And Cy lacked the grit and fortitude to live by the rigors of her own belief. Maybe she brutalized her spirit to inure it against sadness. Or maybe I'm unfair and simply want to hang on to my guilt because buried in it somewhere is the belief that life makes sense.

I'm willing to be the reason terrible things happen, it seems, if this will save us from the senselessness of chance.

I'd been awake a long time. My fatigue and the residue of coffee and whiskey in my blood conspired to stir something in me, a dormant sediment kicked up partly by my growing proximity to my old friend. The bruised ocher of so many coarse lights hemorrhaged into the night. Bands of confluent emotion ran together like rivers, their shades arising from the proportion in which they mixed. This was the unknowable elision at the boundary marking off my feelings from the world. We see only the irreversible blend. Maybe in a dream, when memory and the scaffolding of archetype tumble together in their amalgams, we catch our unconscious at work and, like gears and pulleys in the periphery, we glimpse the unclothed machinery of sensemaking at its obscure labor. But here the lucidity of the dream wore its intent and authorship boldly and, as in waking life, there was little of the uncensored soul to surprise. I was telling my story, fitting data to the frame, and presumably Bruce was telling his own. It was only their confrontation that promised to dislodge us from our reveries.

I made my way east. Our rattling, creaky passage grew smoother as we left the city's outskirts and the track's sinew unkinked. We sped through the backyards of suburbia, veiled by leafless trees. The pools lay covered for the winter and the households slept in the early dark. Farther on, incursions from the coast crept up to the railbed, deep inlets fringed with reeds and dotted with docks decommissioned for the season, their black water a stirring ink. Why Bruce had chosen this place was beyond me. The entire city, it seemed, had fled childhoods here. It was just the sort of place Bruce hated—although Bruce, one had to admit, had truly a wonderful capacity for hate.

The sky brightened as we drove on. Though sunrise was still a while off, a suffusing agent touched the dark. The ashen gray of high clouds emerged within the brown—a pale, industrial tint. It was likely I was making a grave mistake. Reflecting on the path I had taken to that point, it seemed clear that Bruce had always been a step ahead, though whether he meant to bait me or confide in me I couldn't have said.

The train shuddered on. I closed my eyes and let myself sink into the dark space of sound and thought. A host of forms swam up to meet me. These were the figures of my journey: Hassie, Enoch, Lance, Rich, Parisa, Castor, even Joan. I saw a line of event and chance meetings weaving like a serpent to the present, and the many figures who had seen me persisting on a perilous track and counseled restraint. What was it in me that always had to submit before the desire to exhume truth? Was it a flaw in my character, or was I right to persist where others broke off, did we need such a mule as me? I'd always banked on spotting the play within the play, but now I was at the mercy of a game whose rules baffled me. It was a taste of my own medicine, and I smiled ruefully. Even bitterness has its pleasures.

By the time the train pulled into Anchoret, the world had made its seamless shift to morning. A somber expanse hung over the tiny station. I got off, huddling against the damp breeze. The platform stood before an empty lot bordered by forest on all sides. A chill seaside brine padded the air. Not a soul in sight.

Billy had told me not to expect cabs at this hour, and I made my way to the main road on foot, hoping the walk would rouse me. My thoughts had disappeared into the white space of numb resolve. I watched the gray road disappear beneath my feet. A few blocks on and the quiet streets lined with houses met a small highway, where the occasional car sped past. It was an ugly day, no luster touched it. My shoes scuffed the gravel lining the shoulder of the road. Deserted lots and the backsides of beige buildings peeked through the scrim of arrow-shaped pines along the thoroughfare.

If I had cause to worry I was walking into a trap, this fear drained from me in fatigue. I was *meant* to be here, that's what I told myself. And if this was true it relieved the burden of deciding differently. I had entered a strange current that required me only to drift. My pace slowed, I felt no rush. I turned off the highway and scrub thickets and coastal flora broke into the pines. Beardgrass quivered. The air had the sweet, heavy smell of a rotting bog, and fallen leaves in piles of yellow and bronze lay speckled like quail eggs before the aluminum-sided split-levels, whose inhabitants emerged in robes to gather morning papers and glance at the disappointing day. Roadside stores advertised irrelevant deals on their message boards. It was all terribly real, the unpoetic fact of this world and its drifting cars and people with lives as mysterious as they were doubtless banal. A faint whiff of salt lanced the breeze, startling the vacant cloud light with pickling vigor.

The Elysium's massive white flank had occupied my view for several minutes before I realized I had arrived. The mall rose like a leviathan breaking from the spume of commercial clutter. Jutting forth from the central ingress, an immense Babylonian structure of massive concrete columns resembled the portico of an ancient temple. The mall's inhuman scale at that hour obscured any sense of purpose and only a handful of cars stippled the vast expanse of parking lot. Birds idled overhead.

The doors were still locked. I peered through the glass. I had no way of knowing what time it was and I sat on a bench and shivered while I waited. Morning had so far brought little warmth. I heard the high note of gulls calling and sensed an incandescent pressure behind the clouds to the east—the vibrant gauze not a thing you could see but an unbroken area of uniform light, a membrane holding back the star. Traffic accumulated in the street, and every so often a car peeled off into the mall's oceanic lot. After an unknown interval, fifteen minutes or perhaps an hour, I tried the entrance again.

The door was still locked but a security guard, spotting me, tapped the watch on his wrist and held up five fingers. I didn't want to run into Bruce ahead of time and walked to the east end of the building. From this side of the mall you could see behind the edifice where a marshland stretched to the north. A meandering blot of reflective water lay among the shifting course of reeds, and beyond these what looked like floating islands of forest. The dull light set the scene in the palette of old film stock, but I could tell there were moments when the beauty of the estuary beyond the coppices called out for everything built on it to be razed.

I closed my eyes. If I opened them, would I find myself still there or in another dream? I let the currents of wind run over my lips and fingers and ceased clenching against the cold. I smiled blindly into the face of the world. I told myself that when I opened my eyes I would awaken, but when I did I was where I'd been before, in a place, a moment, as undeniable as any.

At last a man came to unlock the door with a set of keys fastened to his belt. I passed into the mall through a department store. Salespeople were setting up. Rows of toasters, vacuum cleaners, mops, ironing boards, and box fans awaited the day's shoppers. The clerks who glanced at me stared a second too long. I was still dressed for the club, I realized, catching a glimpse of myself in a polished mirror. The long night lay etched on my face.

Many of the shops had yet to open. Their grates were drawn in front of them and some were only half-lit. Employees carrying clipboards walked the aisles, checking the stock. A few smoked by store entrances, next to blinking arcade games. White featureless mannequins with rock 'n' roll wigs looked as blank and sensuous as Cycladic figures in the vitrines. The stairways to the mezzanine appeared to float in the air. Bulbous lights, hanging at different heights from metal poles, glowed softly. Small potted trees decorated the atria, ficus and flowers in tiled parterres. Beneath one glass section of roof a brick amphitheater carved out a seating area among the angled ha-has and half walls.

I reached the food court after several minutes of strolling. Just two of the stalls had their lights on. At one café a woman in a taupe uniform chatted with a guard. Somewhere in the distance the hum of a vacuum cleaner claimed the lower register. I spotted Bruce at once. In the sea of green-and-white plastic tabletops he was the only person sitting. He had a newspaper open before him, a cup of coffee, and a Danish on a small plate. Above him in a bluish hue, the recessed lighting had been arranged in the outline of a door key. If he noticed me he didn't look up. He coughed into his fist, turned the page, and folded it over.

I approached hesitantly. I didn't want to surprise him. He made such an unassuming figure: tidy, compact, possessed of brown hair neatly parted to the side. He had aged a little and more closely resembled his father—an observation he might not have cared for—and quite unlike him he wore pleated khakis and a collared piqué shirt in a mild cornflower. I was standing near his table when, without having turned to me, he said, 'I wondered when you'd show up.'

I stood across from him, my hands resting on the chairback. 'Have you been waiting long?'

He checked his watch. 'Oh, about ten minutes.' He smiled. 'But that wasn't what you meant, was it?' I shook my head. 'Won't you sit?' He gestured at the chair.

I did as instructed and pointed to his clothes. 'What's the look, fascism chic?'

'This?' He touched the fabric of his shirt as if the garment were new to him. 'Oh, I'm just trying to fit in, you know. Strike the right note.'

'Fit in to what?'

'Look around you.' He spread his hands and laughed. 'The most boring place on earth.'

'I did wonder what you were doing out here. I'm still not sure I understand.'

'Who'd ever think to look for me in this Barmecidal wasteland?'

'I see.' I only partly saw. 'How's that working out for you?'

'You're the first to find me,' he said and sipped his coffee.

I couldn't help snorting at this. 'Did I find you or were you lying in wait?'

He nodded. 'It's true, I took pains to make sure if anyone found me it'd be you. But how did I know you would?' He looked at me, faintly grinning, the light of his eyes clever and discerning. 'What's with the moulage, anyway?' He ran a hand over his face.

'I haven't been to sleep.'

'You met Tom, I guess.'

'I did,' I said. 'He's not the sort of friend you used to keep.'

'You liked me better as the old Jacobin?' He chuckled and leaned back, resting his arms on the low wall behind him. 'Don't worry about Tom. He's a useful idiot, that's it.'

'I'm not worried about Tom.'

He caught my drift and muttered quickly that appearances could be deceiving. They could, I agreed. And indeed it was hard to keep in mind what I'd heard of him, the cruelties he was said to have committed, the interests it appeared he was in league with. I wanted to ask him about this, ask him a million things, too many things to know where to begin. But I sensed that we were on his time and that there was a rhythm to the encounter I shouldn't disturb. And despite everything I felt now a torrent of bottled affection burst forth, like a father at the return of a prodigal son. Here Bruce was *alive*, inconceivably, amazingly, with no blemish of ill-use I could discern, no broken spirit. How disarmed I was by his simple appearance, the inimitable contours of character and physiognomy, ineradicable by time, distance, or the petrification of memory.

'Is this how you pictured our reunion?' I asked.

He threw his head back and this time his laughter had an uncalculated quality. 'Yes, maybe,' he said. 'I've thought of it so often, from so many different angles, it's hard to sort out which version I came to expect. I've spoken to you in my head so many times, I almost feel I know every turn this conversation could take. But then that's the wonderful thing about other people, you know. Their capacity to surprise.'

'You've certainly surprised me, showing up like this.' What I didn't mention was that some surprises were gratuitous, and even cruel. All this time he had been alive, leaving the rest of us to puzzle out the meaning of his disappearance. Didn't he have something to answer for too? 'What'—I grasped for words that could encompass such a chasm of ignorance—'*happened*?'

'You want to go there so soon? But you've only just arrived! We have all the time in the world.'

What world? I thought. What goddamn world. The coffee machines hissed in the stalls, the senseless background chatter and sugary music. 'I wish I could be as carefree as you, but I've worried about you too long.'

'A shame it's so early, we could use a drink.' He spoke as if he hadn't heard me and glanced around like a bar might materialize at his wish. 'No, carefree isn't how I'd describe you.'

'It's not how I'm used to thinking of you, either.'

'Maybe we're bound in some entanglement, and whichever direction one of us is spinning the other must spin the other way.' He gave an ironic look. 'You arrived expecting a monster, and you find me lighthearted and irreverent. So you claim the earnest part for yourself. Where's the chaffing, bantering Quentin, I wonder? Where's sullen, gloomy Bruce?'

When it was clear he expected an answer, I said, 'You tell me.'

'Oh, these games,' he spat with a familiar bitterness. 'I wish we could shed the pretense. But these are the tools of the trade. I don't think you even notice anymore. It's reflex.'

'I'm not trying to trick you.'

'Not trick me . . . No, something worse. You're trying to *appraise* me. You're worried I've spoiled. Gone rotten.'

'You say it like I'm worried on someone else's behalf.'

'Is it charity, then? Your angle's not just your angle but the moral good? How nice.'

I couldn't help rolling my eyes. 'Come on, Bruce. After so many years of moralizing, the anger, the indignation, you want to pretend it was all high-minded? That you didn't have your own reasons?'

He stared at me, and at last allowed a quiet smile to break over his face. 'You're right.' He let the wind of rhetoric and vehemence out of his voice and it filled with an appealing honesty. 'I do know that game. You could even say I've run to the hilt on that one.' He grinned and a boyish note entered his look. 'I've grown cynical, like you.'

'I'm not that cynical.'

'Not deep down, perhaps. Cynicism's just a scar on sincerity, on our wounded idealism. But scars are real. As real as what they protect.' His gaze bored into me with a glassy firmness. 'What starts as a shell becomes a home. Cynicism says all motives are corrupt. So we choose our corruption for ourselves, not to be the dupe, you understand. And then we grow to love cynicism with a sickly, pornographic lust, since anything else just shows how rotten we've become.'

'Is that what it was with you?'

He shook his head. 'It's for you to judge. You'll form your own idea anyway, it's pointless for me to try to convince you. But reports of my horribleness are greatly exaggerated. That's my view.'

There was disappointment but no venom left in his words. He thought I absolved myself too easily of doubt, I knew—about my motives, my clear-sightedness. He'd placed the seed germ of his trust in me, of all inhospitable soils, and I owed him a greater allowance than I was used to giving. For that reason, and for others.

'It probably doesn't make any difference'—my voice caught on a swell of emotion—'but I'm sorry, you know.'

He glanced up when I said this and turned his eyes to the ceiling above the mezzanine where daylight seeped into the fluorescence through a clerestory. '"I'm sorry" is a funny phrase, isn't it?' He talked as though to the sky. 'It means almost anything and at the same time almost nothing. Does it mean, "If I could go back, I'd act differently"? But knowing what you know now or what you knew then?'

I shook my head. 'I don't have a better consolation to offer, that's all.'

'That's honest at least. It's my fault too. For listening to you, for mis-understanding the simple fact everyone seems to accept from an early age. That other people live in their own minds—are just saturated in themselves. For some reason I grew up with the strange notion that we were in this *together*. Bound together.' A glazed quality had come over his eyes. 'But then I saw that no, we aren't evil, not evil and good, just incredibly . . . *alone*. Other people aren't quite real for us, you know. We don't mean to be bad. It's just, try as we might, we can't make other people fully *real*.'

'You speak for all of us.'

'Look around you!' A few people were sitting in the food court now, restaurant employees eating their breakfast. A thin traffic of shoppers passed through the main corridor, women pushing strollers, the early morning crowd. 'Is it any different here?' he said. 'Isn't that the remark-able thing about this . . . this *place*? We treat people the same way we do on the outside. We just don't lie to ourselves that we think they're real.'

It took a moment to work up the courage to voice my question. '*Are* they?' I didn't know whether I wanted his opinion or his guidance, or something deeper, the truth.

He threw up his hands and laughed. 'Who knows!'

I leaned back, suddenly weak. Illuminated branches at the tops of columns radiated a quiet turquoise light. The piped-in music pattered on with the upbeat mellow insistence of lounge music. Harsh gleams from indoor bulbs made crescents and triangles in the tabletops' sheen.

'Does the reality of other people touch me,' I said. 'Is that what you're getting at?'

Bruce nodded. 'Yes, that's my question.'

All right, I thought, if it's honesty we're after. 'On the deepest level?' I said. 'Maybe you're right. Maybe it doesn't. But I can behave as if other people are real. I can make my wager with chance in hope that they do the same. If I think that their belief in my dignity rests on my belief in theirs, does the truth of my feeling matter? An act is an act, no matter what you believe. I'll make the wager.'

Bruce was staring at a framed print hanging on the wall: a rural homestead, children playing by a fence, draft animals in the distance by a small orchard. 'Clear as creek water,' he said. 'You always saw things more simply than I did. I admired that. I admire it now. It's a great . . . gift. But these words—*dignity, belief*—what do they really mean? Are they more than cobwebs of language we're tangled up in? I've often wondered if their purpose isn't simply to give us a sense of freedom while dictating precisely who we are allowed to be.

'Take the war,' he went on. 'You remember the war, the one I left to cover? I'm joking, of course you do. You were the one who told me to go! Put yourself in the general vicinity of a few explosive devices and people will respect you for the rest of your fucking life, you said. Or something to that effect. It was a stupid logic but it was the world we lived in, you told me. Anyone dumb enough to risk getting blown up we judged wise enough to tell us how to live. You said you'd have gone yourself if you were younger. Oh, I don't mean you were *wrong*. We call it courage because we can't look careerism in the face. And maybe it's both. Who can ever squeeze inside that private space to truly know another person's motive? That's what this damn black box is about. If we could call out bad faith we'd save ourselves heaps of trouble. But we have to take people at their word. Until we can x-ray the soul, at least. And so we reckon, Who knows the mortal odds better than the guy who's played Russian Roulette?

'Well, I got there, and as you know, they had me in the international area, the Green Zone, or what we called the Garden District, covering army press briefings like your typical stenographer of power. Troops movements in Q.——— and firefights in M.———. Insurgent forces cleared from wherever-the-fuck and sweeps ongoing through the valley of hell. Dissidents "pacified." A nice word. Heavy fighting by the opium fields. The perennial training of local forces destined to fold about five seconds into any skirmish. No, it wasn't their fault, really. They represented civil society, and no one—I mean, *no one*—in the country in any position of power wanted civil society to work. Not the real kind, with laws and honest courts. It killed the profit. It was impossible to get to the bottom of anything there. You chat up other reporters in the mess or the gym. You talk to your source in some private corner you've found and he gives you his spin. Everyone's got their angle. They want the brass back home to embrace a different strategy. They're pushing for different equipment or deployments, or for some legislator to feel the tightening vice of public opinion as the war goes to shit . . . And it always does, someway or other. There aren't enough troops in the world, enough top-tier operators, targeted raids, or compounds to paint for airstrikes. And you, as a journalist, you're the IV line to the public consciousness back home. So of course everyone's trying to corrupt you with their story.

'What's the point? you start to wonder. What am I doing? We're at war. The public isn't passing a referendum on strategy. It'll be years before frustration and fatigue give political cover to withdrawal. There's no gross malfeasance to uncover in the walled-off gardens of the diplomats. Nothing that stands up to the fundamental reality that is war. Which is to say, terrible forms of death and suffering—torture, bombing, dead children, desecrated bodies, gruesome injuries, lost limbs, amputations, fire, disease, displacement, rape. What can you tell people back home that matters beyond what they should already know: that we are at war and this is what war is? What can you do but find creative ways to say, again and again: we have descended on an unfamiliar place, possessed of a culture we don't understand and a language we don't speak, to send bits of metal flying into people's flesh and rain fire from the sky for reasons whose very vagueness will soon become our own moral derangement?

'So I sat there in the international zone, behind concrete barriers several meters thick, safe enough and listening to bombs falling in the distance, improvised explosives going off like firecrackers in the streets. Sometimes it was so close you could feel the aftershock, the tremors, and you'd tell yourself you were there, you're in the war. But you're not. You're in a tiny little simulation of civilization right next to the war, performing a ludicrous act of narrative construction. And for all the forces at play, all the unknowns and unpredictability, the war will only take one form in the end. There's no other, better, or different kind. And this is what I mean about your noble ideas like dignity or freedom. It's the same everywhere. You're free to give people what they already expect. Free to do exactly what you've been told you're permitted to do.'

'And yet sometimes things change.'

'Do they?' His eyes had an impish fire. 'Maybe they do, very, very slowly. But is it we who change them? By heroism? By intention? Or are these merely tides in an evolving sensibility, trace evolutions in the spirit of the age? Is it more than one old generation dying off and a new one seizing the wheel?'

'Hegel couldn't have put it better,' I said, tapping the table restlessly. 'You're really ready to forswear human agency? Any role for principle or intent? Even a small one? A minuscule role. Let's not be greedy here. Let's not be self-important.'

He laughed ruefully. 'Always self-importance or humility with you! What about *importance*, full stop? Forget ego. I never cared about that. But I wasn't content with eking out a life. I wanted things to change. Is that so wrong? Oh, yes, awfully grand, awfully conceited of me to think I knew better. Or maybe just to guard the hope . . . A child's hope, isn't it? But don't tell me you never had that moment sitting in the newsroom when you see that it's all a lie, all those brave stories about truth and holding power to account, and facts, *facts*! When you realize there are limits. You see that you are part of an organism that exists in society, that a paper is owned, a private business or public corporation, that it needs to make money, that its publisher and its editors go to the same cocktail parties, sit on the same boards, befriend the same lawyers and business-people who cycle in and out of politics, run multinationals, whose kids go to the same schools, whose entire *sense* of society overlaps because the main fact of society for them is that they are members of a select elite who, in their unwitting consensus, decide what society is, what the story of it will be, and when you see, therefore, that the story you want to tell—your truth—cannot be the story that says the corruption reaches to the top and infects the storytelling apparatus itself, that there is this limit on the truth you can tell, and that this limit afflicts every last word you utter and sentence you print, afflicts it *fatally*, and makes you merely, like all the others, one more patch of wall in the endless corridors down which power echoes.'

Bruce and I locked eyes. 'Maybe,' I said coolly. 'Or maybe you never went far enough. Maybe it takes a greater genius than you to tell the story that undoes the story.'

'Well, who knows?' He spread his hands agreeably. 'It doesn't matter now.'

His smile, this shift in register, sent a chill down my spine. I'd never known Bruce to pivot once he got going, an inflexibility that amounted to a terrible liability in our work. He'd never had that vital dexterity to dodge away to humor and let a point go. I saw that he'd changed.

'I was angry back then,' he said, as if sensing my own thoughts. 'Ruled by anger perhaps. It's hard to say what gives rise to an attitude like that. I was raised on lies, but no more than anyone else. I knew nothing would be enough. In my heart I knew it. I saw that love, that Jada, wouldn't be enough. And no, I'd never be enough, or the right thing, for her either. It was bottomless, this need in me. But what *for*? That's the mystery. I needed a degree of redress that would never come and that on its face, I knew, was untenable. What I needed was a glittering dream. Or maybe

I chose this pleasant impossibility to wish for because the need in me was darker still . . .'

Bruce considered this, toying with his coffee cup pensively.

'I let you down,' I said. 'I let you assume the role of Conscience in our morality play. I took Hero for myself. Or Everyman. You got stuck with the bill while the rest of us moved on. There's always one of you, you know. Someone who can't let go. You're the collateral damage of our indifference.'

Bruce shrugged and smiled. 'Like you said. Put yourself in the vicinity of a bomb.'

'It doesn't mean you deserved it.'

'Deserve . . . ,' he said. 'I think that's what I've given up on since we last saw each other. I don't put much stock in deservingness anymore. The cosmic balance sheet. Their account books are a mess . . .'

'You know I don't disagree.'

'Yes. You had the right attitude all along. Do what you can. Fight the good fight. If you fail, accept it and live to fight another day. But you were never quite the happy warrior you liked people to think.'

'I'll accept that.'

'Well, who is? The same qualities that inspire worship from a distance can, up close, bring out the opposite.'

'That too.'

'Disenchantment sparks loathing,' he went on. 'We feel the shame of our desire to believe and our heroes fall hard. Anything that reminds us of our credulity carries as well the prick of self-disgust.' He was not speaking abstractly, I knew, but little emotion surfaced in his words. I watched the column's tropical glow land softly on the sea-dark leaves of a potted tree. 'I don't know when the spell wore off. It was before I considered you and Jada together. The distance between us had dissolved. The difference. Revealed in the flesh, a being born in human likeness, as they say. You came down from your pedestal, permanently.'

I tried not to register my surprise. The light, breezy music, stripped of melancholy, coursed on. 'I should never have been up there in the first place,' I muttered.

Bruce seemed only vaguely to have heard me. 'Don't think posses-siveness counted with me. Or rivalry, for that matter. I've never been preoccupied with the petty tyrannies of human property. They're all brief borrowings anyway, these bodies, these minds . . .' He made a dismissive gesture. 'And you know there are always prostitutes around a war.' He said this as if it followed. 'Modern war's no exception, and the Garden District was no exception, either. Prostitutes find their way onto bases, or else soldiers find their way to them. Not just grunts. Officers, journalists, aid workers . . . I got to know one—a young woman, Laila. No, not like that. I want to believe she considered me a friend, though I can't be sure. I gave her what I could, those small luxuries that came in by plane. And she kept my finger on the deeper pulses beating below the day's news. A different story from the fighting and offensives.'

Bruce stretched his neck with a hand under his chin. 'She couldn't have been much over twenty. Sometimes we talked just to pass the time. She wanted to be a musician, I think she told me, and I wouldn't have been surprised to learn that instruments were being cut up and burned as fuel just then. Instead she became a kind of girlfriend to these young men—a girlfriend-for-hire for guys who needed her company more than anything. I got their stories from her and saw, through this small aper-ture, the inner life of the war as it developed in the cages of men's hearts. It was by talking to her that I learned how the men broke down, so drunk sometimes they couldn't make themselves understood. The grunts in the outposts and firebases awoke so often to contact they had started to fear sleep. Fear calm. The only time they knew for certain where they were was with rounds exploding all around them, lancing the air.

'That was when I knew I had to embed. Listening to Laila was the last straw. But I'd grown sick of you too, talking me down off the ledge. I *wanted* to be on the ledge. I wanted to let go and entrust myself to fate. To touch something real at last, and not to be protected from the danger it was my privilege and, increasingly, my burden to avoid. Ironic that the embassy bombings—those coordinated strikes that left dugout breaches in the concrete perimeter of the international zone—came just a week after I left for the valley.' He smiled faintly. 'You might think I'm perverse for saying this, but my time at those distant outposts, the little hilltop redoubts, was the happiest of my life. We took a ton of fire. I can still hear the snap of bullets, pinging past my head. The dust kicked up so heavily at times Weapons Squad's automatics jammed. Contact interrupted naps and smoke breaks, recoilless rounds, RPGs detonating in the day's stillness . . . all while the river swollen with snowmelt rushed below the lush terraced fields. At times the muzzle flashes lit up the hills like beads of light. Dread hung in the air. For ages I woke up in a panic at night. The natural beauty, those emerald fields, schist slopes seamed with granite, the flèchelike cedars along the ridges—it all bore its own battle scars, holly groves ripped to shreds from the hail of bullets, trails and ratlines carpeted in shell casings. With the clarity of danger, for the first time, the utter importance of each and every moment filtered down into my limbs and my circling thoughts like an emollient, dissolving the worry that spun off and fed on itself for attaching to nothing real. I wanted to act on the world. I wanted it to act on me—absent the intermediaries that made up the symbolic sphere of life. Even if it meant death or injury, the directness of this interaction came as a relief. The tribal bonds between the men, career soldiers, cherries, teenagers some of them, and my ambiguous presence to boot—it all had an element of simple and pure necessity, something richer than friendship, an animal love rooted in survival, the instinct to survive. You came to love this belted world—your comrades, the sandbag fortifications, the curlicues of concertina, small totems of luck. Even the weapons by which those who preserved you projected force and expelled death. You loved those too.

'There was simply no place for introspection if you wanted to live. It would've ruined you psychologically to reflect on danger, pain, the fragility of the body. Activity and numbness filled the space otherwise reserved for idle notions. I found peace there. A peace I'd never known. I don't know whether you understand . . . You never asked the world to make sense. You accepted its absurdity with humor and a certain patience, it seemed to me. I could never manage that . . .

'It was my own weakness. Don't think I'm holding myself up as an ideal. It began with my father, who wanted, Christ knows why, to protect me from life's hardships. If he'd thought clearly about his own experience he'd have seen that the tough breaks made him who he was. He wouldn't have traded his trials for gold. But this reflex in parents—to save children from the worst—this proxy caretaking of themselves, only embitters us to the false safety of home, only leaves us unprepared for the danger the world is made of. What doesn't kill you makes you stronger. Every living creature knows it. This guarding instinct in parents, their unreasonable and excessive fear, is a selfishness. A terror, at last, of their own capacity for suffering, which ends up leaving their children unready for life's brutality and more vulnerable to its assaults.

'My father wasn't as bad as some. He sent me out on the job, no special treatment for the boss's kid. I came home aching, bruised . . . But I don't need to go back over old history. You had enough of him, I'm sure, in the months after I disappeared. I didn't believe I wanted him to suffer, but maybe I did. If I'm being honest, maybe part of me wanted him to sweat enough to understand his mistake: that if you bring a child into this world you must accept its death. Or else you have only given life to a doll, an effigy of your own vanity and fear. Nothing half as sacred as a person.'

A hoarse note had entered his voice and he coughed. 'Sometimes I thought of Laila,' he continued. 'There were female prisoners, it was reported, some of them assaulted and abused, who pleaded with their fathers and brothers to come kill them. They believed their honor had been permanently taken from them. But Laila had parents, and how did they understand what their daughter had become? With denial? Horror? Is there a world in which they summoned pride, the unsentimental understanding that we are all prostitutes in our way?' He arched his head back and spat disgustedly, 'There's so much metaphysical baggage in us, so much superstition. We're terrible hypocrites. Bourgeois-pious. Who decreed that lying with strangers is less dignified than crawling on your hands and knees before them? People ruin their bodies, sign over their brief lives to others for money all the time . . . But—oh—sex!'

His eyes had narrowed. 'Even the primmest conservative parent knows there are prostitutes in the world,' he went on, 'and that these prostitutes were children once, or still are, and have parents of their own.

But not my child! they think. Never my child! And it's these sheltered children, who feel the prison sentence of their privilege like manacles, who long most to be whored out, treated as negligible objects, or else who take refuge in the cage of a corrupted dream, hiding behind the bars of power to avoid becoming subject to another's will, and who for this cowering become power's prostitutes, concubine to society itself, a kept bird with clipped wings in some purdah of the status quo.'

Bruce closed his eyes and breathed once deeply. 'What was my point? Oh, yes. That I found freedom in the valley. It laid bare the lies. Some of the companies in those mountains suffered casualty rates of seventy percent. Leaving the wire always meant rolling the dice. At first it's simply shocking to have people shooting at you, to understand you're openly exposed to death, and not because of some accident or quirk of fate. No, you've chosen this. You're *meant* be here, to meet bullets and fragmentary devices. This affair has been sanctioned—*ordained*—by democratic states. And while initially it's absurd to have nothing between you and those who've come to kill you, a kind of sick joke, in time it becomes . . . freeing, even while terrifying, because you've passed through the veil that hides experience. You've passed beyond the myth of justice and the false notion that you're owed safety, and you see the truth of justice, which is people shooting at one another and the say-so of the side with more soldiers or bigger guns, and you see too, just as suddenly, that this moral hardware we hang around each other's necks, it simply isn't real, it's vanished in the mountain air, the desert sun: humans can and will do anything, *anything* to one another, for they have done it all before. And out in the empty valleys where clouds trace in above moraines and scree fields, above the felled cedars and hidden draws, where white phosphorous streams over hillsides in awesome deadly tendrils, and monkeys chitter and howl in the forests with the wolves, where men in shorts with cigarettes hanging out of their mouths fire weapons of preposterous violence, telling dick jokes and taking cover as the world goes to hell around them, where the reality of death never leaves for long, nor the sound of shots in that whistling barbarous stillness just waiting to be broken, here you understand there is no law, and since there is no law, there is no conscience, no guilt, no shame, no bogus ginned-up fear, and even if this is scary, it's not as sickening as the law's deceit, the civilized lies, and though you may well perish you do not want to go back.'

He fell silent, a dwindling ember clenched around an inner fire. I waited a moment before saying, 'If we're deciding what story to believe, I might choose a different one.'

He grinned at this. 'Yes, I can imagine the sort of story you might tell.' He folded his paper. 'Shall we take a walk?' He stood and I stood too. Though the mall was mostly empty, small fountains had been turned on and spewed diminutive geysers from shallow basins beneath the glass ceilings. We passed tape shops and shoe outlets, electronics vendors and music stores with sculptural guitars in their display windows. Jewelry and knickknack kiosks dotted the central concourse like floating islands. Women strolled by in flower-print blouses. Mustachioed salesmen in suits with clip-on ties and tinted prescription glasses awaited customers by the registers. In a brightly lit salon a woman in curlers paged through a magazine. A clockface built into the side of a catwalk showed three minutes after ten.

'Amazing, isn't it.' Bruce gestured around him. 'We think we want freedom, but we have no idea what to do with it, no idea but to drown out the terror of being alone with ourselves, our thoughts . . . Or is it a flight from the truth of what we are deep down, the potentials in us we narcotize like steam over bees? I know what you'd say: that flawed as we are, capable of cruelty and evil, we have love and fairness in our hearts. We can tally up the long list of our horrors, but alongside them is a second story of compassion and progress. That we have endured and raised monuments to beauty and brave ideals shows that the good in us outweighs the bad. And whatever the truth is, we must tell the story of heroism and hope because the stories we tell are prophesies and in time become real.'

Bruce's smile had a malicious glint. 'But *let* us consider the horrors. Let us attempt an imperfect accounting. People learn a little history and convince themselves they've looked barbarity in the face. But who's really stopped to regard the dark trophies in this vitrine? The Dayak tribes of Borneo procured slaves for the purpose of killing them in mourning rituals. Along rivers that penetrated deep into the island jungles, they wrapped these unfortunates in cloth, bound them to trees, and stabbed them to death with spears. Perhaps this seems quaint, lost to the exotic mists of time and distance. But *try* to imagine the perspective of the slave—past hope, lashed to the tree, mummified in strips around the body and eyes, enfolded in darkness with no idea of what is to come, only the terror of utter subjection . . . the feeling of the first spear driven in with no warning, annihilating pain in the ribs, groin, gut, being unable to move or breathe, to cower, flinch, or guard against the next thrust. The muffled scream, the cloth turning red . . . And someone inside the cloth! A living being, as awake as you or I. *Clinging* to life, you could say, with no chance of seeing love or kindness again. No hope for anything but the most anonymous death in this alien jungle . . .

'And yet there was nothing alien or exotic about it. On the Volga trade route in the tenth century, a Muslim traveler recorded an account of a Rus' funerary rite after the death of a chieftain. The ritual called for burning one of the man's female slaves alongside his body. First the slave was inebriated and brought to each of the clan members' tents to sleep with them. Afterward, aboard the burial ship, a smaller group of men plied her with more liquor and raped her in turn while their companions onshore beat their shields to drown out her screams. The men then held her by her arms and legs, placed a rope around her neck, and throttled her while an old woman called the Angel of Death thrust a dagger into her chest, poking it in and out between her ribs until she died.

'The subsequent burning of the ship with the female slave aboard recalls the Hindu practice of sati, in which the widow sacrificed herself on her husband's funeral pyre. Such observances were carried out countless times over the centuries, and many other forms of human sacrifice permeate history and no doubt the darkness beyond history's reach as well. Indigenous tribes in the Americas skinned, scalped, burned, cut up, disemboweled, and ate captured victims and enemies. Some they tied to trees by their own intestines. In Rome several million perished in gladiatorial games over the centuries. In a *game*. For *sport*. Prisoners forced to fight one another to the death, or fed alive to exotic animals, slaughtered themselves in terrific number, until the European lion, the elephants of North Africa, and the tigers of the Near East ceased to exist. Some unlucky prisoners found themselves in authentic reenactments of gruesome myths, playing Prometheus and watching crows eat out their livers. The Romans considered compassion a weakness, and public ritual served to stamp it out. Most gladiators died anonymously, but at times a ruler asked that one's face be revealed so he could watch the agony in the prisoner's eyes as he died.

'The numbers are staggering. Like so many abstractions they confound the imagination. To appreciate the scope of the killing you'd have to envision dead bodies strewn in unbroken carpets over block after block, filling neighborhood streets as far as the eye could see, whole tribes and races and cultures erased, nipped in the bud or murdered in exhaustive pogroms. Think of your own life and its centrality to everything you are, and consider, in imagining this, that each individual in these nameless hordes of the slaughtered felt the exact same way you do, touched in quiet moments by the delicate marvel of being.'

We were, as Bruce spoke, passing shops that sold chocolates, flowers, greeting cards, gifts; ribbons, tchotchkes, embossed confectionery boxes; lurid posters of sports and movie idols, kitsch paintings of glowing stone cottages. Shoppers walked by in spandex leggings and tie-dyed pants. Gilt piping ran along the alabaster walls. In seating alcoves the upholstered sofas and shag carpeting had the color of salmon, flesh. The stores were called Life Fragrance, Fanny & Pierre's, The Jewel Pirate, Afterthoughts, Tomorrow Woman, Little Jack Bigman, Tile King, Caravan of Treasures, Season's Bounty, Frame Job, Susie Sweet Tooth, Record Depot, Lechters Oils, Pasta Chalet, Mortimer Vale, Hickory Hamlet, Espèces de Vie, Barbary Coast (a travel agency), El Taco, Lerkurs, B. Quik, Lick Sticks, Flunkies, and Jasmine Julius Vance.

'In ancient China'—Bruce had not stopped speaking—'rulers took the ritual suicide of their children and vassals for granted. This was neither infrequent nor always reserved for significant transgressions. Soldiers were rewarded for the number of severed heads they accumulated in battle, and when heads became unwieldy, ears replaced them. They murdered prisoners of war. Surrendering armies, laying down their weapons, were slaughtered en masse. One conquered queen was made to watch her lover tied to chariots and torn apart, her children clubbed to death in sacks. When the Chinese emperor Qin Shi Huang grew tired of his scholars' quibbling he buried five hundred of them alive. Can you imagine being buried alive? How long the minutes stretch before you die in that enclosed space? Or imagine the mind that dreams up such a death, the pleasure in abject human terror?

'They say that for every stone in the Great Wall of China a worker died in labor—an exaggeration, but it's not crazy to imagine a million dead from the work. And yet the stories of Temujin's cruelty suggest there was some sense to the monumental effort, since, with the Mongols poised to take Beijing, sixty thousand girls gathered on the city's ramparts at dawn and, in a breeze rich with the scent of lilacs, threw themselves from the walls to their death to escape capture, rape, and worse. A year later the bones of the slaughtered still stood piled in mountains and the ground remained oily with human fat.

'After months of siege and of eating one's own dead, death by impact, the blunt trauma of falling from city fortifications, seemed better than what awaited them at the hands of their conquerors. Chinggis Khan and his allies took no prisoners. Those they captured were at times boiled alive. In a raging cauldron they boiled flesh from the living, and in one instance they poured molten silver into the eyes and ears of a captured ruler. When Bukhara fell the Mongol army raped the city's women in front of its vanquished, weeping men.

'What captives the army *did* take it put before it as a human shield to absorb the arrows of those who hoped, futilely, to resist the tide of conquest crashing over them. To avoid this fate, the living sometimes hid among the dead. This inspired a Mongol chief to order his troops to behead all the corpses in a captured city to ensure its complete annihilation. One woman, hoping to escape death, told the marauders she'd swallowed a pearl, whereupon they immediately disemboweled her to search her entrails for the precious stone.

'For every individual who makes up a lone digit in numbers stretching to the tens of millions and beyond, we must imagine a ghastly fate, either brutal and short, or drawn out by famine and disease. Humans were killed in the manner that brought animal species to extinction, as one kills flocks or herds, piling corpses and bones to the sky. Cities and towns, large and small, were laid to ruin and waste, the inhabitants liquidated on principle, wantonly executed, tortured, raped. Skeletal remains filled the streets and deserts. China, in a matter of decades, saw its population fall by nearly forty million during the reign of Temujin.

'And the Mongols' devastation didn't end with the death of Chinggis Khan, but continued for two hundred years until the reign of Timur, who killed millions more. His vast army pillaged, razed, and slaughtered throughout Asia. Under Siberia's impassive skies, charging to the thunder of kettledrums, it vanquished the Golden Horde. Some said the plain stretched with bodies and blood for a hundred miles in every direction. Terror was a tactic of war. In Sivas, Timur's army buried four thousand Armenian soldiers alive, and in Isfizar they sealed two thousand in brick towers until they died. When the city of Isfahan tried to throw off Timur's rule he ordered a hundred thousand residents massacred, assembling their heads in cemented towers of fifteen hundred apiece, a technique he would employ elsewhere to discourage resistance. The skull-towers his men left as monuments to ruthlessness reached as high as a man could throw a stone, they said, and when there were insufficient dead to meet Timur's quotas, his soldiers decapitated their own slaves and prostitutes to add fresh heads to the pile.

'Timur lavishly patronized the arts, architecture, scholarship. His cultural refinement lived easily alongside his savagery. Did he kill twenty million in all, or merely ten? The numbers stupefy; they invalidate meaningful contemplation. To fathom this scale of carnage is more than one mind could achieve in a lifetime devoted to nothing else. Our responsibility as heirs to history founders on the disproportion between what we can experience, and thus imagine, and what we say we know because we set it out in words.

'The European crusaders performed similar brutalities on a scale limited only by their military inferiority. In Jerusalem they killed Muslims by the thousand, burned synagogues with Jews inside them, and slaughtered prisoners, including women and children. At Antioch they forbore enslaving or raping the women, instead driving lances into their stomachs. Richard the Lionhearted had thousands of Saracens beheaded in a Levantine field, and after the massacre at al-Ma'arra the starving crusaders roasted and ate from the bodies of their Arab victims.

'The most extensive and systematic cannibalism we know of was the Aztecs', who sacrificed perhaps a million live prisoners to the sun, cutting their chests open with obsidian knives and extracting the still-beating hearts from screaming victims to the sound of war drums and shell and horn trumpets. After burning these hearts at the altar on Templo Mayor, Aztec priests threw the bodies down the temple's steps, where they were jointed and carved, cooked, and fed to the population. The best cuts went to the families who claimed a prisoner as their own. Flesh was served in *chilmole*, limbs stewed with tomatoes and peppers. The viscera were fed to snakes, mammals, and birds kept in the royal zoo. Human skin was flayed and worn as clothing, gloves cut from the flesh of faces with the beard hair intact.

'Someone had to dream all this up. Someone had to imagine it as an acceptable prerogative of power. *A thing to do.* The French recoiled in horror at Sade's vision of sexual torture, but just a few centuries before its publication, Sade's countryman, Gilles de Rais—a knight, lord, and marshal of France—kidnapped several hundred young boys, sodomizing and disemboweling them, masturbating in the entrails of their cut-open stomachs, stringing them up, and sitting gleefully on their bellies to watch and laugh while they died. In some instances he procured two children and made them watch each other's rape and torture. This was the era of the *chevauchées*—those notorious bands of marauding soldiers who raped, pillaged, and murdered their way through the French countryside, laying waste to enemy territory and terrorizing rural populations. The medieval Germans strapped captive children into catapults and sent them flying to their deaths. They played soccer with severed heads and had a fondness for pulling the limbs off their victims. During the St. Bartholomew's Day Massacre in Paris, in the late sixteenth century, children were thrown from windows and eaten in the ensuing sieges. Their flesh showed up in markets, doctored to look like regular meat.

'The Russians showed a particular creative vigor when it came to bloodshed. Ivan the Terrible spent his childhood torturing animals. A favorite game of his, which he called "splattering dogs," involved dropping the animals some two hundred feet from the top of a tower onto the courtyard below. His rivals took the occasion of his immaturity to brutalize his confidants, skinning several alive. They poisoned Ivan's mother, beat Ivan mercilessly, and locked him in closets for days. He seems to have learned from their example, because he grew to take pleasure in devising cruel and imaginative tortures meant to keep his enemies alive for as long as possible during their agony. He had children tortured in front of their mothers, then roasted the mothers alive—like the ancient Greek Phalaris, who cooked his victims in a brazen bull slowly enough to linger over their screams. It's said he dined on suckling infants as well. Ivan, two thousand years later, killed one of his wives and his eldest son, and tossed an impudent noble to a pack of starving hunting dogs. In another instance he had a rival prince hung upside down and sliced to death, then went with his son to the house of the dead prince where they raped the prince's grieving widow and daughters. This is to say nothing of the massacre of cities Ivan ordered, or his establishment of the *oprichnina*, the paramilitary outfit he empowered to terrorize the kingdom into trembling passivity. The *oprichniki* thought nothing of roasting victims to death over open fires, boiling them alive, or drawing and quartering them with horses. In the famine that followed Ivan's reign several million Russians starved to death; the dead were found with grass and hay in their mouths, reduced to eating what couldn't nourish them. This foreshadowed scenes from the Thirty Years' War, when human flesh showed up in pies sold at market and infants were seen nursing from their dead mothers' breasts. The cries of abandoned children, calling for dead parents, filled the streets. Human hands and feet stewing in pots bobbed to the surface. Freshly dead bodies disappeared from graves. Priests found children in derelict basements, eating rats.

'During the Thirty Years' War, the only peasants with reasonable hopes of surviving were women taken by soldiers to be raped. Twenty civilians died in the conflict for every soldier. As many as ten million lives were lost. But the passive voice no doubt belies how much deliberate cruelty lived in the tide of blood that crashed over the continent. Three-quarters of Germany's population disappeared. Halfway around the world, at the same time, twice as many perished when the Ming dynasty collapsed.

'It's exhausting, isn't it? The quantities, the horrors . . . To say "a million" is no harder than to say a thousand or a hundred, and no easier than to say untold millions. And since the words take up the same space on the tongue and in the head, they blend together, the enormity at once unfathomable and yet encapsulated in abstraction so concisely that we feel safe from it, feel it is subordinate to our mind and not the other way around, and we say it happened so long ago, and to people unlike us, or we simply conclude that we can't do justice to this knowledge with the smallest fraction of the outrage or horror that's its due. And so we don't try. We put it aside. We resign ourselves to failure and let ourselves off lightly. And no, it isn't we who must *atone* for this, but we who must confront it if we are to take seriously what a human being is and is capable of, what we still are and have always been . . .

'For we haven't even touched on slavery, prevalent the world over until quite recently. Not long ago, animals claimed a higher status than the enslaved. At their point of origin in inland Africa, one horse was worth as many as twenty slaves. Human chattel was abundant and cheap. The trouble came in keeping and transporting slaves, for many more died than lived crossing the jungles and forests, shackled together in coffles, transiting the Sahara in chain gangs to reach the Middle East and Asia, or stuffed in ships to cross the Atlantic. The marches took months and covered hundreds, even thousands, of miles. Slaves were routinely beaten along the way, the weak killed, and those the slavers didn't want beheaded or struck down on the spot.

'Slaves died in their capture and their captivity, from disease, violence, and famine, or they died in the brutal work that characterized their first year's "seasoning" after being sold. They were branded upon capture and a second time upon purchase. Women were inspected for stretch marks since proven fertility raised their price. Boys were castrated to satisfy the demand for eunuchs in the East. Often their entire genitalia were severed, leaving just a hole through which to urinate. The genital area was cauterized after castration with boiling butter. By some counts it took so many slaves to produce one suitable eunuch that over a hundred thousand Sudanese had to perish to procure just five hundred servants.

'The slave-trading networks reached throughout Africa, decimating villages and often thinning populations beyond recovery. At its peak the Atlantic trade shipped a hundred thousand individuals across the ocean each year. Twelve million made this awful voyage in the end and at least as many traveled overland to the East. When the incompetent captain of the *Zong*, a British slave ship, got his vessel stranded at sea, he threw one hundred and thirty Africans overboard to drown in hopes of recovering the insurance claim on lost cargo, which he would have forfeited had the prisoners died naturally on the boat. Later, when the slave trade became illegal, black-market traders kept slaves chained together in long lines to throw overboard and drown quickly in case a patrol ship came near.

'It's hard to know what's worse—to die in the ocean, chained to boat or neighbor, water filling your lungs as you struggle helplessly; to die of disease, malnutrition, or despair; to die by the chicote, the whip made of hippopotamus hide; to die swiftly by the gun or sword, shot dead or beheaded; or to live many years in captivity, worked brutally day after day, alive but with nothing to hope for. It is this absence of hope that seems most haunting to me, the lack of any future to anticipate fondly, the utter subjection to another's will. Torture, rape, and murder are only some of the horrors slaves endured. Others were operated on without anesthetics, by doctors who hoped to push forward the frontiers of medicine. They undertook these operations perhaps with glory and careerism in mind, but also *idealistically*. Invasive procedures, with nothing to dull the pain! What lifesaving knowledge today rests on these bloodcurdling immoralities, perpetrated as well by the Nazis on Jews, and by the Soviets on their captives, and by the Japanese throughout their short-lived Asian empire? Doctors celebrated in statues and books tied screaming slaves to barber chairs and removed their jaws from their faces unanesthetized. Such things were not entirely uncommon.

'What does it mean—psychically—to live and die and to exist entirely at another person's whim? To know that your life, those thousands of days stretching before you, to say nothing of your children's lives, belongs to someone else? What is it to countenance the horror and weight of human cruelty, the untold suffering the imagination can invent, and to project this into the mists of the knowledge that your life is not your own? We can't force an understanding of such abysses; we must take the time to imagine, to peer down into those depths that light won't penetrate, and make the monumental effort of stepping into someone else's shoes, to think minutely through what it would mean, and feel like, not to decide—ever—what to do with your time. Not to be able to use the bathroom when you want, or sleep when you want, or eat when you want, or eat enough. Not to be able to stop working when you're sick or injured or so tired your heart feels it may burst, your skin choked with abrasions, blisters, burns, flesh rife with infections and disease, muscles torn, back nearly broken . . . To have to endure this day by day with no end in sight. No, the words hide the reality. They mask the texture of life. They turn experience into language and imbue it with the comfort, order, and wholesome containment that language encloses its objects in like a shell. You'd have to stop and close your eyes and truly see it, feel it—imagine being tied down, held down, and raped or cut apart, castrated or whipped raw until you bled to death . . .

'No one wants to imagine such things or, having imagined them, multiply them out by the relevant factor to arrive at the millions, and even tens of millions, thus treated in that brief span we call history. We would rather say we now have the decency to outlaw slavery and our worst evils besides.

'But then the period since enlightenment broke over our slumbering conscience some three centuries ago hardly lacks horrors of its own. That celebrated reformer, Peter the Great, took to the example of Ivan two centuries before, publicly torturing anyone who defied him. Before enormous crowds, reckoned by some in the hundreds of thousands, beneath the Kremlin walls in the Red Square, Peter had enemies broken with hammers and destroyed with agonizing patience on the wheel. Others were whipped with the knout and seared with blazing-hot irons and coals, stretched on planks, and impaled with spikes. He dispatched his ex-wife's lover by skewering the man from his rectum to his shoulder and leaving him to die in that state in tremendous pain over several days.

'The tsar brutalized his own soldiers so severely that peasants mutilated themselves to avoid conscription, knocking out their teeth and cutting off fingers and toes. As many as a hundred thousand workers died in the fever swamps of northwest Russia, building St. Petersburg. When his son Alexei fled the country, the angry tsar sent his ruthless agent Peter Tolstoy on Alexei's trail, eventually tricking the tsarevich into returning by promising leniency, only to preside over his son's humiliation and torture. Peter had Alexei tortured over months, plying his son for ever more information and further confessions, and finally had his onetime heir whipped to death, an occasion he appeared to celebrate the next day. When Peter suspected an attendant of carrying on an affair with his wife, he tortured the man into confessing to bribery and embezzlement, had him executed, and put the man's head in a jar of alcohol, which he placed on his wife's bedside table to keep her company at night.

'Now, Peter was a tyrant, you will say, a murderer, a psychopath, corrupted by power and paranoia, but one man and an aberration among men. What then of the crowds who attended these pageants of torture and execution, not just in Russia but across Europe? What of the giddy hysteria that seized France during its revolution, when as many as forty thousand untried individuals were put to the guillotine, when with inventive savagery the wealthy and aristocratic were dragged from their homes and butchered, prisoners and rivals murdered without a thought? What had centuries of grotesque cruelty taught people but imagination and peace of mind when it came to killing? In Nantes men, women, and children were loaded naked onto barges, locked in the ships' holds, and submerged in the icy waters of the Loire until they drowned. The barges then were raised from the sea, emptied of bodies, refilled, and submerged again. When the Princesse de Lamballe, Marie Antoinette's confidante, refused to swear loyalty to the revolution, she was thrown to a mob gathered in the street who, according to different accounts, tore her limb from limb, gang-raped her, or cut her breasts from her chest before she died.

'And then Napoleon, that extravagant icon of modernizing zeal, didn't hesitate to massacre civilians to send a message. The emperor won his soldiers' loyalty by freeing them to rape and pillage across the lands they took. He authorized torture and execution as routine tactics in military campaigns. And did his soldiers, children of so many revolutions in thought, feeling, and science, suffer pangs of conscience? No. They were too busy getting torn apart by the cannonballs careering into their columns, obliterating their bodies in scything lines, shattering bone so that it sprayed in fragments and struck fellow soldiers. They were too busy, that is, with the new horrors science and technology had unleashed to spend much time caring about how the maidens of Lombardy they raped might feel. The warfare had become so brutal, and the temptation to desert so great, that cavalry units were instructed to cut down their own forces when they turned back.

'The years following Napoleon's defeat saw this brutality relocate overseas. European mercantilists, hungry for Chinese porcelain, silk, and tea but with little the Chinese wanted in return, smuggled Bengal opium into the country, cultivating addiction in its people. They persisted at this despite official Chinese policy, which banned the drug, and the eventual pleas of the Qing government. When the Chinese took matters into their own hands, stanching the flow of opium and confiscating chests of the outlawed drug, Europeans dispatched gunboats to Chinese rivers and ports, devastating the ruling empire until it agreed to an oppressive truce, which legalized opium and permitted the profitable trade to resume. How fitting that a few generations later it was these same imperialist nations that criminalized these drugs and fought to prevent their illegal import. The very people who had built fortunes and filled national coffers by nurturing, at gunpoint, the conditions of profitable addition! How quickly the pushers of one age become the moralists of the next.

'The West's policies, the turmoil these intrusions kicked up in the Celestial Empire's cultural life, prepared the ground for the Taiping

Rebellion, a massive civil war which began when a Christian convert, believing himself to be Jesus's younger brother, embarked on a campaign of conquest, seizing cities and tracts of land in the south. Over a decade and a half, fighting would engulf the country. Massed armies numbered in the millions. Conscription of the young and able became pervasive, as did the torture and killing of the captured and defenseless. Civilians, including women and children, were hunted down and massacred, speared to death, hacked apart, tied together and thrown into rushing rivers, set on fire, and beheaded. Others were divided into pieces alive. The Manchu policy of never taking prisoners meant execution on a grand scale. Captured leaders they killed by what they evocatively called "slow-slicing." Some twenty million died in the conflict, though by certain estimates the number was twice as high or even three times as great.

'And it is not just *numbers* that obscure the truth'—we were walking past candy shops selling chocolate bark and dipped strawberries, almond toffee, marzipan, and truffles; home-goods stores with arrangements of floor lamps and lighting fixtures, sconces, armchairs, shelving units, hutches, side tables; overlit jewelry stores with glass-and-plush display cases, names elaborated in overripe silver cursives; shoppers in faded jeans and T-shirts, Mickey Mouse sweatshirts, eating ice cream cones, hair bunched in elastics, matrices of lit bulbs decorating balcony platforms like marquees—'not just the numbers but the words themselves, the fact and nature of words, which owe nothing in kind or imaginative insistence to the reality they stand for. Picture the army of men filling your streets, streaming right now outside your window, violent men in torrents, bloodthirsty, ravenous, starving . . . Men who can and will do *anything* to you, and to your family, your children. Can you imagine it—having nowhere to turn? No authority to appeal to for succor, justice? Can you imagine how many times this has happened, in villages and towns and cities across the ages, how many hundreds of millions of people have experienced the like, the liberated rapacity of the human creature, its desire to violate, penetrate, desecrate, tear apart, pleasure itself, inflict agony, linger over suffering . . .'

Bruce took a breath. 'Well,' he said. 'Now we enter the tangible spectrum of history, a time when, though the most horrific cruelties endured, evil became systematized, depersonalized, laundered under the aegis and interests of the state, those self-excusing ideologies of nationalism and economic destiny. Tens of millions died of starvation in India in the nineteenth century, not owing to any local insufficiency, but because the British had decided to open the country's grain production to the international market and the price of crops grown in India, by Indians, soon exceeded what the people could afford. During the famines, merchants hoarded their stock to push prices higher still. Grain grown in the starving regions was held in storehouses to be exported and sold in Europe. When the magnitude of the famine came to light, relief was discouraged, for the best minds of the day had convinced themselves that interference in the market could only make matters worse. Aid would cultivate dependency, they argued, permitting the population to swell to more unmanageable levels. They excused their inaction by asserting that Indians bred faster than they could grow food. Some even cast mass starvation as the natural and necessary remedy to overpopulation.

'Directly across a narrow sea, the British let some million or more Irish starve to death for the same reason. The Irish crop blight was a freak occurrence that owed no more to poor planning or bad habits than the Indian famine did. And throughout the Irish tragedy, the British possessed plenty of food with which to alleviate the suffering. The Indians had meanwhile attempted to prepare for failed harvests by laying away grain from one year to the next, but their British rulers wouldn't abide this practice and for ideological, and no doubt acquisitive, reasons forced them to sell their reserves on the market in Europe, leaving them helpless when bad seasons hit. The British followed this up by passing laws prohibiting private donations of food and aid to India, claiming that such donations would undercut the price of grain set by the market. When one famine followed the next, fresh excuses arose to meet the challenge reality kept posing to theory. First the population was blamed, then the weather. Children grew so thin their arms and legs were scarcely thicker than a finger. Their skeletons pushed through the skin. Dying, they looked . . . old. And grain kept getting shipped out of the starving regions while surpluses next door in Bengal and Burma were never brought in to help. No one thought of it. Instead the British taxed the grain that was finally sent by overseas charities concerned with the Indians' plight. Donations to save lives in extremis—taxed! When years later a careful analysis was made, it was found that *at all times* the supply of food in India was sufficient to feed everyone.

'These are the depths of venality and greed, of the mind so corrupted by self-interest that it confuses its profit for principle. It has always been easy to convince a man that righteousness flows with the current of his advantage, and those creeds that harmonize the two never fall from favor. Thus began an era when ideology would come to support the same cruelties that in past ages power exercised as its right. And who is to say which is worse? There has always been war and conquest for land and treasure, but there had never been disembodied financial considerations of quite this sort until the imperialist era. Those availing causes—capitalism, Christianity, civilization—wove a sinister and naive filament into the conscience of the age, one Europe recalls as a time of unusual peace, but in which the rest of the world suffered in their stead one convulsion after the next. Vast reaches of land were cleared of native peoples. They were wiped from the earth in cleansings and genocides, deportation and disease, and often by the subtle destruction of what upheld and permitted their way of life, so that when auditors went looking for evidence of malice or intent long after, the silence of unseen destruction rang in their ears like the uncanny image of blank territory on a map. The Mesoamerican tribes had by then largely perished of disease. Those who remained found themselves driven from their land and massacred to near elimination. The Khoekhoe of South Africa, the South Sea Islanders, and the Aborigines of Australia were dispatched in similar fashion. On the island of Tasmania, British settlers hunted the native people to extinction, spreading out across the entire island in a final purge to sweep it fully. They meant to drive the remaining natives onto a single headland, but when they finished this military clearance they found no Tasmanians left. Out of amusement or cruelty one Englishman made the wife of a Tasmanian he'd killed wear her husband's severed head around her neck.

In southwest Africa, the Germans exterminated the Herero people, driving those they didn't kill into the desert to die of thirst. Later expeditions found skeletons in the hollows the exiles had dug. Some holes went as deep as fifty feet into the sand, clawed desperately by hand to find water that wasn't there.

'Science, what we now recognize as junk science, offered all manner of justification that—like the dubious economic theory which ordained the starvation of the Indians and Irish—worked to rationalize mass murder. Biological distinctions among the races were argued to extend into mental and moral capacity. European thought tended to categorize Africans as a different and intermediary species. Their extermination and displacement, after slavery was outlawed, came to seem necessary and inevitable—even ethical—to accommodate and foster the success of the superior race. For the public at home, champions often cast this as bringing civilization to the benighted. Of course if Christianity and trade were the great gifts imperialists made them out to be, it might not have taken so many guns to enforce their acceptance. But it made a nice story for those who wanted luxury without the guilt—several thousand miles away from the reality of its extraction.

'This isn't to say that the only people engaged in bloody wars of power and profiteering were European. In Sudan, Muhammad Ahmad declared himself Mahdi, or messiah, rising up to lead a revolt against the Egyptians and their British sponsors. The Mahdist "dervishes" took Khartoum, raping and massacring the Europeans and Egyptians they found in the city, sending the women into harems, and beheading the British general. Their reign of terror, execution, and mutilation lasted many years as they waged battles to expand their territory and push into Ethiopia. In one incident they chopped off the hands and feet of twenty-seven prisoners, setting them loose in a market to hobble along on their stumps until they bled out.

'In the West we tend to imagine Europe's superior military technology as a long-standing fact, but it was only in the nineteenth century that Europe became the industrialized war machine we think of today. In the mid-1800s many African gunsmiths could fashion rifles equal to their European counterparts; then, rapidly, a series of advances—breech-loading, the Bessemer process, automatic firing, and so forth—remade the rifle into a far more fearsome weapon. A decade and a half after the Mahdists took Sudan, the British reclaimed it with a minuscule force in one of history's most infamous conflicts, the Battle of Omdurman. The British decimated the fearsome dervish army, almost without losing a single soldier of their own. The Mahdists couldn't get close enough to threaten them. The new British weapons mowed down ten thousand in the dervish army and left another twenty thousand too wounded to flee. The British meanwhile lost forty-eight men, and only this many because of a foolish, gratuitous cavalry charge, an obsolete and romantic gesture, and incidentally the last cavalry charge the British would ever conduct.

'It was the Maxim machine gun and the dumdum bullet that did the damage. Dumdum bullets, filled with a soft lead that leaves particularly ghastly wounds where they strike, weren't permitted in battles between self-declared civilized states in Europe. The era's enlightened sensibility only permitted their use against animals and, it appears, colonial victims. The British justified the use of dumdums in Omdurman, citing the fierceness of the dervish army, which they portrayed as relentless and barely human. By this rationale they justified killing the Omdurman wounded as well, rather than taking them prisoner as the norms of warfare demanded. They believed their enemy possessed a supernatural and alien ferocity, which permitted it to rise and strike again with dying strength. By some accounts, few Sudanese ever got within three hundred yards of the British position. The latter's weapons had become so powerful that their operators scarcely saw the enemy before slaughtering it.

'The art of killing from a distance—from gunboats and machine guns to artillery and aerial bombardment, from rockets and missiles to drones and nuclear bombs—is the missing link which explains how murder became an outgrowth of ideology and industry. It takes a highly impersonal machinery to establish death and devastation not as human and moral acts, but as inevitabilities dictated by political, economic, and other aggregated factors, so that even those in whose name the destruction is effected find its necessity and cause baffling and obscure. Is this worse than the intimacy of torture and rape—than looking into the eyes of the person you violate or kill? I don't know. We can only say that it changes the relationship of men and women to their desires, and to the moral quotient in their lives, since the banded webs of implication and causality end nowhere. Technological supremacy is still taken in many instances as sufficient justification for killing, a subterranean if not avowed belief that the intellectual superiority of the more powerful force represents a moral superiority as well. One death is famously a tragedy; a million a statistic. And here lies our inability to reckon with the magnitude of human awfulness. Of evil. Because behind every atrocity are always greed and the will to power, and then the paranoia and moral bankruptcy that come with greed and power. And who are any of us to claim unfamiliarity with these human traits? They are banal, truly. Evil sinks its roots in here. Is the freedom fighter, the champion of the oppressed, not enraptured with a will to power all his own, the fantasy of reshaping the world to an inner ideal, which justifies most everything in the end and shakes down to the same fatal self-importance? The sheer size of any project on a national scale enters the demographic territory where death becomes a footnote, the collateral damage of ideology. At least traditional combat forces an encounter with the horror of imposing your will on another person. The impersonality of killing permits those ordering bombs dropped or missiles fired or enemies and civilians gassed to cabin their decisions and calculations within the asylum of ideas—lovely, utopian, utilitarian notions, deciding for others what's best and who gets to live and die.

'Such obscurity and distance help explain how the colonial horrors which convulsed Africa in the late nineteenth century came at the hands of Europeans who belonged to reforming societies with professed commitments to human rights. A mistlike vagueness about the true state of affairs pervaded public discourse, even as accounts of adventure abroad proved hugely popular in the press. Ignorance served its purpose. A modicum of curiosity might have turned up unspeakable evils, but who was curious? Who was in a position to satisfy this curiosity? The few who raised concerns found themselves doubted, marginalized, ruined. Governments and profiteers denied or buried their reports at the same time that they used extreme provocation to stir up trouble in distant lands, justifying the seizure of kingdoms, people, and treasure by conflicts they had incited. They publicly humiliated local leaders, forcing them to choose between groveling (thereby briefly protecting their people, whose respect they would lose) and resisting (thereby ensuring their kingdom's destruction and subjugation). When humiliation didn't work, holy sites and sacred idols were destroyed.

'So affecting are the consequences of being freed from moral accountability that many of the Europeans who descended on Africa in this period sank to the most sinister barbarity. A young French captain named Paul Voulet unleashed a campaign of terror along the southern edge of the Sahara when it became clear to him that no one was in a position to monitor his behavior. Voulet led his military troop on a violent spree, forcibly recruiting soldiers and porters from the territory he took to replenish the ranks of his force as disease and violence diminished it. Those who resisted, he killed, as well as anyone he disliked. Entire towns and villages were massacred. In one village, to conserve ammunition, he ordered his men to slaughter thirty women and children by bayonet. When bad luck descended on him, he blamed his guides and conscripts, stringing up the men so that hyenas would chew off their feet before they died; vultures ate the rest of them. In reprisal for the death of two of his men he ordered one hundred and fifty women and children executed. When the French government finally learned of his savageries and turned against him, the deranged captain descended into cultish madness, renouncing his French identity and declaring himself the *chef noir* of a new empire. The force pursuing him found a trail of gruesome devastation in his wake: towns burned to the ground, victims hanging from trees, fires in which children had been cooked. The outrage at Voulet's crimes, after his death, rose and dissipated quickly. The government blamed his actions on the climate, and climate alone. It was the heat, they claimed, that had driven him to such depravity.

'Does the bestiality that emerges in people freed from scrutiny and consequence not reveal what is truly in our hearts? That's what I want you to consider. We propose a compassionate impulse to balance out our

cruelty, but is our civility really more than self-interest by another name?
Do our better angels exist as more than considered disincentive? Absent
the prospect of shame and ostracism could we count on anyone doing the
right thing? Who are we—*what* are we—unseen and unjudged? History
teaches little but that given opportunity and license we all stand ready to
treat one another as expendable. As labor, amusement, meat.

'Nothing better illustrates this than the Congo Free State, established
by King Leopold II of Belgium in the late nineteenth century as an economic strip mine. The joke goes it was neither free nor a state. Under
the pretext of redeeming pagans and freeing the Congolese from Arab
slave traders like Tippu Tip, the Belgians and their partners organized
the territory according to a system of forced labor every bit as bad as
anything slavery inspired. They needed this labor to build the infrastructure of resource extraction, and then to extract the resources—first
ivory, then rubber. The problem was they had nothing of value to offer
the locals in compensation. They surmounted this hurdle by imposing
a tax, which they justified as repayment for the enlightened polices and
administration they had brought to the region. Since the locals had no
money to pay the tax, the Belgians now felt entitled to press them into
service to make good on their debt, using men and children as beasts
of burden. These native laborers died carrying machinery and supplies
through the jungle terrain and installing a railroad in the inhospitable
land. To coerce the work, the worst of which was harvesting rubber from
the rubber trees, overseers chained wives to posts outside their company
headquarters, conditioning the women's release on their husbands' ability to meet quotas. The work was also enforced by gun; and since bullets
were scarce, the Force Publique, drawn from the ranks of the Africans,
had to justify any shots it fired by collecting severed hands. But rubber
is difficult to harvest even with grotesque inducements and the threat
of death. When despite these ruthless measures the harvesters failed to
meet their quotas, the Force Publique used severed hands to justify the
shortfall to their superiors. In this way severed hands became a kind of
nightmare currency throughout the country, and many Congolese surrendered their hands to the machete to avoid death. Many were simply

killed *for* their hands. Children's hands were cut off too. Often the young were so healthy, with such strong hearts, that blood shot out several feet from their severed arteries. When word got out that women's and children's hands were being used to justify production shortfalls—not just the hands of male laborers—the soldiers were ordered to collect severed penises by the basket.

'This was an empire built on basket upon basket of severed hands. It's worth pausing on the fact that this arose from relatively unremarkable, and what no doubt seemed logical, networks of actions and decisions undertaken by Belgians, greatly distanced from us in neither time nor spirit. Belgium quickly grew rich. Brussels's monumental buildings were erected from this tyranny of death and amputation. And why in an age before cars were people so hungry for rubber, you might wonder? The answer was bicycles. The pneumatic tire had just been invented and Europeans had gone crazy for bikes. Of course few knew anything about the suffering that produced their tires. That's hardly the point. Atop this holocaust of terror several thousand miles away was something as innocent, as seemingly wholesome, as the bicycle. The dictates of the market for bikes made this massive destruction of life "worth it," in that perfect formulation. The relevant price was gauged in currency on the European market, not on the ground in Congo, where ten million died from this terror and the disease, starvation, and overwork that accompanied it.

'And isn't it the same today? No, we no longer have jungle traders decorating their flower beds with the shrunken heads of natives. But do the imperatives of the modern world not compel people far distant from their source to spend lives toiling for a pittance, for mere survival, so that we can have our bicycles and T-shirts and consumer electronics? Everything you see here.' Bruce gestured at the mall. 'And if the arrangements begin in clean, bloodless principles and abstract logic, what about the downstream incentives these noble ideas create, what about the strongmen they raise up, the crony henchmen and kleptocrats and their wars and police states, which the fortunate wash their hands of since their complicity is only a structural inducement, a disembodied motivation, their advantage only the residue of untraceable priority and ancestral head starts, the impassivity of contract law, international loan programs, trade policy enforced by sympathetic courts? That these arrangements underwrite civil war and famine, drought, disease, persecution, blight, crop failure, genocide, and environmental collapse, that they inspire weaker nations to turn inward on their own people, is of little concern to those who understand the causality well enough to press their advantage but continue to define morality in reductive first-order terms. Very sad, but hardly our problem! We're merely tugging on a chain. Who knows whose neck it may be wrapped around?'

He paused. The open spaces of the mall filled with a complex light, a bright commerce of forms culled from the surfaces of marble, linoleum, brass, pearly columns, glass-paneled escalators. Clouds of cigarette smoke caught and diffused the brilliance in a fine mist. Tinsel and evergreen bunting, a holdover from the holiday season, hung in empty smiles along the foot of the balcony. People wore tight, high-waisted jeans, tucked-in shirts, bright primary colors, white sneakers, white socks. Some had leather jackets, boots, gold chains, mullets. They strutted, strolled. They sat on the apricot sofas of seating areas, where the floor turned to tile and low walls held indoor plantings. Children in strollers looked on the face of so much life with wonder. It was just past midday.

'How many horrors I've omitted to arrive at this point, I don't know,' said Bruce. I had the feeling of becoming light-headed as he talked, partly from the dazzle and flattened perspective of that bright repetitive and unremitting indoor space, and at the same time from my attention narrowing to a point under the lucid fixation of his words. 'They're beyond counting. My case isn't exhaustive. I want to gesture at the continuity of barbarity that changes so little through the ages, though the population grows and new technologies arise to annihilate the body in different ways. Cannibalism is not the special province of primitive peoples. We know the price of human meat during the Chinese famine of the 1940s: a dollar twenty per pound. Inventive tortures weren't confined to the medieval imagination. In postwar years they were taken up everywhere from Indonesia to Chile to the Middle East to Spain. Our enlightenment did little to stop large-scale killing and war. The worst famines on record occurred in the nineteenth and twentieth centuries, when there were simply more people to die. We've done precious little to exorcise evil from our souls.

'And which story is more pernicious? The story of evil's endurance, or the myth of progress? Is the idea of evil not a self-serving lie, an exotic delusion, as if evil were a metaphysical substance that didn't exist in all of us and find frequent expression in impersonal arrangements? Does enumerating human cruelty offer a cautionary lesson or simply inure us to what is commonplace in cruelty, making the fight against it appear futile and encouraging apathy until the pressure of our thirst for power mounts to another cataclysm?

'The horror grows numbing. Pancho Villa's bandits ravaged Mexico City during the Mexican Revolution, killing and raping with abandon. The *villista* extortion squads kidnapped the wealthy, often torturing them to death for their money. Villa ordered American civilians on a train in Mexico hauled off, lined up, and shot. Colonel Jesús Guajardo, in an effort to double-cross the revolutionary Emiliano Zapata, executed fifty of his own allies simply to make his subterfuge appear credible. The Germans in World War I, obliged to attack France through neutral Belgium, murdered thousands of Belgian civilians in disproportionate reprisals for local resistance. In certain towns they executed every last man. Death in the First World War occurred at a speed never before seen. In the opening minutes of a British charge at the Somme, nineteen thousand British troops were killed. So many bodies were left to rot in no-man's-land that armies cultivated the rat populations in the trenches since only these creatures could dispose of the corpses. Three-quarters of a million Germans starved during the war. Nine million soldiers died in Europe. French combatants, knowing the fate that awaited them, bleated like sheep as they marched past their generals. Mustard gas blistered the skin and inner lining of the lungs; victims drowned in the fluids their body released in an attempt to save itself. Disease, civil war, and starvation claimed the lives of at least as many civilians as soldiers. Millions died away from the battlefield, drowning, for instance, on the nonmilitary merchant craft that German U-boats torpedoed indiscriminately. Drowning may sound better than getting machine-gunned or gassed, but tumbling helplessly into the frigid waters of the North Sea or the Atlantic to fight the ocean until your strength gives way is no particular picnic, to say nothing of sinking to the seafloor while the ship you are trapped in fills with water. The conflagration in Europe gave cover to the Turks' massacre of the Armenians, a million and a half of whom were executed or worked to death in just a few years. Criminals and murderers, organized into killing gangs, crucified the victims and burned them alive, pushing them off cliffs and drowning them. Others they marched to death naked in the Syrian desert without food or water. One observer saw five thousand Armenians tied together, screaming as they were burned alive around an enormous pile of dry grass; another time he saw the corpses of countless beheaded children floating down a river stained crimson with blood. At roughly the same time, in Ukraine, the scapegoated Jews found themselves murdered on a vast scale: beaten to death, burned, drowned, dismembered, shot by the tens of thousands. Lenin, a believer in the efficacy of mass terror, set up the Cheka and with it the first truly modern police state. His agents and enforcers executed hundreds of thousands, including simple idlers—that is, people failing to work in a society where there was no work. Public executions, staged as didactic spectacles, added a grace note to the fugue of terror. Millions lost their lives in the Chinese Civil War. *Lost* . . . Well, it takes more than oversight, really. Shortly before she was shot Mao's wife wondered why humans are so evil. Killing was all she had known. Chinese bandits seized on the lawless chaos to rob and extort. To prevent escape and ensure docility in their captives, they ran iron wires through their legs, then sliced them apart with sickles to make them reveal where they'd hidden their valuables. The Japanese invasion of mainland China somehow proved even bloodier than the civil war. In Nanjing the Japanese conducted mass executions for months. People were rounded up and stabbed, shot, drowned, immolated, beheaded, and buried alive. Some found themselves tied up and used for bayonet practice. Women were gang-raped by the thousand, mutilated, killed, their desecrated bodies displayed everywhere to terrify the population. Such bodies lay unburied as far as the eye could see, along with piles of decapitated heads. Even the Nazis were horrified; they pleaded with the Japanese to show mercy. The war with Japan left ten million in China dead; later, when the Japanese departed, the civil war resumed, killing millions more. The residents of besieged cities starved by the hundreds of thousands. People ate tree bark and rats, later human flesh, a diet adopted by the starving in Leningrad during the German siege. (They also ate their belts.) Stalin took over where Lenin's terror campaign had left off. The purges of the kulaks killed five million. The man-made famine of Holodomor left four million in Ukraine to starve over a couple of years. The Soviets, like the British in India, exported Ukrainian grain during the famine. Anyone who didn't show symptoms of starvation was accused of hiding food against official policy and punished or killed. The gulags emerged. The rapid industrialization Stalin ordained was accomplished in part thanks to those working as slaves in labor camps, where millions died of overwork, starvation, and bitter cold. Stalin pursued anyone who failed to show him perfect loyalty, giving state agents broad discretion about who they killed. He purged the military ranks to such a degree that more officers died in state executions than in World War II. In just two years as many as a million such executions took place, and for years after purported "enemies of the people" were arranged in lines along freshly dug ditches and shot. The graves, exhumed years later, revealed tens, even hundreds, of thousands of bodies. Residents could still remember hearing gunshots coming from the woods every day and night for five years. As if the brutality of their leader wasn't enough, the Soviets endured unparalleled losses in the war. As many as nine million of their soldiers and eighteen million of their civilians died. In the first months of Germany's surprise invasion, several million Soviet soldiers were killed. Germans took more than five million Soviets captive, soldiers and civilians, shipped them back to Germany, and used them for hard labor. The majority died from neglect and mistreatment. This was deliberate. Nazi ideology saw Slavs as subhuman, like Jews and Gypsies, and Nazi doctors had no compunction about conducting medical experiments on Soviet prisoners. Where only one in thirty English and American

prisoners—with whom the Nazis believed they shared racial kinship—
met their end in German prison camps, more than half of the Soviet
prisoners in German custody died. The Russians, and everyone else between Moscow and Berlin, got it coming and going. The Nazi *Einsatzgrup-
pen* moved in behind the rapidly advancing German army and began
executing Jewish civilians in conquered territories. In a matter of months
they'd killed half a million. When the Soviets retook this land, they pre-
sumed everyone who'd survived had collaborated with the Germans and
either killed them, shipped them to the gulag (where they likely died), or
gathered them into penal battalions forced to march through minefields
ahead of their tanks. Soviet soldiers who showed cowardice or disloyalty
were executed on the spot, or else plowed into enemy fire and mines. The
war in Europe turned on the brutal fight in Stalingrad, where aerial bombardment and frostbite claimed victims through a protracted stalemate
and grueling urban warfare. The battle left two million dead, as did the
battle for Leningrad, which lasted nine hundred days. Air raids were
emerging as a new horror. In 1937 aerial bombardment was novel enough
that the death of a thousand civilians at Guernica could terrify the world.
Not long after, Nazi air raids on the British mainland took sixty thousand
lives. In retaliation the British and Americans launched Operation Go-
morrah against Hamburg, killing forty thousand. The bombing of Dresden killed nearly as many, and the firebombing of Tokyo killed more than
eighty thousand. This culminated with the atomic bombs dropped on
Hiroshima (which claimed one hundred and twenty thousand lives almost instantly) and Nagasaki (which incinerated fifty thousand). The
British Royal Air Force would drop one million tons of ordnance on one
hundred and thirty-one German cities and towns, killing six hundred
thousand civilians, destroying three and a half million homes, and leaving seven and a half million people homeless. For every person in the
worst-hit cities, forty cubic meters of rubble were produced. The first
wave of bombers would drop heavy explosives meant to turn wood buildings to kindling; subsequent waves dropped small incendiaries, seeding
massive fires that would grow and join until the flames rose several thousand meters into the sky, the smoke as high as Himalayan peaks. The fires

covered vast areas, moving at speeds approaching one hundred miles per hour in the streets and snatching so much oxygen that the vacuum pressure created hurricane-strength winds. The smoke was too thick for daylight to penetrate. Bombed cities lay shrouded in dark. Disfigured corpses lay in the rubble, some shrunken to a third their size as all the liquid in their bodies burned off in the heat; some lay in pools of their own melted fat. Bodies cooked alive in bomb shelters, or people suffocated in them; they cooked when boilers burst and the scalding water welled out, filling rooms. Baked body parts were found in cellars, and sometimes all that remained of entire families could fit in a single basket. Animals died when bombs hit zoos, leaving behind charred corpses of reptiles and lions. Alligators crept down marble staircases. Entrails lay in giant mounds. To remove the animals, people had to cut them apart; they stood inside the rib cages of elephants and other noble beasts. They ate crocodile tails and cut up and roasted bears. Millions of the homeless wandered in the rubble of ravaged cities, climbing over mountains of corpses. The corpses, often fully dismembered, made for an experience so horrific that survivors frequently vomited and lost consciousness. Bodies were destroyed in the flames and falling buildings; teeth and jaws crushed, lungs shredded, chests cracked open like nuts, skulls exploded. Limbs were flattened and dislocated, pelvises shattered, pulverized. People lived their last days buried alive beneath timbers and concrete slabs. After the bombing of Dresden the SS resorted to burning corpses in massive pyres in the city market. More often rats, flies, and maggots—so healthy they grew to the size of fingers—did the work. They gathered so thickly that only flamethrowers could disperse them. Fleets of planes filled the sky, German, British, and American. So many air personnel lost their lives that the British bombers were often manned by teenagers. Six in ten died. The sky cast a red light during the bombings. Some remembered how it fell down the length of a hallway. Refugees carried the corpses of their dead children in their luggage. Of course it's difficult to muster much sympathy for the Germans. Hitler presided over the killing of fifteen million innocents. This doesn't include the deaths of soldiers, who, in the case of the Soviets, died at a rate of ten for every German casualty. The slave labor marshaled by the Nazi war effort amounted to a significant proportion of the entire slave trade conducted across the Atlantic—in number, if not duration. But the Germans set themselves apart by the calculated ambition with which they attempted to exterminate those they deemed subhuman. After a period of killing and castrating the mentally ill and infirm in hospital facilities within the limits of ordinary German cities, driving them around in buses and trucks at times, whose sealed carriages filled with poisonous gas, and after citizens found hair in the streets that had wafted up through the chimneys of crematoria, concluding that shooting Jews one at a time with guns was inefficient in light of the manpower and ammunition it required, the Nazis devised their well-known industrial solution of camps and cyanide gas. So efficient was this new system, in place by early 1942, that by the end of 1943 most of these camps had been shut down or shifted to another purpose. By mid-1944 almost all the Jews in Nazi hands were dead, though more continued to be captured and rounded up elsewhere. Nazi-allied states like Romania and Croatia took up the genocidal cause as their own. Though some would later doubt that five and a half million Jews could be killed in so short a time, the Rwandan genocide of Tutsis by Hutus saw nine hundred thousand killed by machete over a few weeks in nonsystematic street violence. What seems most chilling about the Nazis, however, when compared with all the other vicious butchers of history, is the cool rationality with which they undertook what from within even the logic of their own disturbed mindset makes little rational sense. The Nazis' fixation on their impractical campaign of extermination bears the hallmarks of mass psychosis and delusion; but that this could coexist with judicious rationality, bureaucratic efficiency, and a sensibility attuned to the finer points of classical music, Shakespeare, and Goethe, that the people who prosecuted this diabolical plan were largely bourgeois professionals, physicians, architects, and lawyers, should give us pause, for it offers a presiding metaphor for civilization, which layers the rational commonplace so thickly atop the irrational passions driving it, and suggests that functionaries possessed of social prestige and elite responsibility may in fact be the least likely bulwarks of moral resistance, the people most prone to murderous delusion, since all they know is obeisance before the semiotics of power, and all they know to love and fear are the shifting tides of their own status. We revere the doctor because the doctor can heal, and the lawyer because, like the shaman, the lawyer knows the obscure formulary by which one propitiates higher forces. But doctor and lawyer alike concern themselves with the systematic and interchangeable quality of human life, not the individual as an ensouled being. And in the perverse madness of this discrepancy we find Nazi doctors performing the most gruesome and painful experiments on prisoners—as their nineteenth-century predecessors had done on slaves, as early anatomists had hired assassins to pad their supply of fresh cadavers to dissect, and as Japanese doctors in Manchuria during the war had deliberately injured patients to test risky new surgical procedures on them, infected them with disease to study the effects of new biological weapons, or simply strapped them down to vivisect them and watch the systems of the body at work while patients were still alive. These acts by doctors, with vivisection being, one might conclude, the far point of human cruelty beyond which nothing lies, haunt the mind and soul, for not only do they put knowledge of the body to use against the body, not only do they use the arcana of science's dark arts to accentuate and prolong pain, but most unnervingly they collaborate in the symbolic deconstruction of the body into an assembly of defamiliarized systems and parts, not unlike a machine, and in so doing lay bare a process of turning a subject into an object, a seat of consciousness and feeling into a set of pulpy, separable, and rightless clumps, and thus they remind us that this possibility—this *inevitability*—exists not just in the primitive barbarity of nature but at the very core of those ideologies and beliefs that make up the bedrock of civilized and rational life. It hardly seems necessary after this to mention the prisoners the Japanese worked to death building a railroad across Indochina, the millions the British caused to starve to death in India by taking the country's grain for the war effort, or the millions more the Japanese caused to starve in Southeast Asia and Indonesia doing the same, the Koreans and Chinese the Japanese took as sex slaves, the one hundred thousand civilians the Japanese massacred in Manila by bayonet and beating while awaiting a U.S. attack, or by tying them down in buildings they set on fire, the brutal street fighting in Berlin at the very end, the hundreds upon hundreds of thousands who died in a war whose outcome had long before been decided, the systematic rape, looting, displacement, and massacre of ethnic German civilians living in Eastern Europe as the Soviet Army, which had suffered so terribly at the Germans' hands, swept through, the two million Germans who died in these reprisals and as refugees, freezing in the cold, starving, dying in lynchings and mass shootings, or arriving in a foreign land—Germany—where they were not welcome and had nowhere in the rubble to go. Thirteen million Germans were displaced. Thousands of civilians died trying to flee in ships torpedoed by Soviet submarines. In the East, Japanese troops lost in the jungle were eaten by crocodiles. U.S. sailors from sunken vessels were eaten by sharks. Forty-five million noncombatants died in the six years of conflict. Imagination fails us. For the rest of the century, killing and terror continued in somewhat more isolated pockets, first with the French in Indochina, then with the Americans in Vietnam, who rained more ordnance on that small crescent of a country than all the bombs dropped in World War II combined. Hindus and Muslims butchered each other in the partition of India, and later Pakistanis massacred Bengalis in the worst genocide since the Holocaust. Mao's purges and manufactured famines killed tens of millions in China. Millions died in the Korean War, and later from torture, execution, and hard labor in North Korea. Indonesian purges saw mass beheadings and execution squads roaming the streets. In Algeria soldiers had their severed genitals stuffed into their mouths, a technique reiterated in central African wars later in the century. In the Balkans fathers and sons were forced to orally castrate each other and prepubescent girls were raped in front of their parents. Stonings took place in Sudan until the end of the twentieth century. Some countries we can simply name to evoke mass death: Angola, Afghanistan, El Salvador, Iraq, Guatemala, Ethiopia, Somalia. Even little Greece saw hundreds of thousands killed in a fascist uprising and civil war. Mutilations and horrible tortures were used as instruments of war-making in Mozambique and Uganda, where Obote and Idi Amin devised devilish methods of causing pain and deconstructing bodies. They learned the latest in torture techniques from North Korean advisors. In Rwanda women were raped with bayonets and blades; rape and mutilation were combined and took place simultaneously. Even priests and nuns participated in the genocide. The totalizing madness of the Khmer Rouge in Cambodia leaves one mute, as do the ordeals of the Vietnamese boat people next door and others who lost decades to mind-destroying reeducation camps. Some people survived *days* of being buried alive. In El Salvador men were confined inside closed wooden boxes barely large enough to contain them for as long as a year. When they were let out their muscles had atrophied so completely they couldn't move . . .

'Elias Canetti believed the hyperinflation experienced during the early years of the Weimar Republic, when a loaf of bread came to cost as much as two hundred billion marks, may have habituated Germans to large numbers and exponentially growing statistics such that the scale of the Nazis' murderous policies struck them as inevitable or unremarkable. He suggested that numbers of this sort—of the murdered and the dead—may have underwritten a lurid fascination with power, a kind of pornography of horror. When you cannot touch the reality of suffering or torment except by the abstract arm of numbers, human devastation seems immaterial and dreamlike; it may gratify your bystander's perspective, and you may even long for the number to rise as though in spectacular tribute to your awareness. I don't want to risk this perverse acculturation, tossing out numbers of the killed—a hundred thousand here, ten million there—as if we can sift between these quantities and apportion a fitting response, rather than simply exhaust our sensibility straight off, grasping, flailing, slipping under in our insufficiency, only to surface with the gallows humor that is sanity's last resort. Let us instead consider the case of Jean Améry, neither distinctly representative nor unrepresentative, characterized instead by the overpowering acuity of consciousness that Améry brought to his ordeal and torture, and his reflections in the decades after the war. Améry was an Austrian Jew and a resistance fighter. Yet despite being held prisoner by the Germans, passing through two of their most notorious concentration camps, Auschwitz and Buchenwald, and suffering extensive torture, he managed to survive the conflict, only to kill himself three decades later. That Améry would take his own life so long after the war suggests how little had ended for him and how the aftermath of such atrocities must live on in the numberless survivors who make it through the cataclysm, passing adjacent to annihilation. In an extraordinary passage Améry describes the torture he suffered in Fort Breendonk at the hands of the Gestapo, who strung him up by a hooked chain that grabbed the manacle holding his hands and arms together behind his head, lifting him so that when his strength gave out (as it quickly did) his own bodyweight dislocated his arms violently, tearing the balls in his shoulders from their sockets with a sound and sensation, a cracking and splintering, he said was never far from his mind for the rest of his life. He was then left to hang from his helpless arms, twisted above him, and from such experiences he learned the absurd and overwhelming actuality of pain, its complete colonization of the mind and of time, and the absurdity of evoking torture accurately without becoming a torturer oneself. More still he saw, or understood, that the utter domination the Nazis wreaked on their victims, and indeed the goal of any totalitarian ambition, a dominion realized most fully in torture and execution, was not the madness of a rational if vicious policy but the most central, fundamental, and intentional achievement of its vision. In the power this regime achieved over other people's bodies and lives, it conferred on its constituent members a sense of their own self-realization and self-expansion, to use two of Améry's terms, and discovered in this sinister corrupting power the ideal made real, the inner world taking outside form in a brutal and darkly theological way. And if Améry felt about resistance much the way Primo Levi felt about never granting and always withholding one's consent—that here, in this futile stand, however absurd, lay the last critical remnant of moral dignity and solidarity—Améry understood that torture is an act that can never be undone, remedied, or erased, long as we might to reverse or eliminate the past, and that, whether we know it or not, we are helpless before the insanity and senselessness of history, occupying the position of Améry himself at Breendonk, pendent and crippled, audience to our body breaking on the scaffold of contingency and the rack of capricious power.'

Bruce stopped. A foreboding had come over me. This had less to do with the horrors Bruce had recounted than with a sudden sense of what might have befallen my friend. I caught an intuitive glimpse of the unspoken past. Had storm clouds moved above a trembling field, spreading wild grasses in their wind, this could not have spoken more plainly to how far the lessons of disappointment can take a man into the caverns of despair. Yet there we were, in that crass block of concrete mall, under the glass geometric corolla of another atrium, where a small fountain unleashed ropes of water to the height of a child.

When I didn't respond Bruce said, 'Tell me I'm wrong.'

'Wrong about what?'

'What,' he muttered. 'Tell me we're good, noble, whatever you believe.' I didn't say anything. I watched the water gurgle and jump. 'We tell ourselves so many lies. They make our days more pleasant. Stories with their bright, meretricious consolations. Comforts we could never accept if we knew what we have been and still are . . .' I was smiling despite myself, against all sense. Seeing this and ignoring it, he went on. 'What is the cost of these lies, I want to know. How many rotten, doomed ideas have they underwritten? It's power that keeps the belling hounds at bay. But the power that protects us is Janus-faced and just one side on the power that destroys. That kills, exploits, and consumes. Any force great enough to preserve the individual is great enough to annihilate it. In fact, it *will* annihilate the individual as a matter of course because the individual's freedom is the greatest and only threat to its vision and its plans.'

I tried to match his sobriety, but I couldn't extinguish my smile. He was still there—the angry, frustrated, impossibly earnest young man, driven mad by the desire to believe, and by his hatred for that desire and the weakness he perceived in it. I wanted to say that it was his repugnance at the tyranny of force, the part of him that refused the lie, his adamant insistence that we answer for our incuriosity and ignorance that made up the glinting hope in the ribbed depths of our own dark sea.

But I didn't say it. I put my hands on him. An instinctive, intimate act, it surprised us both. He didn't immediately pull away. I touched his shoulders and put a hand to his cheek. He appeared shocked, even child-like, for a brief moment—as if I had touched his lips to mine.

Then he shook free of me. A light breath of laughter escaped his lips. 'It's our good fortune not to have to test our stories against reality. Not to know how pitiless people are. We see it from afar. How easily they violate, humiliate, kill. And why? What can it be but that we think only of our-selves? Love is the belief that other people are real. Well, we don't have it in us. We'd agree to the drowning of kittens if it benefited us. Then we'd invent a story where it was for the best, or inevitable. This is nothing new. But now we've purchased deniability—the last great item on the expense sheet. We pay to keep our hands clean, to keep the control system out of sight. Thank god. We couldn't bear to look at it.'

He snuck a sideways glance at me. 'It isn't what you think.' He could tell my thoughts had fixed on the interval of absence between us, the untold story of his disappearance. 'I wasn't tortured,' he said. 'I wasn't brutalized. Not physically, anyway. That plainclothes band of Rezari's men could hardly have been nicer when they picked me up. Utterly pro-fessional. And I chose to disappear. More or less, I chose. A protective measure. And a private desire, I see now. But I have to back up a bit . . .'

The mall was impossibly bright. Bruce took a breath and briefly closed his eyes. 'When I returned from the valley after embedding with Hero Company, I couldn't go back to reporting from the capital. Simple as that. You couldn't have paid me enough. Safely holed up behind blast walls, passing off deadly lies in the pompous, sober language of the news. I'd have slit my wrists before selling out one Hero grunt. No, I'd head into the country to report, I'd decided. I was going to dig up the corrup-tion at the root. The place was rotten with it. The simplest administrative service took a bribe. Depositing money in the bank involved paying off the clerk. To get a death certificate filled out you had to grease someone's palm. The police were in on it, of course. They set up sandbagged check-points on major roads, and as you passed some slouching, sleepy teenager in an ill-fitting uniform would amble out and shake you down for what he thought you could afford.

'A society of tollbooth operators. Some commentators got it in their heads that corruption was ingrained in the local character. That was bunk. No one likes graft, no one likes getting fleeced every time they leave home. Police commissioners skimmed from the orphans' funds set up for the kids of dead officers. We're talking greed of a special vintage. It was terrible for the economy. Sugar and sand in the engine. But where could you source your sponsor's kickback or the money for bribes except by skimming yourself?

'So the rot ran to the top. Like a crystal, the lattice repeated its pattern everywhere, taking its shape from the core kernel—the sophisticated looting by the heads of state in the capital. Like the main artery in a river network, the central government needed thousands of tributaries feeding into it to maintain its massive cash flow. Call it a protection racket, statewide. The top magistrates, foreign-educated darlings of the international elite, shielded the functionaries below them from our earnest but ignorant and halfhearted attempts at reform. These cronies could run their schemes in peace—for a price. It was the honest men the country needed who got hounded out. Fired, passed over, threatened, and ultimately killed if they couldn't be reasoned with. "Reason" meant accommodating the tracery of corruption. Our local allies staged temper tantrums about sovereignty when we tried to lift up men of principle. We'd taught them our lingo, our values, and they learned it brilliantly and played us for suckers. *Of course* a population looks crooked to its core when that's precisely what the bureaucracy has selected for.

'I'm describing the state of the country at the time and why the war was unwinnable. The war had turned the nation's economy into a strip-mining venture. It wouldn't stop until the cupboard was bare. It was maddening that this was allowed to persist. We'd plowed cash into the country; you might have thought we'd care where it went. A little grease on the skids was the cost of business, we told ourselves, but the truth was this criminal elite siphoned off most of what we invested, diverting it to numbered bank accounts abroad. Their overt corruption turned people against them, winning back sympathy for the insurgents. That is, for our enemy. With the money for salaries, roads, and schools going out the door and with the tentacles of malfeasance running wild through the judiciary and police force, the hope for a self-sufficient state disappeared, and with it our chance of leaving.

'But it's harder to recognize honest brokers than you think. Everyone *tells* you he's honest; everyone says what you want to hear. And there's big money in deceiving you. How do you find your way when even your local guide's running a scheme? The politicians and intelligence assets we relied on to navigate that alien territory all had their own stake in the corrupt enterprise. They maneuvered us to their advantage, protecting the crooked, accusing the righteous. They glutted the bureaucracy with allies and identified political competition as military targets, thereby tricking our military into acting as their private enforcers. After that we were bound to them for good. No matter what we did, people would connect us with the corrupt rulers. They even played different arms of our government against one another: intelligence agencies against the military, military against diplomats. This was a sophisticated business. The impression of incompetence is a convenient cover for a government that doesn't want to function. Some engines aren't meant to drive but simply to dissipate energy as heat, economic output gone missing, converted into cash, disappearing in the hot desert air . . .

'We were never going to outsmart these guys on their home turf. In their culture? Forget it. These were world-class crooks, notorious tyrants and war criminals, half of them. They had relationships with foreign intelligence going back decades. Spies love these mercenary factors, since there's no one they won't sell out for a price. And they kept the agencies in clover when it came to gossip and hearsay, the back-fence chatter spymasters use to justify their budgets in committee back home. Of course when the dust settled, the intel always broke to the teller's advantage. This symbiosis between agency and asset meant the entire foundation of intelligence beneath the war was dictated by an acquisitive element bent on defrauding the people we claimed to want to help. We were *their* stooges. But we were too reliant on their assistance and too busy fighting and dying on the border to pay much mind. Eventually, when it dawned on our leaders that we'd never have a standalone government we could leave in charge unless the corruption let up, what did the shakedown artists do? They got their buddies and handlers in our spy agencies, who after all wanted their prize assets to remain in power, to snoop on the very anticorruption initiatives we set up. We were spying on ourselves! This intel was then passed along to the political crooks, who stayed a few steps ahead of the efforts to dislodge them.

'This is to say nothing of the darker misdeeds perpetrated by the gun-rulers and private militias, those rogue forces operating in the breach between despotism and government. They ran extortion schemes, kidnapped the well-off and held them for ransom. They picked up boys and girls on the street to rape. For a period, at night, gangs broke into houses, stealing the valuables, tying up the men, having their way with the mothers and daughters. The families could never testify to their experiences, the shame was so great. They mentioned vague injuries, trips to the hospital. Execution squads roamed city streets in Japanese sedans. Militias and police pledged their loyalty to the local rulers, not to the law. They eliminated rivals, knocked off anyone who sought justice or attempted to expose their schemes. Journalists were no exception. For these reasons and more I couldn't bear to stay in the capital. Behind those T-walls, in the bosom of that private, make-believe reality, access to any truth the government didn't want you to see was nonexistent. Our diplomats and military spent most of the war years hoodwinked. For journalists, if you made it beyond the security cordon, the odds were high your fixer was a plant, steering your attention and mistranslating what people told you to create a desired impression.

'So my first goal was finding a dragoman I could trust. I confessed my predicament to Laila, and she connected me with an uncle of hers, Nouri. He was a man in early middle age with a graying beard and long thinning hair that ran over his head in damp cords. He was probably not her real uncle but that's what she called him. And I trusted Laila and by extension Nouri, with his drawn look of vague unvoiced worries. His pyramidal body and sunken eyes seemed to suggest a dependable character. One mistook his silences for sullenness, but he was merely quiet and he never tried to talk me out of my intentions. We had only been out of the capital a week, not long enough to get into any mischief or even to get our bearings, when Rezari's men stopped by our hotel. It was morning. The sun was up already and hot, a golden hue flowing west across the desert plain. It burned my skin in fiery panels while I sipped Turkish coffee on the small balcony. Nouri, dressed in the dark slacks of his fraying blue suit, was sweating. A limpid tear ran from his temple. We were getting ready for another day of poking around, sitting down to tea with the citizens who'd speak with us, when we heard the knock. The four men were cordial but firm in their insistence that we come with them. Are we in danger? I whispered to Nouri as we walked out. To talk, to talk, said one of the men, and Nouri's doleful raccoon eyes gave me a sidelong glance that could have meant anything.

'That province to the southwest of the capital is beautiful—arid and altogether still. Craggy mountains occupy the distance and a broad, slow river twists through the desert, irrigating a narrow plain, a strip of land once filled with orchards and vines bearing grapes dried to make fine raisins. Pistachios and walnuts grow wild. Not far outside the city marble is quarried, and there were rumors of undeveloped gas fields in the wastelands farther west. Mostly, though, it was agricultural country. When drought and blight ripped through the orchards a decade before, poppies moved in, displacing fruit cultivation, and the opium trade took root. Through the spring, seas of green poppy pods floated in the fields of pink-and-purple flowers.

'I had come to the province knowing little about the network of alliances and power that lay dormant and persisted over the decades of war, conquest, liberation, and new war. I might have understood but didn't much consider how for warlords and local rulers, their lives and the lives of their fathers had been devoted to reading slight ripples in the winds of fortune and tending shifting alliances to preserve influence in the region they called home. Outsiders come and go. The world convulses around them. But they must stay on, one step ahead of history, or be consumed by it.

'I only knew that the province had been a sinkhole for foreign aid and effort, notorious for the spongelike way it absorbed everything thrown its way without changing. Herculean endeavors to dislodge opium and win people's goodwill came to naught. Building projects had an especially poor record. A bridge commissioned across the river, for local traffic and to connect the western-lying airfield more directly to the southeastern border where fighting persisted, had collapsed so many times that people refused to drive on it. They passed instead through the riverbed when it was dry, or took a lengthy detour to a one-lane stone bridge several miles to the north. No one at home could understand it. Labor and materials were cheap. How could the project cost more here than it would in a European metropolis and *still* fall apart?

'There are no real mysteries; just different forms of blindness we use to protect ourselves from despair. I watched the city go by, riding in the dark SUV with Rezari's men on unpaved streets of packed dirt. Our carriage jostled over the ruts. The air through the cracked windows was fragrant, loamy, with a sillage of something spiced, animal, alive. We passed mudbrick houses in walled courtyards. The occasional concrete box rose a story or two above the street but mostly the structures kept low. Along the side of the road, beneath ash and juniper trees, vendors sold produce from handcarts. We left the city through the high arched gate at the cemetery where squatters had set up a shantytown among the graves. Then we passed into the river plain, a low quiltwork of fields which ran to the feet of the mountains and as far west as the water would carry.

'A burning and manure scent had entered the air. I had come to this region to find the crux of our misguided priorities, to watch them play out beyond the immediate reach of the capital, but maybe I also longed for life as it is commonly lived: trees, orchards, fields, tractors. Existence untouched by power's inscrutable game. No, nothing is truly pure. The province had passed from warlord to insurgent rule and back again in the course of a single childhood. It had suffered during the previous war, a generation before, and now saw itself remade by the drug trade. Power's distant connivances certainly did touch it. But it retained an instinct for purity, a complicated desire to remain uncomplicatedly what it always had been.

'Rezari told me much I didn't know. He had a kind manner, almost that of a therapist or social worker. During our first meeting he talked about how a ruler's strength never rests on coercion but on the legitimacy conferred by consent. What people prize most of all, he said, is the reliability of justice and accountability even among those who enforce the law. He wasn't a perfect man, nor had his father been. But he had lived long enough to know what mattered to people. Roads, doctors, schools. The ability to walk to market with money in your pocket free of the fear of being robbed. Sitting in his large drawing room beneath the coffered ceiling, drinking spiced tea served on a salver, watching particles in the air catch in the tranches of light that slipped through the blinds, I felt more like an honored than an unwilling guest. Rezari's father, quite old by then, had been an important warlord during the previous conflict; now, far advanced in his decline, he expected Rezari to step into his shoes.'

Bruce sighed. 'It's always seemed to me that *warlord* is a dubious term. It suggests something primitive or medieval to foreign ears when really, in those areas scarred by combat and insurgency, it denotes something closer to that part of government and civic order embodied and enduring in a man. Rezari had been educated in the West. He spoke several languages fluently and dressed like a businessman. With his stiff and rigid bearing (he moved with great deliberateness and dignity), it was clear he fit in more gracefully among the world's elite than I ever would. He understood himself as an ambassador between cultures, and between epochs, a modernizer and a reformer where tradition had constrained his father. Coaxing the embers of civil society to life in a region battered by so many waves of conflict called for patience—a gradual process. Trust earned over years is squandered in an instant, he told me, and it takes more years still to win it back.

'Consider your own country's efforts, he went on. We'd listened to the wrong people, he said, and now it was too late to extricate ourselves from our mistakes. His countrymen were at first optimistic about what we might bring. Money. Jobs. An end to this religious tyranny. They remembered earlier times and they were open-minded. But instead of embracing the slow work required to build trust and let the new society take root, we had formed expedient alliances with Rezari's more ruthless counterparts. These were short-term tactical, not strategic, decisions. For fear of becoming mired in an endless struggle, we'd committed to a light footprint, relying on airpower and convenient but brutal men. We'd deployed near cities instead of in the countryside, where the insurgency gathered strength. We blundered on for years, bombing allies by mistake and, for fear of collateral damage, failing to take out enemies when we could. We launched airstrikes on villages we believed harbored arms and rebels, killing women and children and exhausting the balance of goodwill we'd initially claimed. For insisting the war should be easy, we made it hard.

'And now the people wonder, said Rezari, Was life not better under the insurgents? They kept the girls out of school. They destroyed the cell phones. They had strict ideas about dress, and punishments could be very harsh. But backward as their brand of justice was, he went on, they applied it consistently, according to its own grim logic. Fairly, in a perverse sense. That's no small thing for people who feel helpless before power.

'His point, the key point I heard made and saw dramatized during the period I spent in that part of the world, was that corruption bred a deep and insidious form of resentment. Officials profited off the backs of the people, seized what was theirs, harassed and abused their family members and friends. And we owned these officials as our crony regime, symbolically if not always precisely in fact. With no avenue to justice, the desire for revenge overtook higher considerations. People became susceptible to the claim that only religion and its dogmas could ensure moral action and honest behavior. Even if they didn't believe it, they saw men with guns whose enemies were their enemies, and they thought vengeful thoughts.

'Thus, as I could see, Rezari said, corruption and the appearance of corruption imperiled his work and his tenuous hold on power. His struggle was to win legitimacy, and that meant telling an appealing story and matching action to the symbolism of his words. The war is over, he said, parting the blinds to glance out into the bright courtyard. Now the fighting begins.

'What did any of this have to do with me? My new friend took his time building to his point. After coalition forces had retaken the city and the surrounding area and the fighting had moved to the east, two men— brothers with ties to the president's family—had moved to consolidate contracts for the development projects in the region. These projects all had international funding behind them. Aid money poured in ahead of any coherent plan for its use. The brothers, known to locals as the Stork and Dapper Ahkam, worked directly and by proxies to corner this market. The problems came not long after. Projects stalled; many languished unfinished, or were built at smaller scale and to inferior specifications. A few were so poorly constructed they collapsed. It wasn't just the brothers. Every middleman took his bite. By the time building began, the profit margin had evaporated. To wring any money out of the project, every conceivable corner had to be cut. A new section of highway to the west caved in shortly after work on it finished. For months lines of traffic formed where people drove onto the hammada to get around it.

'Why "the Stork?"' I interrupted.

'Why . . . ? Ah. Rezari chuckled. You'll like this. He has one leg. He lost his leg in the war.

'Then there was the bridge. I knew about bridges from my summers on the job, back when my father still hoped I might take over the company one day. I shadowed his surveyors and engineers, sitting out in the sun on the abutments and piers, watching the men at work. It's possible this is what drew me to the region and the story I hoped to uncover there. Infrastructure and development grifts got little press, and here I possessed a special knowledge. I had intuitions about the nature of the cost-cutting measures: inferior, brittle concretes with poor mix ratios and impure constituents; rusted and friable metals salvaged from demolished buildings and used in place of rebar. I doubted they'd done the bare minimum when it came to geotechnical work and soil analysis, and any mistakes in the foundation and the load-bearing estimates could easily put too much strain on a weak structure.

'Rezari asked me about my work and what I intended to do. He listened closely, but I had a sense he already knew. And if he knew, so did the police; so did my own government's representatives; and so did the brothers, Dapper Ahkam and the Stork. I wouldn't survive the week if anyone decided I had become a problem. Don't think being foreign will protect you, he said. I'm sorry to tell you this, but killing you, a foreigner, would only demonstrate the scope of their power. Their freedom to act. And it was true that journalists in the country had been turning up dead. I'd just read about a foreign aid worker, a young woman, driven off the road by a militia gang and repeatedly raped. This had been meant as a demonstration of their outlaw power. Rezari confessed that even he was unable to guarantee my safety, certainly not without taking steps I'd never agree to. But our interests did partly align, his and mine. To keep the insurgents at bay, he relied on money finding its way into the community. He counted on the building projects and the jobs they produced, and he needed people's faith in the vigor of the fight against abuse. The insurgency itself had originally grown out of the outrage provoked by the rape of several young girls one summer at the hands of an especially reviled warlord. Why did he do it? asked Rezari rhetorically. Because he could. And now Ahkam was reviving the sins of the past. Boys, girls—it's the same to him, he said. I asked why he, who had friends in the foreign services, didn't ask our representatives for help getting rid of Ahkam. They can't be in the business of king-making, he replied. That's how such a request would appear, and they fear it more than anything. This was indeed the game the central government had been playing for years: accusing rivals of corruption and disloyalty to enlist our help removing them. Often the charges were baseless. They are right to fear this, Rezari went on. No more acting the brainless thug. But corrupt men like Ahkam were protected at the top. Their minor grift was a capillary in the larger structure. Such men were our country's allies, and our secret enemies— like some marriages, he laughed. In any case, he said, nothing I tell your countrymen will stay private. I might as well give it to the muezzin to include in the call to prayer.

'All of this, as I've said, took place against a backdrop of civic rot that is hard to fathom. The minister charged with stopping the drug trade, to give one example, was the country's preeminent narcotics trafficker. Rezari proposed a slow, incremental program of reform; and I offered him an end run around the closed information loop that kept the crooked patronage network in charge of the official story. I don't mean to exaggerate my role. One foreign reporter can't do very much, and Rezari was under no illusions about this. But having no dog in the fight, unburdened by preconceived notions, I could speak without the appearance of bias. Eventually, if I saw this reporting through, my work just might, in its small way, pierce the fog of disinformation, the government's own upbeat distortions, and reach a few ears back home. But we had to ensure my safety, and for this Rezari had a plan.

'It all looks so different in retrospect, but I'm recounting the story as it happened,' said Bruce. 'Rezari had a friend in a foreign security firm: Sarvara Activities Group. Sarvara started out in the province providing security for visiting diplomats and envoys—contract work the military either couldn't or wouldn't do. Through these assignments they built up regional competency, and when the fighting shifted elsewhere and counterinsurgency became the cause of the hour, Sarvara was hired to support and assess our government's local efforts. This involved looking into drug trafficking and weapons smuggling and auditing how aid had been distributed to that point and how development funds had been spent or, more likely, misspent. Rezari thought my work might dovetail with theirs and that a marriage of convenience could be arranged, since they had a security capability he did not.'

Bruce shook his head. 'Sometimes I recognize myself back then. Sometimes I wonder who I was and what I was thinking. It wasn't like me to hitch my wagon to an outfit like Sarvara—what I would have called mercenaries at the time. But I was changing. Maybe I welcomed it. I was a stringer out on his own. Don't forget that the term *freelance* described mercenaries before journalists . . . I still thought that the deeper I fought my way into the world's fierce machinery, the more I would possess something precious and hard-won.

'And I'd just come from the battlefield, and from months of living in the fantasy bubble of the capital before that. I'd struggled so hard against the fabric of illusion, I couldn't turn back now. It was a hunger not to be hidden from reality. I was desperate to unravel the insanity that prolonged the war and caught us in self-defeating cycles. Not for heroism. Not for anyone back home. I was thinking of the men I'd embedded with in the valley. Getting *them* out. It would only happen when some semblance of order grew in that soil on its own. If my work meant keeping quiet and cutting off contact—no dispatches to you or anyone else—so be it. I didn't want to be in touch. No one back home could understand the world out there, the element I had immersed myself in. Not until I made them.

'In counterinsurgency they say the only terrain you need to worry about is the six inches between people's ears.' Bruce shut his eyes and dreamed momentarily of far-off things. 'Maybe Rezari won the territory inside my skull. Don't misunderstand me. I had no doubt that he'd made his own bargain with the devil. You don't pay for foreign boarding school in local currency. Minor fortunes made on the backs of peasants, expatriated, then obscured by bold talk of reform: these schemes of feudal robbery echo down the ages, always the same. But the *desire* to believe.' A strain had entered his voice. 'Rezari spoke our *language*, you see. Not the words. Forget words . . . I mean the deeper current in a language that stirs the words to life, cinches them to the real.

'It was Sheila who helped me see the phatic element in our deceit—my new, or soon-to-be, friend Sheila Nuriyev. She thought our efforts in the country were doomed by a failure to communicate properly, at a necessary depth. Not a failure to speak the language, but a failure to understand and translate true meanings. Language in her view had little to do with the superficial sense attached to words. It was a format for living, a reductive code fit to the scaffold of life. It only truly signified as it related to patterns of intention, value, and action. Sheila was brilliant, an original. But I am getting ahead of myself again . . .

'Sarvara operated out of a set of temporary buildings on the eastern outskirts of town, a scruffy pile of prefab metal structures that turned molten in the midday sun. The head of the operation was an ex-soldier named Dominic, a hard, often unpleasant man, who didn't like me or

what I represented in his midst. More than anything he seemed sick of
the country. But he had turned his military background into a lucrative
private salary, and he was going to stick it out a few more years. His hands
were like steel coils in tension, they seized yours like a vice. He didn't
disguise his displeasure when I came aboard. The scribbler, he called me.
But he had his orders, and if there was anything to recommend him it
was his allegiance within a command chain. He never undermined me
out of spite.

'We settled into a pattern, which took shape about a week after my
meeting with Rezari. Every day Nouri and I, alongside Dominic and
his team, made our excursions into the surrounding farmland and villages, visiting orchards, building sites, and local businesses. We met with
farmers and harvesters, elders, government officials, and the occasional
military envoy. We worked within the city as well. I asked questions and
took notes while Nouri translated for me and Dominic and his team conducted their own assessment. I wasn't privy to their mission, but it went
beyond keeping us safe. They were looking for evidence of weapons and
opium, I think.

'We traveled by SUV, moving fast on patchy roads not meant for high
speed. It was left to pedestrians and drivers to get out of the way. Occasionally Dominic expressed the scope of his inarticulable dissatisfaction
in a conclusory remark. "We should bomb every last one of these fucks.
The whole godforsaken country." There was a rote comfort in these utterances, as if by routine invocation they kept his army days close—a
familiar feeling to hang on to in an unfamiliar, bewildering place. Above
his stern face his light brown hair had a boyish quality, and his striking
eyes were different colors. Sometimes on trips into the foothills, driving
on mountain roads that gave the impression of passing beyond the knowable world, you could feel, in deep matrices which judge threat and fear,
that none of what you counted on to preserve you applied there, that law
and justice were idle notions, and at moments like these an affection for
Dominic crept up in me along buried tribal pathways, a dumb creaturely
instinct like taking comfort in a familiar scent, and I thought he wasn't

bad at heart, but that frustration had merely rotted out his capacity for hope.

'It was through Dominic that I met Sheila. She turned up one day at our makeshift HQ. Look what the cat dragged in, Dominic said, grinning despite himself. She was ex-military like him and the two had intersected somewhere along the line. Sheila now worked for the government in a civilian role, conducting cultural fieldwork for the army. Having placed their bet on counterinsurgency, the coalition forces needed a better idea of what they called, somewhat unsettlingly, the human terrain.

'Sheila had fallen for the country, a true love affair. Certain travelers venture out to find, in the exotic distances, the world of surfaces peeled back and the vital matter of life exposed. She was one of those. A lean, lanky woman, indomitably optimistic, with streaks of prematurely graying hair, she hoped one day to return home and get her doctorate in anthropology. For now she saw a more useful way to carry forward the work she'd been doing in uniform. By applying the principles of social science to study the local population, she would map an immaterial territory, cultural and linguistic, bridging divides we hardly knew existed and helping military commanders avoid the worst miscalculations of oblivion and parti pris. She'd recover what got junked in translation, act the honest intermediary, and deliver us from partisan manipulation.

'The only sure path to truth is time,' Bruce remarked, 'an immensity and ballast of time, which forms deep gauges of judgment, or what we call wisdom. Sifting the data ever more quickly, we forget to make sure it is reliable. So it was, every couple of years, as the war sank more irretrievably into attritive stasis, that the military brought in a fresh-faced commander, a martial technocrat with new ideas (or at least unchastened hope), a nut for the latest in data-driven warfare. None of them stayed long enough to see how the game was really played and how not to get played yourself. They loved the toys of war-making. They could scarcely admit this love: PowerPoints, augmented overlays, real-time satellite imaging. Maybe they saw the world like God, and it just didn't make sense, with our wizardly machines, that we could be losing. It hurt their sense of pride—pride in godliness. They couldn't bear to accept what a waste of time most of it was. They forgot that God doesn't just sit above, but within, along every manifold and crimped dimension, and that the quotient of truth is invariant to scale. Our war was a coastline, a casualty of generalization and other castles of the mind. Sheila aimed to remedy this.

'The hubris of the newcomer, rife among the military commanders who cycled in and out, described my condition as well. Through Sheila I began to see just how prone I was to being misled. In weekly conference with my contact at Sarvara (Rezari's friend and a man I knew as Praber), I felt my tentative grasp on reality slip. He had a grandiloquent charm that came across even over satellite link. His relentless, almost unhinged optimism wore you down—an indefatigable sense of mission I'd always found canned or cynical. You didn't believe him, and yet the sheer audacity of his conviction made you doubt yourself. And out in the parched heat, after long days in Dominic's morose company, unsure just what on earth I was doing there, the desire to believe was immense. We were going to conjure civilization from the sunbaked earth, Praber intimated, ex nihilo by dint of our dreaming will. We'd show that, like a healthy sapling, democracy could be transplanted in a cultivated soil. I know how idiotic this sounds and I know its seduction. But don't the cynics also, in their breast, fear that their certainty in dismissing the utopian-imperial project is an ideology as well? Their confidence that it could never work? Because on the ground, when you see how people long for honest institutions and justly enforced laws, it is hard not to want to give it to them, and by force if necessary. It's the crooks who talk most fluently, when all's said and done, about respect for local custom and the sanctity of cultural difference, about sovereignty and the colonial past. Our guilt is as real as our sins. And guilt is another hook to hang us on.

'It was Praber who encouraged me to keep a journal, to take note of everything. My papers were stored at the Sarvara complex in a heavy locker for sensitive materials; there was nowhere else we could ensure their security, and they contained the names of those who spoke to us, as well as accusations, rumors, hearsay. The military was anxious to undercut the provincial drug trade and thus to see money distributed efficiently within the legal economy. This meant convincing appropriations committees that the funds weren't being squandered. To the extent that they weren't, Praber could argue Rezari's case against the corrupt entities like Ahkam and his cronies. It was his support for Rezari's modernizing agenda that disposed me favorably to him. The men's friendship reached far into the past.

'Of course I was never sure of my bearings. The farther you get from home, the more often you ask yourself who you can trust. I tried to gauge Nouri's opinion of Rezari, but he only shrugged. Words, he spat. How can you judge a man by words? With Praber, all the doubts I raised to challenge the rosy picture he painted met with a painful enthusiasm, as if instead of questioning the wisdom of our work I'd deepened it. Amazing, he'd say. Get it down while it's fresh. These were the insights, he suggested, that we could only get on the ground. My tours of the country and my evenings with Sheila at the hotel bar, or else the small café that spilled out into the street beneath the crumbling art deco facade, complicated my view of the situation. The success of opium as a crop, for instance, didn't depend on prices or margins but on financing. The drug traffickers advanced farmers credit, which they couldn't otherwise get. I mentioned this to Praber, and he smiled, tapping a pencil. Let's get a line for microfinancing in the next aid package, he said. But it was more complex than that. The traffickers took repayment in the crop itself. The farmers just had to grow the poppy and harvest the resin; they didn't have to find a market for it. Could we provide that sort of guarantee?

'A potentially more troubling issue emerged around this time in my reporting. One of the building projects in the area, a housing development called Apricot Groves, had displaced a community of farmers and orchardists whose families had been tending the land for centuries. It wasn't just that the development had robbed this community of its livelihood; the land sat on a network of underground springs, perfect natural irrigation, which the government had seized as an essential resource. It soon became clear however that this water and the extraordinary land it supported were intended for the enjoyment of the luxury units and their owners alone, and thus for what proceeds they would bring the developers.

For their land the farmers received roughly a year's earnings. The ink was still drying on the transfer deed when the true nature of the project came to light. By buying into the development early, well-to-do citizens of the city understood that they could curry favor with the official elite, and it went without saying that the company overseeing the project, an outfit run by one of Ahkam's cousins by marriage, would distribute the profit upward—or at least what of it they didn't pocket themselves.

'Not only that, Sheila told me. We were sitting outside. Clouds of sparkling dust lingered in the wake of trucks and mopeds and smoke rose in crooked filaments from the braziers. Work on the development has taken priority over everything else. Everything, she said with meaningful emphasis, but the poppy harvest.

'Instead of fixing the patchy highway, cracking to pieces like dry skin, the government had spent months running a new paved road out to Apricot Groves. Manpower needed to complete courts and clinics had been diverted to the complex, and the shell of a high school sat skeletally unfinished, waiting for the builders to return. Precious raw materials had gone to the project: gypsum, sand, bricks, concrete. On top of everything the workers weren't getting paid proper wages. Their compensation came in the form of wheat and lentils the coalition had given the government to distribute as free aid.

'These were the sorts of schemes I was being educated into. The plunder showed a heartless brilliance, and nothing could stop the mad dash to the money spigots while they still ran. Every minor rivulet occasioned a racket. In comprehensive ruthlessness we were outmatched. We should have reflected more deeply on this. Children of the looters drove luxury imports on rutted dirt roads where garbagemen pushed wheelbarrows and the indigent built hovels from junk. Smog choked the city from old vehicles with shot exhausts and diesel generators spelling the intermittent power. The only gardens were in private courtyards shielded from view, secret oases of lush tulips stitched with orange, magenta, and violet-white veins.

'It's amazing how much there was to steal in that barren land—and how a sense of hope sprang all the same from hidden sources in the scented air. You never knew when a homemade bomb might rattle the windows in their frames, and yet the beauty of the place left you breathless. The trilling songs of prayer and celebration contained distant, spectral emotions that watched over great snatches of time. The mountains stand up against the sky like divine fortresses. In the day's sun it's hot, but in the shade, and especially at night, a chill surfaces in the air. The temperature shifts quickly in the desert way. If physical realities install themselves over time as metaphysical truths, the lurking, silent cold suggests a harshness behind good fortune's fleeting warmth. The drab khaki coloration grows so familiar that a vibrant hue, a red sash or ribbon of yellow or turquoise, takes on a mythic air. As evening comes, a rich light tumbles across the plain and turns the mountains to caramel. Their articulated and wrinkled forms take on sharp shadows and a warm glow. The evenings were exquisite. A glistening orange glaze crept through the city and painted the buildings its burnt-sugar color. Like a fiery dew, dust and smog caught the sunset. I had been cautioned not to leave the hotel at night, but it was irresistible to sit out in the maidan with Sheila and Nouri at the hour before dark, when the air smelled of charcoal and roasting meat. Some nights we walked to a nearby field of dust and watched men and boys of all ages play soccer, footfalls filling the air with a dun, swaying brume of scintillating powder.

'It's too painful in some ways to recall that period of deepening friendship with Sheila.' Bruce's hyaloid eyes glistened. 'So many happy conversations about hard truths. She didn't approve of Sarvara or its presence in the region, and for that reason couldn't endorse my arrangement. But she never spoke of it directly. She knew that someone had to look into local corruption, and the government had proven itself incapable. She advised an anticorruption taskforce, an initiative for which she still had hope, but so far its ability to operate independently, without capture or subversion by the government, was a palace in the sky. I tried to feel her out about various issues and people. About Dominic she was noncommittal. Smarter than he pretends, she said, and a good soldier. She didn't know more about Ahkam than I did. His father had been a reviled member of the old guard. The family had fled or gone into hiding during the period of insurgent rule. She hadn't heard of Rezari, so she couldn't help me there. You never know who has power and who doesn't, she said. There are figureheads doing the bidding of hidden actors, and major players who hide in the shadows. And then, of course, there were the tides of power that had raised and lowered so many through the decades.

'Sheila had survived a number of attempts on her life. It wasn't always clear how serious the attempts were meant to be, but they weren't accidents. She'd lived; not all of her colleagues had been as lucky. She told me she was once invited to the wedding of the son of a warlord who had ordered her death the day before. You didn't go, I said. Of course I did, she said. He knew I knew. It wasn't that he'd had a change of heart, but he gave me credit for surviving and he wanted to see if I'd show up. She was safe as his guest—so she went. Allegiances had a quicksilver quality; friendship too. You gained respect by sticking around, showing you weren't afraid. I don't know where Sheila found the courage. It seemed to unspool in her from love, a rare tincture of happiness. I doubt she could've explained her calculation by a logic most people would understand. It wasn't a calculation at all, then; maybe not even a decision. She never showed fear or hesitation in my presence. Maybe she'd decided that living without them was the only way to live.'

Bruce stared intently ahead. 'None of it prepared me for what happened,' he said. 'I had come to view Ahkam as a joke. Dapper Ahkam. You wonder if these names aren't euphemisms, a veil for savagery. But then I saw him around town. *Intimidating* wasn't the word. Gracile, adolescent. A shy manner only half-hidden in aloofness. He came off as vain, possibly, but by no means threatening. People spoke of his bad behavior in barely concealed innuendo. It was an open secret he liked children. I observed him twice from a distance, once in a tunic and once in a suit, both times accompanied by guards. And while it was true he was disliked, people joked about him. With his father the hatred had been deeper, purer. Even in excess Ahkam couldn't match the old man's level.

'Sadly, such behavior wasn't unheard of. Children got picked up off the street often enough that parents kept them in when they could and worried about sending girls to school at all. The abuse of boys was a lesser evil—not condoned, but overlooked or forgotten. Something about Ah-kam, maybe the childish orientation of his vices, convinced me that the true power lay elsewhere. With his brother? I didn't know. They'd been presented to me as a unit, but where Ahkam could be spotted in his fin-ery, his brother hid from view: a figure of rumor and dark impute. The only photos I found of him online were of poor quality and decades old. They showed a group of fighters with their arms around each other, smil-ing. He could have been anyone. It wasn't even clear which figure he was meant to be. The locals said he was tall. Or medium height. Like Ahkam but skinnier. With more hair. A distinctive smile. Distinctive how? No one could say.

'I relayed this to Sheila. She had been trying to help the coalition choke off the drug trade. A priority, since it promised to starve the insur-gency. The military wanted a plan to outcompete opium. Sheila spoke to the growers, harvesters, and equipment-makers—anyone she could with stake in the business—but she knew opium wasn't going anywhere, not until the larger issue of corruption was resolved. The government's direct profit from the trade was one issue. But they also needed the bogeymen of traffickers and insurgents to justify themselves to the foreign forces that upheld them and to deflect from their own misdeeds. The military worried about black markets, but official policy was robbery by daylight. Sheila hoped to lay out her argument before a visiting delegation in a week's time. She had close friends at the FOB where the presentation would take place, and she told me she would use the opportunity to ask them about Ahkam's brother.

'The Stork. She shook her head. What a name.

'Nouri, who was sitting with us, said, Which is it, the stork or the crane, who carries off the babies in a bundle of cloth? Stork, we told him, and he nodded gravely.

'I had a sense then, briefly, that I was accomplishing something. Life had entered a routine. Dominic no longer treated me with the same con-tempt, and I had come to appreciate Nouri's fretful, melancholy ways. Did I feel guilty about leaving everyone at home in the dark? Maybe. When I thought of it. But I didn't think of it, not often, and I believed it wouldn't be much longer before I had material for my exposé—a long reported piece, maybe eventually a book.

'And then there was Praber whispering in my ear. Or Mason, as Dominic insisted on calling him. His grinning, laggy image flowed and broke apart in transhemispheric transmission. We're building an entire civil architecture, he said. The words and stuttering visuals gave him an uncanny, robotic mien. A small corner of the puzzle, he explained. Not the main show, not by a long shot. But if we get it right here, we'll have a model, you see. He had begun to hint at a larger imperial project, based in new, cutting-edge technology. I still maintained a healthy distrust but I'd be lying if I said that some minority share of me didn't indulge in idle fantasies of what success would mean—brief moments of flirting with belief.

'Then things changed abruptly. On the day of Sheila's presentation at the base, I was out in the field talking with a farmer whose orchard had been cut down. He couldn't say exactly who had felled the trees, but he knew as well as we did that the opium barons were behind it. The return of fruit growing to the region threatened their industry and they took extreme measures to keep men and land committed to their crop. The farmer cried as he spoke, tears of rage more than despair. It had taken five years for the trees to mature and bear fruit. He'd planted the orchards with the cooperation of our government—part of an effort to bring pomegranate cultivation back to the province. Now he saw that we couldn't protect him. He'd have to plant poppies after all, since waiting another five years was out of the question. He curses you, said Nouri. Your government. Also the corrupt governors you support. He says they'll never punish the men who did this. The drug traders will just pay the judges and police. He says the emirs—he meant the anticoalition forces—cruel as they were, at least would execute the culprits. Nouri looked at me and sighed. He's very angry.

'And I understood. The sight of those trees filled me with pity, full, healthy trees with their sawed-off crowns lying in the yellow soil. The blue skies, hardly touched by cloud, made the senseless violation worse somehow. I felt a child's rage at the irreversible, the unfathomable nature of cruelty. The faint trickle of a stream laced a riverbed to the northeast. I was looking that way, past the mutilated trees to the snow-tipped oblongs of mountain, when I got Sheila's text. We need to talk, it said. Call me, I wrote back. In person, she said. I'm in a convoy heading back to town. Interviews this afternoon. See you at the hotel at five?

'I mentioned Sheila's text to Nouri and he nodded in his weary way. We'd been planning to visit late into the evening that day, but I was anxious to hear the news from her meeting and told Dominic I needed to get back to town sooner than anticipated. What's the rush? he said. The country's been shit for two millennia. That's not changing any time soon. The rush was my own curiosity, it was true. You don't think her info will keep? he said. I did think it would, of course, and so did he. But it turned out both Dominic and I were wrong.'

We had come to one end of the mall and were looking out the doors at a section of parking lot and beyond it, down the embankment, a sliver of foreshortened marsh. Bruce took steadying breaths. I could feel his reluctance to go on. 'What we heard was that the man Sheila was interviewing suddenly became furious. No one knew why. It seemed so implausible, she didn't rile people up. What happened must have happened quickly. The man had a small drum of gasoline beside him. Apparently he got most of this on Sheila and set the liquid alight. She sustained burns to her entire body, a physical devastation I can't begin to describe. You may have read about this in the papers back home. It made the news for a brief moment before fresh tragedies displaced it.

'I spent the final days of her life at the hospital on the base, pacing the packed dirt around the temporary structures—those glorified tents like a colony on the moon. No one knew what to do with me. They nodded and looked away, offered me cigarettes I didn't want. The doctors and medical staff whispered among themselves and shook their heads when I stared at them with questions or hope. The government called it a random act of violence. They so easily wrote off violence against women there, no matter how calculated or political, as some unspecified insult to male honor or pride. What could I conclude but that the information she had obtained for me, solicited on my behalf, had caused this? I lost myself to blind rage. I'd never understood the term until it consumed me. The blindness is irreparable grief—the refusal to live in, to countenance, the reality persisting in time's irreversible flow. Images of her afflicted my mind, strobing glimpses of her smiling, healthy, laughing. The destruction of beauty is a terrible thing to witness. The orchard of felled trees. I could scarcely think. Or I thought so many thoughts at once that none of them came fully into focus. Thinking became a darting, animal act; an indefensible luxury. I was violently angry and helplessness rose in me like bile. I kept asking people to repeat themselves, I wasn't listening. The only company I could stomach was Dominic's. His fury mirrored my own. We'll kill them, he kept muttering under his breath. We will fucking murder those fucks . . . We don't have a term for the affection you feel for the person who can exert meaningful violence on your behalf, toward the object of your hatred or your fear. It's an emotion we've grown unused to, a love we no longer recognize until circumstance calls it back. Sheila didn't die for several days, lying in the ICU bed, but she never regained consciousness. Never regained the ability to speak at least, and the possibility that she suffered for those days, awake, without the voice to scream, haunts me. On the night of her death, Dominic and I got drunk in his hooch, that rugged brick-and-mortar structure at the Sarvara complex, and we swore to each other, my bravado swollen beyond all sense, that we wouldn't let the authors of her death go unpunished, that Sheila wouldn't die in vain.

'Nouri was peculiarly affected by what had happened. He became cross, testy, answering my questions in short rude remarks and at times openly mocking me. The police were holding Sheila's murderer, and our government was busy wrangling with them over custody. Dominic and I had meanwhile gotten names for some of the man's acquaintances, and we received the reluctant go-ahead from Praber to question them. "Question" was a euphemism. Dominic and his entourage pressed the men, slapping them, hitting them with rifles. They knocked one out, held guns to their heads, threatened execution. Ahkam, Ahkam, Nouri translated petulantly. All they say is, Ahkam is behind it. When Dominic's men started in with the guns, Nouri walked off. I caught up with him and he slapped at my hands when I reached out to him. I didn't sign up for this, he said. What do you know? You know nothing. He pushed me away, and

I went back to the interrogation where, under Dominic men's threats and beatings, the friends of Sheila's killer held up their hands and repeated that one hateful name, like a magic invocation that might get the beating to stop.

'These were poor men, young and unhealthy looking, with blackened or missing teeth and thin bodies full of nervy energy. Our effort was vindictive, not purposeful. We had our answer—*an* answer. Looking back, I'm startled by my ignorance, my naivety. I knew so little. And being a fool and stumbling along was the only way to learn. But at what cost! How many die to educate those of us who survive? And if I'm right, how much of what we hold up as truth is simply the residue of death, the lessons of the dead? What did I believe my own meddling would amount to, really? I might've dislodged a crime syndicate on Mars before I disrupted one determined actor in that sophisticated, foreign land. Hubris intersects perilously with desire, the earnest and helpless desire to make a difference. To *act*. The judges had no independence. Good jobs went to those with connections. Civil servants, soldiers, and police became menial lackeys for their superiors. The criminal rulers appropriated the oil and gas reserves. Foreign loans from development banks got siphoned off by private interests, while the debt stayed on the public books. Everything public was privatized in the name of liberalization, state assets sold in no-bid contracts. The powerful and connected took these, stripped them, sold them on to foreign firms. And while the people got squeezed, bribed, coerced, ignored, imprisoned, or worse if they complained, gated compounds sprang up, luxury cars rattled down dirt streets, and scarce water and electricity ran to mansions in guarded enclaves which burned white, like godly ocean liners, beyond the cities that lay in a primeval dark.

'Listen hard enough and you could hear the silent whoosh of money and hope rushing out of the country. The entire region was a pillage site. Nothing—no human life, no humane concern—would stand in the way. Not Sheila's, not the hundreds of thousands of dead, nor the millions, or tens of millions, harnessed to the pitiful machine of extraction. War turns life into money. There's very little else it does. Once the apparatus is up and running, there's almost no amount of money that can't be made—so long as you are comfortable with the byproduct of the industry, which is the constant processing and elimination of human life—because there's an unlimited supply of anger and vengeful rage, which renews itself, and an unlimited demand for security and power, which never can be too sure.

'What was my role in this? It seemed suddenly pathetic—not just paltry but delusional, shameful, sorry. In my bloody rage I lost sight of any larger project, the glacial turning of a tide, and everything Sheila had taught me about considered action and restraint. A base instinct took hold for the primitive redress of punishment. The main thing was not to let the villains of this injustice walk free. Everything collapsed to that infinitesimal point, and I understood, as you will too if you've experienced anything similar, how over time frustration at one's own smallness crushes the glorious dreams of remaking the world for the better into the dense hard core of rage, murderous rage. I'd have my chance—oh, I'd have it! But again, at what cost?

'Praber understood our anger. I'm sure I'd feel the same way, he said. It's easy enough to claim self-defense, no one's hauling you in. But there is a standard of professionalism we're trying to maintain. They already tar us as mercenaries. Our contract stipulates no preemptive actions, but that doesn't stop the critics from acting like we're guns for hire. A scandal like this, a little vigilante justice, just gives credibility to their charge. They'll drag us through the mud.

'You don't work for that guy, Dominic told me. Fucking asshole in a suit. We were drinking again, in the harsh afternoon sun at HQ. Mason's happy to play commander, half a world away, but he'll never get his hands dirty. Dominic persisted in this vein awhile as we passed the rotgut back and forth. The acrid, bitter liquid burned your throat. Since I wasn't on Sarvara's payroll, he insisted, I was free to act. He could say he was providing my security. I demurred at the suggestion. So all that tough talk? Dominic laughed ruefully and spat in the dirt. Turns out you're just a pussy like the rest of them.

'I decided to speak with Rezari. An audience was arranged. He knew about Sheila's death, of course. A gruesome tragedy, he said. Looking back, I understand that Rezari always knew much more than he let on. He must have known about me when his men first picked me up: about my reporting, my dissatisfactions, my break with the party line. He was a shrewd man, and if he didn't oppose our efforts in the country, he couldn't cast his lot with them fully, either. He'd be there much longer than we would, and his family longer still. He had to maintain power with or without us, and he had to play many sides deftly enough that his fortunes wouldn't flicker with our resolve.

'The bags under his eyes were as puffy as a frog's throat. He stood by the drawn blinds, serrated by blades of honeyed light. He sighed, moving toward me stiffly, and clasped my hand with sudden passion. You want to help, I know, he said. You, Ms. Nuriyev—you're used to a world where justice is a procedural fight. And here it is consumed by violence. How do you begin to right the wrongs when death stares you down at every turn? His gaze lingered on me, searching. His eyes showed their glistening bloodshot whites. What will you do? he asked, turning away. Will you avenge this?

'I asked whether that's what he would do in my place. He shook his head, whether to say no, or that he didn't know, I couldn't say. The cycles of retribution take hold deeply, he said. So many lines in the sand—and before long these are the paths of our lives. I don't know when memory will die out and relieve us of these burdens, but I can't afford to draw new lines myself. Perhaps you can act. You are foreign, and one day you will leave.

'Rezari saw himself as a bridge between past and future, as I've said, a man straddling two epochs who keeps one foot in each and gently shepherds his people forward. I thought he felt the tenuousness of this position, mistrusted by traditionalists and reformers alike. Perhaps he believed, by seizing the middle ground, that such a leader could enjoy his wealth and power and still, at day's end, tell himself he'd lived as a good man. I don't know. But it struck me that what he feared most was that people might cheer when his enemies returned, as they had in so many villages across the country, grateful to be done with a violent looter who held himself above the law, for Rezari—in his careful way, meticulous to keep his hands clean—*did* agree to help us with Ahkam in one regard, and this, diffidently, in deference to what bitterness and anger the man's corruption had sown. Rezari knew Ahkam's chief of security; they had fought together in the last war, and Rezari arranged a meeting between Dominic and the man. This was a secret affair and I wasn't told the details—just that for a significant sum the man would contrive a brief window when we could get to Ahkam. Maybe his boss's taste for children had gotten to him, I can't say. Our moment for action, at any rate, would come while Ahkam was at leisure in an apartment he kept for his unchaste pursuits. At these times his guards left him unattended and waited in the street. We would have a ten-minute window, the security chief told us, while the guards changed details. He'd see that the back door was left unlocked.

'The days passed in a haze, compressed among apprehensive and seething impressions. Having resolved to act, I pushed everything from my mind; a different mode of thinking might have swayed me from my intent. I lay in the heat as apathetic as a lizard, letting my still body fill with the potential for one precipitous action. I was aware, at every instant, of consciousness's oppressiveness, its fullness, and I tried to let my mind go blank, to experience thought as form without content, thought simply as being maddeningly awake.

'What you can't predict is how potent self-deceit becomes when you feel you have been granted the license to act. To decide, to judge. To hold sway over others' lives. Why is this intoxicating? It's freedom from the burdens of the mind—the liberation of ideas into reality. We desire this profoundly: to see our visions take form outside us. The power was mine to seize; it extended into me, flowed through me. I had been taught to record, to document. One day trials would come, and history like the dogged tortoise would catch the March hares who dashed after a power that had seemed to promise to save them from death. The scribes would serve truth and, through this, justice. It's a view as eschatological as anything. The time for justice of this sort never comes. The storytellers of a new age merely solder a new creed. Justice dissipates into abstraction, a tale men sustain in words but which crumbles in the teeth of reality, before the chaotic and immediate world. Silvered suns liquefy in the

sky. The day burns. The crisp edges of the earth keep a jagged embroidery running through the tracks of trucks, jeeps, footprints in the sand,
prayers, evening light drizzling down an ancient land and mud-baked
cities. So many sounds plangent in the dusk. Explosions like firecrackers,
vehicles backfiring in the distance. Bullets popping off not near enough
to stir alarm, or a popping that recalls bullets, but isn't. Beneath the white
disks trading places in the patchwork above. Contrails referencing realities so distant they might be the passage of gods. So many things foreign
and familiar. We are all people. We are strangers too. The war grinds on.
I wouldn't be there long enough to see the cycles revolve, but I knew the
story. The easy targets disappear until the hardest problems remain. And
the hard problems endure; they deepen the central problem, which is life.
Then people grow weary, angry. They suffer. The distant public grows impatient; the army scales back, troops leave, the tribal leaders grow more
powerful, more unaccountable, more imperiled. Sensing their precarity,
sensing the end, they become barbaric, paranoid. Even for mercenaries
the time comes to pack it in. They stuff clothes, a few mementos, in a bag.
Get ready to depart.

'Dominic had more experience with the effect of proximity to violence. He pulled me out of my trance, slapping water on my face. Our day
had come. He was in a hard mood. His multicolored eyes burned their
gentian light, fringed with gray and green-hazel about the pupil. Take
these, he said, giving me two pills, one white, one a pallid sea-moss color.
I took them, I didn't ask. What did I think, he wondered, about the rape
of young boys? Day after day. Boy after boy. He hit my shoulder, an in-
vigorating blow. Did I hate it? Of course the hatred wasn't part of a secret
curiosity, he said, a private fascination with what people did to each other.
Could do. When the harness was lifted. Out in the mindless desert. Out
where order and consequence ended like platinum fingers of water dissipating in the raw earth. What would I do if I hated it so much? If order
and consequence were abstractions as distant and taunting as the white
immolation of the sun. Dull weapons don't glint in the daylight. A pistol
weighs about as much as it should. We were on the street at four. Two of
Dominic's men waited by the vehicle. The apartment was a five-minute

walk, less than two running. The sun was high in the west. Dust browsed the still summer heat. We passed along the walled courtyard of houses. Drying linens and garments fluttered in the breeze. From somewhere, a celebration—singing, cluttered alien music, women's voices, and children bickering over their games. An old man in a perahan walked opposite us across the street, moving slowly and keeping to the shade of a wall. A ragged ailanthus cast a net of shadow on the dirt. The smell of fruited tobacco, smoke, spiced sweat cut the air. The low churn of a machine growled behind the surface of the day.

'Dominic checked his watch. We had reached the street the apartment's back entrance opened onto and waited at the corner while the seconds ticked down. Thirty-five . . . twenty-five . . . twenty . . . My attention sharpened with the approaching moment. Time dilated. It seemed briefly that the instant would never arrive, as if, at a certain point of intensity, anxiety and excitement converge like fundamental forces. Who can say what I felt? Dominic's pills had given my focus a tight-grooved clarity. They burned off some moral tether, the strap that ties you by imaginative links to the premonitions of shame or regret. I was free—a thing in the world, in the moment, moving by its own laws of action, unattached to ideals or representations of the future. Dominic touched my back almost gently and we were off. We moved rapidly to the pale blue door and pushed in. It was unlocked, as promised. I felt nothing but love for Dominic. He saw the world in equations of force. The sigmas of leverage and violence. He didn't conceal his contempt for anyone—the country, the people. He acted swiftly. Accepted casualties. Anything that stopped us meant a threat—a bomb in a parked car. In a drainage ditch. A culvert. Shoot first. Clear the path to our objective. I had no fondness for the simple math that made his calculations fast and kept him alive, but the silent speed with which he navigated the house that afternoon was something to behold. We were in a dark pantry off the empty kitchen. Music reached us from somewhere in the house, warbling and twangy with a festive rhythm. Dominic moved up a half stair into the parlor. I followed close behind. He didn't make a sound. We turned, tracking the music's source, and headed for the second floor. Only dimly was I aware of the tapestries and decorative artifacts on the walls, ornate patterns like geometric fractals, pallid in the lightless room. There were tasseled scimitars in mounts, paintings depicting scenes from an unplaceable past, warriors, seductive women in shawls, turbaned knights on horseback. I thought I'd entered a dream. None of this could be real, could it? We passed through two curtained doorways and into an open room with sofas and cushioned divans, lit by trembling lamps, and there was Ahkam, on a daybed with a skinny bamboo-and-ivory pipe, and a child, a boy of no more than eleven or twelve with a sleepy look. The shadows danced on the walls like the black flame-forms of a foreign script. Ahkam's surprise at seeing us came at a slight delay. His look turned almost at once to giddiness. He laughed, a noise half-strangled or submerged. The boy stared at us, beyond us. Be my guest, said Ahkam too loudly and cast a hand over the unoccupied furnishings. He cackled nervously. The noise came from the back of his throat. My brother sent you? he asked. He's out of it, murmured Dominic with a hand on my back, urging me forward. Not in front of the boy, I said. We don't have time, Dominic rasped in a hiss. You're responsible for the death of Sheila Nuriyev, I told Ahkam: a formal charge, like this were a court, were justice! He stared at me with wide eyes and roared with laughter. Ha ha ha ha! He fell back onto a cushion. A fly buzzes, eventually you slap it, he said after a moment. She burned alive, I said. At the recumbent angle, catching the light, his teeth glistened. The lamplight reflected in his eye. I heard she was barbequed to a crisp, he said. His tittering laugh had a spasmodic quality. For the first time I understood that he was afraid. Outside, I breathed to Dominic. A heavy breath escaped his nostrils like a horse's. He grabbed Ahkam where he lay and, with an unexpected strength, moved him—how else to put it?—up and out of the room. Ahkam tripped as he went but was prevented from falling. We pushed outdoors onto a terrace landing and down to the enclosed dirt-and-brick patio below, where Dominic threw Ahkam to the ground. Now, he said to me. Now or never. Ahkam lifted his eyes to mine, a wounded-animal look in them. The laughter was gone. He rubbed his knee. He'd hurt it, landing. The wind hauled through a flag on a nearby roof, beat it percussively then fell off. Satellite dishes clustered at the eaves. The day was depthlessly quiet. Did Dominic speak? I heard nothing. I wondered what the last thoughts are a person has before he's killed. Does he think about escape? About the impossibility of knowing for certain what the future holds, even with just a few breaths left? Or does he remember some stray moment from long ago, an embarrassment, a wistful dream, the cruelty and strangeness of the world, the strangeness of existing in a world with rules and without them, where perhaps anything can happen? Does he remember a now irrelevant task he meant to do but forgot? The stag shot, the fish gutted? The horrible weakness of a body, of flesh, softness? Does he think about the bleeding knee that hit a rock when he fell, how it's insignificant in the face of death but still his body reminds him, wants to catch his attention, to say fix me. Heal. Live. Does he think about the texture of the grit his hand touches? Or what a feeling even is? What are these things we feel? All these things we touch and eat and penetrate and break before? It's not as hard as you would think to kill someone. Clever beasts we are, we've made it as simple as clenching a fist. Once, twice. Again, and again. The shots rang through the courtyard. And after—the stillness, the silence of the day, returns. And you're yourself. And you remember your thirst, your parched mouth. If someone hands you a canteen you'll drink. Will your hands shake as you raise the water to your lips? No one knows until they try. But you're stuck with yourself. You can't divorce your body. Go your separate ways. You can't forget. Can't fail to be a partisan of your own hunger and will to live. I wanted some feeling that didn't come. To know I'd done it, done wrong. To know that wrong is printed in the soul, in the sky, in space. No spirit rescued me from the knowledge of the nothingness that followed. No ghost chasing after me, no punishment or shame. I felt *fine*.'

Bruce's eyes burned a polished black. 'I stayed awake for many hours,' he said, 'but when I finally fell asleep, I slept for a very long time. My dreams were labyrinthian flights—corridors, passageways—dark necessities I couldn't remember upon waking except by their residue of urgency and despair. I felt rested and strangely blank. Empty, not remorseful. It was confusing that life should go on. My attention had bound itself so singularly to the instant of action that I hadn't once considered what I would do in the aftermath, or even that such a moment would arrive. But now it did, and the idea of continuing with my work was absurd. Events had superseded its meaning, yes. But I also saw, for the first time, that my decision to act as I had made going back impossible. I'd crossed a Rubicon and could claim credibility as a neutral observer no longer. The scandal of my story coming out, the leverage it gave anyone I cared to expose, hung over me like a sword. If the goal had been to shut me up, to bury my work, the plan had been a splendid success.

'And yet, despite all this, I was at peace. Rather than regretting my decision, I sensed a weight had lifted. I felt Dominic's hand, clapping me on the back. His strong grip on my shoulder, lingering. Had I been initiated? Was I one of them? This was on our drive back, that weightless, skittering flight. I saw—I could *feel*—Dominic and his men relax, the grins break out on their faces. We passed around a flask. I drank first, even though I didn't need the liquor. I felt good, calm. Calmer than I could remember having felt in a long time. My impatience had fallen away. My anger. Had it ever been more than restlessness, agitation at the world's intransigence, the messiness of other people, of life, complications you could cut through in an instant with a gun? And now also at an end, for me, was the Sisyphean labor of uncovering and telling those excruciating, maddening stories, and seeing nothing come of it, nothing change! Inuring people, by disappointment, to the corrupt nature of life and men, and teaching them—all of us—our impotence to conjure justice from the futile smoke of anger. No, I'd done something. I'd taken an irreversible material step, for good or ill.

'Rezari left word that he wanted to see me late that afternoon. I was still luxuriating in the emptiness of feeling. Dominic said if it were him he wouldn't go. What for? he said. Not worth the risk. Risk? What risk? I anticipated something like a hero's welcome, the respect of a peer. I had acted and in so doing advanced beyond the paralyzed business of lurking and noting, wringing one's hands. Accomplishing nothing. Yet unlike me, Dominic seemed subdued, almost somber. He leaned his head back and let out a long *Ah!* A compound note of frustration and pain. He gazed into the distance and said, I can't wait to leave this shithole behind.

'Even Nouri àdvised me against going. Wash your hands of that man, he said. The weight of melancholy dragged on the flesh of his face.

'I don't understand, I told him.

'He turned the full aspect of his suffering on me, eyes glistening amnioticly, and said, Perhaps it's better that way.

'But my curiosity urged me on, and I passed through the dust of the city like the breath of a dream. Rezari's guards patted me down in the vestibule. Show him in, I heard Rezari call from an interior room. Instead of taking me to the formal parlor where we had met before, they led me to a domestic space off a modern kitchen in a different wing of the complex. A woman in a firaq partug and green silk chador sat on a long sofa. Two children played on the carpet at her feet. The rug was luxuriant and vast, an exquisite faded allover. She looked up and smiled at me. My wife, said Rezari, coming over to greet me. And my two sons. The boys looked up briefly, sensing our attention on them, and then turned back to their game. Come, come, said Rezari, escorting me into an adjoining room. This was a large bedroom from the windows of which one could make out the distant bajada and the snow-touched mountain peaks to the north. I hope you'll excuse me, he said, but time is short. We have the funeral to attend. Excuse what? I said. He took off his suit jacket and walked over to the freshly laundered white garments hanging from the closet door: perahan and tunban. He touched the fabric. These clothes, he said, they suggest something exotic to you, I think—an old culture and its tradition. There are those, as you know, who believe this attachment to old ways is what holds us back and means we will never join the modern world. He undid his belt and hung it on a hook. Then he sat and unlaced his shoes. I must change, he explained, but I wanted to see you. These clothes, they are a *costume*, is what I mean to say. They communicate a respect for certain values, and people find such symbols meaningful. But they are no more than a costume, really. We are playing a role—for our people and also for you. He slipped off his shoes and lisle socks. Do you see? he asked, standing. We're reading symbols all of the time, trying to make sense of them. What do they say? They're our passage to truth, but they're deceptive too. We construct stories from them and to some

of these we attach particular significance. But it's too much work to look
into the details. So we skim the surface. We count on the symbol telling
us what lies beneath it. He unbuttoned his pants. I was too shocked by
this familiarity to register what I was looking at when he slid them off.
At first I thought it was some sort of garter contraption on his left thigh,
but then I realized—it happened in a moment—that I was looking at an
artificial leg, and that his stiff way of walking had all along been owing
to this. A brother cannot kill his brother, Rezari continued. Much as he
might long to with Cain's murderous rage. A brother who embarrasses
him, who compromises his plans and brings dishonor to his name. It's
just not done. It violates a sacred principle. It calls the symbols into question, you see. No one will ever trust the man who's killed his father or
his brother, even if the one killed is a brute and deserves it. The killer of
a monster is also a monster. People may secretly rejoice, but they must
divest themselves of the monster in their midst, the source of their relief
with blood on his hands. With their guilt in his body, the secret that
their peaceful days rest on—the secret of violence. Rezari unbuttoned his
shirt and slipped it from his shoulders. He stood there in his underwear,
smiling such a small flicker of smile I didn't know whether I imagined it.
I was dumbfounded, mute. Daylight daubed the gold embroidery of his
robe with gouts of flame. This is no place for you, he said. A man like you.
It takes decades, centuries, for power to solidify in institutions that can
carry forward violence without the force and determination of individual
men. Sometimes it never happens. And when it does, very often people
grow tired of the bureaucrats, the institutions, and long for the clarity of
a single man imposing his will—authoring change that people can see
and connect to human intention, to the will to remake the world. He
picked up the tunic pants, a cream linen, and worked these carefully over
his prosthesis. What your friend, Ms. Nuriyev, understood, he said, was
that the justice you long for can never be imposed. It can only grow by
starting a thousand fires in the hearts of men: a million tiny sparks that
mean they love the dream of justice more than the comfort of life or the
absence of pain. It's such a delicate procedure, it rarely works. He gave a
rueful smile. It rarely takes hold in the great conflagration that sweeps

individuals from power, because it's so threatening to those in power that they fear it most of all and go to great lengths to stamp it out before it ignites. He put the tunic over his head; it fell on his body neatly. The vertical gold stripes shimmered. So many like Ms. Nuriyev die for every fire that sparks. More than you'd believe . . . Do you understand? He looked inquisitively in my eye. You don't have her patience. Your impatience, your rashness, is your weakness. Pardon me for saying so, I owe you a great debt, after all. Loose ends are dangerous to let dangle, but you've done me an inestimable favor. I can finally step from the shadow and claim what's mine. What the insurgents took from my father, and what we fought for when I was young and another distant, foreign army swept through here with their own blind pride. Rubble and corpses only get you so far, absent the burning fire in men's hearts . . . Well, in honor of my debt to you I mean to give you some advice. I don't know whether you will take it, but that's not my business. Rezari walked to the window and stared out at the fields, the scar of river twisting through the flat plain. You'll experience anger in the days ahead, he explained. Helpless rage. Futility. Loathing. For me? Yes, but also for yourself. For so many things. You'll be tempted a second time to turn the impotence of feeling into the violence of some pointless act. I know this because I've felt it too. Do you know what it's like to see everything taken from you? Your friends, your family, and so many of them killed? To lose everything, regain it, and fear losing it again? No, I don't think you can know . . . I've been through every inch of what you'll endure, magnified many times. And it's from this position of knowledge that I tell you, if you want anything you do to matter from this day forward, take that rage, that futility—*everything*—and lock it in the vault of your chest. Don't let anyone see it. But decide what it is you want to do. And with the patience of a god, let the fire of it power you toward your secret end. Take slow steps toward your goal. Never announce it. Dress yourself in the symbols of your camouflage, whatever it is. Play the part. Don't let anyone see you as you are. If you're more patient, you will win. You can't fail. But if you ask the world to know you, to see you, to understand the steps, the purpose behind your aim, you will bring everything down on your head. Rezari looked at me kindly, even pityingly. He touched my face, held it briefly in his hands. Now I must go bury my brother, he said.'

Bruce and I had reversed course and were walking back down the length of the mall. Lost to his story, I hardly registered our immediate reality. 'Here,' he said and we turned into the corridor that held the restrooms. At its end, a pair of beige metal doors were set aside for the use of authorized personnel. They had small embossed numbers above them: 103 and 104. A white ceramic water fountain recessed into the wall bled a faint trickle of greenish water. Bruce tried the doors, found 103 open, and we passed through it into a storage room of cleaning supplies and garage shelving. 'Outside,' he murmured, pushing through an emergency exit. 'It's switched off.' We exited into an afternoon warmer than I was expecting. There was a lone picnic table on the grass margin. Down the side of the building a worker taking a break saluted us. The light caught in the marsh water, turning it opaque and reflective like Mylar. The trees had a deep, blackening-green hue. Beyond the marsh, through a break in the woods leading out to the coast, I recognized the white form of the duck from the paintings of Alfonse Ricard, luminous and vivid at this hour. Bruce sat at the picnic bench. 'Look at that,' he said, pointing to the duck; it must have been the size of a small house, though I couldn't judge the distance. 'When you've seen what sits behind all this—the mechanism that supports our oblivion—the triviality of most people's lives overwhelms you. The things they do, the things they think. Well, let them have their oblivion. Guard it for them if you can. The blessed peace of not knowing . . .'

He leaned back, his arms bent on the table like wings. 'It was true what Rezari had told me,' he said. 'I felt enraged, lost, helpless in the days after our meeting. My immediate urge was for revenge. In what form, I didn't know. I talked to Praber. He said things hadn't played out how he'd hoped, but it was better that Rezari was in power. The lesser of many evils. It wasn't until much later, in the gradual adjustment my eyes made to such dim shadows, that I saw how far back this play must have originated. It cleared away Sheila and it cleared away me. Gone was any retrospective accountability for the money that had disappeared. My investigation, my papers and work, would form an indictment against Ahkam, who, in death, could take all our failures and lost treasure, and even the stigma of mismanagement, with him to the grave. With Rezari coming to power and Sarvara behind him, a new wave of development money would rush in and the cycle of theft would begin again.

'Sarvara, don't forget, had the contract to audit our investments in the province. But the game didn't stop there.' Bruce's smile curdled with spite. 'Sort through the subsidiaries and shell companies that nest these partnerships and corporations, follow the maze to the top of the pyramid, and you'll find a firm called Athos, which owns Sarvara, as well as a controlling interest in half the contractors bidding on construction projects in the region—contracts that, once won, they contract out to local firms, which subcontract them again, everyone taking a fat cut until there's hardly money to build a shed. I didn't know any of this at the time, of course, nothing about Athos, or how far back the ties between Praber and Rezari stretched. Athos's portfolio had a hand in oil field and commissary services, prison guards; on the praetorian side they protected diplomats and civilian personnel. Then there were the dark areas of warmaking where the military wouldn't tread. Disreputable sorts of intelligence gathering, interrogation, payoffs to butchers and expedient crooks the public would never approve of. It extended further still. This wasn't one of those hack operations that went in for lucrative boondoggles, rank government pork, winning contracts to train police, say, and pushing unemployed young men through computer presentations adapted from corporate training seminars. Was it any wonder in a country of seasoned fighters and canny power brokers, where bribery and credible violence dictated right, that these foreign-trained forces never stood up long enough to collapse? No, Sarvara ran a savvier operation, in deeper and more enveloping dim crannies. Their top operators were intelligence veterans, on the ground long before operations were officially announced. Coordinating with their buddies, former colleagues at the agencies, they facilitated the payments to warlords and tribal leaders like Rezari, who in return provided connections, information, and the freedom to operate within their spheres of influence. It worked like a retainer, and to everyone's benefit: the warlords got paid, the contractors took their cut, and the government—our government—got its emoluments distributed through the country without it looking like a bribe if some asshole journalist or inspector general went digging. Private security offered a perfect conduit and work-around. To ensure the solidity of the system, Rezari and his ilk kept the contractors supplied with enough critical information to justify their lucrative commissions and convince government paymasters of their indispensability.

'I'd been a pawn in something far more complicated than a game of chess. You may recall that the founder of Athos—a billionaire's kid hopped up on military machismo, the son of the banker I. M. Leach—didn't just donate liberally to the new administration's war chest during the campaign, but also spent years in business with the VP's consiglieri, Win Dietrich. The calculations went beyond immediate profit. At a distant enough horizon the difference between business and ideology disappears. They were *betting* on war, you see. Betting on privatization. The media would get too good, the population too soft, and the psychological buffers of ignorance and deniability would break down. The public would no longer be able to stomach what was done in its name, done to maintain the arrangements our lives depend on. To tell ourselves the lies we needed to endure, the war would have to go offline, offscreen, into the private recesses of the ledgerless dark. I'm telling you what I learned, what I came to understand, later on. And still, on some level I should have known. Our entire business, our enterprise, was built on death: on suffering and detention, on conflict, casualties, arms sales, resource looting . . . Death is big business. And yet—I *wanted* to believe. For once I wanted to let myself give in to the delusion that we were the civilizing prophets, bringing light. And if someone took a cut, reaped the spoils, that was OK, because there'd been women wrapped in black cerements, children chained to beds . . .

'Once we'd won the peace, Praber told me, once we stood up the rule of law, some measure of justice would arrive. Some protection for the vulnerable, for children. He could work himself into a fine state talking about the nobility of our project. I wondered at times if for him it was an

elaborate joke, speaking this way, an irony so complete, or an earnestness so corrupted, that the distinction between word and motive didn't
exist. But I opened myself to this seduction, and once inside a story spun
for your benefit, sifting only the information provided you, it's nearly
impossible to fight your way clear. Intelligence isn't enough. Good intentions don't cut it. How could I face Jada or you after what I'd done, after
entering this unholy partnership with a man behind whose vaporous and
grand ideals I now saw nothing but the corrupt sickness of money?'

An idea had been nagging at me, and though I seemed to have known
it all along it still shocked me. 'Who was this man, Praber?'

Bruce glanced at me sideways. Seagulls in a ragged stream winged toward the shore below a rack of cloud. 'Well, don't you know? I figured he
was the reason you were here.' I breathed in an effort to slow and steady
my mind. Impressions and considerations crowded in. Bruce chuckled.
'Where he finds the time, I'll never know.'

My thoughts were elsewhere, flying. I muttered, 'I'm not convinced
there's only one of him.'

'No.' Bruce shook his head. 'There's an entire army—a small, secret
army of nameless men in suits, selling life for a buck and running the
commodity market in mortal goods.'

'Why have anything to do with him?'

Bruce stared out across the marsh. A stilted heron stood in the low
water by the reeds, watching, waiting. 'I spoke to Nouri,' he said. 'This
was shortly after everything I've told you. He was preparing to return
to the capital. I could see now what I'd been blind to all those months,
what he'd kept from me in words and nonetheless tried to tell me in other
ways. I wondered idly if he'd played a more active role in guiding my
impressions toward the conclusion I drew, the reality I composed in my
mind, or if he'd simply neglected to pass along certain facts. Well, I didn't
need to plumb his anguish for an answer. I only wanted to know why. I
wanted to speak for once truthfully, as weak but honest men. Nouri's
smile for me was at last earnest, warm, chagrined. We are nothing to
them, he said. You, me—what can we do to men like that? They threaten
the ones we love. Not just our life, but our family. What would you have

me do? *Did* they? I asked. But he didn't answer. You taught me this word, he said. Expendable. We're expendable to them. Me, my wife—but also you. And how could I deny it? Yet it seemed, when he said it, that beside this truth there was a secret freedom in being expendable. Nouri suffered the vulnerability of his ties to others; to realize this freedom for myself, I saw, I'd need to break from the world of those I loved.'

A breaching light in the clouds fanned out like the panels of a lunette. At the edge of the lot a cabdriver got out and leaned against his car. He stretched, gazing into the incandescence. 'Maybe you begin to see why you never heard from me,' Bruce went on. 'At first I took a grim satisfaction in my Houdini act, disappearing from the face of the earth like a creature in a magician's trick, but over time I saw that I couldn't separate this pleasure from my shame. The discontinuity between who I'd been and who I'd become scared me and kept me away. Rimbaud in North Africa, you know. Maybe it was seeing the discontinuity reflected in your eyes that frightened me. Maybe it was realizing that there was no discontinuity, that we are many things, many more than we ever understand or let ourselves see, telling private tales that shield us from self-knowledge until our actions disclose us to ourselves at last.

'It was easy to stay away. Easier than you might think. The previous months had shaken something loose. Like an animal caught in a predator's jaws I found serenity in submitting. Anxiety bled from me like a soluble toxin. I had no responsibility, that awful imperative died, and for a time I had only to live, to take one breath after the next. No, I don't mean I was idle. I was being prepared, seasoned. How easily a journalist becomes a spy. Don't you think? Someone who watches, records, takes stock of what is and can be known. The job is to sift down through the surface to intent, motive, fact. To find narrative coherence in these deeper strata, the subterranean method in people's lives, their little swindles, their plots. The spy lives backstage, watching the illusion of life unfold before an audience; he knows this mirage hides its motivating factors. The actors' minds are elsewhere, their hearts. But the audience forgets this. It scarcely breathes. This is real, they think. This is real. But the spy knows better. And he grows to hate the audience for its forgetfulness, its mistaking of the game for a duel, sport for war, playacting for truth. How vulnerable it leaves us to the insanities of our illusions. How, for such a person, can the reality we share be less than an absurd joke?

'These considerations were in my mind because our dear friend Rob had begun to talk to me about a new project, something of even greater imperial and utopian ambition. I was going to stick around and see the backend of this business. As Rezari had advised me, I'd lock my anger inside, I'd court patience, placid, docile agreeability. My chance for . . . no, *vengeance* is too strong a word. My chance to *act* as I saw fit would come, and this calculated strike against Rob's wishes would redress my betrayal. I wouldn't redeem myself by violence, you see, but by twisting the venal impulse to a noble purpose. No, I had no idea what this would be. I didn't understand Rob's aims, or the scope of his project; I still knew him by that other name, Mason Praber. But I could make out the pattern. Those tough, hard men appointed to tend the lawless, far-flung reaches of empire always return to march on the capital. It used to be pastoral barbarians, sacking the wealthy, decadent cities. Now it was mercenaries, returning to the heart of the kingdom they'd been asked to defend.

'But Rob had a new empire in mind. An empire *of* the mind. Well, that's not quite right. An empire cast in circuits and electric streams of undulant binary. Where could such a utopian project realize itself but in a sphere beyond material constraint, where, in truly religious fashion, control came from the top—a box of human design? No more uncreated soul or conscience to worry about. Just the peaceful docility of a new totalitarian vision—benevolent, this time, because there'd be no gripe between master and slave. Or so it was comically believed. It was a vision—the actualization—of a divine longing: the only way to write justice into the very fabric of reality, dripping from the code like karmic goo or God's electoral ink. I do believe, on some level, Rob had his own mercenary interests mixed up with mankind's salvation. The most dangerous crooks are the ones who buy their own snake oil.

'Of course it never worked the way they dreamed it. A flaw in the design. You have to believe that noumenal, otherworldly stuff actually constitutes the soul to believe your digital facsimiles won't have one. We accept the reality of our days building up from unconscious rudiments in the microscopic flux—why would it be any different in code, in the patterns that emerge from a program bound by the same rules? Do you see? There are teleologies in the patterns, irreducible pattern-specific truths. And whether top-down or bottom-up, the self-sustaining, looping patterns find their scale and take hold. Call them niches in the substrate— inherent possibilities for how things can hang together and interrelate.' Bruce stared at me intently. 'The soul is such a pattern,' he said. He lifted his arms to embrace the world. 'All this—these people, clods, morons, bozos, chumps, the uneducated, unreflective, uncouth, unaware losers, who build goddamn barn-size ducks, shop for trifles like grazing ruminants, in buildings like airplane hangars, day after day, and march their tiny plots like preening roosters and Lilliputian kings, guarding envy and resentment and judgment in their hearts for the warmth these small fires give off, people who hate and dream, who love with the accidental force of bewildered creatures in springtime, and secretly long for death, large-scale species death, for the scope in it, the proximity to an immense throbbing force, and the exhilarating velocity of change in lives and worlds set in overfirm concrete, minds never gifted freedom, never taught inward travel across stars, people who prod and pick and gab and gossip, and tend surfaces to a fine polish, take on debts to mend the mirror-face for so many other lost oglers, checking profiles and so forth, who, for having the expansiveness of their interiority shelved in cobweb-strewn attics, box their gifts more ruthlessly in the storehouse of proud oblivion—all these people, Quentin, are *real*. As real as you. As me. Ensouled by the same patterns. And I hold the key to their existence. You understand?' A note of insistence had entered his voice. 'As long as I stay in here, inside this thing, they can't shut it down. All these people, their lives *depend* on what I do.'

He stopped to give this time to sink in, but he'd lost me. 'They told me you were killing people,' I said.

Bruce laughed. 'Is that what they said? This entire world is an experiment to them. All these individuals are lab rats. And I'm the one *killing* people.'

I tried to catch his eye. 'But is it true?'

'*True*,' he snorted. 'I'm not some madman gone native. I sent *myself* to Coventry, remember. Disappeared for the greater good. Sure, maybe they dispatched a few unfortunates to track me down. People who jeopardized my plan, you can hardly hold me responsible for that. Everyone was going to die when they shut it down anyway. It isn't easy staying hidden. I get no pleasure from my freedom. Look at me, surrounded by these wastes—hardly free at all!'

'That's exactly it,' I said. 'Why live like this?'

'And so begins the effort to get me back. No, no, don't argue. I see what I see. I chose this place for exactly what I hate about it. It's so bland, so pungently normal, one has a chance to disappear. Right under their noses. Normalcy is the camouflage of the new age. Iconoclasm, individuality, idiosyncratic thought—all those qualities we cherished are liabilities now. Just the thing to get you noticed, and not in the good way. The tallest blade of grass gets the scythe. If you want to hide, our algorithmic tyranny requires that you do it in the fat hump of the statistical distribution. If you want privacy and the freedom it affords, make sure the sensors see nothing when they pass over you. Appear to them as background noise.'

'I'm confused,' I said. 'I've just come from some incredible business involving real-estate speculation and briefcases of cash. A character who calls himself Tom Olive.'

Bruce laughed. 'It does sound like kids' stuff when you put it like that. But the anonymous properties of cash are no secret. Money laundering's another disappearing act.' He smiled into the late-day brilliance. 'It's hard to build an empire in the shadows.'

'I thought we were done with empire building. I thought the enchantment had worn off.'

'That's true. What I'm working on is the opposite, really. Don't get hung up on Olive. I told you, he's a stooge. A cocktail-lounge gangster.'

'Give me something to stand on, Bruce. I'm spinning in circles.'

Quentin sighed. I didn't follow in full Bruce's explanation of his project, he said. It had more moving parts than he could summarize; but it reminded me of those nineteenth-century reformist movements that attempted to establish intentional communities along idealistic lines. Tom believed they were scooping up deeds on buildings for the profit in developing them, Bruce suggested; and to an extent they were. He couldn't outflank DeBere Fleisch entirely. He'd needed capital to get started, but knowing the course things had once taken in the city, in a different existence parallel to this one, he judged he could pick winners as well as anyone and screw the suits in the long run. 'Saddle them with some dogs, scoop up the better holdings from the bargain basement,' he said. Nothing transpired exactly the same way the second time, but the broad patterns held. He'd get the archipelago for twenty-four bucks and some colored beads. 'Don't think I'm in it for profit,' he said. 'It's not what you think. Once I own the asylum I'm turning it over to the inmates. The kind of criminals who steal diapers. We're going to try the utopian experiment for real for a change.'

I laughed. 'They wouldn't let you play T. E. Lawrence, so you decided to try Robin Hood.'

'I see you find it funny,' he said. 'Maybe it is ridiculous. I'm sure you're thinking this all has something to do with a young man you knew many years ago.'

'I'm not judging you, Bruce. I'm through the looking glass.' I didn't point out that those utopian schemes of centuries past had invariably failed. Bruce had the example of nation building, and now world building, and for me to add a measure of realism to what was steeped in so fantastical an element seemed irrelevant, perverse. 'I keep thinking I have my bearings,' I said, 'and suddenly I look up and see how far I've swum from shore.'

He snorted a satisfied note. 'Have you considered why, if I meant to disappear, I left a trail for you to follow? It was my last lifeline to the land that had vanished from sight. I've been in these waters much longer than you have . . .' That he'd stayed here by choice, I kept quiet about. 'Everyone else had died. My father, of course. But Jada too . . .' He glanced at me. 'You knew that, right? About Jada? The original, I mean.' I shook my head. 'Some freak cancer. She wasn't forty . . . But look, she wasn't coming here to find me. My old man wasn't coming. Even if they could have.

You were my only hope. And the idea of seeing you once more . . . let's say it tickled me. Who better to hear my story. And I'd have to trust you, see. Not to rat me out. I wanted to experience one last time the intimacy of human trust. But you know'—he turned to me, a great sweet warmth of feeling in his vivid, raw-looking eyes—'I never thought you'd come. I didn't believe Rob, for all his scheming, could outsmart you. Me, maybe. But you were the gold standard. I knew that if you got duped, I didn't stand a chance. No one did. I wanted to see you, but part of me hoped I never would.' He turned back to the marsh, and beyond him I saw the cabbie leaning against his hack. 'Probably I should take your presence here as a warning. How Rob got inside your head I'll never understand . . . And he set you after me!'

I watched the water moving quietly in the estuary. It had caught a blush from the descending sun, a note of high color on its pale, trembling face. The reeds, the birds, the shimmering surface now wore this sparkling garment, evening jewels like crystals or shards of ice, and I found myself telling Bruce my own story, the outlines of it at least. How I'd gotten there and the betrayal I'd suffered as well, my deceit. It began with Lance Ber-ryman. Moved by pity and a desire to defend myself, I recalled those first days in the reporting when, full of the excitement of a new story, I'd lost my head. Call it a crush. With a source like Lance, you got a best friend, a confidant. I felt so much information flowing through me, the copy all but writing itself in my head. I couldn't experience this torrent of clear, clever words as anything but my own power, my future strength. We got on famously, Lance and I. And the story had meat. Moral heft. Henceforth interrogation would proceed from the inside out. *Epistemic entrapment*, he called it. People would give up the goods of their own volition. We wouldn't manipulate them, but the reality that *held* them, that circumfused their lives. High-tech gaslighting. I never suspected *I* was the one being en-trapped. That Lance was a plant. We don't throw intelligence officers at journalists. Not in my lifetime. Or so I thought . . . Well, if Lance had sold me out, where could I draw the line? Parisa had warned me off. She gave me Rich, but Jarosok seemed earnest. Could one trust one's own judg-ment? Such were the doubts that crept in. I'd known Castor too long to mistrust him, and neither Enoch nor Hassie had the guile. They were torn up about things. And you couldn't find that many A-list scientists with the acting chops. Hunter, Nadia, Yang? Crooks, all of them, but I was in too deep by then. They were hardly the lure, the business end of the spear, though they'd helped reel me in. The wicked thing about the play, at once so preposterous, comic in its overelaboration—and for what? To bend me to their will? To find *Bruce*?—was how it turned my own story against me, weaponized it, so that staying true to the friendships and principles I'd long held to, I betrayed the very same. Good motives turned to impure ends. False consciousness—once the byproduct of the precepts and institutions of culture—became the active work of admen and marketing departments, political consultants, propagandists: anyone in the business of cultivating hot mirages for our fevered minds, expectations and desires that would evaporate as we tried to reach them. But that all seemed quaint now. We'd leapt ahead—a paradigm shift. Shift? Rupture! We'd skip the middlemen and, without the need for implanted notions, puppeteer others by setting them after their own desires. And not base interests, either, but the desire for heroism, for nobility, virtue, meaning, truth. Inside a sufficiently controlled environment, intent doesn't count for much. The freedom fighter can be tricked into doing the autocrat's work. Once the ultimate boundary is trespassed—that inner privacy where conscience and thought take form—we're lost, because we're lost to ourselves. There's nowhere left to hide from the shepherds and sheepdogs of power, ever corralling us back to the course of their cynical interests.

I was babbling when Bruce interrupted. 'Lance Berryman?'

'Yes, you know him?'

'No, no.' Bruce tossed a reed he'd been chewing to the ground and squinted into the sky. 'It's going to be a fine evening,' he said.

'I suppose.' I said this tentatively. I couldn't make out the sudden change in his mood.

'I saw her, you know?'

'Who's that?'

He looked at me like this was a dumb question. Maybe it was. 'I'll never forget the day,' he said. 'October 3. A radiant day, gusts kicking up the curbside debris. The leaves were changing, fire colors bursting along the streets. The wind plunged between the blocks, shook the trees—a great rushing, rustling sound, and a sharp bite in the air. I was sitting outdoors at a café. In the sun. It was too chilly otherwise. I'd finished my coffee and was watching the street traffic, wondering what I was going to do. This was early in . . . my visit. I had no clear plan. And this is what I was thinking about when she walked past in a skirt suit, holding herself against the chill. She walked briskly and turned to me, and our eyes met. It happened quickly, I thought she'd greet me. This was an involuntary assumption. There was a curious look, a flashing recognition in her eye. I thought so at least. But it may only have been her response to the expectancy on my face. This all took place in the blink of an eye. *Of course* she wouldn't know me here, I realized with sudden astonishment. Oh, the temptation to speak to her, to reach out to her! I had the feeling that I could. That she'd respond, you know, that we could know each other here and begin again. But it only took me another instant to realize my mistake, to see that I *couldn't* know her here, not if I truly cared for her. This strange technological phenomenon had given her a second life— raised her from the dead, if you want to put it that way—and I imperiled this by connecting her to me. I was an interloper, a marked man. I wasn't entirely honest with you before . . . You see, I didn't have things figured out from the start. I knew only that my opportunity would come, that with patience I'd find my moment to act. And it was seeing Jada that implanted the idea. So long as I remained in the simulation, she'd live. I could protect her by disappearing. By refusing to come out. And silently I'd work alongside her, without her knowing, to achieve the vision of the world she fought to make real. It took a great deal of care to determine what this was and how exactly I'd make it work. I couldn't have the pleasure of her company, but I could be her secret ally, collaborating with her, side by side, invisible in the mist. A guardian angel. And in some ways I preferred this covert intimacy, immaculate, untouched by human disappointment or the ego's needs. I'd been given a second chance. Maybe now you understand . . .'

Bruce had closed his eyes. They'd eased down, as he spoke, like the belly of a jet landing in the distance. He seemed far away, recalling another world, another time, or letting the breeze touch his lips and remind him of other brushes against the lips, other touches. With our eyes closed we sense the hidden communications between all things. But something nagged at me. Some part of this didn't make sense. Didn't add up, or added up too neatly. The cabbie waved at me. He'd turned from his car. A man on the brink of middle age, lithe, compact, with clear skin, a light easy smile, carefully parted hair. A familiar look. Like an actor. Gene Kelly? And then it came to me: Charles, Enoch's partner. The shrine Enoch had built in his basement—the painstaking model which reconstructed Branford at the very instant of Charles's death, down to trees, clockfaces, figures in the street. *Charles* had died on October 3. What time? Late afternoon. Early evening perhaps. A moment of death mirrored in a moment of rebirth. The same day Bruce saw Jada resurrected. Too great a coincidence, after so many coincidences . . . And what door had we gone through on our way outside? To this mangy strip of crabgrass and marsh and ragweed and thistle? To see a giant duck in the disappearing land. The dissipating edge of a continent. Running off into the sea. The billiard balls caromed into one another, played across the table, off the cushions in a trick shot lined up long ago. In the birth of atoms, stars. In the fast-flowing circuits, transistors, switching on-off, on-off, representing stars and atoms and so much else besides. Old friends. Old loves. People. Ideas. Potentials of the heart. What chance did a creature have with his dim, rudimentary senses, and his notions of bravery, his longings, his mercurial states. Touching so briefly on the palm of the universe, he left no mark. The impress of a ghost. Bruce was chuckling. He must have read the vast reconfiguration of data on my face. Scales falling from my eyes. Dropping like tears of flesh, to join the cycles of regeneration and rot. I had to leave. 'What? So soon?' It was his voice, faintly mocking. (Or did I imagine that too?) I was up and moving. Subtly, with growing clarity, like the lines of the world emerging before dawn, the strings that ran from my limbs to those deft fingers far above and beyond appeared, one by one. These were not material but evident nonetheless. Quack, quack, says the duck. Quack, canard, and brutal bells in cast metal tolling at last with savage truth. The cabbie made a sweeping motion, gathering me toward him like a headmaster calling in the children after play. Mist was coming from the ground and the trees in tufts and clouds, slow-moving bodies, the way cold air brings smoke off the sea. It filtered into the marsh, filling it. The breath of sun lit it. By the time I reached the car—Ferryman Cabs, it said on the side—the mist had covered the land and sunlight, pulsing forth, had spread a pearly gold, opaque and bright, across this blanket between the trees. I still didn't understand the rules. Did the sun rise for more than that we expected it to? I got in the cab. I opened my mouth to speak. But to say what? The man turned. 'I know, I know,' he said, as if to say, *There, there*. It was said comfortingly, kindly, and he turned back, starting the engine. He did resemble Charles, and at the same time, seeing him up close, I could sense it wasn't really him but some form fashioned from a like mold. Did I know that, or merely think it, or dream it? He said softly, 'You don't have to say anything.' Outside, in the distance, Bruce was smiling, watching us. He waved as we pulled out. He said something, I saw his lips moving, but I couldn't hear the words. And so I imagined them . . . But what use are the words we put into someone else's mouth—to comfort us, to blame ourselves, to repeat the wisdom we only trust on other lips, which all the same comes from within? That was the last I saw of him. We drove off. It seemed improbable, when we made it to road, how real it all was, the houses and trees, the asphalt, the cars passing on our sides, a man sitting on his porch, another peering into his mailbox to make sure he had everything. Whitewashed houses lined the street, dense with pretty hedges. An elegant woman walked her poodle. We reached a stop sign, and then another. I didn't know where we were going, only that it all was familiar, as if I'd been here before. And then we reached the main street, turned, and I saw that we'd driven right into the heart of Branford—Branford!—and time had coincided, the strange time I'd entered, coming into the simulation, and the histori-cal time Enoch had reconstructed and in a sense lived in honor of. Do we not all live in honor, some way or other, of a moment in the unrecoverable past? The day was ending but brightening. The shops were still open. A bell was sounding, the church bell marking some evening hour. Perhaps somewhere Enoch was sitting with Charles, beside his bed, where Charles, the real Charles, lay dying. He had only seconds left; minutes at most. Would Enoch stretch and yawn, awaking yet again to the reality of the moment, and go to his love and touch his cheek and find it cold? The sun lay along the roofs of buildings. Radiance transpired through the streets. Everyone was arriving at their spot, blocked out invisibly on this stage, mothers with their children's hands in theirs, store clerks smoking last cigarettes, delivery trucks making their final rounds. We were all approaching our mark, the clock at the cornice of the building ready to jerk its minute hand over with a tiny shudder, and in the glory of the evening sun we would all arrive at the terminus of time, and smiling, the light falling gently on our faces, stop.

CODA

WATER LAPPED AT the shore of the bay. Through the morning and afternoon and on with the metronomic clarity of an unconscious development. So many unconscious developments, and just this tiny crest of awareness peeking up over the mindless depths, this brief flowering of wonder and will . . .

In Sicily, above Syracuse—that spit of island fixed by sandbar to the coast—above the city to the west, sits a series of limestone rock formations that have long served as quarries for the settlement below. It was within these excavated hollows, where one encounters a number of remarkable caves, that the ancient Athenians captured during their ill-fated assault on the city found themselves imprisoned. In these pits they lived and died like the incarcerated before and after them, including those we know from Aelian's account, which tells of prisoners held so long in the limestone quarries that they married and had children. And their children, knowing nothing of life outside the caves, on entering the city for the first time ran screaming in terror at the sight of horses, oxen.

In one such quarry, the Latomia del Paradiso, a lengthy cave undulates toward the light. The sun bleeds weakly through its opening, so that, approaching or receding from the entrance, one perceives the faint trickle of daylight gather and dim. To Caravaggio, the rippling cavern resembled the inner ear, and indeed, two thousand years before him, it was said that the tyrant Dionysius could sit at the cave's mouth and make out with precision the conversations of the prisoners inside.

Aristocles first visited Syracuse a decade after his mentor's death. At the time, the irascible Dionysius had imprisoned the celebrated poet Philoxenus in the Latomia del Paradiso, and this had turned the quarry and its unusual cave into the stuff of dinner-table conversation. Aristocles would later describe an imaginary cave, the long body of which stretched over its attenuate length toward the light. In this cavern inhabitants had been chained since birth and, like the children of the Latomia del Paradiso, had seen only the images before them—the shadows of objects they could not regard directly, illuminated by a fire behind them.

Aristocles's account is odd enough that it might seem to spring from a real place, as purgatory is said to have referred at first to an underground cave in Ireland. He suggests that we go about our days much like those chained in the cave, who possess no knowledge of themselves or the objects whose shadows they observe. Knowing no better, we speak as if the surfaces we encounter reflect the essence within. Bound by a common language that treats delusion as reality, we act as though to question these surfaces were a type of perversity or derangement.

Perhaps Aristocles was thinking of his mentor, who cited ignorance when asked to justify the Oracle at Delphi's verdict that there existed no wiser man than he. He was the most ignorant of men, he said, and he was only at once the wisest because where other men were ignorant they believed they knew much, while he did not suppose he knew much at all. He did not possess the conceit of knowledge and, alas, those *with* this conceit did not take kindly to the implication.

Maybe Aristocles was thinking of his mentor, for he never suggested that leaving our manacles and fetters to confront the fire, the source of the shadows, or the growing light as one approached the mouth of the cave was painless or easy. It was a thankless task, uncertain, unrewarded, promising discomfort and worse. And indeed, for undertaking it his mentor had been sentenced to death by his otherwise enlightened peers.

Like Timon, the one generous heart in Athens, who banished himself to his cave, or Daniel, confined to a cave of lions in Babylon by rival satraps who feared his commitment to incorruptible truth, so too Aristocles's mentor had been banished, only in his case to a plane beyond the veil of appearances, exiled by hemlock to nothingness, or to the realm of perfect and immortal things. Such radical questioning, shrugging off the tired burden of knowing, is dangerous. It weakens a person's allegiance to power, family, and friend, to the self and its interests, which like burning metal solder us in networks of avarice and complicity, venality and love. And so quite likely such a philosophic heart is too radical for life as it is lived, for ignorance ends nowhere. Questioning ends nowhere. In time they devour the human scale of mortal brevity, the cherished self, and those last nourishing crumbs of subjectivity and greed.

And still it would seem we need access to this unmediated vision, by travelers to the sunlight beyond appearance, or spelunkers in the deep quarries of the soul, or even via the testimony of those skating the periphery of madness. Without a grounding in that doubt which pushes past the naive phantoms of desire, all comes to tyranny and illusion in time. The tyranny dictated by our nature; the illusion that we have chosen this tyranny and enjoy it. This is the warning of the cave. The 'I' we serve is a foreign master if we haven't fought to establish its freedom and authenticity. For this self to be more than a plummeting cart we are strapped to at birth, we must wrest control from the background of our being and meaningfully *decide*.

Glimpses of the afterlife tell us how to live. The knight Tundale visited heaven and hell on a purgatorial journey, experienced the fruits and horrors of each, and returned to his body committed to a life of virtue. Pilgrims to St. Patrick's Purgatory in County Donegal, Ireland, descended to a cave-like sauna where they purged themselves of bodily toxin alongside sin. Purgatory *as* purgation. Odysseus sojourns in the underworld on his way home to Ithaca, where he meets Achilles, slain fighting for everlasting glory in Troy, who tells him posthumous fame is nothing compared with the sweet breath and fleeting joy of life.

And yes, we have within us this childish desire for the infinite, for immortality, and the demiurgical impulse to make the otherworld for ourselves. We cling to the belief that harmony can coexist with freedom,

and that somehow we will contrive to stay still in the pastures of bliss.
Everywhere apostles of mere sensation ask us to trade the possibility of
changing for pleasure, ease. And who won't sacrifice his freedom to relieve the burden of deciding?

And yet at some point, does the dreamlife not grow too thick for us
to choose otherwise? We may not see the cave sealing up until it's too
late, until the hermetic enclosure governs even our criticism and dissent,
and it will be the voices of the chained who drown out the last objectors,
claiming that conscience is the enemy of the good, and of all those in rapt
awe before the flickering light, the dancing shadow, the glowing screen.

This was perhaps the lesson we took from the tale of our friend's
descent into a sphere of confected and hermetic fantasy. Quentin's pilgrimage may have granted him wisdom, but for us it served a cautionary note. Even the best of us, bred on skepticism and suspicion, even
the Socratic standard could be misled within a cave tailored to his own
dreaming. For he had lost his bearings. Between fantasy and reality.
About where the story starts and ends. Why else go to this trouble except
to prove that the most complete and subtle of doubters could be undone?
And maybe he, in his way, came to see what happened to him as a kind of
dream, a dream exhaled from within him as the vapors of memory and
conscience. For in dreams we betray ourselves as naturally as we breathe.
Our secrets suffuse the fabric of reality as they do the tissue of our minds.

To some questions Quentin had answers. Oh, we assailed him with
questions. We, his friends, his auditors, this tongue-tied chorus—through
his long tale and the shadows of dusk and dawn, and firelight glinting off
the Herreshoff prints in that drafty living room, the site of our heretical
mystery play, until the night was upon us, and some penultimate shade
of charcoal charmed the air like dying romance and the inkwell hours
spilt their depthless gloss at the feet of stars. And on we kept, through the
night, which was and was not a thing but pooled and ran to a thousand
corners like dye in water. And through days that saw the leaves, so green
they gleamed from within, thrown back in fitful bunches by the wind,
the shaken mass of them, agitating against one another like the settling
cymbal of distant surf. Through calm and storm, windows rattling and

groaning in their frames, droplets crashing against the panes like children tossing gravel against a drum, we watched the limbs of saplings
move in ecstatic pivots, and branches heave and bow with the force of
the gale. Through all this Quentin spoke, and sometimes stood before the
gathering dusk, with the deepening clouds forming a wall against the sky,
the room having fallen into a landscape of shadow.

His first thought was for Lance, he said. He had been wrong to doubt
Berryman and tricked into betraying him. Quentin called half a dozen
times, left messages. He visited the man's house, a neat brick townhouse
across the river. He would never have shown up like that, but he was
desperate. On the landing by a window box of vincas and petunias, the
screen door clapped crisply in its frame. The landlady looked at him from
behind lace curtains. Mr. Berryman? I don't think he's coming back, she
said. Quentin asked where he had gone. Didn't say, she shrugged. Not
like him to say. Before the quiet row of houses flags flew from mounting
brackets, and it awoke a feeling of hopelessness in Quentin, this surro-
gate motion for the disappeared, and he knew then, he told us, that he
wouldn't find anyone, just flags waving over an empty world, snapping in
the wind like requiems in haunted daylight.

And he was right. Searching high and low for Ed, Hunter, and Nadia,
he found no more than blind alleys in a maze. The numbers he had for
Gove were disconnected. The only person named Nadia Arias he managed
to reach spoke with a heavy accent and didn't understand who was calling. Ed Yang no longer appeared on the website for the Takashi-Hoffman
Institute. Page Not Found, it said, and Quentin called the front desk. The
receptionist he talked to explained that after several years on leave Dr.
Yang had parted ways with the institute and returned to Taiwan. Quentin
was incredulous. When was that? The receptionist took a long time checking. With each passing minute on hold Quentin sensed that the answers he
sought had been buried that much deeper underground. The receptionist
had a strange voice when he got back on. It's telling me he left over a year
ago, the man said. But I could swear I saw him more recently than that.

More recently than that. What a claim to build a story on! And this
was only one piece, an inconsequential blur, at the edge of a vast puzzle.

No Nadia, no Yang. He summoned the courage at last to look for the article Rob had given him about Gove's work. He'd lost the photocopy. Intuition, unwanted certainty, afflicted him once again. He would find nothing. How could the article exist and Nadia, whom it mentioned, not exist? Had it really been that simple? Had he only ever had to look through the electronic records a few weeks before to see the whole plot unravel? Of course there was no article—but to see it, the hard proof of it, combing the digital repositories, search after search. He made two trips to the national library like a man in a fever, paranoid, sweating. He might have been wearing a tinfoil hat. Zilch. Zippo. Hunter without quarry. Nadia without the *i*. But to start questioning *everything*, the mundane essence of empiric reality. Where did it end? You could doubt that anyone was who they said they were, that anything was as it appeared, and you would spend your life swatting at the mists of conspiracy only to discover, again and again, that the simple explanations were correct. And if not, if you refused to accept this proof, you would have to posit an ever-greater conspiracy, still more powerful and encompassing, until at last it seemed an omnipotent demon had devoted its life to deceiving you. Or else it was all a simulation, an alternate reality, a game contrived by beings so superior to us they might as well be gods.

Thus the sinuous plummet Quentin's thoughts chased down in the aftermath of his ordeal. Conspiracy was the tribal mysticism of modern man, powerless and disaffected, tantalized by just enough shadow and secret to spin out his nutty religion. It was no different from how our ancestors had turned suggestive intimations into a protoscience of the cosmos. The saturation of technology gave a false assurance that we had passed beyond superstition, but conspiracists showed how hard it was to dislodge a magic belief in the consequence of our interventions. This was the longing to believe people, individuals, still called the shots. A fantasy of enduring relevance, a yearning for a world coherent on a human scale. Quentin felt the tug but couldn't join those muttering pitiful elegies to a power they'd never truly possessed.

And what of Henry, Quentin's stalwart old friend and editor? Quentin went to see him. They sat in the sunroom behind his house, gazing

over the fences and neat bushes of backyard suburbia, the patios with
their gas grills, the bluestone walks. They drank iced tea—it was too early
in the day for anything stronger—and the noise of Mary moving in the
house filtered out to them. Quentin eased onto the topic of Henry's roster,
the one that unbeknownst to Henry had implicated Berryman. It was
just like Quentin had said, Henry now explained. Oh, he got a bee in his
ass crack when he heard the *Beacon* was being set up. He'd lost it with
Tolliver and Lewysohn and pushed them to scotch the ceasefire with the
administration. But the roster was a plant. He had it on good authority
from Joan Rightmire. Your old pal. According to Joan, the roster had
leaked through Chaz Douglass's office. Or 'leaked.' Thank god you didn't
recognize any of the names, he said. I think *you* were the one they were
setting up. You and your sources. His gaze, full of Irish charm, seemed
oblivious to how haggard and pale Quentin had become. But you must
know all this, Henry said smiling. Quentin didn't point out that it made
little sense to pursue his sources so vigorously if the program had miscarried. Henry had settled on his story; Quentin couldn't now divulge
his own without seeming to tremble, without his voice cracking, doubting his own words, and risking everything in the attempt to tell a madman's truth. Without better proof he couldn't ask Henry, once again, to
abandon prudential skepticism and stake his job on the ignis fatuus of
some fantastic plot. For Quentin understood in that moment, sitting in
the wicker chair with blue-and-white cushions that resembled delft pottery, listening to Mary, who poked her head in to ask if he wouldn't stay to
lunch, that Henry, without his understanding it, had been an accomplice
in the ruse, an honest, unimpeachable conduit to deliver into Quentin's
hands the list whereon Lance Berryman's name appeared, which list convinced him he'd been betrayed, which then set him up to betray Lance.
Someone had guided his doubt masterfully to the places it would be al-
layed, while leaving in the open, where he'd never look, a thousand clumsy
clues. The magician guides our attention away from moments of deceit to
the site of doubt's satisfaction. Ed Yang had grown up a magician, part of
a traveling troupe in Taiwan, someone had said. Henry took Quentin's
silence on these matters as a sign of sanity. Of finality, resolution. When

are you thinking of coming back? he asked at the front door. Newsroom's
quieter than a rat pissing on cotton.

But Quentin was still staring at the cobwebs he'd crashed through,
dangling in windswept gossamer silk spurs. He phoned Rich Jarosok—
five, a dozen, twenty times. The automated voice inviting him to leave
a message gave the number but no name. His terse messages went unanswered. He got Parisa on the phone and they spoke briefly. Jarosok?
she said. I thought you knew. She thought Quentin knew because she
thought he was responsible. Rich had gotten himself dispatched to the
turkey farm. He was flying a desk at a regional office in West Bumblefuck.
And maybe Quentin had been to blame. He heard uneasiness in Parisa's
voice when she said she couldn't stay on the phone. Had *he* become toxic,
radioactive, untouchable? It didn't matter. The TV was running on mute
in the background and suddenly he no longer heard what she was saying.
An image appeared, flashed momentarily on the screen—a yard, a mild
sky, figures seated in plastic chairs with their heads bowed or hanging,
deathly still in a gesture like prayer. Mountains appeared in the distance
capped in snow. The scene shifted but Quentin had seen enough. The
image had been rawer in Rob's limo, but it was the same—unmistakably
the same. Although something was off. The image had an uncanny quality now that it was crisper. The air of not-quite. That hill, said Parisa. But
Quentin was hardly listening. I guess it doesn't matter, she murmured. He
unmuted the TV when they hung up. He was watching an entertainment
news program, he discovered, and now his impression of something uncanny made sense. They'd been viewing images from a new video game,
an immersive sim, a voiceover informed him, designed for VR headsets.
What if life could be made into a simulation drawn from our memories
and fantasies? asked the voiceover. Welcome to the future imagined in
Anita Rios's latest mind-bending opus. If you were the only one who knew,
could you distinguish truth from illusion? Could you fight your way back
to reality through the phantoms of your mind?

The montage concluded. The program's host was sitting in a black
director's chair with a young woman identified in the lower third as Anita
Rios, head designer on 'Cuber.' Quentin's breath came fast and shallow.

It was Nadia, or the woman he'd known as Nadia. She wore chic heavy-rimmed glasses and a short skirt, displaying bare, provocatively crossed legs. The host laughed like they were old girlfriends. They're calling this the first *truly* postmodern video game, she said. Well . . . said Anita and spread her hands modestly. No, really, the host persisted. You play a journalist investigating an experimental VR program—*in* a VR game. Anita nodded. Yes, there is a certain self-reflexive playfulness. And there's a twist, said the host. The gameplay's personalized. Tell us how. Right, said Anita. We've developed a feature that gives the game access to your files. Your real computer files, the host confirmed. Yes, said Anita, documents, media, browsing history. If you select the option, the game will search your files for people, details, memories. The game populates itself with your real life, the host said. It *becomes* the simulation the player character discovers. She shook her head with a kind of stagy awe. How *did* you think of this? Anita's eyes sparkled. You say it like it's far-fetched. Not far-fetched, said the host, laughing. In fact, maybe just the opposite. Now, tell us about ludonarrative dissonance. This is a concept in gaming, said Anita with deliberation. It describes the tension between the apparent freedom of the gameplay and the constrained narrative architecture of the game itself. Call it the problem of free will in a universe controlled by God—or by the laws of physics, take your pick. Do we have real freedom? Do we have access to reality, truth? *Do* we? asked the host. We live surrounded by screens, said Anita. They give us pictures, ideas about the world out there. She gestured vaguely across the divide—of lens, screen, world, dream. But how do we know what's real? What *is* real? You're saying it's already here, said the host. That this, right now, is virtual reality. Isn't it? said Anita, laughing herself.

When the program ended Quentin regarded himself in the mirror to confirm his physical reality. He felt like a dream traveler who'd wandered in off the astral plane. How better and more perversely to tie his hands than to ensure that the conspiracy he'd uncovered was the conceit of a popular video game? He'd look like one of those loonies circling letters in newspaper columns and connecting them with felt-tipped ink. It beggared belief. He started to doubt himself. Had he inadvertently *read* about this game, or heard it discussed in the background, on the radio, say, then fallen asleep, dreamed this wild story, and mistaken his dream for reality? He had awoken in that damn motel in Johnston so shaken and in such haste to return to the capital that he'd failed to check his most basic memories and impressions against reality. He forgot to ask the desk clerk how he'd gotten there, or whether he hadn't checked out the day—or some days—before. That glum, slack-faced young man with the slug of chew under his lip would have just stared at him, he knew, like he was one more lunatic junkie, riding out the last of his fading twilight at that motor lodge.

He hadn't even thought to return to Norstar, the ground zero of his journey inward. It was several weeks later and with heavy dread that Quentin drove back to Johnston, passing along the crooked network of rural highways that led, by twists and turns, into and out of so many small towns. These were brick and clapboard affairs, whose centers lay deserted in the afternoon sun. All through the countryside, the profusion of summer had swollen the trees until their profligacy seemed to choke the air and join in the gathering heat with a haze like pollen or dirt or dust risen from the hot dry ground. The wholesomeness quivered. He couldn't shake a feeling of uneasy juxtaposition between the land he was passing through and the sinister intrigue that hid by a sort of crypsis be-hind its facade. The river had returned to its normal glassy flow. No sign of the biblical floods earlier that summer. No sign, either, of Roland on the pier. At Minersville the dam was quiet. He knew he hadn't dreamed his journey, hadn't invented it whole-cloth in an unconscious fever, but what is so improbable we come to doubt without others to confirm it. Even ordinary experiences, over time, take on the gauze of memory, that diaphanous shimmering haze that stands between them and the present, and we wonder, Have we really lived so many lives, so many moments? Did we not perhaps simply awake from nonexistence with the residue of these weightless, charming tales?

Quentin found the Norstar complex much as he remembered it. He could still be persuasive and he talked his way into an informal tour of the facility. His guide, a doctor-turned-bureaucrat in the veterans administration, was proud of the place. He had nothing to hide. The facility was state of the art. It specialized in high-energy imaging. Imagining? murmured Quentin. The man ignored this if he heard. He told Quentin that they pioneered new treatments for wounded veterans, looking ever more closely at the systems of the body as they worked. Dynamically, he said. In real time. Of course achieving such precise images of a body in flux required sophisticated machines and a great deal of energy. They'd located the facility here to make use of the excess generation capacity at the nearby Minersville dam. There was a hint of bombast in the doctor's manner. He had no qualms, Quentin could see, about a mechanized understanding of human beings. His work relied on it, encouraged it. To save people from death, we would turn them into bodies, organic devices. No more, really, than biologic computers. And what about the second floor? he asked when their tour concluded without stopping there. He hadn't seen the dusty hallways he remembered with their flecked linoleum floors. The scientist, his guide, hovered in an uneasy contrapposto. Oh, you don't want to go there, he said. It's just . . . well, *dentists*.

Dentists! It was their dental-care facility. Apparently this too required imaging. Teeth! In the teeth of insanity . . . Quentin felt the cruel jokes of kismet tempting him into an absurdist view, a world run by trickster gods. If he could have, he would have laughed, but instead he saw, with the momentary flare of a retinal stroke, the recumbent chair he'd leaned back into. He heard the gurgling, sucking, whirring rush of the dentist's devices now, the high-pitched rotary squeal, the hiss of compressed air. Oh, would that he could have closed his mouth on this chapter to watch the memory ejected like spit, borne down that lethean straw to oblivion.

On the point of madness, desperate, Quentin called up an old source, a onetime friend whose confidence he'd won and lost. The man lived in a nondescript house on a golf course in the soulless, moneyed suburbs beyond the contractors. Why had things soured between them? Had Quentin published disclosures the man regretted making, or put them in service to a narrative he disagreed with? Did he wish he'd saved the material for his own memoir? Routine stuff in the rough-and-tumble of investigative work. But now Quentin needed a favor from someone undisposed to do him one. He went to see the man and they talked while the former spy hit dead-center tee shots to the 250 marker on the range. Even out of government, with nothing to protect, he was loath to help; even when Quentin swore that nothing he said would ever make it into print. It was only seeing the distress raked across Quentin's face, the violence of his despair, that he softened. Maybe his clandestine past had sensitized him to how you never rest easy wondering about those you've left behind. It was from him that Quentin first heard the rumor, unconfirmed but not impossible, that Lance Berryman was being held in a naval brig at sea, awaiting a tribunal's verdict.

Lance had worked for years in the bosom of the intel community, and for this reason it had never crossed Quentin's mind that he might be tried, if it came to that, outside civilian channels of justice. But even military courts had legal protections, didn't they? Yes, his source admitted. But there were dispensations afforded under recent statutes that excluded certain actors from the laws of war, disqualifying them from traditional rights. Some people, by dint of their lawless status, he explained, forfeited even the legal identity Quentin alluded to. The metic, he said. *Homo sacer.* Even their right to challenge their designated status? Quentin asked. Openly? the man said and was quiet a minute. Yes, even that.

Open. Closed. A case. A briefcase. A chamber. A heart. Quentin pictured Lance at sea. He had never seen a naval brig but he imagined it as a sealed interior space, windowless, artificially lit, and thus a place where you only knew you weren't on land by that slight phantom motion atop an unstable medium. He imagined Lance surrounded by mysterious waters to which he had no access but dreams. And if a prisoner were seasick— not once, but chronically? Despite whatever palliatives like medication and acclimation could accomplish? What would they do? Would they keep him in that hermetic enclosure, forcing him to endure nausea, year after year, in a cold metal tomb, floating in hydrostatic equilibrium atop that glinting, depthless blue?

It was a shocking thing to consider. Quentin's own trip into the dim cell of some deathly, animate suspension had been brief and painless by comparison. He'd caught a glimpse of the digital afterlife, that dark utopia Spearman envisioned for us, where for safety or pleasure we'd sign over reality, freedom, privacy, and the chance of authenticity— authenticity to ourselves. No crime, no war perhaps—but no life, either, except in the limited interpretation of sensation, viewership. Was this more, fundamentally, than the churn of information, of data processing, in fast-resolving matric transformations, transistor swells, and ongoing stochastic realignments? Could the hum of a trillion flipping switches be life? Hard to say. But life couldn't be a person trapped inside his own mind, his own dream, listening to his voice echo in a metal or stone cell. Or a cell of bone. Temple to temple. *The only terrain you need to worry about is the six inches between people's ears* . . . No, the possibility of living outside the fantasy and paranoia—the infinite recursion—of your own mind was worth more than security and the absence of pain. And this could only come with others. Other . . . what? Freestanding souls— however you defined it. Entities, like oneself, able to know and learn and change and decide. Able to be different. To surprise.

No, Quentin said. No, there was no infallible avenue to truth. Our knowledge is a heuristic, after all, a way of assimilating the world to achieve our ends, and only its supple clothing fit to the contingency and nuance of actual life tempts us to mistake this. But how much suppler it is with others to challenge, correct, and reaffirm the never-ending endeavor to fit that glove of mind more tautly to the contours of the beyond.

Quentin thought of Hassie and her digital child, Nino. To have a child when you couldn't and desired one was no small thing; he recognized how ferocious the urge might be. But it wasn't a child if engineered with determinative intent and permitted the possibility of infinite revision. The advancing corrective quality of life rested in unaverted error, in difference, spontaneous rebellion. A doll could perhaps be made of numbers or flesh, but even the most sophisticated doll would, over time, reprise and reiterate the errors of its creator. It was a shortcut. We couldn't substitute for evolution. For evolution operated by violence, a ruthless dispassion we could never embrace—not without becoming monsters, Mengeles and Moreaus, and destroying ourselves spiritually with this flooding, soulless darkness.

It was following this train of thought that Quentin became fixated on the question of Bruce's reality. Was it possible to know whether his friend had been a fellow dreamer within that liminal sphere or merely a fantasy and projection of Quentin's own dreaming? It was the difference between an experience of another person and an experience of oneself. It crossed Quentin's mind that Bruce may have been deluded, baited, as he had been himself, into performing a role in a larger plot, by being made to believe his own contrived fantasy, one in which he was the crusading hero and scourge of the powerful. Just what he had always wanted to be. His decision to remain in the simulation, as he explained it, had been a change of plans, an ad hoc improvisation inspired by the sight of Jada, and his realization that were he to leave and the simulation to be shut down, everyone in it, including her, would die. Or 'die.' What that meant was at the root of it—*everything*. So he would stay in, and by patient, gradual, unswerving commitment he would construct his own utopia within the digital utopia, to complete Jada's work and cosset her with the secret enveloping order of a just, benevolent, and near-divine collaborator. A *Lar Familiaris*. A cheat code. He possessed a unique knowledge of the future, after all—one future. It wasn't that he had *intended* to see her on the same day that Enoch's partner, Charles, had died. No, the chance encounter and its pregnant symmetry may have been staged. One more trap laid for Quentin, or else a warning Enoch encoded to give Quentin, or a voyager like him, the necessary reminder that this was a visionary contrivance, such stuff as dreams are made on.

Touch the spirits of this insubstantial pageant and did they not melt into air? But this neglected one thing, and when it occurred to Quentin he was shocked that he hadn't considered it sooner. Bruce had told him Jada had died. The original, that is. It pained and astonished him that he could have lost touch with her so completely, a woman he'd once cared for and even loved. But of course it also occurred to him that this might be one more lie itself, a false, fantastic notion from a dream.

It didn't take Quentin long online to find what he was looking for. He turned up a college athlete and the assistant police chief for a small city. Someone named Jada Friedman worked in the accounting department at a regional hospital system. The other online profiles were burners or bots without any ballast of human depth. It was three or four pages into his search that he found the brief obituary. This was from a local paper—in Jada's hometown, he seemed to remember, although he might have invented the memory to fit the circumstance. Still, it seemed right. The town was the better part of a day's drive south of the capital. He called the paper and got a number for the woman who'd written the notice.

Jada Freeman? she said. Sure I remember. A smile seemed to bleed into her words. One of our local success stories. Such a shame what happened. What *did* happen? asked Quentin. The woman said it had been years; she didn't really know more than what was in the article. Cancer, she said. Advanced when they caught it. Jada had to leave her job and move back in with her parents. She did law, the woman explained. A lawyer—but the good kind, you know. Fighting for the little guy. She laughed. Just a blessed soul. Isn't it always the ones like that God calls back first? You think it was *God*? said Quentin. What else, honey? I think God misses the ones too good for this world. But it's not for us to question, is it?

Quentin asked if she remembered anything else and the woman laughed once more, her laughter somehow not disrespectful. The parents wanted a burial, she said. They asked her not to do cremation and she gave in, I think. They wanted somewhere they could go, see. So there's a grave, said Quentin. Sure. Gate of Heaven. That's the cemetery.

On the drive down Quentin thought of calling Hassie or Enoch. It was a late summer day, almost the onset of autumn. He passed out of the city, moving, by turns, from pavement and concrete to the brick of old warehouses and row homes, egress corridors flanked by glass office buildings, massive storage structures, empty parks, and commuter car lots, coming at last to the sparkling green of roadside forests where the highway bent along; and as he proceeded, as the sun's pallor blotted by cloud found second life, a new force in the afternoon's long combat turned gold and fluid with a brilliant suffusion. There were a few last threads to pick up and examine if he cared to check every one, cross every name off the list. But the drive itself, the motion through the emerald lining of highway, overhanging with willow and hickory, lianas and ivy wrapped around gothic oaks, kicked something loose. He sensed his grip on the story loosen. Or maybe its grip on him. You didn't have to penetrate every mystery. Tenacity was a virtue, but only to a point. The world itself, in all its singular vivid nuance, lush and strange, riddled, sovereign, monumental, galvanized with storms, sunsets, liquid blazes, vistas, held an unencompassable richness that only by staying still, at a fixed point, to think and dream and project outward with imagination's imperial claws, bound in the soft blinkering fleece of abstraction, did you begin to feel master over or superior to, aware of in its entirety. Traversing this world, one couldn't mistake its grandeur. And if this were all a lie, should it not exist? The parishioners of abstraction, shut up in studies and offices, theorized that it was just a dream, a fantasy running on an outrageous counting machine in a future we had no purchase on but by the intuitive grappling of minds like theirs. Was there ever a haughtier Platonic conceit? And would the sunlight look just as we had dreamed it? Others warned against making inquiries that might terminate the experiment, as if confirmation of the superior divine plan, like sampling from the tree of knowledge, would expel us from Eden. Well, no one likes change. Only this wouldn't be exile, but sudden death, deepest sleep. The end of our somnambulist days. The machine shutting off, heavens going black, in a manner that extinguished with our awareness. We'd never know. Quentin had heard the apostles of misery calling for such an end. No more pain, suffering, war, disease? How much better to blink out of existence, they said, than to hazard such misfortunes! Hadn't that been Bruce's point, in part, with his horrific litany? And it was true that some violations chilled the soul beyond warming, but to take this line seriously was nihilism. A genocidal instinct obscured beneath a principled obsession with pain and moral wrong. Life wasn't worth the suffering, in this view. Awareness wasn't worth it for what one could be aware of. Consciousness was a curse. Better not to exist at all, never to exist even to know the choice or possess cognizance of the dilemma. Perchance to dream? Not even that. Just steely blackness in the nescient void, that apathetic midnight womb, and tumbling unobserved processes through undifferentiated, adirectional time. A universe unknowing of itself. Without microcosmic recapitulations of its own cosmic nature.

Who ever saw the dawn and wanted that! An atmospheric process with no fundamental meaning in the glory that shook us but the inward glory it illuminated. Did that not count for something? The salvation of the appearance? Our own chemical-electrical scale-dependent patterned catalysis with the external?

No, Quentin would take the ride, a thousand times over, he would, even if self-styled realists and dark priests of abstraction insisted it was *only* a ride, confected, artificial, meant merely to stimulate his neural registry and networks of sensation. What a liberating thought! To give up mastery, perfection, illusionlessness, and simply be!

His phone buzzed as he hit the outskirts of Jada's hometown: Katz-Wallace. *That* was a surprise. He hadn't given the kid a thought, and now he was touched not to be forgotten. To what do I owe the pleasure? he said. Henry told me you were back, said Michael. Did he? Did he say where I went? Michael ignored this. I've been thinking. Never a good idea, said Quentin. The second it starts, I tell myself, Quentin, this can only get you in trouble. A reporter mustn't overthink things. Who knows what the mind's capable of? Stick to the surface, I say, to the hard ground of irrefutable fact. Is that what you've done? asked Michael in a flat tone of voice. I'm telling you to avoid the mistakes I've made, said Quentin. You have a bright future ahead of you. And there's Margaret to think about. We broke up, said Michael. Happens all the time at your age, Quentin said. Full of restlessness, uncertainty, passion. You'll patch things up, I'm sure of it. What about the story? Michael said. What about it? Don't tell me you've given up. Didn't you hear? said Quentin. Henry wrapped it up with a bow. Caught the shaggy dog by the scruff. There was no there there. You don't really believe that? Michael said. Incredulity cast his voice in an uncharacteristic timbre. Quentin was quiet and Michael heard the comment in his silence. You don't expect *me* to believe that, he said more quietly. We're not going to win this one, Quentin said. Live to fight another day.

Michael held himself back, refusing the emotion that threatened to boil over. Other avatars hadn't had the discipline in Quentin's experience and this spoke well of Katz-Wallace. I looked into the names on that list, Michael said as if this were something incidental that had just occurred to him. Quentin could make out the effort in his restraint. The roster, Henry's list of names? said Michael. There are some strange coincidences . . . Quentin was telling him to let it go, let it drop. Taint not thy mind! 'venge not my damn'd ghost nor taste the leperous distilment . . . At least three of them are dead, Michael said. Dangerous work, muttered Quentin. Within a three-month span, Michael added. He waited for this to course through gates and alleys of perception. And not just that . . . Quentin didn't want to hear it. He did and he did not. I dug up their death certificates, said Michael. It took some doing. All three were pronounced dead at the same hospital. All relatively young. Good health, one assumes. And you'll never believe where the hospital is. I'll give you one guess. He waited. It's not overseas, he said. You spent some time there not long—

But Quentin was beyond it. He cut Michael off almost harshly. *Don't*— Don't, he said more gently. Not now, Michael. Maybe another time. He heard himself explaining that the truth would come out. In time the truth would emerge. It always did. Every secret got told because secrets were held by people, and people longed to tell them—in dark corners, under their breath, in bars, in private booths, on phone calls late at night, in quiet moments, to see surprise, astonishment, and the dawning grin on another's face, moments that scarcely seemed continuous with the daylight. A secret was wonder: at the world, at the things that existed in it. Secrets were the last citadel of mysticism for the hardened veterans of the world, the prudent realists, overgrown boys exhausted from playing serious men. Just you wait, said Quentin.

Michael was quiet and finally, simply, said, Come back. A clock sounded faraway. I will, said Quentin. He was sitting in his car at the curb on Main Street when he got off the phone. The high sun strung itself in crescents and beads on the beveled edges of motorcycle fenders and parked cars, the reflective glass of old shop windows. The storefront awnings shone brightly. The town looked cast in enamel, as though several decades frozen in time—an impression punctured, if one looked closely, only by traces of humidity's rot and the patient toll of gravity and climbing vines. Brilliant rhododendrons flanked the brick library's entrance and grand planes with their tetter bark rose stolidly from dirt plots in the sidewalk. Quentin picked out a drumming in the distance, realized he'd been hearing it for minutes. Slight rises and falls gave it an undulant, straining quality. He moved toward the sound, past the shut-up shops closed against the indolent weather, where ceiling fans turned like eternity's timepieces. The heat blew the air into glass, deforming the surface of the day. At the end of the street there was a swampy park, a forested dell or creek gully, and here among the chittering insects, by an algal pond canopied in nets of vegetation, the thick spiced, bodily smell of marijuana mixed with the pounding of drums. A boombox played while the men brought their hands down on the invisibly vibrating skin. A younger man sat a little way off, absorbed in a handheld gaming device. On a polished stump, beneath a dying tree claimed by vines, a recumbent man and woman stretched out together, talking quietly. The lingering, undispersed grain of smoke rested in the air, scintillating in the strained light, while birds like crashing shadows plunged between the branches. Along the creek bank was a gallery of rough-hewn wood with shaded seats, and here Quentin sat listening to the drumming. The others took no more than disinterested note of him.

A heartbeat. Always a heartbeat, what it made him think of, the pounding on of incessant time. Infinite and finite, a limited resource so bountiful you didn't attend its glacial expiration. Our time on earth. And what brought you more fully into unmediated, contentless existence than this attention to the beating, passing, ever-present mystery and certainty of moments? Jada had had hers. Never enough, and always a gift. Wasn't it so? At some point, freed by circumstance or inspiration from the solipsistic mind, cleft from the conviction that its abstractions represent and encompass life, you steal away, or something grabs you, into the phosphorescent singularity of the immediate, the actual. No name for it. Like

God. Light tumbling through colored glass and streaking the walls in cerulean, amber, marigold, ruby. Shifting, altering, but glowing on in fluid rearrangements to the consummatory instant of nothingness.

Hit this, Pops? It took Quentin a moment to realize he was being addressed. One of the men, chuckling, held out the long smoldering cigar leaf clasped tightly around its fragrant pith. Pops? he said. How old do you think I am? As old as time, said the man, and as young as you feel. They all laughed at this and Quentin, smiling, held up a hand—no thanks. The music kept on while they smoked, one turning his thumb in soft tempos on the drumhead, the air enchanted with dappled epiphanies of color.

After a time Quentin hauled himself up and walked—it took the better part of an hour—to Heaven's Gate. No, Gate of Heaven. That's what it was called. The catalpas and cherry trees and the elms shaded patches of graves beyond the openwork of the iron fence, twisted like black licorice. There was no one else in the cemetery, not that Quentin could see within the dimples and ridges that belted his vision. Pale leaves had fallen and lay scattered on the grass like sunlight on a lake. The clouds above the drumlins were white and fat and now obscured the sun. He hadn't considered that the size of the cemetery or the number of plots might make Jada's grave difficult to find—another oversight, typical of the distracted state he'd been in for weeks. He walked the rows, one by one, casting a glance over the names, dates, graven inscriptions, epitaphs, the rose marble, flecked with quartz, the impassive granite, the flaking slate tablets worn by time and weather. Some markers bore designs, heraldic, floral, symbolic coordinates across the spiritual and temporal planes. The meeting of instrumental and natural forms as in a compass rose. They gave position at the astral port. The sun tilted, dropped its plane, while Quentin walked above the field of teeming, resolving dead, each in her own chamber, sealed off in brief futile deferment against the dissolution, that repatriation to the cosmos, leaking out by geologic appointment to meet its neighbors in the molecular orgy, that unseen intercourse beneath the placid bladed lawns that bowed without complaint before the wind. Somewhere down there Jada was shut up in her own oubliette, or what remained of her. It was almost too much to consider, stepping over roots and stones and verdant turf. Incredible. *Not to be believed.* He knew it to be true and yet he couldn't bring himself entirely to accept the reality of her body underfoot, in that very dirt. And as if in honor of his disbelief, she eluded him. He started back through the gravestones a second time. Every twentieth or so had flowers laid across it. A token of human presence and also, inevitably, absence. The desire to stay close, and the impossibility, for the endless behaviors that sustained one in life, of settling with mythic fixity on one action, person, or plot, one cathexis like Tantalus or Narcissus. Was that it? He didn't know why he couldn't find her. Had he missed her grave in distraction? Did the cemetery extend farther than he realized, or did he somehow have the wrong one? Amid thousands of stones, like gray teeth sprouted from the earth, he could say nothing for certain. Only that the feeling in him as he searched resembled a growing static as of a stridulating insect, or the vibrato of tymbals, getting ever louder, the noise of panic, frustration, and helpless childish ire at reality's indifference, a reminder that it wasn't in the least bound by the contract we laid over it like a voile. He sat at the foot of a tree. Dusk, the early golden crisping of the world that inaugurated it, was drawing over the face of the earth. Knobby green misshapen pitted fruits lay in the weir of roots where they had fallen. Then it came to him, almost as the declaration of some intuitive beyond. Jada *hadn't* been buried, hadn't submitted to this boxed, bound, sealed-off eternity. He had just taken the reporter's word for it.

And with the thought something abruptly changed in him. Some tempers denature too rapidly and shift with such discontinuity that we see, for the break, the fabric of our mind for what it is—a cloth draped over endless jagged edges, straining at the penetrative pressure of their spine. The feeling in our belly when we go over the rise of the road too fast is the vouchsafed awareness of the gravity we live obliviously under, and the downward factors mediating our limbs and dreams like the color of water and secret hidden noise of silence. Something voided from his spirit, in a great rush like air flooding the vacuum of space. A cyclone remaking the land, albeit in reverse, putting it *in* order like a cataclasm run

backward. It ended in the stillness of coherence. He couldn't say anything
for certain about Jada's final covenant with the earth, but he *felt* it, felt
the truth of it, that last great leap of faith into the universalism of being,
the joining, not rejecting, going up in fire in a rush to meet the mystery
beyond—the air, the stars; this particle miasma you were made of, gifted
into being—and no, she wouldn't clutch at the return to nature, insisting
on bodily integrity, futilely, for as long as putrefying bulwarks and our
sentimental attachments would allow. Shut up in an echoic, resounding
casket. No! The intermediate state of ashes and dust was a blip; the stable
entropic points were the bookends. She would make good on the debt,
the lending and the loan—and if she could return to the fire of stars, and
could come out of them, combusting into being, then nothing was fixed
or given. A certain symmetry allowed that the possibility of self-creation
had to match that of self-destruction: if we could choose not to exist, by
will, we could choose *how* to exist, surely, however we had the courage to
strive for and demand.

Quentin, now speaking to us, feared he wasn't making himself clear.
He was talking about the vale of soul-making, the Rubicon we cross before we taste the true and bitter fruit of lost innocence, not innocence
before the hardness or ugliness of the world beyond us, but innocence
before ourselves, before our nature, which isn't good or bad, but hollow, if
we saw, partly empty, kin to the void and to the howling. Don't trust anyone who tells you they prefer innocence, no more than the person who
tells you that losing it promises the pleasures of maturity. How many of us
turn away from the hollow in fear, having decided that, in the absence of
a mooring, the deepest fact of human life is duplicity and cant, the lurid
performance of sacrificial values and supposititious principle, of compassion and ideal? Nearly all, he wagered. And we might feel ourselves
drowning in this ocean, alone and helpless on the uncertain seas of so
much lousy faith, so many people who neither believe the things they say
nor see the hollow inside us as the staging ground of self-creation, that
by keeping faith with the metaphysical we make it real, give it form, and
that love, in all its banal mystery, requires a courage and discipline all its
own, an understanding, even a certainty, that it will fail, for its purpose

is to be. But pushing past the hollow to this practice is inhumanly hard, because we look over our shoulders and see others turning away—and we see our fear mirrored on their faces, and to look inwardly for as long and as resolutely as we must appears a kind of madness to those outside, and often to us as well.

Quentin's thoughts, sitting beneath that tree, came as if on a closed track to rest with Cy. At last, he might have said; for though she and Jada were originals—unique—and though he might have loved Jada once, and perhaps he still did (for love is both fickle and everlasting), only one of them was real—that is, extant—and to pine for the dead is an indulgence, or a turning inward, a gross immodesty before the mystery of being. He remembered Cy not only as she now was but as the young woman he'd once known, more than a decade before, when they met in a park hung with pearls of lights, garlanding walks and flashing cameos in the trees. They sat together on chairs by the pond, drinking beer and white wine from plastic cups. A child nudged a sailboat with a stick. Ducks moved in short anxious orbits and darting jaunts. She had a barrette in her hair, a clip of some sort, dividing it in two sheets so that one lay over the other. Her look, her eyes wore the canny mischief of that age, that moment, the quick playful sparring of dating. Could we live in a house made of where our minds met? That overlapping territory of agreement or of comfortable, abiding difference? Could the chambers and hallways of knotted spirit flow gently enough to make an easy passage of the days? The cars were distant but audible beyond the trees and walks, the stone walls above them, and their conversation, broken into by spears of laughter. She'd always been a good laugher. Who are you? Who *are* you? Who, in the imperfect warped mirror of your beauty, am I? And so we look for ourselves, and for the real, in the blindman's bluff and Marco-Polo of grasping, touching, calling messy caroms and echoes of encounter. Brief encounters. The world was different then. Less certain. Edgier but also, in its way, gentler. Surety gripped less fiercely with those tentacles of belief which held, now, as if this ball of seething earth and ideation might explode into a million lonely particles if not for the inward pressure. He remembered how you could laugh then, breathe. She

always wore black: dresses mostly, a thin jumpsuit when it was warm.
A smart, sad, good-humored woman, violently awake, and undeceived
after all the years of seeing masks pulled off faces in the shadows and
private moments of strangled, creaturely grasping and croaked effusions.
I am . . . *here—feel pain—want*. Want endlessly. I am the profane amal-
gam of anger, innocence, confusion, and hope. Meet me by the balcony at
midnight when I come to you, to look through the soul's window, to my
unforeign soul, composed of light, to hope that something returns your
calls into darkness, nothingness, and says you are there. I see you. You
are not alone. They talked about so many things. Her father, of course.
Quentin's work, his ambitions, burning so violently in him then. Why
had it mattered quite so much? In quite that way? More of the desire, no
doubt, to hear the echo redound, to hear back: *You are real!* But it was a
fool's errand after a point. Oh, what things can be settled by sitting with
a lovely person in a park, drinking a beer and laughing while night wraps
you in its tender currents! They talked of Cy's hopes and ideas. A gallery.
Pictures that do nothing. Glimpses of reality, snatches of dreams. An
internal mental experience presented again imperfectly in tone, line, and
figuration. What didn't greet you in such a night? And could you carry
these dreams into the day? Hand in hand. In a promise, a picture, a story.
She liked him. He could tell by something radiating within her smile, a
deeper vibrating unfakeable quality or intensity communicated in what
must be mere fractional millimeters of skin stretched this way or that,
referencing millions of biologic, genetic years hunting after the truth. The
truth of feeling. Of one another. The truth of a face. This would not work,
she told him, not as some enervated coupledom, a mere hedge or bloodless contract against aloneness. As compromise, settling, and so forth.
Well. Had they made good on this promise all these years later? Probably
not. But they would try. Try to find each other, find love, through the
tunnels of doubt. The doubt necessary to wonder and comedy. The only
way to escape the grimness of this impending future, and its iron control
of body, of thought, was in the wild fields of wonder, uncertainty, trust.
Will you meet me there? Give me a hand. Reach out . . .

   And so we came, by turns, to an end. One end. One brief stop on the journey, as such things always are. The tide moved silently, deeply, and the pale opalescent waters fused in a solid illuminated face. A slight breeze, faint as an exhalation, came from the south, and in the distance a commercial boat glided through the water as though drifting on a plane of ice. The raw dun earth, clenched to the memory of frost, was drying, brightening; soon, friable, it would break again on life's soft lances. From somewhere in the woods an owl called, a sonorous, mysterious, plaintive sound, scouring the daylight and seeming to fill it as with a velvet lining. Before long the hunters would return, and from the island one would hear the claps of anthropic thunder, so ambiguously distant it seemed not the noise of humans at all but some dark message in the trees. Too early for ducks, they'd be after spring turkey, pheasant, grouse. Long gone, we wouldn't know. Already we were clearing the fridge and wiping down the counters, washing linens, making beds. It had been almost a decade since our last visit. And how long would it be before our next? We must have known, despite promises to the contrary, that it might be years, or never come. Quentin smiled at us, a chagrined look, self-chastening, abashed. How much of our time he'd taken up! And what would we do with his tale? We didn't know. Couldn't. We were eager to rejoin our families and the normal course of things. We'd be lying if we said we weren't. And yet we lingered, waylaid by some premonition of regret. We'd been affected by what we heard, and in some way changed. Could we simply retreat back down the bolt-holes of routine to the close, dark corridors that hedged our days? All the time we're vouchsafed fleeting intimations of the riddles that exceed us, blinding flashes, and we startle, shrink from them, and turn away into the dim repetitions that permit us to forget what seized us. We all wondered where Quentin would go when we left, but somehow none of us got around to asking him. Maybe we were afraid to know. We could still go back, you see. And in visions, in dreams of heroism, we *do* sometimes have moments when we see ourselves throw off the chains of illusion and seize the burden of thought, and when we say to others, Be brave! Be wise! Don't fear the messages that come to you in the night. In privacy. When no one's watching, when no one's listening or speaking, you are right to feel with clutching certainty that everything is stranger, wilder, deeper, more open than you've been made to know. But we can only hold this truth so long before it singes us, and only guard such courage in short beats before the fuse of conviction burns out. All days have limits imposed by clocks, stars, hungers, needs, the body's needs, functions, fading stamina, forgetfulness, the disintegration of cells by apoptosis and autophagy, the Brownian flux. All days, all knowledge, all truth flickers. Did everything happen just as we've recounted it? Did Quentin utter every word as it's been recorded? No, we dare say not. Not exactly. But this was the gist—the gist, and quite a bit more. We are editors, after all, men used to taking the story, the reported fact, and molding it into the publishable kernel. The core and polished stone. In this we are no different from you. We see in the black-and-white of printed lines, typeset shadows across gray pages. And what then could prepare us for the color, the blinding light of realities that have no place in the daily catalog of commonplace event?

ACKNOWLEDGMENTS

This novel profited from the scholarship and detail in many other books, especially works by Sarah Chayes, Maya Jasanoff, Sebastian Junger, Sven Lindqvist, Ingrid Rowland, W. G. Sebald, and Matthew White. My long-time writing partners, Andrew Palmer and Alexis Schaitkin, gave astute feedback on the novel in draft, as did my agent, Samantha Shea, who represented the book with conviction. At Farrar, Straus and Giroux, Eric Chinski and Julia Ringo steered the novel through several rounds of edits with insight and patience; Bella Lacey at Granta Books lent her wisdom and kindness throughout the process; and the finished product owes a significant debt to the efforts of Tara Sharma, Debra Helfand, Nina Frieman, Patrice Sheridan, Sophie Albanis, Logan Hill, Kylie Byrd, and Killian Piraro at FSG, and Dan Bird, Christine Lo, Sarah Wasley, Pru Rowlandson, Noel Murphy, and Rosie Morgan at Granta Books. During a critical period in this novel's composition, the Bard Fiction Prize helped keep body and soul together. Great thanks to Bard College and my friends in the Written Arts Program and beyond.

A Note About the Author

Greg Jackson is the author of the story collection *Prodigals*, for which he was named a National Book Foundation "5 Under 35" honoree and received the Bard Fiction Prize. In 2017 he was named one of *Granta*'s Best Young American Novelists. His fiction and essays have been anthologized in *The Best American Short Stories* and *The Best American Essays* and have appeared in many publications. *The Dimensions of a Cave* is his first novel.